BETWEEN THE BIRCHES
BOOK TWO

HARBINGER

KP ROBERSON

Author Note

This book contains sequences of graphic violence, gore, and disturbing imagery that may be unsuitable for readers under the age of eighteen. This book also contains dark ritualistic magic leading to murder and attempted murder, one instance of innuendo where they threaten to SA someone, multiple deaths, and dealing with grief after loss. There are also non-explicit scenes of consensual sexual acts between adults, some of which are slightly on the spicy side.

Edited in part by: Katie Bell & Carter Elise Key

Cover art by: KP Roberson

ISBN 9798985627374 (paperback)

Lunar Ridge Publishing LLC

178 Bracketts Way, Ste. 7 #116

Blairsville, GA 30512

www.lunarridgepublishing.com

Harbinger is dedicated to my readers.
Without your support and encouragement, I would find less joy in writing or sharing my world with anyone. Undoubtedly, I would not be as sane of a person as I am today...as questionable as my mental stability remains.

Edited in part by: Katie Bell & Carter Elise Key

Cover art by: KP Roberson

ISBN 9798985627374 (paperback)

Lunar Ridge Publishing LLC

178 Bracketts Way, Ste. 7 #116

Blairsville, GA 30512

www.lunarridgepublishing.com

Harbinger is dedicated to my readers.
Without your support and encouragement, I would find less joy in writing or sharing my world with anyone. Undoubtedly, I would not be as sane of a person as I am today...as questionable as my mental stability remains.

Prologue

Grief is like a serrated knife, smoothly slicing tender flesh as it cuts and bleeds on entry. When it retracts, it burns and aches, doing twice the damage on exit. —KP Roberson

SHE AWOKE WITH A start, the nightmare's vice-like grip loosening its hold on her chest. Echoes of her family's screams, as vile creatures with razor fingers tore their flesh to ribbons, caught in the synapsis of her awakening. The stale stench of vomit clung to her nostrils, almost real enough to taste.

She reached for the man she'd married thirty-two years ago. The soft sheets were frigid underneath her aged fingers. Fear caged her lungs as the hair at the back of her neck and arms stood on end. Pushing herself to a sitting position, her gaze landed on the faint glow emanating from behind the bathroom door.

"Charles?" Theresa's frail voice wavered. A low, familiar grunt from the other side reassured her enough that she could breathe through the desert forming in her mouth. "I'm going to the kitchen for a glass of water."

Theresa slipped out of bed and into her orthopedic pink slippers, casting a furtive glance at the ensuite door before padding down the hallway toward the kitchen. The sound of rushing water echoed behind her, fading into a squeak from the bathroom faucet.

She passed several of her fondest memories framed behind glass. To her horror, the familiar smiles of her children and grandchildren twisted into too-wide grins or grotesque, melting faces.

She gasped and shivered, skin crawling. Her heart thundered as she whizzed past. She was almost at the end of the hallway when her slipper caught on a loose nail in the hardwood. She stumbled, grabbing the wall for support and left the shoe behind.

Theresa didn't look back, not even when she made it to the kitchen sink. Her frail lungs struggled to keep up with her racing heart as she gripped the edge of the porcelain.

Moonbeams slithered through the thin curtains, gifting Theresa with light to see without flipping the switch. She kept her gaze on the window over the sink, watching the clouds lazily glide across the night sky.

Deep breath in, slow release.

When her body realized she was no longer in danger, she swallowed the lump in her throat and reached for a glass.

A dark figure passed silently in the reflection of the window. The mason jar slipped from her fingers as she jerked her hand back, falling to the laminate countertop with a crack. She squeezed her eyes shut, hoping whatever was outside was a trick of the limited light. But the scent of rotten eggs wafted from the hallway. Flashes from her nightmare, raw and angry, taunted her with sadistic promises.

Theresa shuddered, rubbing her bare arms as she clutched her stomach. Her eyes flew open to see her breath coming out in a visible white puff.

A loud thump came from her bedroom, and she whipped around.

The icy tendrils of dread seized her core when she heard nothing else.

"I'm coming, Charles," she called out, rushing back down the hallway as fast as her brittle bones would allow.

Swish-clap. Swish-clap. Swish-clap.

If he'd taken another tumble, the stubborn man wouldn't stay put for long. "Don't you dare move until I get there," she added, her voice louder now, bolstered by the sense of urgency.

Reaching the doorway, a flash of heat and the heavy scent of copper knocked her back a step. Her hands flailed until the thin wooden door frame halted her retreat. Theresa swallowed her heart and forced her watery gaze to focus on the large mass filling the bathroom doorway. Its skin, blackish-green and leathery like a crocodile, was studded with pulsing, puss-filled lumps.

It's not real. I'm seeing things.

Despite her pep talk, evidence pointed to the contrary. Theresa's knees rattled as she stepped into the room. She gripped her cotton pajama shirt to keep her heart from leaping out of her chest. Her husband had fallen. She couldn't let her nightmares bleed into reality.

Like photographs shown on a slide film projector, the scene was revealed in slow clicks of clarity.

The soft halogen glow bathed the bathroom walls in a pinkish hue. The creature's hunched shoulders flexed, causing something on the floor beneath it to jerk violently.

A pair of blue and white striped pajama pants.

She shook her head. *Charles is wearing the orange and white football pajamas, I'm certain of it. He must have spilled the dirty clothes basket when he fell.*

She edged toward the bathroom, cringing when the crunching and slurping sounds became louder. Even though it wasn't real, the noise was maddening. She peeled her fingers away from the soft fabric and covered her ears, forcing her gaze to the next segment of her waking nightmare.

A glossy red stain bloomed on the bedroom carpet where it met the white bathroom tiles. The pajama pants jerked again, directing her wide-eyed gaze to what pulled them.

Theresa expected to find Charles reaching for her, but what she found instead caused her chest to collapse under the pressure of a terrible truth. He couldn't greet her with his luminous smile that chased the dark clouds away, not without his head. A sob escaped before she could catch it.

The creature stilled, emitting a deep, rumbling growl as it slowly turned towards her, towering head and shoulders above. Bits of skin and fabric clung to its maw between red-stained, needle-like teeth. Blood oozed between its gums and coated its chin, dripping to the carpet with soft pats. The burning coals in place of its eyes searched her soul and reflected her fears back at her.

It's not real.

Somewhere between grief and madness, Theresa's mind hiccupped, allowing a whisper of courage—or stupidity—to enter. She raised her hand and placed it on the vile beast's arm.

Solid, uncomfortably hot, and rough to the touch. The rumble in its throat turned into a roar that bleached her blood white.

Theresa stumbled backward until her backside met the footboard. Her jaw worked like a fish out of water, but terror had robbed her of her voice. To make matters worse, her crumbled heart had created a vacuum, collapsing her chest cavity and immobilizing her.

The creature purred when terror saturated the room. Pins and needles rippled underneath her skin, severing whatever hold it had. Theresa made a run for the door seconds before it lunged with its arms outstretched, grabbing. The bed creaked and splintered. There came a pained moan, but Theresa didn't slow, not when she had forward momentum. The instant she did, the monster would get her.

Theresa bolted back down the hall—her other slipper lost somewhere between here and hell. Her vision narrowed in slow motion, the hallway stretched longer than it should have been. The creature was closing in, pressing against her back with searing heat and the stench of burnt hair. Panic clawed her lungs, depriving her of the oxygen needed to make it to the kitchen's back door. If she could make it, she could run to her neighbor's house for help.

The vile odor singed her nose hairs and coated her tongue; Theresa swore off deviled eggs forever if she survived. The flickering flames in her family photos blistered her skin with their heat. The constant assaults sapped her strength, but the angry grunts and shuffling carried her when she was ready to give up.

After what seemed like an eternity, the hallway spilled Theresa into the kitchen. She made a beeline toward the periwinkle door, aware of the heat and stink at her back.

Her hand closed around the doorknob, but it wouldn't turn.

Theresa whimpered, her hands trembling like rattles on a snake as she tried to grip the lock to turn it, but the damned thing wouldn't keep still.

A huff of hot air against the back of her head had warmth trailing down her legs. The tremble had spread to the rest of her body, but she managed to turn and face her end.

Out of the corner of her eye, Theresa spotted the knife block to her right. She kept her gaze trained on the creature, wondering why it didn't finish her.

Maybe it was full of Charles. He always did have a big head.

The random thought caused her bottom lip to quiver as a manic chuckle slipped out. No one was coming to help her, and even if this was a dream, it wasn't worth living without her loving husband.

Theresa wrapped her fingers around the dull edges of the butcher knife handle and yanked it free. Hot tears washed away the sulfur stinging her eyes.

The creature moved too quickly for her mind to register. Sharp, stinging in her midsection broke her trance. Theresa looked down to find her shirt open to the breeze, colored in red that spread like drops of food coloring in water. The cut wasn't deep enough to kill, so toying with her must have been its game. Well, she was done with it all.

Theresa stabbed forward with the knife, barely able to keep a grip when it pierced the tough flesh. Black blood bubbled from the wound, pulled by a string connected to her blade. The monster blinked rapidly, tilting its head to the side. When it raised its sharp claws to bring doom, Theresa slashed across its chest, flinching as a splatter of sticky blood whipped against her face. The creature bellowed, swiping at her hand, but her fingers were locked in place forever.

Pull the knife out, stab it back in, repeat.

As Theresa continued her mantra, the creature's arms flailed wildly, causing sharp pains across her cheek, chest, and arms.

Manic giggling spilled from her lips with each strike until her movements slowed, becoming sluggish. Her cackles had morphed into stuttered sobs. She wasn't sure when the creature stopped moving, only that it had. Her gaze met its dying eyes. Satisfaction settled in her bones as the light snuffed out like a cindering coal.

Sinking the blade in one last time, the creature slumped to the kitchen floor with a wet squelch, landing face down. A tarlike substance flowed from its slackened maw, pooling around its head.

The adrenaline left as quickly as it had come, and Theresa dropped to the floor with a yelp. She looked down at her plain nightgown, now torn to shreds.

Funny, she didn't remember owning a red one.

The pain in her midsection pulsed like a live thing, sending her into cold sweats. She winced as she ran her hand through the sticky mess on her forehead, letting her hand drop into her lap.

Her breaths came in short pants, her lungs giving less with each inhale. She stared blankly across the kitchen, pins and needles probing her toes as she contemplated whether she had time to get to the phone.

The shapes in her line of sight wavered like a desert mirage, then cleared. A withered figure appeared above the monster, its red eyes burning with malice and delight, as if it found her suffering euphoric. Dread suffocated her remaining hope as its lipless round mouth curved into a menacing grin. It pointed to the ground, where the remains of her fallen foe lay.

Her gaze lowered, locking onto the bewildered face of the man she had sworn to love for the rest of her life. His milky eyes were unseeing, haunted by her heinous actions.

"God, no..."

Her choked sobs sounded foreign, even to her. It wasn't fair that their final moment together was so horrid. She couldn't understand what they had done to receive such a fate. They went to church every Sunday, they loved and supported their son when he came out, they doted on *all* of their grandchildren regardless of whether they were blood-related or not.

As her vision flooded with watery grief, she helplessly watched as the creature drew back its clawed hand. Though her body wanted to move, her spirit had given up. One quick swipe was enough to end her suffering.

Chapter 1

BETH

SHE SWIRLED THE GLASS, watching the red liquid slosh around before tipping it back. The sweetness hit her tongue, and she closed her eyes for a brief prayer for strength. Keeping on the edge of comfortably numb and falling apart was the only way she could go through Tom's things.

Beth placed her wine glass on the dresser next to the closet. Her fingers ran over the soft fabric until she found her first treasure and pulled it off the hanger. It was the red polo shirt with white trim Tom wore on their first date.

She clutched the garment to her chest, burying her nose in its layers while her shoulders shook. His cologne had faded with the passage of time but with her eyes closed it was there. When she pulled it away, wet blotches had formed on the front. She sighed and returned to the bed where she neatly folded it. Placing it near Tom's pillow, she smoothed the wrinkles.

"This is gonna be more difficult than I thought it would be." Beth sniffled as she returned to the shared closet.

Nestled behind layers of shirts, a black bag hung. As Beth's fingers lifted the garment bag, her heart took on water, sinking to the depths of the rocky ocean that had become her life after Tom died.

Each step toward the bed was fraught with peril, the muscles in her head warring with those inebriated by the drink. Thoughts of Grady's hugs and his kind sapphire eyes skulked at the edge of her inhibitions. Here she was, mourning her dead husband but she couldn't stop thinking of his best friend. She couldn't deal with both, so anything attached to Grady was tossed back inside her secret closet and drowned by the juice of wilted and aged grapes. There had been at least a bottle's worth since she sent him away.

When her knees met the mattress, Beth remembered what agony awaited her in the black bag. She rolled her bottom lip between her teeth, scraping at the scabs left behind from dehydration. She pulled the plastic key. Each zippered tooth parted with deafening clicks, promising agony. It was almost enough to render Beth's heart and lungs useless, but she *had* to do this.

Beth knelt to unzip it all the way, but when she stood and parted the flaps, the sight was a punch to the gut. Hiccups caused her slobber and salty tears to mingle at her chin. Tom's navy tuxedo had been pressed to perfection, marred only by a fleck of white icing on his collar.

"What's a drop of icing when I get the whole cake?" Tom had said when Beth frowned and dusted it away. That night, he'd shown her he wasn't talking about baked desserts. They'd worshipped every inch of each other until no spot of skin was left untouched. The memory left her body tingling, aching for one more day to say all the things she was afraid to admit before, to make sure he knew she loved him with her whole being until the second he took his final breath.

Even now.

Beth's lips parted with a scream as her demolished soul toppled into a heap. She fell against the bed, dropping to the carpeted floor where she took out her frustration, gripping the fibers as if they held the cure to her anguish. She'd begged the reaper to bring him back, so that the missing pieces would cease their endless torment, but she knew nothing could save her from this.

This kind of hurt was persistent and mean, not just a rite of passage into the understanding of mortality.

Tom's death had left a permanent scar on her soul she would wear proudly.

When she'd bled her ocean dry, Beth uncurled from the fetal position and rolled onto her back. The weight on her ribcage had lightened, but her center still clung to an anchor of disparity. With puffy eyes, she stared at the stippled ceiling, watching the edge of her vision pulse in time with her heartbeat as she traversed the mountainous peaks on a journey of self-discovery to end up lost.

Beth sighed, relieving some of the pressure in her lungs.

She grabbed the quilt with both hands and pulled herself up until she was on her knees. The effort drained the strength from her arms, but Beth was able to stand with another last tug.

She plopped onto the bed, letting her gaze wander freely until it stopped on the bottle of rose water sitting atop an envelope with her name penned on the front.

Tom's goodbye letter.

Her chin wobbled, and her heart rate skyrocketed, thumping loud enough in her chest she was certain the neighbors heard. The air in the room thinned as her vision blurred.

Not again.

Taking a deep breath, Beth counted to ten as she exhaled, clutching her chest and squeezing her eyes shut. It took several more ragged breaths to reset her brain, slowing her heart from marathon speed to more of a jog.

Rising to her feet, she braved crossing the chasm between the bed and dresser to bury her grief once again in the temporary waters of Red Moscato.

"This one's for you, Tom," she whispered, her gaze flickering to the wedding pictures above their bed before she tossed the drink back.

The bittersweet liquid soothed her thoughts like a sensory deprivation tank, a crutch that helped her straighten her back and forge ahead on the promise that tomorrow would hurt a little less.

Joining Tom's polo shirt was the glass bottle of rose water, the magical moonstone he'd made for portal travel. Tom's lucky fishing hat had turned invisible or else he'd given it to Grady. She slipped into the bathroom and picked up the half-empty bottle of Tom's orange and cedarwood scented body wash. It was the same kind he'd used before they started dating. After she was brave enough to tell him how nice he smelled, Tom bought it in bulk.

This was the last bottle.

Beth continued her descent until the waters became too muddy to carry on. Grabbing a moving box from the back of their closet, she made her way foot to the bed. Placing her most precious memories of the man who filled her days with so much joy and love, one whose passing left an ocean-sized cavity in her chest, gave her a sense of peace.

The last things left to go inside were the three framed pictures above their bed. One black, one white, the middle with a winter wonderland providing the backdrop to the happiest day of her life.

Beth climbed up the middle of her mattress, snorting at how the wall tilted on its own. She gripped the headboard and planted one foot on her pillow. With the grace of a baby giraffe, she pushed herself to stand, deciding at the last minute to headbutt the wall.

"Fugggg," she slurred as her body fell in slow-motion, landing on the mattress with a bounce. On the rebound, the back of her head picked a fight with the baseboard. Beth's body curled into a ball, her fingers searching along the ache to find a bump and a dot of wetness. "Son of a nutcracker."

This was stupid. She knew better than to stand on her bed while drunk. Grady would be disappointed if he found her like this…which was a sobering thought that cut her in a different way.

Despite wearing the special necklaces Myrtle had made to block his thoughts and emotions, she could still feel the tug of the magical thread connecting them. Yes, she loved Tom with all her heart and soul. She'd buried a piece of herself with him, but her love for Grady was rapidly changing in ways that terrified her. Hence, the ill-advised drinking game she had devised as a distraction.

"Pull yourself together, woman."

Beth shoved off the bed and straightened her back. Putting one foot in front of the other, she closed the distance to the oasis of filtered water in hopes of regaining some form of clarity. She was ashamed to admit the only fuel she had given her body was in the form of fermented grapes. Cooking was the last thing on her mind.

Opening the refrigerator door, she blinked several times and frowned at finding food inside. More to the point, she had no recollection of making a key lime pie from scratch...or going to the grocery store. Why did she—

"Shit."

Fennick Rayon.

In a bout of loneliness after sending Grady away, she'd invited Fen over for dinner. It was supposed to be a simple thing, to thank him for stopping Curtis's attempt on her life. It had seemed like a good idea at the time, but that was before she was three sheets to the wind.

Her gaze flew to the waning light streaming through the living room window. Wasn't it lunch when she grabbed this last bottle of wine? The digital clock said she had an hour to prepare before he showed up for the home-cooked meal she'd promised. At the thought of food, an earsplitting growl rumbled from deep beneath her ribcage.

Beth grabbed a water bottle from the fridge and chugged it. As she gathered her breath, her gaze landed on the crumpled plastic bag holding the end pieces of a loaf of bread. She closed the refrigerator door and teetered across the kitchen. Once the pitiful snack was devoured, her bladder promptly announced a visit to her porcelain seat was due.

Afterward, Beth watched the bubbles swirl down the drain, unable or unwilling to look herself in the eye. She'd let herself go, she knew that. Who wouldn't after becoming a widow?

Rather than let her thoughts turn bitter, she splashed cold water on her face and patted dry with the warm terry towel. With her focus sharpened enough to get her shit together and cook, Beth headed back to the kitchen.

"Set the steaks out to rest, preheat the oven to...whatever the potatoes need," she said, recounting the steps for preparing dinner. "And, um, broccoli. Yes. Don't forget it this time, dum-dum."

Rounding the bar, Beth patted herself on the back for walking in mostly a straight line. She was halfway to her refrigerator when the front door slammed open.

Beth jumped, pulling her arms tight across her chest to keep her heart from popping out through her ribcage. Her front door hung by the top hinge of the splintered frame. Behind the perpetrator, light from the waning sunlight created a frightening silhouette. It took two heavy steps forward, stealing her bravery.

"What—"

"I've come ta tie up some loose ends," the shape rasped in his deep southern drawl. A chill spilled down Beth's spine.

That voice haunted her dreams. For reasons Beth didn't care to admit, her brain couldn't communicate to the rest of her body the need to *move her ass.*

The devil took her lack of reaction as an invitation to step inside her inner sanctum. Curtis's soiled clothes were covered in rust-colored paint and hung loosely from his bony frame. His chest heaved like he'd run the entire distance across town. The foul cocktail of body odor and cheap whiskey knocked the air right from her lungs with its potency.

This time, though, Beth was on her own. She forced a swallow, dislodging the lump in her throat. Facing her demon wasn't part of the mourning process, but she was going to make him pay for interrupting it.

Beth scrunched her nose and covered her throat with her hands. She pleaded with her magic to work this time, otherwise she'd be keeping Tom company.

Curtis pounced with a snarl; his eyes wide enough that they were almost white. When his muddy boots stomped on Beth's spotless white tile floor, her stunned muscles finally got the message. His fist flew toward her face. She raised her arm to block it, but her head rocked back like a boxing bag and copper coated the tip of her tongue.

He punched me in the fucking mouth!

A tingling started in her fingertips, but it wasn't enough…yet.

Working with a drunkard's instinct, Beth stumbled sideways, barely dodging his other fist. His rancid breath clouded her face, stinking worse than sauteed ramps and garlic cooked in a dirty boot. She gagged, giving him an opening. Curtis grabbed her by the shoulders and drove his knee into her ribs. What precious, untainted air she held evacuated her lungs as she bent at the waist.

"As much fun as it is to watch you bleed, I got other shit to do," Curtis rasped.

Rage built a plateau over her grief, fortified by preservation. How dare this man come into *her* home during *her* sob fest?

Hell to the effing no.

The tingling moved to her palm like a line of lit gasoline. A wry grin spread on the corner of her lips.

Beth raised her palm toward Curtis and called on her lightbringer guardian magic. She didn't have time to aim, but the blast range was close enough to send her attacker flying. It also knocked her on her ass.

Glass shattered in the living room, followed by what sounded like a thump on the carpeted floor. There was a moment of silence where relief waited at the boundary, but Beth was lucid enough to know better.

Tentatively, she reached for the countertop and gripped the edge with her fingertips. Beth pulled herself to stand and peeked over the bar.

The floor below the broken window was missing a body.

"Fucking bitch. Die already!"

Curtis vaulted over the bar like some comic-movie villain. The thin ribbons of blood across his face and hands only added fuel to her nightmares…and he was blocking her exit.

Beth didn't have time to think. It had been days since she went outside to renew her energy. Anything she used would be taking from herself, unless she took from him.

Remembering how she'd used Elliott Larson's life-force to fuel his death, she sank into the puddle of what remained of her magic and let her instincts drive. Her knuckles glowed white when she punched Curtis square in the gut, leaving a burnt patch on his shirt. Blue sparks showered her kitchen floor.

Her next strike glowed brighter, landing on his cheek with a hiss. The nauseating stink of burnt hair and seared flesh reminded her of a sleazy burger joint using week-old oil in the fryer. The wine in her gut soured. Bile choked her.

A sudden, stinging pain in the top of her thigh caused her to cry out. Her wide-eyed gaze swiveled toward the pocketknife in Curtis's hand. He sneered and stabbed the pointy end at her stomach. Beth spun along the countertop to keep her footing, narrowly avoiding the blade.

Desperation facilitated cleverness. Enter the toaster to her right.

She kicked the side of his knee and yanked the cord free from the socket while he cursed her with a grunt. She grabbed the toaster in time to block his next hit, deflecting the blade with a metallic clang. When Curtis reared back for another shot, Beth slammed the small appliance into his face with as much force as she could muster. Her body was so tired that, when the knife clanged to the floor, she almost cried. Instead, she held the cord on the short end and swung the toaster like a mace.

Beth learned two very important lessons: Inebriation does not vacate the blood stream after water and food; and her aim was shit.

Curtis cursed when her failed attempt at another headshot missed by a mile, grabbing the appliance and yanking it from her. As he tossed the toaster over his shoulder, Beth noticed a glint of silver on counter next to the wine bottle on the counter.

Fight or flight, drunk or not, she wasn't ready to die tonight.

Beth's vision went white around the edges. The empty well of her magic stirred and time slowed. As her hand shot out and gripped the open corkscrew tight, she prayed to the goddess to guide her aim. Beth stared at the target with an intense focus she'd never be able to replicate in a million years.

Curtis's jaw was set; his lips curved in a deep frown. That all changed when he registered what was coming. Before he could do anything to stop her, time sped back up as Beth buried the corkscrew in his jugular. Blood spurted from the wound like a fountain, flowing in sanguine rivers over her hands and down his neck. Beth jerked her hand away just as Curtis opened his mouth like a sputtering fish and coughed, sending a splash of warm stickiness across her face. His hands gripped her shoulders, but there was no strength in his hold.

Beth shrugged him off and took two steps back, hands shaking violently as he fell forward with a squelch and a crunch. Lifeless eyes stared at her accusingly while his jaw remained open at an odd angle.

She tore her gaze from the carnage and grabbed at the roll of paper towels. Pulling several handfuls loose she scrubbed her face with a vigor her mother would be proud of, but her busted lip stung like a sonofabitch.

Curtis sputtered and wheezed from where his spot on the floor. She dropped the soiled napkins and swiveled not so gracefully on her good leg. Both hands were balled into fists in front of her face, ready to kick his ass again even though she was done for the day. Hell, probably the week.

Sorry, Fennick, but dinner is canceled. Beth cracked a smile at her internal dialogue, *"Look, my dead friend's dad tried to unalive me again, but I stabbed him in the neck with a corkscrew. Here's your raincheck for dinner sometime next year. Okay, byeeeee."*

During her brief mental check-out, a noise coming from Curtis snapped her back to the present. Her taut muscles stung with overuse when she tightened them again, but the only movement was his body deflating with one long, wet exhale.

Beth relaxed on a sigh, letting her arms droop at her sides. She stared at him for a good long while, unsure whether he was playing possum or not. To be sure, she chose her least favorite wooden utensil from the jar on the counter and jabbed Curtis in the shoulder with the tip.

He didn't move an inch, meaning her personal bogeyman was finally dead.

The wooden spoon clattered to the floor. Beth followed, leaning against the cabinets to catch her breath. The dark clouds that had arrived with Curtis parted, letting the sunshine through. The heaviness that came with looking over her shoulder lifted, and she could breathe again.

When Beth closed her eyes, the sunshine disappeared and the band around her chest tightened again. The darkness behind her eyelids called for rest. She wanted to, but there was something she had to do first.

Beth took a deep breath and regretted it immediately. Curtis had emptied his bowels while she took a break. The nastiness coated her tongue, making her shudder.

Should I call the sheriff's department before or after I clean myself up?

The logical answer was, yes. Her gut instincts suggested otherwise. Chances were, some busybody had already alerted the sheriff's department. Her *not* calling would certainly be a red flag. But no one would begrudge her washing that awful taste from her mouth first.

Beth crawled to the furthest counter from Curtis and pulled herself to stand. She limped around the body, throwing a quick gaze to the front of her apartment as she headed to her bedroom. If anyone *had* called, you wouldn't be able to tell. The outside world continued without care.

She went straight to the ensuite bathroom and turned on the water. The red water swirled in mesmerizing patterns as she scrubbed her hands raw. Chancing a look in the mirror, her chest dulled at the sight. If she showed up to a haunted house looking like she did—hair sticking out from her ponytail, blood smeared face, and wild eyes—they'd hire her on the spot.

The absurdity of the thought caused her to crack. When she noticed the crazed woman in the reflection appear, her smile dropped. Beth's sharp intake of oxygen parted with a shudder.

The ugly cry caught her off-guard. She couldn't bear the sight. She sunk until her butt landed on the closed toilet lid. The feelings Beth had bottled up over the week finally burst free, all because she killed a man.

Burying her face in her hands, she wailed, she screamed, she let it all out. When there were no more tears to cry, Beth blew her nose and stood on shaky legs.

Yes, Beth had defended herself against a man who'd gone mad with grief, but he started it. Thinking like this sounded juvenile, but it didn't change the facts. Losing Jeff was a tragedy, but Curtis blaming her was bullshit.

Beth rested her forehead on the cool glass mirror, giving her tired neck a break. Her thoughts eventually quieted and the heavy thump, thump in her chest stopped racing. She pushed away from the mirror and flipped on the cold water. Cupping her hands, she filled them with the means to wash away her sins, watching them swirl down the sink and taking her fear with them.

She needed help.

She *should* call Grady.

"I don't want to." She swallowed the lump forming in her throat. The woman in the mirror testing her resolve didn't give her an inch. She finally conceded with her own stipulation. "After I call the sheriff."

Beth patted her face dry with a towel and limped to her bedroom. The cell phone weighed like a sack of potatoes as her finger hovered over the lock screen photo. The two men who shared her heart were so happy, so carefree.

Before her tear ducts found a secret oasis, she pressed the home key and dialed 9-1-1.

Chapter 2

GRADY

GRADY STEPPED OUT OF Jeff's bedroom into the hallway, focusing his heightened panther senses to scan the rest of the house.

Big mistake.

The stench of decay coming from the center of the house flooded his nostrils. His hand flew to cover his mouth, but the cough bounced off the walls. He may as well have shouted 'hello.'

"Stupid," Grady softly cursed himself, pinched the fabric at neck of his shirt, and jerked it over his nose. The thin material did little else but point out how badly he needed a shave.

Before he went further, Grady listened for any other heartbeats. Best not to be surprised after announcing his presence. Outside of the heavy thump in his chest, there were no others outside of the fast skittering of several rats.

On the way to the kitchen, his gaze fell the dusty rectangular frame hanging crookedly on the wall. Behind the grimy glass was a photo of four barely teenage boys in all too familiar woods with shoddily built tents in the background. It was one of the happier memories of summers past, of simpler times before learning of death cultists and magic.

A time when Tom was still alive.

The companion he'd kept since that dreadful day squeezed its way into the too cramped space in his chest again. Grady stamped it out before his thoughts wandered to Beth for the thousandth time.

Keeping his wits sharp when death clung heavily in the air took precedence, especially when something sinister happened here. The slimy essence he associated with Ja'azul lingered, skating across his skin like rusted nails.

Still, he continued toward the source. Curiosity often won the toss of the dice when magic or occult things were involved.

The unswept hallway led him to the cluttered foyer before the kitchen. Grady's nose and eyes crinkled in disgust as he kicked aside empty beer bottles and crumpled newspapers. The glass clinked against the baseboards, camouflaging the faint squeaks of disturbed critters, before rolling to a stop in the kitchen arch.

Mrs. Putnam took pride in a spotless home, so this level of filth was a far cry from normal. His stomach soured, but it could have been the smell.

The closer his steps brought him to the kitchen, the less his t-shirt helped. The stench permeated his nasal passages and coated his throat with its bitter tanginess. Swallowing helped keep the bile at bay, for now.

A white plastic cornucopia lay open on its side; a feast for the furry hosts who had taken up residence. He stepped over the litter, and his boot slipped on something sticky and wet.

Grady's arms shot out to his sides for balance. The rodents circled his ankle, their wiry hair scratching the denim as they fled to a less human-infested section of the house.

Without his scant barrier, the full force of well-composted rubbish slammed into him. His lungs stuttered. His stomach convulsed. Closing his eyes, he found the quiet place in his mind, settling the panic overtaking reason.

I can breathe. I am fine.

Calmness settled in Grady's gut and breathing normalized. Opening his eyes, he swiveled on the planted foot, turning his body sideways to clear the obstacle.

Once both feet were firmly on the ground again, he gripped his nose and tried to breathe through his mouth instead. Whatever was in this bag reeked like a decaying corpse.

His gaze fell to the tiled floor where maggots wriggled to escape their rubber prison. He lifted his boot, leaving a dark red impression stamped on the floor. More of the red substance was splattered across the foyer walls, against the glass on the back door, and beyond, into the kitchen. It was as if someone had dropped a half-full bucket of rust-red paint from the top of a ladder.

Grady gulped, his esophagus becoming a dredge for the suffocating odor. Gripping the countertop with both hands, he edged his way into the kitchen. Negligence be damned. He'd left evidence of his trespass in the form of a smudged trail with his shoe type and size.

Better than ending up on the floor, covered in someone else's blood. The thought turned his already spoiled gut. He focused on steadying his breaths to keep it from boiling over.

At the bend of the countertop, Grady paused. The source of what singed his nostril hairs was behind him. All he had to do was turn around and the mystery would be solved. His brain wouldn't send the signal. Something in the back of his mind wouldn't let it.

Grady peeled his fingers away from the edge of the countertop. They pulsed in time with his chest. A flash wave of cold prickled his entire body. In that gasping pause, he turned. First with his hips, followed by his head. The hazy image took seconds to load. While his brain processed the details, time was unkind enough to freeze.

"Fucking hell."

Practically at his feet, lay the remains of Marla Jean Putnam.

His throat clogged with thick, stringy saliva. The remnants of his last meal threatened to contaminate the scene further. Vomit sputtered behind Grady's pursed lips as he scrambled to the edge of the cabinet where he emptied his stomach on the floor. The additional smell caused him to dry heave.

Grady wiped his mouth with the back of his shaking hand, staring at his most recent fuck up.

Pushing away from the countertop, he distracted himself by studying clues. Jeff's mom—

Nope. No personalization.

The *body* looked like someone's dissection project gone wrong. The organs were arranged around the *outside* for a macabre display. Her eye sockets were messily hollow, as if someone had taken a melon baller to them. Huge, furry brown and gray bodies surrounded her body, chewing at her gray, bloated flesh. They were in her hair and clothes, wriggling about like oversized earthworms digging through dirt. Only, it was human being...someone he knew well.

The image would forever be seared into his brain.

Their squeaks and the wet sounds broke something inside Grady. Rage bubbled like lava, boiling in his gut until it spilled from his mouth.

"Get away from her!"

They scattered as he swung his arms. Others hissed in protest when he stomped the ground. The rest watched from the shadows with their beady black eyes, waiting to reclaim their meal.

He wiped his clammy hands on his pants and bent at the waist, resting his hands on his knees until air came more easily to his lungs. Unable to look at Mrs. Putnam anymore, his gaze searched for something—*anything* else—nearby.

The toes of his shoes fit the convenience. It didn't last long. Eventually, his curious gaze slipped from its shoddy cage, cautiously closing in on the body in front of him. Strange black markings took shape. The larger, a circle. Beyond were smaller symbols, some were smudged past the point of recognition, but he could almost recall seeing them before.

The longer he studied the markings, the more they seemed to glow with a dark aura that caused his skin to feel like it was covered with frantic, biting fire ants.

Suddenly, a light burned in the attic of his memories.

These symbols.

He'd seen this blasphemous act done in real time once. Once was enough. Only, that was in a particular part of the woods, and this was not.

And the sacrifice is fresh.

"We've already lost."

Grady ducked his head against his forearm to wipe away the line of sweat hurtling toward his eyes. He'd outstayed his welcome at the Putnam house.

Pushing to his feet, he left out the front door. He didn't care who saw him anymore.

Anyone in town would recognize his truck, and he'd left enough tracks behind that a blind person could follow.

The only thing he cared about now was getting to Beth.

His truck rumbled to life, and he threw it into drive. The tires squealed on the curbside, leaving behind the rancid burnt rubber smell.

It hurt when she asked him for time to grieve Tom's death alone. While he was keen on giving it to her, she'd have to grieve alone later. Again, things had been set in motion several steps ahead of them. They'd need to get in front of the wave before the storm hit.

Rapidly tapping his steering wheel, Grady lowered the gas pedal. As trees and houses he'd known his whole life whizzed past, Grady's thoughts wandered to Tom's last request. *'Be happy,'* he said, placing Beth's hand into Grady's. This was always at the forefront of his mind. But saying and doing were two vastly different things, and neither was an easy pill to swallow.

Despite Grady's love for Beth, the blockade keeping him from jumping the fence and running headlong for his own happiness was the Tom-sized hole in their lives. While his best friend left behind a widow and parents who adored him, Grady had survived to pick up the slack as nothing more than a glorified second pick. He'd hammered this point home by dropping the 'L' bomb in the same breath as his goodbye, all wrapped in a funeral day bow.

A buzzing sounded from the bench seat. His gaze flicked to the worn fabric long enough to find his phone and grasp it.

The second he saw Beth's name flash on the screen, his stomach somersaulted. One-handed, he pressed the button and answered before the next ring.

"Are you okay?" He winced at the breathy quality.

"Yes. I mean, no. Not really..." Her voice trailed off like she had turned away from the phone. A muffled sigh came through the receiver. "I...need your help."

Grady could practically see Beth wringing her hands.

"I'll be there in five."

No response.

"Beth?"

The line went dead, and his gut churned like a paper shredder.

"Fuck."

Grady dropped his cell in his lap. The engine in his Dodge Ram roared as he tested its speed. Three minutes later, he parked next to Tom and Beth's Subaru Outback. Heat radiated from the hood in waves as the block underneath popped. Most of Grady's attention was focused on the broken window and busted door hanging by the top hinge.

His body moved on instinct, taking the steps two at a time, and praying to the gods he wasn't too late. At the top of the stairs, his knees buckled at the sight. Blood covered the kitchen floor, and in the middle of it was a man. Realization sent icy spikes down his spine.

Did Beth hang up on me because she was in danger?

"Beth!" He roared in desperation, unable to tame the wild beast ready to burn the world to keep his one and only safe.

His feet carried him across the living room toward the master bedroom. He *needed* to see with his own eyes she was still breathing. Her soft voice stopped him in his tracks.

"You're here."

Beth stood just inside her bedroom, her wide eyes glossing over. A strip of terry cloth was wrapped around her left thigh as she wiped her hands with a pink towel. She looked like she'd fought a black bear, bottom lip swollen and split, hair sticking out all over. Her chin wobbled as fat tears spilled down her cheeks.

She was covered in so much blood.

Grady choked on his words as he rushed over. His hands went to either side of her face, holding her in place as he surveyed the damage. The tightness in his chest made it feel like he was breathing from a pinched straw.

He should have been here sooner. If he'd come straight to Beth's instead of playing investigator, she wouldn't have been attacked in her home again.

"Don't." The firmness in her quiet voice struck him. Confusion wrinkled his brow, and her eyes softened. She closed her eyes on a long blink and whispered, "It's not your fault."

"How—" he stopped himself, knowing the answer already. They could read each other like a book, which was another reason he needed to tread lightly and not further overstep her boundaries. "Never mind. You're freezing. Let's get you a sweater."

And keep you busy, so I can check the rest of the apartment.

Wrapping his arm around her shoulder, Grady led Beth into her bedroom. Touching her made his magic tingle like hundreds of fairies giving his skin warm kisses. He did his best to ignore the feeling and tuned his panther senses to 'seek intruder' mode. His inner hackles lowered when he found them alone.

Grady looked around, following Beth to the closet. It appeared to have exploded all over the room. She offered no explanation as she rifled through her drawers. She turned back to him, slipped her arms through a plain heather gray cardigan, and crossed her arms. Grady tipped her chin to meet her gaze head-on. Her split lip and the bruises blooming on her cheek gave his anger convulsions. "I'm going to check out the rest of the apartment. Stay by my side, okay?"

She nodded, her pitiful frown and big, puppy dog gaze made him want to pull her into his arms. It felt wrong not to hug her, but Grady took a step back, then another. He ached to kiss her wounds, knitting each one shut, because, dammit, he *loved* her. The *need* to protect Beth was exactly why he resisted. She'd asked for this space. His leg muscles twitched against the movement.

A man lay dead in the next room. This was neither the time nor the place.

Grady stalked from the bedroom taking in every detail, building a narrative that matched the damage. Heat boiled in his gut. He used it to keep him grounded in the moment.

"Mr. Putnam." Grady growled, stopping just before the linoleum.

"Yeah. Caught me off guard, but I killed him." She studied her fingers as she made fists.

She turned them over and repeated the action. The shaking had stopped, but she sounded zoned out. "Stabbed him in the neck."

Sure enough, the corkscrew Grady had gifted the Newmans as part of their wedding present now poorly plugged Mr. Putnam's artery.

"Resourceful." Grady scrubbed his hand down his face.

His gaze dropped to her delicate neck when her fingertips grazed the curve. Smooth, unmarred skin held no signs of fingerprints like the last time Curtis was here. Clearing his throat, he shifted his attention back to the problem elephant in the room.

"I called the sheriff." Beth murmured before going to the couch and fluffed pillows. "They should be here soon, I think."

"Why did you—" Grady bristled, causing Beth to jump. Panic threatened to pull the plug on his Zen. She didn't know what he'd been doing before checking on her. "You did the right thing."

However, the clock was ticking. There was no way the sheriff's department knew he had been at the Putnam's house, not yet. Still, they couldn't dawdle. When Grady looked up, Beth was lint rolling the couches. He gently placed the palm of his hand on the middle of her back. She leaned into the touch, stopping to look over her shoulder. The lost look in her eyes wounded his soul. He couldn't leave her alone now.

"Pack your suitcase."

"What? Why?" Her eyebrows sunk in confusion as her head tilted to the side.

"Your apartment is a wreck, Beth, and I, well..." Grady scratched his itchy neck. "We're going to the Grove, where it's safe."

Chapter 3

BETH

BETH PLACED A STACK of clothes in the open suitcase on her bed. The diamonds in her wedding ring glinted as she smoothed the top. She stared at the double-band of gold around her finger, remembering the day she said, 'yes,' like it was yesterday rather than months ago.

Flashes of her husband's stormy gray eyes, filled with love and joyful tears before they sealed their promise of eternity. Had they only known how little time they'd really have.

Regret tugged at her ribs. If she hadn't made such a big deal of his yearly excursions into the woods, Tom wouldn't have invited her along, and none of this would have happened. Instead, she buried the man who had held her heart like it was made of porcelain, who livened her days with his goofiness, and warmed her nights with wild fits of passion. Tom's loss had weakened her on a sub-atomic level, leaving her knees susceptible to gravity.

Heavy, warm droplets fell to her chest. They were swallowed by the same black hole pulling her to the floor. She welcomed the numbness encompassing her heart. If she couldn't feel, it couldn't hurt anymore.

Something in the cosmos must have heard her pleas. In lieu of relief, though, they summoned more suffering. Grady appeared in the doorway, his hands in the front pockets of his jeans. He stood just outside the room, as if his presence wasn't welcome in the space. His watchful gaze echoed the pain she was reliving, but he didn't come to her.

She hated herself for wishing he would.

Grady broke eye contact to study a blank space on the carpet. "I need some stuff from my house. Clothes, and books."

"Okay." Beth used both hands to swipe away the proof of her weakness. She never liked people seeing her like this, especially not Grady. He was always so strong. She could be, too, if today would cooperate. "Let me close my suitcase and we can go."

Beth used the comforter as a crutch to stand.

Grady's face was a flurry of emotion. His frown twisted into a grimace before he pulled his shoulders up and stepped inside. It was like he expected to combust like a vampire.

"It's okay. You should probably be here when the sheriff's men show up." He clicked his tongue, the weight of something chewed on his conscious.

"Yeah." Beth could tell by the hard set of his jaw he was adamant about leaving. She pushed anyway. "But I would appreciate you staying, you know, for moral support."

After a long silence, Grady sighed. "Look, I didn't want to put this on you with everything..." He waved behind him toward the mess where *he* still lay.

That's right. I murdered someone. She was going to jail and had even called the executioner.

Beth's throat swelled with those thoughts, taking her voice hostage. Pressure built behind her eyes, and the room dimmed around the edges. Grady was too busy wrestling his own demons to notice.

He must have taken her silence as permission to continue, "I went to Jeff's house before I came here. Marla Jean is dead."

Wait. What?

"What?" she echoed, trying to fit the clues together. What was she missing? "Why did you go over there? When?"

"Earlier today. Before you called." Grady's blue eyes had turned almost navy as his gaze finally settled on her. His hands were by his side now, making fists. "I went over there to deal with Curtis before he did something stupid, but I was too late."

The air crackled with guardian magic, pushing her toward him. It would be so easy, too. One step and she could collapse into his arms. Beth's stomach balled into a fist. These weren't rational thoughts. It was the magic. She stuffed the feelings as far down the rabbit hole as she could reach and let out a shuddering breath.

"Looks like I dealt with him just fine." In Beth's head, the words were strong, confident. When she spoke them aloud they were barely above a whisper.

Murderer.

"Are you sure you're okay?"

"I'm fine, Grady. Shaken, but fine."

Liar.

Beth crossed her arms over her chest.

Grady cursed softly. Averting his watery gaze, Grady sniffled and lumbered toward her. Blood rushed to her face when he opened his arms for a hug.

Beth fought against falling into his warmth, the last soldier standing on the wintry battlefield. The moment Grady enveloped her, Beth wrapped her arms around his waist and buried her face in his chest. She hadn't realized how touch-starved she was for his comfort, or how he thawed the iciness trapping her soul. One by one, the cracks formed. Her fists tightened on his shirt, and the floodgates were flung wide open.

Gently rocking them, Grady's heavy downward strokes lulled her bones into a relaxed state, helping to clear her brain. He loosened his hold enough to rub circles on her back in time with her slowing breaths. She had expelled all the excess emotions until she was raw.

When his other hand moved to cradle the back of her head, she squeezed her eyes and hid her pained cry as his fingers brushed the bump.

"Sorry," he murmured, pulling away. "I swear, if that bastard wasn't already dead, I'd kill him."

He parted her hair and prodded around the soreness.

"He didn't do this. I did. It was an accident…just before." Beth studied Grady's chest where it was clear the wetness was more than saline drops. In her mortified state, she blurted, "I'm sorry. I got snot all over your shirt."

Grady's frown lines softened when he met her gaze. "It'll wash."

They stared into each other's eyes for the longest time, searching for the comfort neither was ready to admit to needing. All the while, the heat from his body soaked into her bones, warming her to her core. Grady's breath had a sour tanginess about it with the barest hint of sweetness. Maybe it was the drink playing tricks on her again, but it seemed like they were inching closer.

Grady gulped, breaking the tension that had been drawing them in like a half-hearted game of tug of war. Beth pulled away first, hugging herself. She told herself it was a shield, but her heart knew the truth.

"You should probably get going. I'll take care of the—"

Flashing red and blue lights spilled from the living room into the doorway. Beth's brain caught up with what was happening about the time there was shout from the top step, and someone hissing, 'shit.'

Grady stared at her with an expression of calm that contrasted with the pins and needles coursing through her veins. She'd done it again. Took too long to pack, had another breakdown. If—

"Beth." He cracked a wobbly smile as his hand cradled her cheek. With his free hand, his pinkie finger hooked hers and squeezed gently. "Breathe, beautiful. It'll be okay."

A tear rolled down her face. Beth knew what he was doing, trying to invoke the anger she needed for a clear head, but Grady didn't understand how vulnerable she'd made herself. She'd put on her brave front for him.

A parade of stomping boots stopped behind Grady. Beth peered over his shoulder into the barrels of two hot-headed deputies looking for trouble.

"Keep your hands where I can see them." Both men looked familiar, but Beth's memory failed her.

Grady complied, his jaw working as he lifted both hands in surrender.

"Ma'am, are you in distress?" The older man asked. His dark hair was peppered with gray and contrasted with his umber skin. Another prick of recognition fizzled when she met his tired and sad amber eyes. This man had known deep loss.

No matter his situation, heat flashed across her tongue, but she swallowed it, knowing it would only cause more issues.

"No, I am no longer in distress or danger. Grady—"

"Grady Alan Cooper." The older deputy holstered his weapon and grabbed one of Grady's arms and secured his hands with metal cuffs. The younger fellow kept his standard issue trained on Grady's chest, finger gently squeezing the trigger.

Her best friend kept eye contact with her, his face the poster of stoicism.

"You are under arrest for the murder of Mrs. Marla Jean Putnam…"

Everything else was drowned by the pulsing in her brain. Her lungs refused to work as the deputy recited his rights. This was wrong. Grady was innocent. He wouldn't have murdered anyone…he couldn't.

"Hey." Grady's cracked voice broke through her panic attack. "Cooperate with them. I'll call you as soon as I can."

"But—" Tears streaked her cheeks. How could he be so calm right now? Then the realization she was going to be alone hit her square in the chest. "I can't do this without you."

"Yes, you can." Grady grunted when the uniformed men jerked him forward. "Stay *safe.*"

As soon as his back disappeared through the front door, loneliness seeped into the hollow of her heart before she could stop it.

An older man with sharp features and a stripe of white his temples snapped his fingers in front of her face. His hardened steel gaze lacked compassion.

"Ma'am. Can you tell me what happened?"

"He kicked the door in and attacked me."

"I see." He scribbled something in his notebook. "After Mr. Cooper kicked in the door—"

"No. Not Grady. *Him.*" She pointed toward her kitchen floor, where Curtis's body was being looked over by men and women wearing gloves. "*He* kicked my door in while I was in my kitchen and attacked me with a knife." Beth waved at her shoddily wrapped thigh.

"Can you explain why there is a wine corkscrew in his neck?"

"It was available."

"And the toaster oven covered with blood? Was that available, too?"

"Yessir."

"Mm-hmm." He scribbled something else in his stupid notebook. His unflinchingly stony gaze returned to scrutinize *her* wrongdoings.

Beth held it with sheer force of stubbornness. He slowly listed sideways.

"Miss," the steely-eyed rude deputy narrowed his eyes. "Are you under the influence of alcohol or any other recreational drugs?"

"It's Mrs.; Recently widowed." She shifted on her feet and tucked her hair behind her ear. "I drank some wine, but I don't think—"

"Do you often drink at home, or do you frequent the local bars?"

A surge of anger parted the hazy cloud around her reasoning. Since when was protecting yourself from a home intruder considered a crime? It's possible she was making up laws, though. Lingering aftereffects of bolstered bravery and all.

"My having a few glasses of wine in the privacy of my own home isn't breaking any laws. The crime here was that man came into my house without permission and broke my things while trying to kill me." To make her point, she put her hands on her hips and jutted her chin.

It was a bad move.

Deputy Asshole's face darkened, and his face puckered like a butthole. Keeping a poker face at the correlation was worthy of an Emmy or an Oscar. Beth couldn't remember which was which. What was important was keeping composure in front of a man who was itching to put a hurt on someone.

"Do you personally know or have had any dealings with the intruder?"

The abrupt shift in the line of questioning stirred unease in her gut. Grady was in their custody, and the truth would find its way out.

"I was friends with his son, Jeff, sir."

"Are you aware of the recent death of Jeffrey Putnam?"

"Unfortunately, yes. It's a small town, but Jeff was always nice to me."

Until last weekend, she almost amended, but the words couldn't pass the lump in her throat.

"Were you in any way responsible for the death of Jeffrey Putnam?"

"What? No. Why is this-what does Jeff's death have to do with—"

"Ma'am, I am not at liberty to discuss the particulars of the case, so I'm gonna have to ask you to refrain from asking any further questions."

His edged tone and the set of his jaw cautioned Beth of the dangers should she continue, but that didn't stop her from foolishly asking one more.

"What's going to happen to Grady?"

His notebook snapped shut, causing her to flinch. She swore his lip sneered at her reaction before it snapped back into a scowl. The man's hardened exterior held a perpetuity that was well practiced.

"We'll be in touch, *Miss* Harper. I suggest you don't leave town." He gave her one last once-over before storming out of her apartment.

A sharp whistle came shortly after, and the apartment emptied in a hurry, leaving Beth in a barren home of fractured dreams. The curtains flew inward with a cool breeze, prickling her skin as she struggled to recall when she had given anyone her name. The angry drill sergeant-looking guy had been the only one to address her, and by her maiden name, no less.

The weight of repercussions, isolation, and countless unknowns was so great her knees lacked the strength to bear it all. Her slow descent to the middle of her carpeted living room would have been comical had it been under different circumstances.

"Beth?"

Shoes crunched on gravel, pounding up the stairs with heavy urgency. The scent of cardamom and cinnamon entered the room as Fennick stopped inside the doorway, a bottle of wine in hand, and his eyes wild. When they landed on her, he rushed over. The glass bottle rolled away to clink against the wooden table leg as he knelt by her side.

"What are you doing here?" She hadn't meant to question him so harshly, but he acted as though they were familiar. Outside of saving her life, she still knew nothing of this mysterious new neighbor.

"You invited me over for dinner, remember?" His fingers brushed the hair away from her cheek and forehead, leaving warm, familiar tingles in their wake. The act was tender, much too intimate for her comfort. She scooted back from him. His hands faltered, finding their rest on the carpet. "There are officers just outside. I can call them for assistance."

"No. I don't want them back in here." She shook her head.

"Will you tell me what happened?" Fen asked, his gentle voice soothing the edges of her isolation like a warm spring creek. The effect annoyed her.

"My attacker—the one you saved me from—came back, and I killed him. Then, these guys interrogate me like *I* did something wrong." Beth chanced a look into his hazel eyes. They were as gorgeous as she remembered, even with the pinched brows wrinkling his handsome face. "By the way, I'm gonna have to cancel your 'thank you dinner' tonight."

She lazily slung her arm in the direction of the kitchen. Hell, she wasn't sure when or *if* she'd be cooking anything because the sheriff's people didn't give her a straight answer.

"Ah, yes." Fennick frowned, but a smirk played on his lips. "By the look of things, I would say you defended yourself splendidly and live to fight another day."

He stood, dusted his jeans, and offered her his hand. "What do you say we get out of here? My apartment is clear of anyone wishing you harm and I find myself with an open schedule this evening."

Beth raised her gaze to his height. She hadn't realized how tall he was until now, towering over her with a lithe body that pretended to be slight and weak. But there was power there, rippling with each purposeful movement.

"I dunno," she answered, placing her hand in his. The familiarity rang again, stronger but different. She ignored it for now, stuffing it with the other emotions swirling around as she pulled herself to stand. Fennick made a decent anchor. "I'm afraid I won't be good company tonight. I should probably pack and call my parents."

"Nonsense. I would be remiss in my duties as your neighbor, should I not extend some hospitality after such a horrendous event." Fennick dropped her hand. "I will not keep you long, only until I am sure you are mentally well to tackle whatever comes next. What do you say?"

The twinkle in his eyes warned of how dangerous spending time with this charismatic gentleman could be, yet learning more about her new neighbor would be a welcome distraction. Safety wise? She figured the sheriff's department would be keeping an eye on her. Besides, it's not like she was looking to hook up with the guy. Her poor heart was full as it could be while divided between the grave and a jail cell.

"Sure. Why not?" Beth ran her hand through her ponytail, snagging on several knots. She must look like a hot mess. "Uh, you go ahead. I'll clean up, first. Meet you in ten?"

"Of course." Fennick bent over to retrieve the wine bottle, tipping his chin. "In the meantime, I shall open the wine and rummage for some food."

As soon as he left, Beth's lungs shuddered until they were empty. Once she had her bearings, she straightened her back and tackled the task of making herself look presentable. Ten minutes later, Beth was on her way.

As she stepped outside, a man hooked Grady's truck to the wench on his tow truck. The metal clank and loud whirring made her stomach sink like quicksand.

She was halfway up the stairs leading to Fennick's apartment when she stopped.

What am I thinking? I'm going over to my neighbor's apartment after a home invasion and my best friend being arrested.

She squeezed her eyes shut, wincing at the bruise forming underneath her eye. This was stupid, but her mother's brand of southern hospitality had been burned into Beth's etiquette training from a young age. Rather than make a run for it, she was compelled to cancel to Fennick's face.

Beth took a deep breath and continued her climb. Before she could raise her hand to knock, it opened to reveal Fen's charming smile.

"Punctuality is a virtue."

She grinned, but she probably looked feral. Her eyes were too puffy for it to spread right. "Look, Fennick, I appreciate your offer, but I think it's best if I head to my mom and dad's place."

As she spoke, the ground beneath her feet rocked like a boat on the lake. Her hand shot out, gripping the trim around his door.

"You are in no fit shape to operate a vehicle, Beth." Fennick pinned her under his defiant gaze. Beth relented with a short nod. He waved toward the minimalist living room, placing a hand on her back. "Please, come in and make yourself comfortable."

A modest array of mismatched furniture was arranged in such a way that it complimented the small space. It wasn't the style or décor she expected from someone as refined as Fennick, but rather like how she expected her former neighbor, Jeremy, to have decorated the place.

"It is not much, but I was somewhat rushed to find a rental after my previous lease ended." Fen's hands were on his hips as he studied the space with a frown. "I am fortunate the former tenant did not mind parting with the furniture when I took over the lease."

"Ah. That explains a lot." Beth sat in the faded brown accent chair next to the corner fireplace and tucked her hands between her knees. She winced when the action pulled at the clean cloth she'd tied around her thigh. It chafed the wound and saturated it red. She hadn't thought to heal herself before coming over. At least she had enough of a brain to switch her jeans for shorts.

"Do you mind if I take a look?" Fennick gestured to her leg. He must have sensed her hesitation because he added, "I used to care for wounds in third world countries where medical practitioners were scarce."

The coil of stress in her chest loosened a stitch. "Sure. I'll just add 'doctoring your neighbor's stab wound' to my 'thank Fen' list."

His laughter rang in the living room as he left toward the hall. It was a handsome laugh, if you could describe it that way, youthful as a summer day but hearty like a drunken sailor. Beth rolled her eyes, busying herself with untying the knot when he returned with a first aid kit.

"When the police arrived, did no one look at your wounds?" Fennick dotted a cotton ball with alcohol and cleaned the area. She sucked air quickly through her teeth, clenching her jaw. "Apologies."

"You're okay. And no. They chose to bombard me with the FBI edition of twenty questions." Beth watched his nimble fingers cut gauze to size. When he opened a round silver tin filled with a sweet-smelling green paste, she asked, "What's that?"

Fen paused, rubbing the mixture between his fingers before spreading it on the gauze. "It is an herbal poultice made with aloe, dried calendula and chamomile, tea tree oil, and elm bark. It will help your cut heal and stay any infection."

"Cool." Beth's fascination piqued. Her new neighbor seemed to have many layers to uncover. "Did you make it, or do you buy it from somewhere?"

Fen's hand paused before he whispered, "I made it."

The softness of his voice and his sudden curtness hinted at a deep melancholy. Beth wondered if she'd unintentionally struck a nerve.

"There." Fennick stood and put on a forced grin. "Tomorrow, you shall be right as rain. Let me know if the soreness lingers, and I will redress your bandage."

Without waiting for her reply, he disappeared down the hallway. The shutting of a door left Beth to wonder if she should leave, or if she should stay and hope the awkwardness faded. Once again, her carelessness had potentially cost her a friend...and left her alone with her thoughts.

All she could see was the concern etched on Grady's face as they handcuffed and dragged him out.

'Stay safe,' he'd said. Curtis was dead, and Tom's sacrifice had given them years to get ready for the coming battle. What else was there besides Grady's situation?

She buried her face in her hands and groaned, wishing today would take a hike.

Chapter 4

RICH

THE LIGHTER FLICKERED TO life, transforming the white paper into a smoldering cinder. As Rich inhaled deeply, the acrid scent of burnt tobacco permeated the air. Bitterness burst across his tongue, sending a temporary buzz straight to his cortex.

Rich stared at the broken door of Beth's apartment and shook his head. She hadn't recognized him, but he couldn't blame her. Several years had passed since he'd been a parent volunteer for the high school track team. Since Deena's disappearance two years ago, Rich hardly recognized himself these days.

A heavy sigh, a cloud of smoke… If only the headache they found at the Putnam residence would as easily dissipate. At least they had the guy responsible sitting in the back of his cruiser.

Staring at the cinders he took another long drag before ashing his cigarette with a practiced flick. A second nature habit picked up during academy.

Smoking was supposed to settle his nerves, and it did for a while. Back then, he smoked all the time—at least three packs a day. Bea hated it, always complaining that he came home 'smelling like a damned ashtray.' Rich had tried to quit, several times. For a few years he was successful, hoping his efforts would save his already crumbling marriage. Quitting one bad habit didn't count for much when he had so many.

He pinched the bridge of his nose and groaned. Carrying too fucking much baggage had given him a permanent slouch. Today had added a shit ton more.

The crime scene images from earlier flashed behind his eyelids. In the twenty-some odd years Rich had been an officer of the law, he'd never seen anything like this, not in real time. The ritualistic symbols drawn with days old blood were unlike anything he'd researched, but it was the filth, and rats…the desiccated corpse of fifty-four-year-old Marla

Jean Putnam that scarred him most. Those fucking rodents had been nibbling away at the evidence. Their only clue had been some smudged boot prints and vomit until an eye-witness statement put Cooper's red Dodge Ram at the scene. It was the breakthrough he needed to keep Sheriff Blaylock off his ass.

His boss's idea of 'disciplinary action' looked a lot like bullying. The Sheriff made his own rules and changed them to fit his narrative. Thing was, when Blaylock told someone to jump, they asked how high, or things became...difficult...at work. If not for his daughter's disappearance, Rich would've left two years ago. Despite being told in no uncertain terms to 'drop it or he'd be demoted to janitor,' Rich was still digging for evidence. Being one of the few people of color on the force in a predominantly white neighborhood didn't garner any favors in Mayes Hill, so people were tight-lipped. His interest in the occult didn't help, either. So far, the only things he'd found were dead ends and a failed marriage.

This was not the start Rich expected for his first weekend off in several months. And the cigarette wasn't helping.

Rich shivered. He opened his eyes and took one last pull on the cancer stick. Staring at the useless thing, he scoffed and tossed it to the ground, stamping the butt with his boot. Smoke curled from his nose and lips, wrapping around his head like a cloud before the wind carried it away.

"Stanton, the sheriff wants to see ya before we wrap up." Deputy Wilson tongued the tobacco in his cheek, spitting brown juice in the gravel off to the side. He shifted back and forth, casting his wary gaze between the squad car and the apartment.

His partner had the energy of a Jack Russel Terrier. Rich didn't understand why the sheriff assigned the young man to work with him. The rookie was just a kid; fresh out of academy at twenty-three.

Same age as Deena.

"Alright. Meet me at the cruiser, kid."

Wilson's head wobbled like a bobble-head doll before he jogged over to stand with the younger officers. Rich wished he could share in their excitement. Having busted the perp before he could cause more trouble looked good for the department and even better for his retirement. However, the cavalier way the clues were glued together bothered Rich. The boot prints and vomit were fresh, but the body had been laying there for days. Unfortunately, he'd learned to turn a blind eye to a lot of the rot happening downtown.

At least until he found his daughter.

Blaylock turned to greet him. Something flickered in his sharp, blue eyes. Rich was too preoccupied with keeping up his poker face to bother figuring out what was eating at his boss this time.

"Stanton," Sheriff Blaylock greeted while scratching the side of his short salt and pepper hair. "Take these files back to the station and type up the report. I want it on my desk by morning."

A crisp manilla folder was thrust into Rich's chest. He had to grab it before the pages slipped out. The rookie came to stand next to them with a water bottle in hand.

"But, what—"

"Wilson," the sheriff interrupted, making Rich's face hot enough to fry an egg. "Tell the boys to shut it down and pack it up."

"Yes, sir." The kid turned and jogged back to where their coworkers huddled.

"Sir," Rich ground through his teeth, "I thought we were gonna question the offender tonight?"

"We are, just not you. I need you"—Blaylock poked a finger into Rich's chest—"to keep the paperwork clean and tight. You're the only one who gives a shit about whether it's done proper or not."

Rich narrowed his eyes in thought, ignoring his aching sternum. "Can't it wait until tomorrow, after the questioning? Sir, I've never let you down before."

The sheriff grunted and stopped abruptly. The buddy-buddy gig was up as he moved to stand in front of Rich. Disdain curled on his lips. "Not with this prisoner. If we play our cards right, we'll be able to pin his daddy's death and the others found in the woods on this delinquent."

Rich frowned and shook his head. His boss was reaching more than usual. Cooper was seen leaving the Putnam's house and, soon after, arriving at the widow Newman's place. He could have been responsible for the ritual, but not the Putnam woman's death. Knowing how mild-mannered Beth was in high school, Rich didn't peg her as the violent type. Cooper must have been the one who killed Curtis. Then again, the young man didn't have any wounds indicating he'd been in a fight.

There were too many questions and not enough evidence to support the facts either way.

"Before you get any *ideas*, this isn't Grady Cooper's first run in with the law." Sheriff Blaylock's steady steel gaze penetrated Rich's dark brown eyes. "Given the number of deaths in recent weeks, the townsfolk need to feel safe. Capturing the person responsible for it all will do just that."

A deep sigh left Rich. If you smell bullshit, there's a heaping pile nearby, and this was strong enough to make his eyes water.

"Is this gonna be a problem, Deputy?" Sheriff Blaylock asked as he took a step closer, exuding the menacing aura Rich had become all too accustomed to.

They were close in age, but Rich hadn't been born and raised in Mayes Hill, Tennessee like the rest of these good ole boys. Instead, he'd been reduced to a simpering lap dog cowering in the shadows while the devil gallivanted in broad daylight. There wasn't shit he could do about it.

"No, sir." Rich's chest caved with forced obedience. The urge to bruise more than the man's pride seized him something fierce. His grip on the manilla folder tightened a fraction.

"Good." His boss studied him closely before clapping him on the back harder than necessary. As he sauntered away, he called over his shoulder, "Don't forget the report, Stanton."

As always, all manner of ill-intentions crossed Rich's mind when the Sheriff left him to do his dirty work. One day, Rich would discover what secrets Blaylock hid, and it would be a glorious day of comeuppances.

There was more to this murder and others than Rich was led to believe. If his hunch was right, Sheriff Blaylock was at the center of this misinformation maelstrom.

One way or another, Rich would discover what was going on at the station. Secrets had a way of being found if you knew where to look.

Chapter 5

GRADY

GRADY HAD BEEN SITTING in the back of the squad car for ages. He cringed internally, knowing the phones pointed his way were recording his misfortune. By this time tomorrow, all of Eastern Tennessee and North Georgia would know his face. He'd be infamous.

A mysterious-looking man crossed the front of the cruiser. Grady scooted forward in the seat to get a better look. He was tall—pushing six feet plus—and his wavy dark brown hair went just past his shoulders. He carried himself like someone who was used to getting his way.

The stranger spared him a passing glance, eyes sparkling in the flashing lights. He raised his chin like they were two acquaintances passing on the street, but Grady had no damn clue who this guy was. Last he heard, Beth's neighbor, Jeremy, still lived next door, so what was this guy's business?

Grady's skin flashed with heat, followed by a shivering cold. The mystery man waltzed past all the uniforms, and not one of them raised a single damn eyebrow.

"Hey," he yelled. Anger pooled in his chest when no one paid him any attention. The thick glass most likely muffled any sound, 'cause he sure as shit couldn't hear anything.

Grady craned his neck in time to see the guy run up the stairs to Beth's apartment. If Beth was in trouble, he was powerless to help...unless he was ready for the rest of the town to find out about his well-kept secret.

Grady tossed his body weight back and forth. His teeth ground and crunched as he rocked the car, trying to get their attention. Obviously, these pricks didn't give a fuck. He stopped, kicking the back of the passenger seat before sliding back and dropping his head against the headrest.

What the hell kinda good are these assholes if anyone can walk onto a crime scene unnoticed?

He willed the burning pricks at the corners of his eyes to go away by counting the threads in the upholstery. When that didn't work, he tried closing his eyes, attempting to meditate. His inhale was too sharp, and his wrists pulsed with impending blood loss.

There was no calm or inner peace, not when he was at the end of his rope. His Adam's apple bobbed on a hard swallow as his imagination ran rampant.

Beth, welcoming this stranger with open arms. Him, kissing away her troubles like Grady should be doing. *They probably met at the grocery store.* But that thought felt wrong. There was something else going on; a thought scratched at his subconscious. A mysterious man showed up the first time Curtis tried to murder Beth. Could this be the same guy?

A whole new level of terror threatened to shred his insides. Was this man the reason she held herself back? Because he'd been her savior, her knight in shining armor?

His stomach wrestled with his other organs for real estate in the shrinking space. Swallowing didn't help anymore, not with the passages closing. The air in the cabin became unbearably hot. Sweat appeared in an instant, but it did little to cool his overheating skin.

In a last-ditch attempt to calm his erratic emotions, Grady leaned against the window. The glass cooled his forehead enough for his brain to reset.

Beth wouldn't do that. She loves me. She's still grieving because her husband just died, dumbass.

While she'd only had days to process, Grady had spent the equivalent of months in the Grove. Building, sanding, painting, staining...using the tools of his trade to work through things. It had been therapeutic, allowing him to come to terms with falling in love with his best friend's wife. The worm eating his brain was whether he could ever live up to what she had with Tom.

There was also an unvoiced fear he kept buried deep under lock and key. A question of whether Beth loved Grady without the draw from their magical connection.

The stranger reappeared, turning a bottle of wine around in his hands. He stopped suddenly. Turning his gaze to Grady's, the man lifted his upper lip a fraction. Grady's eye twitched and his nostrils flared when heat flashed across his face. He didn't know the man, but he instantly didn't like him. No amount of rational thinking would change it.

A passing deputy blocked Grady's sight. He ducked back and forth to find the man, but he'd disappeared. Grady's annoyance was short-lived when both front doors opened, bringing a blast of fresh air. His lungs greedily replenished while the car dipped like a listing boat.

The doors closed and an uncomfortable silence followed.

The younger deputy, Wilson, turned to face him with a shit-eating grin. Clutched in the palm of his left hand was the portal moonstone. "If you know what's good for you, Mr. Cooper, you better 'fess up. The quicker ya do, the easier it'll be if you know what I mean."

Grady didn't grace him with a reply. Instead, he returned his attention to Beth's place as they drove away. She never came out of her apartment.

He'd fucked up again, leaving her alone, only this time she was left to process killing someone in self-defense on top of everything else. At least with Curtis dead, Ja'azul had no one else to perform the sacrifices.

Once Grady was out of this current mess, he and Beth had all the time in the world to continue learning magic and find a way to banish Ja'azul to his home dimension, wherever it was.

The cruiser pulled into the precinct parking lot in the back of the building. The older deputy opened his door and ducked down, giving Grady time to glance at the nametag. Stanton grabbed Grady's left arm and tugged. To keep a shred of dignity, Grady exited on his own.

"You'd better have a good lawyer if you wanna see daylight anytime in the next decade or three," Stanton growled, his low voice full of annoyance.

Looks like I'm not the only one having a bad day, Grady scoffed internally.

Night owls ogled Grady as they led him inside, further stirring the gossip pool. They dragged him down a poorly lit corridor. Keys jingled and a pop clanked. The door's hinges screeched like a screaming banshee with a head cold. His temporary lodging offered a bed, a toilet, and a sink. The whole room smelled like bleach.

They shoved Grady into the room, yanking the metal bars shut behind him. The lock clicked into place. As if he was stupid enough to try and escape.

"Back up and put your hands through the bars."

Grady complied, sighing when the metal cutting into his tender flesh dropped away. He tentatively rubbed his wrists, rolling his head to release the stiffness in his shoulders and neck. He turned to face his detainers.

"When do I get my phone call?"

Wilson snickered and ignored Grady, strutting back down the hall with his thumbs hooked in his belt like he was the cock of the walk.

Rich narrowed his eyes as he studied Grady like he was gum on the bottom of his shoe. "I'll talk to the Sheriff."

"Thanks," Grady mumbled quietly as the day's events smacked into all at once.

He lumbered over to the cot and dropped onto his back. The hinges creaked, playing a 'bed of nails' version of Whack-A-Mole of with the thin mattress. Finding a spot that didn't shank him in the kidney, Grady laid his arm over his forehead to block the harsh fluorescent light and stared at the dingy white popcorn ceiling. The constant buzzing only served to irritate his mood, probably by design.

His other hand covered the stone underneath his shirt, fingers tracing the outline through the fabric. If only he'd thought of having them take the necklaces off earlier. He could be talking to Beth, making sure she wasn't too shaken after taking a man's life. And without his portal stone, there was no hope of getting out this weekend.

"Fuck!"

Grady's frustration edged on panic. The side of his fist hit the wall. It wasn't enough, so he punished himself again. His pinkie finger pulsed from the impact. Hearing Beth's voice would alleviate the twisting in his gut, the weight crushing his heart. What if they didn't let him call?

What if the mystery guy is moving in on your girl?

He shot to his feet, gripping the sides of his head as he wore a path between the cot and the door. A dull ache formed around his head like a squeezing fist centered above his eyes.

I should have left with Beth instead of hanging around.

He could be consoling the woman he loved, bonding over their shared trauma instead of leaving things to chance. But Grady was stuck in this cold steel cage like an animal.

The concept paused his frantic war march. His beast's fur swept soothingly along the underside of his skin.

If they're going to treat me like a caged beast, I may as well act like one.

His fingertips blistered as claws forced free of their fleshy confines. A throaty snarl coaxed its way from his mouth as teeth elongated. He would rip them all to shreds, starting with Wilson and Stanton. They were the ones who took him away from Beth.

No, no, no, no, no. This wasn't him. Somehow, his panther was putting feelings into thoughts.

He needed to calm down before he lost his head and dug a deeper hole. Proving his innocence would be harder to accomplish if he wasn't of sound mind. Grady gripped the bars of his prison with both hands, resting his forehead on the cold metal. Instantly, the loss of heat calmed the rising beast. The panther hissed, but he receded to the shadows, taking with it any outward signs.

Grady slid to the floor as exhaustion turned his bones to gelatin. His chest caved inward toward the black hole swallowing insides. He was pretty sure this was what dying felt like.

You can't give up now, not when Beth needs you.

The voice resounding between his ears didn't sound like Grady's, but their words did the trick. He wasn't prone to breakdowns, but he'd never loved someone so deeply that his gravity depended on their nearness.

A ragged breath brought him to his knees. A stronger breath brought him to the side of the cot. Whenever he was lost or needed a reset, meditation was the key to finding his center.

Grady propped his back against the bed and crossed his legs. He sloppily rested his elbows on his thighs, palms up and began his breathing technique. Deep, five-count breaths in, hold, release, repeat. Once his mind was somewhat still, he focused on the events of the evening, in order, searching for clues to help clear his name.

His thoughts took an unexpected left turn toward Tom. His best friend never strayed too far from Beth, even in death. Now was not the time for Tom's memories to resurface. Not when Grady's anger stalked the outskirts of his calm, waiting for an opportunity to be unleashed. Why couldn't Tom had fallen for someone else? He could have had any girl in school, but chose the one who didn't want anything to do with him. He chose the one girl fate had destined for Grady.

While he was cooped up at the Grove, the question eating at Grady, plaguing him daily: How could he prove himself worthy of Beth's affection, worthy of his best friend's approval, if he couldn't keep one simple damn promise?

The conundrum perplexed him in a way that left him dizzy and unsettled. The same could be said in his current predicament. Naturally, this particular state of mind made hunting a safer outlet than sawing wood. There was no popping out to find game this time.

Groaning, Grady refocused and repeated his mantra. This time, he meditated on being led outside the apartment. The deputies—Stanton and Wilson—pushed him up against their cruiser, nudging his legs apart for a brisk pat down. The younger deputy had pocketed Grady's portal stone, but he missed the necklace. His cell and keys were still in the bed of his truck, which was hooked up to a tow truck.

In the back of the cruiser, he saw the mysterious man carrying a bottle of wine. He'd been a man on a mission. Single-minded. Determined. When the guy came out of Beth's apartment, it was as if he sensed Grady watching. He *wanted* Grady to see him, to know he was with Beth. For what end, Grady hadn't figured out yet.

Before losing visual, the man looked to be heading toward the neighboring apartment. If Tom and Beth's neighbor had moved out, that was news to him.

Grady put a pin in the odd neighbor for now.

Moving to the next recollection, Grady recalled Deputy Wilson turning the moonstone over in his hand; the rattle on the console. He hadn't heard the rattling again, so it was possible they'd left it in the cruiser.

His brief surge of hope was interrupted by the low growl in the pits below. He'd heard the adage 'three hots and a cot' but wasn't sure these guys adhered to the rules.

Grady had no way to satisfy his growing hunger, nor was he able to connect to any plant life through these walls. Thank the gods he was a persistent man. If there was a crack somewhere in this building within his magic's reach, he'd find it.

Chapter 6

FENNICK

THE DESPONDENCY FENNICK WORE behind his jovial mask slipped back into place as he battled for control with the man in the tarnished bathroom mirror. His lungs refused to fill with enough oxygen to sustain him, forcing him to ration the short bursts he was allowed. His long fingers gripped the edge of the porcelain sink until his knuckles locked into place.

Here he was, the most powerful witch on the planet, playing host to his prey in a stolen apartment. All to what end? To satisfy a cosmic god's vendetta against humanity? Oh, how he loathed that part of himself, which was what put him in dire straits in the first place. Had he not made an oath to Ja'azul, his soul would not be damned for eternity.

Fennick had not expected Beth.

Being in her presence was akin to waking from winter's slumber to find the sunshine had melted the snow, allowing life to spring forth once more. As swiftly as he gulped the sweet air of serenity, the festering chill brought back all his pain and hatred when he left her company.

Fennick dared not call this dependency love, for one cannot claim the sun as solely their possession. No, her power called to him, beckoning to the long-dead ruins where goodness once resided. Ja'azul had pitted from him all that was light and left only darkness, but after arriving at her apartment to find her frail and defeated, something in the bottomless pit of Fennick's black heart shifted.

He had touched her. He had felt the damned tingles. What did it mean?

She could never love someone as irredeemable as you.

Fennick mentally swatted away the voices as they snickered. They were right. He knew this, which is why the pain of rejection wounded him less than expected. He must resist temptation, no matter how pure. Sacrificing Beth was the only means to his freedom.

Yesss...Kill her, light*bringer. Give her soul to the master.*

Fennick's grip on the porcelain sink tightened until a hairline crack formed. He stared at the sweat beading above his brow and upper lip as he fought his demons, the voices. Their command grew ever stronger the thinner Ja'azul's veil became.

Beth is here, alone, and no one knows of her whereabouts.

The cleverness of the voices had seen to that, coaxing her next door before she could call her parents. And with Grady temporarily detained, there would be no better time to act.

"No." Fennick's harsh whisper pushed them back. He gulped as control was once again in his grasp, and whispered as if speaking to a mouse, "I will do this *my* way, of my own accord."

"Apologies," Fennick announced as he reentered her addictive aura, though it had diminished in the time she was left alone. Her face was now buried in her hands. "It is unusual for me to disregard my guests in such a manner."

Her muffled reply was unclear, but after removing her hands, it became obvious. Her red-rimmed eyes swam with uncertainty. "It's okay. I should probably go."

Beth stood and wiped her chin with the back of her hand. Pins and needles flashed across Fennick's face and neck. He gravitated to her side, positioning himself between her and the exit. Beth peered over his shoulder, rubbing her hands together. He could practically see her wheels spinning. He had to act fast.

"I must insist you stay for dinner. Your body could be in shock and food will help." Fennick tried on his most disarming smile. "With the current somber mood, I think comfort food is appropriate. What is the name of the pizza restaurant a few blocks away?"

"Benny's." Her gaze was slow to meet his. "It's the best."

Her tongue darted out to pull her bottom lip in. The movement tested Fennick's resolve, but he was not some stripling maneuvering puberty. To prove his restraint, Fennick placed a hand on her shoulder.

"Does this mean you will stay?"

"Yes," she said with tired sigh, shrugging away from his hand. "I'll help you eat the pizza, but afterward, I've gotta go."

"Brilliant. Please, follow me and I will show you to the kitchen where there are libations." Fennick held out his arm, directing her further inside the apartment.

Beth picked at her fingernails, casting another glance at the door before passing him by. His heart thumped, stirring the voices. He gritted his teeth against them. Setting his jaw straight, Fennick turned to address her. "Being that you are the local expert, what do you suggest for a Benny's first timer?"

"You can never go wrong with pepperoni and cheese." Beth's stomach chose that moment to growl, dusting her cheeks pink.

Fennick couldn't help but laugh. "Classic it is." He picked up the land line, but it was dead. "Hmm."

"What's wrong?" Beth crossed her arms and leaned her hip against the counter.

"It appears the telephone company has been too preoccupied to connect the line." Fennick knew better, but the lie slipped from his tongue like silk. Jeremy was...indisposed, therefore unable to make the payment.

"That's alright. I'll call it in." Beth pressed the speed dial on her cell and gave him a friendly half smile. The simple action warmed him bodily.

As Fennick listened to Beth's voice, his concentration slipped. His gaze fell to the corkscrew sitting next to his right hand. Fennick's fingers inched toward the silver tool. Fighting against his will, the spiraling tool ended up in the palm of his hand.

How poetic would it be to impale the female guardian with the same thing she used to dispatch the pathetic one?

"I ordered two large pepperoni pizzas and some buffalo wings, 'cause if you eat anything like the guys, they devour that much in one sitting." Beth snapped his internal debate, staring across the room at nothing with a sad smile marring her soft features.

Fennick leaned against the counter, crossing his ankles and arms while mimicking her demeanor. He attempted to dislodge the sharp tool while being inconspicuous. When he did 'the deed,' it would be done with more dignity.

"Your brothers?" he asked, feigning attentiveness. He knew full well who they were, but pretenses needed to be kept.

"No! Gods..." She jutted her hip and covered her face, shielding her embarrassment. The way her delicate skin tinged with a darker pink was delicious. He drove away the picture of her flush skin after more carnal activities. "Tom is—*was*—my husband. He passed away suddenly a few days ago. Grady is–well, he's our best friend."

"I am sorry for your loss." Fennick pushed away from the counter and grabbed a napkin, offering it to Beth.

"Thank you." She took care to dot her face clean with the scratchy material.

His desire to keep her relaxed in his company necessitated a swift change in subject.

"So, you now know that I have travelled abroad and am a competent healer, tell me something about yourself." Fennick poured wine into the two waiting glasses, offering one to Beth.

"Thank you." She sniffed the drink and swirled the glass, but did not partake.

Fennick mimicked her action before taking a sip. *See? There's nothing in the wine...this time.*

"Well," she began, tucking her chin and shifting on her feet. "I recently graduated college with a degree in early childhood education. This fall, I'll begin teaching at the elementary school."

"How wonderful. I am sure the children will be in good hands."

"Yeah, that's *if* the school even accepts a—" Her eyes widened into saucers and the tips of her ears flushed red. "I think I'd rather have water. I need water. Please."

Fennick waved his free hand at the sink and hid his smirk behind a drink. Beth took a glass from the dish drain and filled it with cold tap water.

"Souls as pure as yours are rare thing, but they all have one thing in common, Beth." Fennick swirled the wine in his glass as he inhaled the sweet fragrance of Moscato. "People flock to them like moths to a flame. The children you teach will do the same."

"Wow, okay." Her chuckle sounded forced, laced with bitterness. "But I'm not so sure my soul is as spotless as you say. I killed a man tonight. Even though it was in self-defense, something like that leaves a mark."

"I have many scars upon my soul, my dear, and have met more people than I can count, but all of them pale in comparison to the light you exude." Fennick raised the glass to his lips, pausing to add, "Your soul, my dear, burns as brightly as the day we first met."

Beth's lips parted but snapped shut, as if her rebuttal had been doused by his enigmatic argument. Doubt lingered in the crinkled edges of her eyes.

Fennick had not meant to push her boundaries to breaking point, but her natural ability to render him senseless was becoming a habit. Blessedly, the doorbell rang, diffusing the anxiety clouding the room.

"Ah! Pizza is here." He placed his wineglass on the countertop and pointed to a shelf, hoping it was the correct one. "Please, plates are there. We will dine at the table if you like."

"Sure."

When Fennick returned to the dining room, a plate had been placed at each of the farthest ends of the table. Beth stood behind the chair closest to the living room, almost a straight shot to the door. Her intention was loud and clear. The snare was set, he simply needed to lead the rabbit.

"Thank you for setting the table." He placed the food in the center, humming when the scent of melted cheese and tangy hot tomato sauce wafted toward him. "I will fetch our glasses and some napkins."

"Okay." His little bird had retreated to the safety of her gilded cage, watching his every move with eagle eyes.

As he left the room, out of the corner of his eyes he detected movement. *Good, she is occupied.* Grabbing another wineglass, he filled both, adding a touch of the very potent sleeping tonic he'd prepared to Beth's drink. The liquid swirled within, settling as he made his way back.

Beth had returned to her post, gripping the back of the dining chair. Fennick noted the modest amount of food on their matching plates.

"I hope you don't mind, but this seemed more efficient."

"No, not at all. I am not one to argue the benefits of efficiency." Fennick winked as he made his way to her end, placing her wineglass next to her plate. Her stomach rumbled again. He turned with a chuckle. "Sit, eat, or the roar from your stomach will rouse the dead. The wine will help settle your nerves.”

Beth nodded and sat in the chair with it turned slightly away from the table. As she thoroughly chewed her small bites, Fennick guessed her manners had been hammered into Beth from a young age.

Throughout their awkward dinner, Beth’s wine had gone untouched. Surely, she had not detected anything amiss. If so, he had vastly underestimated the young one.

Fennick stood, ready to put his plan into action.

“It seems I have a favorite new restaurant when the need for comfort food arises.” He placed two more slices of pepperoni pizza on his plate. Gesturing to the cardboard boxes, he asked, “Would you care for some more?”

“No thank you. I should probably get back anyway.” Beth stood and placed her napkin over the remnants of pizza crust. “I appreciate dinner and the temporary distraction.”

“Certainly. You are welcome to visit any time.” Fennick closed the pizza box lid and came to stand next to her. He raised his eyebrow at her untouched wineglass.

“I had plenty to drink earlier,” she explained, moving to step around him.

“Pity. I was told this particular Moscato was a limited edition.” He lifted her glass to his lips, willing her curiosity to override her caution.

“Maybe just a sip.”

Beth reached for the glass, her fingers brushing against his. They left a trail of pleasurable tingles like sparklers. She jerked her hand back, letting the wineglass fall to the laminate floor where it shattered, spilling across the floor like blood.

“Fuck. Sorry Fen.” Beth apologized, grabbing napkins off the table. Her hands shook as she threw them to the floor. “I-I can’t.”

You tried it your way. Now it is our turn...

Fennick’s hands were also shaking as he gripped her shoulders. “It is not your fault.”

A deep ‘V’ formed between her brows as his long fingers tightened. “Fen, you’re hurting me.”

“I am truly sorry, but there are—”

The voices swelled his tongue, keeping him from warning Beth of the danger. He hated the fear she exuded, the paleness of her skin as realization dawned. This was not the way.

“Let go!” she shouted, sending a wave of force into his body like a huge fist had punched him in the gut.

The surprise burst knocked Fennick’s hands free as he was tossed backward, landing on his ass with a hard thud. The door slammed shut, but he did not have time to catch his breath before the biting shadows pressed in. Those damnable whispers he so desperately tried to block bombarded him before he could catch his breath.

You are weak.

Failure.

The master should dispose of you now.

Coward.

“No.”

His fingers slid between his mahogany locks, pressing against his ears. Stumbling toward the couch, Fennick had barely gone a few steps before the buzzing in his head floored him.

Kill her.

"Stop."

The master needs her.

Kill the guardian.

"No."

Sacrifice her.

"I will."

After her display, Fennick lacked conviction. Her power was greater than he believed. Perhaps she was strong enough to break the bonds of his agreement. If he were not at square one in gaining her trust, that was.

She will never trust you. Never.

"Fuck off, you bloody wankers."

The whispers turned into angry banshee wails. Covering his ears did nothing to save his eardrums. A warm and sticky wetness oozed from his ears and nostrils. The recognizable metallic tang also slipped down the back of his throat.

The harder he fought to silence the voices, the louder they became, pushing on the inside of his skull until his mouth opened with a muted scream.

Chapter 7

BETH

BETH STOOD OUTSIDE HER apartment, arms crossed and shaking, as she contemplated her dilemma.

A single line of police tape fluttered across the open entryway, and what was left of her front door was propped up against the foyer wall. Blood stains dotted her cabinets and in trails across her carpet, left for permanency by an authority who didn't give a damn. A dark stain marked the place where Curtis Putnam took his last breath.

Beth swatted the yellow tape and charged inside, straight to her bedroom. Consequences and 'saviors' be damned. Fennick's fingerprints were undoubtedly still imprinted on her shoulders. Getting the fuck away from whatever brand of crazy he was peddling was worth any flack she got from the department.

She threw a few more incidentals into her backpack, like the deodorant she'd forgotten to pack earlier. A silent 'thank you' went up to the Universe for clearing her alcohol addled mind enough to consider temporary living arrangements. There were a few places she could stay on short notice, her parents' house, the Grove, or Grady's house. The latter was her preference, wanting to be close to him, to feel safe, but the sheriff's department would be crawling all over the place.

The Grove, being the most logical choice, was out of the question. If the sheriff's department came looking for her while she was there, more than eyebrows would be raised. They'd think she'd skipped town and could end up being Grady's neighbor, unable to help.

Her parents' house was the best option. It was close by and currently vacant while her parents were living it up on some cruise ship in the Bahamas.

The thought caused her jaw to clench. They could at least check their phones or text her a thumbs up in response to the several messages she'd sent over the course of the week. She knew her dad didn't care about her, but at least her mom had showed up at her track meets in high school before cutting her off after graduation.

You'd think they would have called her immediately after finding out Tom died, but they didn't. Every single text message unopened except that last one. It was left on read: 'Tom's funeral is tomorrow. I know you can't make it, but it would mean a lot if you sent flowers.'

Would it kill them to show a shred of empathy?

Beth roughly swept the tears from her cheeks and rolled her shoulders back. If her parents didn't have the energy for her, she would give them the same. First, she'd crash at their house. After this, she'd cut them out of her life. Grady always told her they were toxic and that she'd be better off without them. He was right.

Grady. Gods, she missed him already.

Over time, his roots had become so entwined with hers. Grady had fought against insurmountable odds to keep her grounded, saving her at least twice from the brink of death. His heart was as fierce as a lion's and unyielding to the forces bent on breaking him. In a short time, he had gone from her best friend to becoming her everything.

Part of her winced at the thought. Tom had been her world, but he wasn't coming back. His dying wish was for Grady and her to take care of each other, to make each other happy. When Grady was arrested, Beth realized she didn't want to waste any more time. Her heart still beat because of him. Grady was her other half, the level-head to her quick to anger, and the only other person who enjoyed popcorn cooked slightly over. He was the calming breeze to her tempest sea. Most importantly, she loved him with every battered and broken piece of her soul.

Ja'azul was out of players in his little cult, which meant Beth could finish grieving Tom properly and focus on her blooming relationship with Grady once he was exonerated. They'd have time to learn magic without the interruption of world-ending threats and hopefully find a way to banish Ja'azul for good.

There was just one thing left to do.

Her gaze found the wrinkled envelope sitting on the nightstand.

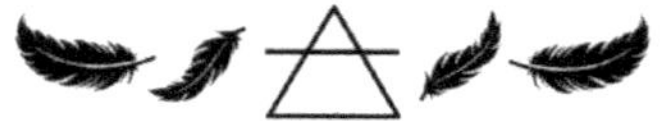

It DIDN'T TAKE LONG before her suitcase and backpack were loaded into the back of her forest green Subaru hatchback. Tom's box got to ride shotgun.

Beth put the car into reverse, not daring a glance at Fennick's apartment before heading across town. When she pulled up to her parents' empty house, the glow from the neighbor's houses on either side gave it an awful eeriness. She shivered, feeling like someone had walked over her grave as she got out and gathered her belongings. The lock and deadbolt took the same key, so she slid the tumblers one by one, cringing at how loudly they echoed underneath the awning on the small porch.

The door was barely open when the smell of rotten food and garbage smacked into her. "Oh, gods!"

She dropped her things inside the foyer to cover her nose and mouth. It was hotter than blue blazes in there.

Beth hurried to the hall. The thermostat blinked like the power had gone out. She pressed the buttons until the panel read seventy-two degrees, and the fan was set to 'on.' She waited but nothing happened. Trying to recall how her dad fixed the power, she opened all the downstairs windows to air the place out. Halfway through her task, Beth remembered he was always going down to the basement to fix the breakers.

Using her cell phone as a flashlight, the beam was enough to guide her around boxes and old workout equipment. The breaker box came into sight when she rounded the corner. Thankfully, it was within reach.

A choir of angelic hallelujahs rang when Beth flipped the switch, and the lights hummed with a glow. The unit kicked on, pumping conditioned air into the house. She stayed in the damp basement for a few minutes, relishing the coolness against her sweat-covered skin.

The quiet left her thoughts to drift. She wondered what the sheriff's office was going to do about the Curtis situation. The odd line of questioning allowed her imagination to roam dark places. Places where she would end up in prison for the rest of her natural life for murder.

Or until Ja'azul was free.

What if they pinned the blame on Grady instead? What if they also charged Grady with Marla Jean Putnam's death? They could say he went after Curtis because the man was seeking retaliation for his wife's death.

The pizza from dinner turned her stomach into a bubbling grease vat. A double murder charge would put him away forever.

Grady would have to be cleared, but how would she go about proving his innocence? He couldn't have killed anyone in cold blood.

Except his father...

Beth ended her internal debate and hurried back upstairs. Thankfully, the atmosphere was suitable for humans again.

She headed toward the source of the foul lingering rot: the kitchen. Her parents may have been terrible, but she planned to camp out here until she could return to her apartment.

The temporary cessation of future worries was a bonus to cleaning. It took a solid hour to evict the fruit flies and clean out the fridge. Several times, when giving up in exchange for a shower and sleep almost won, Beth reminded herself she was doing this for her benefit, not for her parents. By the time she finished, her limbs ached, flopping at her side like wet noodles.

Using her stubbornness as a crutch, she trudged up the stairs with her bags and Tom's box in hand. At the top of the stairs, her nose crinkled at the stench of more rot.

"Heat rises, dumbass."

Beth placed her things in the hallway and opened the nearest window. The warm, fresh air rushed in, but it wasn't enough to get the stagnant air moving. She hurried past the closed door of her parents' bedroom and opened the window at the end of the hall. As the clouds part on a sunny day, the thick air thinned out enough to breathe.

Beth gathered her belongings and crashed onto the foot of her childhood bed. The dust particles were massive enough to be seen in the low-light flooding in from the hall. They incited a fierce coughing fit, giving her sides stitches.

Beth swatted at the swirling nuisances and pushed her tired body to stand. She came back with a damp washcloth, marveling at the amount of dust that had accumulated during her college years as she wiped the comforter.

Her mother abhorred dust, so the neglect to Beth's room was slightly surprising. Their disregard for Beth's existence left a sting in the corner of her eyes, but she wouldn't cry. She was officially done trying to be the perfect daughter to parents who never wanted her anyway.

Her gaze flicked to the bookshelf, and a memory from her childhood charged forward. Eight-year-old Beth handed a book to her mother for story time. It was her favorite, a grand tale of fairies in cottages, magical woods, and a brave princess who befriended a dragon.

"Aren't you getting a little too old for fairy tale stories?"

"Please, mommy. Will you read it?"

Her mother stood, tucking the book against her chest. She loomed over the bed with her lips pursed and cold gaze, reminding Beth of the evil stepmothers in other books.

"No story tonight, Elizabeth. You are almost nine. The other girls your age are playing sports or learning to play the piano, not daydreaming about fictional characters in fake worlds."

"But, mommy—"

"Goodnight, Elizabeth."

Her mother had promptly left, firmly closing the door behind her while Beth cried herself to sleep. It was the beginning of her nightmares where things moved in the dark.

"At least I learned to conquer my fears."

She tossed the filthy rag on top of her old hamper and slumped to her bed. The fabric was slightly damp, but the coolness was welcome against her overheated body. She sat cross-legged in the middle of the mattress. Her brain was too overworked to think, and her body wanted to rest hours ago. Already, the silence in the house crept into her room, reminding her of how alone she really was. There wasn't a single person who felt her company was worth having or else they'd be here.

The only people she seemed to attract to her side were the ones wanting to cause her physical harm.

Beth sniffled and crushed a pillow against her chest as fat tears rolled down her wobbling chin. The one person who never let her down, who was always by her side, was gone. It was all her fault. If she'd protected Tom, he never would've been shot. Maybe, then, he could've been strong enough to withstand the magic Myrtle stored in him to defeat the Agnazars.

Hell, if she hadn't had been so damn stubborn, she could've learned enough magic to draw it out of him.

"Why didn't I take it from him?"

Deep down, she knew why. When she closed her eyes, her reason stared back with his baby blues hidden beneath a curly lock of soft black hair, giving Beth the sideways grin he reserved only for her. It had always been there, growing below the surface with every genuine smile or brush of the hand, each hug that fit her like a glove.

Beth's arms weakened and the pillow she clung to like a lifeline fell on top of Tom's box of keepsakes. Her love for him couldn't be a lie. The hole in her heart was a testament to that.

But she loved Grady with everything she had left.

She pushed the pillow aside and opened the four cardboard flaps. Tom's letter had stayed on top despite the jostling, patiently waiting for her.

"It's time, Beth. Just read the letter."

She snatched the box of tissues from the nightstand and filled her lungs with bravery. Penned on the front in Tom's neat handwriting was her name. She traced the letters and took another deep breath. Lifting the unsealed flap, a sad smile raised the corner of her mouth when she removed the letter. Tom had written it on notebook paper, same as the love letters in college he'd pass to her when they had classes together.

Even folded, she could see the dried tear stains. A new one appeared next to his.

With trembling hands, she managed to unfold the letter, bringing it to her nose. It smelled like Tom, orange and sandalwood. She smoothed it on her lap, so the edges lay flat, careful not to tug at the wet spot. Grabbing a handful of tissues, she took a rattled breath.

Dear Beth,

If you're reading this, my time with you is over. There are so many regrets I left behind, like not taking you to the café on the corner you always wanted to go to or taking you on a real vacation on the beach or someplace sunny and warm. The biggest regret of all is not giving you the family we talked about. I don't blame you, so don't even go there. I know if I had asked again, you would have been open to trying sooner. I wanted to give you the world, and I thought we had a lifetime to accomplish it.

A hiccupping wail echoed in her old bedroom. Tom was right. She wanted to wait a year before trying for a family, but if he'd asked again, she would've given in. Beth's chest burned like someone dug at her heart with a spoon. She made a fist with her free hand

and beat it against the soul-deep wound. When it did nothing to help, she wiped her eyes and continued.

If this whole magic and saving the world ordeal has taught me anything, it's this: don't wait for your happiness. Embrace the good with the bad. Chances are, the good will always outweigh the other stuff. Do this and find the happiness that was stolen from us.

Beth scoffed. *More than happiness was stolen from us, Tom. Does this mean forever is a lie?* She sat on that thought and continued reading despite the tightness in her chest threatening to swallow her whole.

As much as it pains me to say it, I want you and Grady to live a full and happy life.

Beth's breath caught, and her eyes darted back and forth in a frenzy read. The words blurred as she whispered, "How, Tom? How do I move on so soon?"

The answer danced on the tip of her tongue. She couldn't, but necessity required her to. Grady wasn't the only one with a responsibility. Beth's part was very clear. Together, they stood between Ja'azul and destruction. And in order to do so, Beth would need to learn the limits to her magic, and Grady was the person to show her.

If you were to move on with anyone else, I'd be upset. But you both deserve to be loved to the fullest capacity, and who could love you more than I do? The man who I deemed worthy, the man who I consider a brother, my best friend, and the one you were destined to be with.

Yeah, yeah. Grady may be your 'destined one,' but you were always mine. Your broken hearts will heal with time, just be there for each other.

If you still don't believe me, I found a passage in one of Myrtle's journals. It was after she lost Josiah and found Barton. He healed her broken heart like it was nothing but a briar scratch. Seems like permanently completing the bond had everything to do with it. I bookmarked the page so you can find it.

"What?"

No, it can't be that easy.

She shook her head, sending salty droplets to land on the comforter. She wanted to love Grady without the help of magic. Otherwise, the doubts would drive her crazy.

Know this, Elizabeth Marie Harper-Newman: I will always love you, even after death. And—Circe willing—I will always be by your side in spirit.

Now, go and take care of our boy. God knows he's been through enough and I know it hasn't been easy for you, either. Love each other fiercely, be happy, and don't forget me.

All my love, forever and always,

Tom

"Oh, Tom." Beth's hand stilled. "I'll never forget you. Never."

She read the letter twice more, tracing his signature with her fingertips. At the bottom of the page, dried circles of faded blue ink stood next to new, darker ones. She choked on another sob, covering her mouth with a wad of tissues.

Tom was her first everything. She'd never even kissed a guy until him.

"I will always love you, Tom. Please don't ever forget that," she said aloud, hoping to summon his spirit.

The thought of letting Tom go made her chest squeeze harder and her heart heavier, but he was right. Grady and she deserved happiness and love, though it may not be with whom they expected. If Tom wanted her to embrace the good with the bad, she would try her damnedest. Not now, but soon.

Beth carefully folded the letter and placed it back into the envelope. She kissed the outside before holding it to her breast, and squeezing her eyes shut.

"I promise, Tom."

A gentle breeze swept past, causing her to shiver.

"Beth."

Her whispered name sparked a flutter in her gut. Soft but firm knuckles caressed her cheek, just like Tom always did. Her heart clenched as his shining face appeared in her mind's eye. He mouthed the words, 'I'm always with you.' He tapped his chest twice as if to say, 'here,' and faded into the mists of her treasured memories.

When Beth reopened her eyes, she was still in her castle of solitude, but his scent lingered strongly, especially on her pillow. Heaving a sigh, she slipped the goodbye letter back into Tom's keepsakes box. Her bones were exhausted, but a hot shower beckoned with the promise of a more restful sleep.

AFTER A LENGTHY SCRUB to remove all traces of her living nightmare, Beth stared into the foggy mirror. Dark pink ovals formed on her shoulder blades with thumb-sized dots on the front.

Fucking Fennick.

"My apartment doesn't have anyone who wants to cause you harm," Beth said, mimicking her neighbor's British accent.

How stupid she had been. Fennick had seemed so nice one moment, then tried to break her shoulders the next.

Maybe he's schizophrenic or something.

Her gaze dropped to between her breasts where the fluorite necklace dangled. She took it between her fingers and turned the delicate stone. Thin, ribbons of rainbow glittered between layers of opaque blues and greens. Unless someone had the predisposition, it looked like a regular stone, not an enchanted talisman. If she and Grady took them off, they would be able to communicate, to feel the other's emotions again.

The thought of being able to shoulder their burdens together was reassuring. Surely, the officers would have taken Grady's necklace when they patted him down, but their incompetence at her apartment seeded doubt.

"Fuck it." She blew a lock of hair out of her face and pulled the stone overhead.

"Grady?" Seconds passed while she waited for a sign he was listening.

Nothing.

Anxiousness dropped her gut, dragging a piece of her heart with it. Loneliness lurked at the top, waiting to fill the void.

"I don't know if you can hear me. I'm at my parent's house, but I need… If you can, please take your necklace off."

Being able to talk to him, whether he could hear her or not, somewhat quelled the heartache and fear of solitude drowning her. By sheer force of will, Beth made it into bed and nestled underneath the musty comforter.

As soon as her head hit the pillow, Tom's presence returned. Whether he was a figment of her imagination or not, Beth took the gift for what it was.

"Good night, Tom."

The soft heat pressing into her forehead caused butterflies to erupt in her mid-section. As a tear rolled down her cheek, she fell into the first restful sleep in days.

Chapter 8

GRADY

THE SOUND OF GRADY'S cell door creaking open brought him out of his failed meditation. He must have passed out with only the blanket of his failures to keep him warm. There would be a permanent crick in his neck if he didn't get up and stretch. Two officers entered, leaving space for a third.

Grady pulled himself off the floor to sit on his bed. He didn't have a window and nothing else to tell the time by, so he guessed. "Mornin'."

The deputies ignored him as a tall, imposing older man entered with a practiced sneer that promised pain. Dude looked like he could take someone out with only a pencil.

Sheriff Eric Blaylock. His name was written in bold, red print in Louis Cooper's little black book of secrets and lies. This 'visit' was looking worse.

"Well, well, well. You finally gave me a reason to pick your little punk ass back up." He picked his teeth with a toothpick and tsked. "Too bad Gail can't bail you out and daddy ain't here to drag your sorry ass home."

Grady's blood boiled. This asshole had the audacity to speak his momma's name after his part in a generation-long list of murder coverups. Grady wanted to shove the toothpick into Eric's tongue and twist it off, but he knew better. Whatever leash his father had on Blaylock was broken. Grady needed to keep a level head and both eyes on the snake in front of him.

"What? Got nothin' to say?" The sheriff cracked his knuckles and stepped forward, almost nose to nose, filling Grady's nostrils with the scent of expensive whiskey and spearmint gum. "Let's see how long it takes this animal to howl."

The two young deputies on standby rushed into the room. They twisted Grady around and slammed his face against the cold white-painted cinder block wall. He grunted as they manhandled him, trying to show no signs of resistance. They still managed to wrench his shoulder out of socket, leaving it warm with a dull ache. He muffled his discomfort by facing his uninjured shoulder and taking quick breaths.

"I get a phone call." Grady gritted his teeth as they raised his fists, causing his shoulder bone to rub against the socket. "I want my phone call."

"If you're cooperative, I'll consider it." Blaylock's evil chuckle turned his blood to ice. "Take him to the VIP room, boys."

The fluorite stone dug into his sternum. As much as he needed to hear Beth's voice, it was a good thing they still wore their necklaces. If Grady's hunch was correct, he was in for a long and painful day, and the last thing he wanted was Beth to feel it all. Since he couldn't be there in person, at least he could protect her in this way.

Goddess, have mercy.

As they passed the other cells, the thin opaque windows burned with orange light. These fuckers weren't wasting daylight. He clenched his jaw, gearing up for the long day ahead.

The two deputy dickheads jerked him to a stop in front of a door that looked like all the others. Flat gray metal with a thin rectangular window made of half-inch thick glass and metal wire crossed in diamond shapes. Once Grady's cuffed hands were moved to the front, they shoved him into the interrogation chair.

He'd been denied a phone call and hadn't been offered anything to eat or drink. Hell, he couldn't remember the last time he ate. His default mode was burrowing into his work to forget all his troubles. Looks like this time his unhealthy habit bit him in the ass.

Grady sat back in the chair and stretched his legs, hands resting in his lap. He stared at the wall, counting how many times the halogen light above flickered. Every now and then, his gaze would migrate to the door, wishing someone would come in and get on with this charade.

What seemed like hours later, his lower back protested, so he played musical chair until the next extremity prickled from loss of circulation.

When none of that worked, he stood up and paced the room. Eventually, he ran out of patience and laid on the floor along the wall. The cold concrete was blessedly flat, opposite from the miniature man-made stalactites overhead. Whoever thought spackled ceilings were a good idea never had to dust anything in their life.

The door to the interrogation room unlocked, disrupting his internal debate. In stepped the man whose sole purpose was to fuck up his day further.

Grady pushed to his feet, his back popping as he rolled his shoulders back to loosen the taut muscles in his neck.

"Got bored and thought you'd take a nap, did ya?" His jaw worked a piece of spearmint gum, the scent eliciting a low growl from Grady's empty stomach. This only served to make Sheriff Blaylock malicious smirk deepen. "Oh, so now you're hungry? Jesus fuckin' Christ. Does this look like a three-star hotel to you, boy?"

Sheriff Blaylock pulled the metal chair back, deliberately dragging out the high-pitched screeching. Grady didn't flinch. Without breaking eye contact, he picked his chair up, and set it back down away from the table.

The men were stuck in an intense staring contest where the winner won superiority over the other…and Grady was losing. To keep a shred of dignity, he held the sheriff's gaze as he lowered to his seat. Gentleman as he was, he gestured to the chair opposite him with cuffed hands. Blaylock huffed and followed suit, stretching his legs out and crossing them at the ankles.

"Do you speak English?"

Grady nodded in response.

"Please state all answers aloud."

He shook his head.

"Do you understand why you are being held?"

Grady shook his head. He hadn't had much experience with the law, just the one time he was blackout drunk after his mom died and tried to drive home. Since then, he'd kept on the straight and narrow, but he knew his rights. It was about the only good advice his bastard of a father had given him. He'd already fucked up by not asking for a lawyer, not that he knew any he could trust.

Sheriff Blaylock's chuckle turned dark. "Okay. Let's try something different."

"See." He stood and flipped the chair around to sit backwards. "I know all about your little occult hobby. In fact, the boys are taking a little trip to your house today to box up all your freaky shit."

Grady's skin prickled, but relief hollowed his chest. He'd busied himself before Tom passed, moving all the important books to the Grove, but there were still personal items in his room. He gritted his teeth to keep from saying anything. By the looks of the sheriff's sinister glare, Grady's fake poker face worked.

"That's right, boy. We already have all the evidence we need to put you away for a very long time and then some." Something black and jagged swam against the whites of Blaylock's eyes. He leaned closer, emitting an aura of terror that caused ice to spread through Grady's veins. "By the time I'm through, you won't have to say one goddamn word with how high the evidence is stacked against you."

Shit.

Sweat broke out over Grady's face. They'd find his photographs over the years. They'd know how he felt about Beth, putting her in more danger. An involuntary gulp fueled Sheriff Blaylock's ire. His teeth gleamed like a cartoon wolf about to get his mark.

"Boy. Christmas is coming early, and I am just *giddy* with excitement. What kinda secrets are my boys gonna find at your daddy's place, huh?" Blaylock narrowed his eyes and lowered his voice. "That's right. Your old man told me how much time you spent with the Newmans. I bet you and Tom were real close, weren't ya? Like *brothers.*"

Grady's brow ticked as the sweat beaded above his upper lip. The room grew too hot.

"Like brothers who shared everything." Blaylock leaned in close, as if they were beer buddies sharing gossip at the bar. "And I mean, *everything.*" He stretched the last word out, giving it an extra syllable and winked.

Heat flared across Grady's face at the insinuation. The combination of heat, dehydration, and hunger had robbed him of the ability to focus. His panther's ears pricked as it awoke, yawning and exuding impatience.

"I'll take your silence as confirmation," the bastard chuckled as he leaned back in his chair. He scribbled a few lines into his notebook. "Can't say I blame ya. Tom Newman was sure something. Came from a well-off family, popular with the community, and could charm the pants off any girl if he wanted. And you? Well, you know what you are. Being the son of a bastard...what do they say? The apple doesn't fall far from the tree, does it? Of course, weaseling your way into a marital bed...not how I would'a done it. Didn't seem to bother your daddy either."

The palms of Grady's hands stung. He'd gripped his fists so tightly, his short nails had dug into the skin. Inside, the beast stirred, rearing to protect his human counterpart. The large cat wasn't a fan of the Sheriff, either. Grady required concentration to keep the panther contained when he got like this. He was running short.

"Tell me, from one man with needs to another, does Tom's wife taste as good as she smells?"

Flashes of gnashing teeth and claws blinded Grady for a split second. His neck rolled, body shook. Sharp points pushed against his fingertips as his skin rippled with blistering heat.

"Leave Beth alone, you sick fuck," Grady spat, his upper lip quivering. He wanted to bare his teeth but knew his elongated canines had broken the gums. Holding onto his humanity was the only control he had currently.

Blaylock whistled, rising to his feet. "He speaks at last."

He stalked closer to Grady, hands on his belt above a hunting knife and standard issue Glock. Blaylock's posture read 'relaxed and ready,' but his darkened features and mirthful grin screamed 'I want blood.' "Tell me what I need to know, and you can have your phone call."

Grady's fight or flight senses kicked into overdrive. His nostrils flared as he gave a curt shake of his head. It didn't do Grady any good to admit being at the scene, Blaylock would find a way to spin the evidence in his favor. The asshole was simply on a power trip.

"I warned ya."

Grady's head rocked to the side with his next blink. A hand-sized sting burned along his cheek. The Sheriff gripped his chin and jerked his head back around. Grady's gaze flew to the door, foolishly hoping someone caught wind of what was going on in here.

"Look at *me*, you little shit."

Grady gritted his teeth and zeroed in on his aggressor. One hard jerk forward, and he could knock the man's teeth in, securing the Sheriff's first-class ticket to 'Pain Town.'

"Mark my words, I'll get the confession I need one way or another." The Sheriff stood abruptly and straightened his belt. "Oh, and while you ponder holding that tongue of yours any longer, you might think about that pretty little thing you left all alone. Keep up the silent treatment, and I will *personally* make sure Miss Harper is taken care of...and all that it implies."

When the asshole winked, every muscle in Grady's body wound tight, ready to spring at the threat. He curled his toes and dug his heels into the floor to keep from launching from the chair. He knew the man was baiting him. This asshole wanted to add as much dirt as he could to bury Grady in the deepest, darkest hole he could find.

Grady's languid breaths cloaked the storm raging inside. The Sheriff's dark chuckle echoed well past the closing door.

No matter what, Grady vowed to find a way back to Beth, even if that meant showing his hand. For his plan to work, he needed to keep a cool head.

He'd also need to get his portal moonstone back from deputy Wilson.

Deputies dumb and dumber returned to escort him to his room.

"Well, now, lookie here. Mr. Cooper done walked himself into a wall." One of the asswipes guffawed like a donkey.

"Hush it," the other one replied, loud enough for anyone down the hall to hear. "We don't make funna incompetent people. We's the law. Gotta be civilized."

Grady had been holding his tongue for so long he may as well been sipping peanut butter through a straw.

They bypassed the cell he had stayed in last night and stopped at the end of the hall. A thick gray door opened to reveal a tiny concrete room with a narrow bed taking up half the space. From the doorway, he could see the black stripes around the rim of the toilet, which was located conveniently above where his head would lay.

"Charmin' ain't it? Boss figured you could use some time for reflection, and ya won't even hafta leave yer bed for a piss." Goon number one grinned like some diseased monkey with his crooked yellow teeth and pockmarked face.

Goon number two smacked his partner up the backside of his head.

"Gah! Whaddya do that fer, Davis?"

"*B'cuz*, Norton. It's called intre-spection, moron. Why doncha try readin' a damn book e're once in a while."

Davis and Norton grabbed Grady by the arms and shoved him inside. He stumbled into the far wall, barely missing the sink as the door clanged shut. He couldn't make heads or tails of their muffled voices, but they grew quieter until the only noise came from his heavy breaths.

Grady looked around the cell for anything other than the furnishings. No windows, no vent, no seams except between the cinder blocks and the door. Traces of a fresh coat of paint permeated the tiny space.

Great. It's all I'll be able to smell for a week.

He fell onto the thin, threadbare blanket they called a bed and stared at the ceiling. At least the surface at his back was flat. He scrubbed his face and realized they had left the cuffs on.

"Fan-fucking-tastic."

No sustenance, no medical attention, hands still cuffed, and no magic. The loss of the latter was what irked him the most. Since when had he become so dependent on it?

Since you found out you had magic and would be teaching Beth. Since you found out the two of you were destined to save the world...that you were destined to be lovers.

He closed his eyes, willing one of the many dreams where they were together to manifest, but all he could see was Beth covered in blood and bruises. Knowing they now had a matching set of black eyes didn't improve his mood.

Reaching for the invisible thread that linked them, Grady sighed. Being able to feel it so strongly meant Beth was not at the Grove, which only deepened the chasm growing in his chest. However, he allowed himself the selfishness of being able to connect.

The gentle hum consoled the aches in his body, but it didn't reach his heart. There was only one way to fix that kind of hurt.

Grady turned onto his side. His hand closed over his necklace, as the sting in his cheek mimicked those in the corners of his eyes.

"I'm so sorry, Beth. I promise I'll come back to you, just please stay safe."

Solitary confinement was already living up to the rumors.

Chapter 9

RICH

RED AND ORANGE HUES spilled into the sky above the smoky azure mountains as Rich's car crested the hill on the lonely two-lane road. Despite the gory scenes from yesterday, the glorious sight stole his breath. The quiet peace of this mountain community was what drew him here.

Mayes Hill was supposed to be a safe place for his family, far from the daily gunfire, theft, and death of the city. A place where he wouldn't be ridiculed for his open-mindedness regarding cases of the more mystical sort.

He couldn't have been more wrong.

Nine months ago, his wife, Bea, moved back to Woodworth, Georgia, taking their teenage son, Randy, with her. It was almost enough for him to turn in his badge, but he'd be expected to retire this time next year. He had until then to solve the case that kept him from quitting early. Finding Deena—or whatever happened to her two years ago. His family needed closure. The only obstacle had been Sheriff Eric Blaylock and his twisted sense of cowboy leadership.

Fucking good ol' boys.

The hand on the steering wheel turned white, causing the leather cover to creak. He let out a loud huff of air. And now this. A murder case involving Grady Cooper. The kid was twenty-six and had only seen the inside of the jail cell once prior. An overnighter for DUI. He'd been visiting between college semesters and found his momma lying dead on the kitchen floor.

It was a damn shame, too. Gail Cooper was a god-fearing woman who wasn't afraid of anything, except her husband. Louis Cooper had always rubbed Rich the wrong way, sending his heebie-jeebies meter off the charts when they passed each other in town. God only knows why Gail stayed with that bastard. According to what he'd learned, Grady seemed to have taken after his mother. Another riddle Rich had to solve since the young man didn't seem the murdering type.

The cruiser didn't hold any answers. The sooner he got home, the sooner he could sleep on it.

He pulled into his driveway and heaved a ragged sigh. The quaint two-story house Beatrice had chosen when they moved here seven years ago was dark and uninviting. Every time he returned, the place seemed more like a stranger's house and less like a home.

The planter boxes in the windows and around the porch, however, were full of happy pink petunias and yellow pansies, graciously kept fresh by his neighbor, Theresa Gilbert. She and her husband, Larry, were the most welcoming neighbors and they became fast friends. The Gilberts had three kids between them and were blessed with seven grandkids, the oldest of which was close to Randy's age.

Cutting the engine, Rich glanced at the Gilberts' house. They'd be getting up in a few hours to get ready for church. Soon after, there would be a knock on his door with two smiling faces inviting him to join them for Sunday service.

He grinned, sucking air in through his teeth. They meant well, but he'd never been the church-going type. His beliefs edged on fringe sciences and things unexplainable. To have one God who supposedly created everything seemed to be too small a package to house all the mysteries brimming to be discovered. There was *more* beyond what he'd been taught growing up.

After Deena disappeared without a trace, Rich dove headfirst into his work, picking over the case with a fine-toothed comb. He'd even dug into darker corners of the web looking for answers until Bea couldn't stand living in the same house anymore. If only he'd been more attentive to her needs, she wouldn't have had to grieve alone.

Randy's way of handling his sister's disappearance was to stay at his friends' houses as often as possible. They'd grown so far apart with his absence, that Rich didn't know his son anymore.

Rich's eyes stung with the familiar saline, ready to wash away his worries if he'd just let them fall.

Wiping his nose with the back of his hand, Rich searched for a napkin in the console. There was a smooth gray stone sitting in the cup holder. The shiny surface was cold to the touch but quickly warmed in his palm.

"Wilson must've left it." Rich pocketed the stone to return to his partner later and eased his stiff joints out of the cruiser.

He stretched, his body protesting the long hours by cracking like a handful of twigs. It alleviated some of the discomfort, more than his cold bed would anyway.

The promise of sleep summoned a yawn, followed by a growl from his midsection. Food would have to wait. Rich was in dire need of some shut-eye.

He unlocked the front door, dropping his keys on the foyer table. Rich found Zeus, the family bulldog, asleep in his bed near the fireplace in the family room. The dog opened one eye. Seeing it was Rich, Zeus huffed and went back to sleep.

"Good morning to you, too." Another heavy yawn stretched his jaw.

He'd barely made it to the master bedroom and tossed the rest of his pocket stuff—wallet, cell phone, badge, and the strange rock—onto the bedside table before collapsing on top of the comforter. His droopy gaze landed on the framed photo of his family. They smiled back at Rich, taunting him with a time when life was good. His beautiful Bea, their handsome boy, the man who sought redemption, and the one whose face haunted him in his sleep.

The world slowed around him, darkening as a shroud of dreamless slumber descended.

Knock, knock.

Rich groaned at the sudden breach of silence. The fog of sleep dissipated, leaving him disoriented. Flashes of the previous evening came in disjointed fragments: corpses, blood, an empty house.

Knock, knock, knock.

His eyes shot open. Pushing the bed, Rich rolled onto his back, blinking rapidly to work his eyelids loose.

"Coming." It sounded like he'd eaten a handful of gravel.

He planted his feet firmly on the ground. Rubbing the back of his neck, he grabbed his phone to read the time.

2:00 p.m.

"Shit."

The knocking became more insistent.

"Coming!" Rich repeated as he stood and stalked to the front door.

He peeked through a gap in the curtains. The Gilberts' youngest child, Aaron, had one arm hugging his midsection, the other was vertical with his hand covering his mouth. The young man's face was flushed, body trembling as he stared at his parent's house. When Rich opened the door, it drew Aaron's furrowed gaze.

"Sorry to bother you, Rich, but I'm worried about mom and dad," Aaron explained, the words spilling from his mouth in a rush. "They're not answering the door or their phones."

Rich glanced at the SUV sitting on the curb. Aaron's spouse and their two kids were waiting in the car. Rose, their three-year-old, wailed while Sam tried his best to calm her. Their thirteen-year-old, Lucas, was glued to his phone, face drawn in a frown.

"Are you sure they're back from church yet?" Rich asked, remembering how Bea used to get caught up in two-hour long conversations with folks after service.

"Both vehicles are in the garage. I would use my key, but mom had a new doorknob installed the other day. She's going to give us a copy of the new key today." Aaron chewed on his thumbnail. "I'm worried they had an episode. It wouldn't be the first time mom's blood sugar dropped at the same time dad's did."

Rich rubbed his face from forehead to his scratchy beard and cleared his throat. The greasy weight on his gut drug his mood further down yesterday's shithole mess. "Call for an ambulance, just in case. I'll get my tools."

Aaron nodded and jogged to his vehicle.

Rich rifled through his closet, looking for his trusty lock-pick set. He found the duffel bag in the back corner and grabbed the slim black leather case before heading back outside. Aaron met him at the top of his parents' driveway.

"Is the ambulance on the way?" Rich asked, gesturing toward the front door, and veering in that direction.

"Yes," Aaron nodded. "Sam took the kids to stay with Aunt Margaret until we know more."

Kneeling in front of the Gilberts' door, he unbound the strap and rolled the case to lay flat on the welcome mat. Bright yellow sunflower petals created a stark background against the dark leather.

Sweat beaded his forehead as Rich felt around the tumbler with the tension wrench and positioned the rake. It'd been a few years since he'd had to use the set. He hoped it worked within the first few tries. Holding his breath, Rich eased it out slowly as he brought the rake down. His determination was rewarded with a soft click.

He replaced his tools and stood, winding the leather strap a few times before tucking it into his back pants pocket.

"I'll check it out first; you wait for the ambulance," Rich instructed when he reached for the door.

"Oh, right."

Aaron's voice seemed far away as he stared into the house. Rich hesitated before stepping inside. He wasn't good at consoling people, or Bea would've stayed.

"Aaron?"

The Gilbert's son blinked rapidly and turned his tear-streaked face to Rich. He could do this. Just a few simple words.

"Why don't you go sit with Zeus in the living room while you wait? He'd be happy to see you, and you'll have a good view of the ambulance."

"Are you sure you won't need me? What if—"

Anguish turned Aaron's face into a tragedy mask. It was too close to what Rich wore whenever he had too much time to drink...and drinking led to thinkin'.

"Renewed my CPR cert this Spring, and I know where Theresa keeps the insulin shots." Rich squeezed Aaron's shoulder. "It's gonna be fine. I got this."

Aaron nodded and hugged himself as he walked across the grass between the properties. He stopped and put on a wobbly smile. "You're a good man, Rich. I'm glad you and my parents became friends."

The tired organ in the middle of his chest warmed. He almost choked on his reply, "Me, too, kid. Me too."

He waited for Aaron to turn around before heading inside. The house was too quiet. There should be music or television noise coming from the living room. His first stop.

Dread rose up his spine like the tides, lapping further up the shore. It pricked his back, low and dangerous. It niggled at his memory banks.

The living room was unoccupied.

"Theresa?"

Silence.

"Charles?"

Rich's breaths came heavier, more frequently as he headed toward the hallway. *Maybe they're taking a nap?*

The whole house smelled like Theresa had been boiling cabbage but let the pot run dry. *No, not burnt cabbage.* He sniffed again, this time deeply despite his reflex to cough out the tainted air.

Sulfur.

The niggling grew from lazy scratches on a door to determined banging. Iciness seeped into his chest. A warning to not just look but to *see*. These were the instincts he'd read about in his studies, the ones his peers scoffed at. He followed the warning, hoping to reach his friends before it was too late.

Rich's steeled gut already knew the answer; however, he'd made a promise.

In the hallway, Rich found a line of black slime trailing between Charles and Theresa's bedroom and the kitchen. The coldness squeezed his ribs like sharp fingers. He couldn't trust his feelings, so he leaned on his training to guide him the rest of the way.

Rich skirted the dark stain with a game of hopscotch. He stopped in the doorway and shuddered. The bedroom was empty, save for the tangy burnt smell and a large puddle of bloody vomit in front of the bathroom.

The faint cry of a siren drew nearer. Rich needed to check the kitchen. He had to be the one to find them. To catalogue whatever dignity he could because the county EMTs sure as shit wouldn't.

Along the hallway, scorch marks ran up the wall where warped plastic frames were fused to melted photographs, clinging to the wood by nothing more than chance. There was no blackened soot on the ceiling, or the lingering charcoal left by a fire. His fight or flight senses were on high alert.

"Theresa? Charles? It's Rich. If you can hear me, help is on its way." His deep voice was steady, but his chest thumped like war drums as he jogged down the hall.

Please be okay. Please be okay.

As soon as his rubber soles hit the linoleum, the strong, coppery scent kicked his training to the curb. Rich skidded to a halt and his stomach lurched sideways. Suddenly, he wasn't there as a deputy, but as a neighbor, a friend.

"Oh, God..."

Theresa's empty eye sockets stared into oblivion while her mouth was opened into an impossibly long 'O.' Her skin was too tight for her bones, almost as if someone had taken a straw and sucked out all her fluids.

Next to her lay Charles. His torso looked like a human knife block. There were several stab wounds, more than he could count. Charles's face was twisted in pain, and his skin looked the same as Theresa's. Dry, too tight, like it had been vacuum-sealed to his bones.

Bile worked its way up Rich's pipe. He barely had time to turn his head before expelling whatever was left of yesterday's lunch.

Footsteps rushed inside the house, signaling the paramedics' arrival. Rich opened his mouth to call for them, but nothing came out. He fumbled backward as the team hurried by, unable to rip his gaze from the bodies of his neighbors, his only friends. The Gilberts had been the only decent family in this whole goddamn town and now they were gone.

When Rich's back hit the wall, he sank to the ground as the blurred figures hurried around the space. He couldn't hear the barked orders over the sound of his heart breaking. Hell, he wasn't sure who moved him outside or when.

All he knew was, he did not have this...and Aaron's heart-wrenching cry would echo forever in Rich's box of failures.

Chapter 10

FENNICK

THE MORNING'S RAYS FLICKERED through the broken blinds, startling Fennick awake. He lifted his face, leaving a puddle of drool on his mattress. Groaning, he flipped over, and a stampede of elephants trampled what remained of his slumber. The pounding in his skull persisted while he squeezed his eyes shut, trying to recall what had transpired before this unusual blackout. The last thing he remembered was saying goodbye to Beth, and then...the whispers.

He had passed out onto the living room floor, so how did he make it back to his bed?

"Goddess be merciful and tell this incessant throbbing to kindly fuck off," he grumbled with a voice like a rock tumbler.

Fennick pushed off the bed, rolling to his feet. The room warped into a funhouse mirror, pulsing in time with the elephants parading in his head. The scent of sulfur and ash was the final straw, sending him careening to the lavatory.

In all his centuries on this green earth, he had never been so ill. His skull cleaved in twain, pitching the contents of his stomach straight into his porcelain bowl. Every heave, every expulsion of gods knows what brought him one step closer to a troublesome hangover rather than feeling as though he would perish. The exertion melted his bones, leaving him in a heap on the floor.

His reluctance to leave the confines of the apartment was rivalled only by the need to persuade Beth to his cause. The veil of Ja'azul's prison had weakened to the point that his influence was strong enough it felt like a constant huff of icy hot breath on the back of his neck. Somehow, Ja'azul had managed to break through his defenses, almost bending Fennick to his will. While this was troubling news, if Fennick's plan worked, he would be free of this servitude. First, he had to regain Beth's trust after yesterday's disaster.

Fennick completed his morning ritual of washing, dressing, and brushing, which took forever in his current state. When he turned the light off, dizziness rocked him sideways. He clamped his eyes shut, gripping the edge of the counter. His lids fluttered open as a low-budget film played in the reflection of the mirror.

Beth slept on a strange bed while he watched from her side. After a long while, she whimpered, inviting his hand to caress her soft cheek. Her skin was softer than the finest bamboo silk, and his featherlight touch calmed her troubles.

The next frame showed him walking around her room, violating her privacy further by touching her most intimate clothing. He brought a pair of lace undergarments to his face, deeply inhaling the scent of her before stuffing them into his pocket.

Fennick touched the outside of his jeans pocket to find a soft lump. His muscles tensed as heat rushed his face. He continued to watch the train wreck, chest tightening increasingly as it unfolded.

His gaze went to the mirror. His image was distorted, wavy, and his eyes—gods his eyes—they looked like the bowels of Hell. Scarlet pits of flame; smoldering centers surrounded by an endless rage. Fennick wanted to look away, unable to bear the disgust souring his gut at the hideous sight.

But he could not. He had to know the depth of his depravities, even if these were without his permission.

The sensation of watching himself and having no recollection of these events was disorienting. Fennick watched as he traveled the hallway until he came upon what appeared to be the master bedroom. The space reeked of Ungenth, but it was long gone. Fennick's gaze was drawn to the bed, where remnants of a couple lay still and silently screaming. The female bore a striking resemblance Beth, albeit older and with too many gray hairs and wrinkles to count, while the male looked more like a pile of bones in a loose skin sack. The memory faded, leaving a sinking in his soul.

The hairs on the back of his head rose to attention as Ja'azul's warning rang with crystal clarity. Fennick would need to make haste or submit to the doom he had wrought upon himself. He'd made a deal with the cosmic being in order to end to the lie he had lived during his early years with *her;* to breathe the fresh air and to bask in natural sunlight after centuries in darkness. The decision had been the product of desperation and an escape from madness. He was not convinced of his freedom from either.

The weight of everything pulled his head back, making his Adam's apple bob on a swallow.

"Get yourself together man." His voice was akin to that of a frog.

He filled his lungs, expelling the air slowly as he leveled with the man in the mirror. Gone was the hellfire swimming where his hazel eyes had been. Gone was the wavering visage of the shapeless terror. He had regained his former attractiveness, which served these days to mask the fragile glass of his psyche. Hidden below the surface, he could *feel* the cracks growing, reaching, with each passing day.

"We can keep the darkness at bay long enough for our sweet, Elizabeth, to save us."

Summoning the courage to turn from his transient clarity, Fennick dove back into the currents of uncertainty. Previously, braving the deep sea of madness had been nothing short of a picnic. Today, the winds had changed, and Fennick had misplaced his compass. He had until the cover of night to find his bearings before the salty seas dashed his vessel against the cliffsides once more.

THE MID-DAY SUMMER BREEZE wound through his hair, whipping it like kite tails. As he moved with purpose along the sidewalk, the voices stalked him, hiding in shadowy whispers between branches and bushes.

Fennick ignored them, as usual, focusing his attention forward, trusting his feet to guide him to wherever Beth had sought refuge for the evening. His hopes were validated when he came upon a lovely two-story house with her green vehicle sitting just outside. Idly, he wondered if she had discovered her parents yet.

While he regurgitated the various apologies he had constructed on his way over, a passing cloud cast him in shadow. The temporary lack of sunlight was enough to shelter his nightmares. Ja'azul's favorite torment was casting him back to his cell. The one his beloved had trapped him in. He could smell the dampness of despair and the stench of hopelessness as if they were woven into the tapestry of his being.

Stopping in his tracks, Fennick retreated to the only place he could find sanctuary. In the bottomless pit of his ruined soul, he had carved out a space in the corner. There, he could retreat for a moment's respite, but only. The longer Fennick hid, the closer *he* came to finding it.

The clouds parted once more, letting the sunshine burn away the filth. Just as Fennick opened his eyes, Beth stepped outside. She moved with a fluidity of order, not of someone who was still grieving.

Once the home was secured, she turned with the agility and poise of a professional ballerina. Her dark honeyed hair glistened with honeysuckle dewdrops and rubies in the noonday sun. Supple lips the color of dusty rose were raised into a radiant smile, surely the flowers were jealous. Fennick silently begged her to notice him, to grace him with such a gift as he neared.

Even more, the vast pool of power pulsing through her delicate veins *called* to him. Like a moth to a flame, his body craved the warmth only she could supply with her unyielding goodness.

"Fennick?" Beth's melodious voice brought him from his reflections. He noted how her hands were in loose fists at her sides, knees slightly bent, and feet hip width apart. "What are you doing here?"

"Well, hello to you, too." Fennick chuckled, keeping his hands clasped in front and flashing his most charming smile. "Since I have no vehicle, I am learning my way around town by foot."

Stop being stupid and apologize, already.

"Makes sense, I guess." Beth licked her lips and surveyed the neighborhood as she subtly gathered energy from the surrounding shrubbery.

"Honestly, I am glad we ran into each other." Fennick slowed his pace and stopped behind her hatchback. "I believe you are owed an apology for my egregious behavior last night."

"Yeah, I'd say I am." She raised her chin and one eyebrow, burying daggers in his brain with her gaze.

Her magic popped like miniature fireworks. It was exhilarating. Fennick wanted nothing more than to savor the taste of her defiance, but Beth was not a plaything. He needed her cooperation. His survival depended on it.

"Last night, I was not myself." Fennick pulled his brows together and dipped his head. "You see, my nerves were frazzled by the idea of dining with you last night, so stronger spirits were needed for bravery. I fear I went too far."

Beth scoffed. When he lifted his gaze, her jaw was clenched, and she glared at him. "No harm, no foul. If that's all, then…"

She left the words 'fuck off' between the lines, too kind to utter them. She waited pointedly by the hood of her vehicle for him to walk away. If she only knew how much this game intrigued him.

"I am not finished." Fennick ignored the whips of anger lashing out against his skin as he inched his way toward the side of the vehicle. Beth mimicked his movements.

"The trust I violated after such a distressing evening was a social faux pax of enormous proportions. Saying I am sorry does not seem adequate, though I *am* terribly sorry for my offense. Could you find it in your heart to forgive me? Can we start anew?"

Beth paused and chewed on his words like they were gristle. A dark purple oval peeked past the neck of her t-shirt when she shifted her weight to the other foot. His gut was leaden with guilt. Had he been in control, her perfect skin would never have been marred in such a barbaric way.

"Apology accepted. Now, if you'll kindly move along, I have things to do."

Fennick caught the briefest scent of frustration while she rubbed her bicep and twirled her keys.

"Thank you, Beth." Fennick sighed, her forgiveness severing the rope strangling his lungs. "Please let me make it up to you. I am not one to let aggrievance sit. Ageing is for fine wine, not for apologies."

Fennick knew he was losing when Beth's gaze quickly searched the area before settling on him.

"I dunno. There's a lot going on in my life right now, and I'm not looking for complications. Let's just say things are settled and go our separate ways. Water under the bridge."

Fennick's black heart jumped at the thought of her turning from him forever. "Beth, you are the first and only friend I have made in town. Please do not let my first strike be our last.”

The tops of her teeth tugged at her bottom lip. She stared at the ground, rubbing her arm. Her eyebrows were gathered as conflict striped her soft features.

“Please?” Fennick’s soft plea erased the offending creases.

“Fine.” She crossed her arms, raising and dropping her shoulders in a careless shrug. “What do you have in mind?”

“Join me.” Fennick extended his hand while his insides lit up like a fox in the hen house, frenzied with joy and possibilities. When she did not accept the proffered hand, he raised it toward the sky. “The weather is far too lovely not to enjoy.”

“I’m not in the mood to walk.” Beth squinted when her gaze met his. He stepped to the side, so the sun was no longer affronting her. Her stomach growled.

“Suppose we go to lunch in an alcohol-free and public place? It will be my treat.”

Hook set. Line taut.

“Okay. But I’m not walking to town. Get in.”

And she is mine.

Fennick slid his feet together and gave her a curt bow. “Yes, ma’am.”

“Ew. Don’t call me ma’am.”

“As you wish.”

Fennick wanted to jump for joy, but the worry that Ja’azul would detect his mood change kept him cool as a cucumber. He opted for an unhurried pace and rounded the passenger door.

Beth had her seatbelt buckled by the time he hopped inside. While he situated himself, the windows descended, inviting the cooling breeze. Fennick detected a hint of petrichor. Within the hour, a shower would pass to cool the heat of the day.

“What part of town have you seen so far?” Beth slung her arm across the back of his seat and maneuvered down the driveway.

“Most of downtown and on this side of the apartments, but not anything going toward Chattown, Tennessee.”

Fennick leaned against the door to rest his elbow on the outside of the car. It had been far too long since he had enjoyed a leisurely drive, and even longer since he had driven his sports car on the adventurous mountain roads.

“So, about half of Mayes Hill?”

Her attention was divided between him and the rearview mirror. The warmth in her eyes when her gaze found his inched its way into his chest cavity. Would that he could savor the fleeting moments of joy and peace this woman afforded him. Perhaps he would feel human again.

“That would be an accurate estimate.”

On the drive to town, Beth played the part of tour guide. Fennick learned that the bowling alley was ‘the place’ younger adults flocked to on a Friday night and to avoid the Barnes’ place if he was not keen on having the barrel of a shotgun shoved into his face. The corner grocery store was the only place to purchase groceries unless you drove twenty minutes to Ridgeville, the next town over and across the Georgia state line. Downtown was full of family-owned businesses and restaurants whose livelihoods depended on tourism. The locals kept them from going under during the winter months, but they barely survived.

"Most folks either brave River Road every day to work out of Chattown or commute a county or two over. The lucky ones are those who find work in the financial sector. Everybody needs a bank, and there's one in all of Mayes Hill."

Beth turned onto the main road back toward the restaurants.

"Do not be so modest, Beth. Educating the youth is a noble endeavor." Fennick turned to study his chauffeur. She gripped the steering wheel with both hands, staring out the windshield with pursed lips. "You are also one of the lucky ones, and your students are as well."

"Teachers don't get paid much, especially in small Podunk towns where gender equality is some 'newfangled hippy idea' or 'liberal agenda.' It's ridiculous."

"I agree with how absurd modern politics have become. Education creates well-learned individuals. They benefit the community and create job stability. Handicapping schools and starving areas of decent teachers only serves to cripple society."

Beth's stomach growled again, loud enough to shake the seats. She quickly covered it with her hand.

"Excuse me. With all this talk about the degradation of educational standards and pay-gaps, my body is telling me to stuff it and eat already."

"Shall we enjoy a quick bite at the little corner café? Word on the street is their pastry chef studied in France and makes croissants that rival those found on Canal Saint-Martin in Paris."

"No," Beth replied with a dark chuckle devoid of humor. "Today is a greasy diner, heapin' plate of potato wedges and a juicy bacon cheeseburger type of day. And if you want breakfast for lunch, they have the *best* southern biscuits and sausage gravy this side of the Mason-Dixon Line."

Fennick filed her reaction within his memory folder labeled 'Beth.'

"You have been a most gracious host. A greasy diner meal does not convey how thankful I am for you giving us another chance."

"Promise me you'll lay off the hard stuff and keep your hands to yourself." Beth pulled into a narrow side street, parking behind an old brick building, and added, "Then we'll get along peachy."

"An easy promise to make."

She turned her body toward him, hands clasped in her lap. "Doesn't mean a thing if it's easy. Nothing worth doing is."

"You are correct," Fennick amended with a deep nod. "I shall endeavor to prioritize my sobriety and not make light of promises."

"Good." She eyed him for a moment longer before she slipped off her safety belt.

His next words slipped out as if she'd pulled a plug loose. "I, too, have known hardships. Recent challenges have been difficult to manage, and I find myself changing. The man I see is not the one I want to become."

Beth paused with one foot on the ground. It was an eternity before she spoke, "I'm sorry."

Fennick was struck silent by the sharp electricity coursing through his chest. Her pure soul threatened to clear the cold, stone rubble where his heart used to live. Unlike other women of power he had met, she possessed humility. This only made her more alluring.

"If it's any consolation, I understand," she added before closing her door.

Beth stood in front of her vehicle, clutching her purse to her stomach like a shield. Fennick slipped out of the passenger side and gave her a warm smile. His attempt to disrupt the flames of yearning igniting long-dead feelings was feeble at best.

Their moment of understanding was interrupted by a rolling rumble. She winced when a raindrop bounced off her cheek.

"We should go inside before we turn feral with hunger and are soaked to the bone." Fennick held his arm out, signaling her to go first.

The door had closed behind him when the torrent fell, clouding the streets in a gray mist. Fennick barely noticed, for the beauty in front of him had him enraptured. A faint halo of soft gold surrounded her body. When Beth flipped her loose honeyed hair over one shoulder and turned to face the front, a celestial choir sang their angelic tune. His lungs forgot how to function.

Oh, how he wished to be worthy of such a powerful creature, but his transgressions surpassed lifetimes. Perhaps he could allow himself a sample of happiness. Beth could be the spark he needed to light the cleansing fire that would set him free.

Suddenly, his head tilted and jerked. The air grew stiflingly hot.

Please, I beg of you. Not now.

Fennick rolled his neck to loosen the muscles. Beth gave him a wary smile as he took the seat across from her.

In the past, Ja'azul had left Fennick to his own devices. Even now, he could feel the creature's hold crawling inside his brain, seeking passage into the world. Fennick was not ready to deal with him. Not yet.

But Ja'azul's prison walls weren't the only ones thinning.

Chapter 11

GRADY

WHEN THE DOUBLE DOUCHES left him in solitary, his hands were still cuffed—thankfully in the front. After failing to find a sliver of earth to pull magic from, Grady spent the rest of the morning trying to work his new accessories loose without breaking them.

Keeping his mind occupied with menial tasks helped him ignore the gnawing hunger in his gut. Thirst was a different matter. Each time he concentrated, his tongue darted between his cracked lips, but they were drier than Georgia clay during a drought. When he finally gave up, raw red rings surrounded his wrists.

Grady relieved himself in the dirty toilet bowl before settling on his back. The bed was a thin mattress laid atop a concrete slab. He didn't miss the sharp metal springs poking into his back.

Naturally, the quiet gave way to thoughts of Beth. Hard not to when loving her was hardwired into his DNA. Hell, he didn't need their magical connection or destiny to care for her. He'd fallen long before his magic awakened. Tom had just won her affection first, fair and square.

Beth would be awake by now, no doubt worrying when he didn't call. If Ja'azul hadn't been temporarily neutralized, Grady would never have cooperated with the police. However, returning to a mundane life meant going along with the law, even if it was corrupt.

Despite his concern for her well-being, Grady knew Beth wouldn't rest until she found a way to get him released. He was tempted to take off the fluorite necklace and try contacting her. Hearing her voice would give him the boost he needed to make it through the weekend. However, if they caught him with it...

No. He'd not add to her worries.

A tinge of guilt still shaded his heart grey, even though Tom had forgiven him before passing. His best friend's final wish was for Grady to spend as much time with Beth as possible, citing Myrtle's journals about the healing power of the bond between guardians.

When Beth sent Grady away, he may as well have left with his tail between his legs. He waited for her to call. His portal stone was worn smooth from his constant considerings. She never called on him. The hours he spent lamenting his uselessness were the most miserable of his life. Sitting in this barren cell, he vowed that nothing else would stand in their way. Once he held Beth in his arms again, he'd make sure it was where she stayed.

Muffled voices approached his cell, stopping abruptly. Grady barely had time to get to his feet as the door swung open forcefully, bringing him face-to-face with the red-faced monster of his current predicament.

"How'd you do it?" the Sheriff growled, twisting Grady around and slamming his face into the concrete wall.

Before he got his bearings, the Sheriff slammed him again. Stars swam across his vision. Blaylock jerked him back. Grady spat out a gob of blood onto the floor. A white lump swam amid the viscous fluid. He tongued the vacant space and grinned with grim satisfaction.

Finally. The stark white room had a splash of color.

"You were locked in here all night, so there's no way you could'a done it." The man's breath, reeking of whiskey-laced spearmint, brushed against the side of his face, spittle making contact. "Unless you sent your little bitch to do it for ya. Huh? Did'ja?"

Grady's inner panther hissed a warning, loud enough to make the good sheriff tighten his grip. The sound of fabric tearing reminded Grady to stay cautious as he pieced together this new clue.

Another murder meant Ja'azul was still causing mayhem. If he was still sending creatures out, it meant Beth and the townsfolk were still in danger.

I can unleash hell and worry about the consequences later.

Grady took a deep breath and released the animal. It raced forward, eager to defend his human shell. When Grady's face met the wall again, the panther stumbled. Grady's jaw throbbed like a pinched nerve. His panther roared as the lights dimmed.

HE JOLTED AWAKE IN a dark room, his cheek stinging sharply. His stay most likely looked like he'd walked into a hornet's nest and got into a punch fight with the bees. It sure felt like it. Looming above him with a sinister sneer was the bane of his existence, Sheriff Eric Blaylock.

"Rise and shine, princess."

The room pulsed in harmony with the ringing in his head. It suddenly seemed to warp... or was that just his vision blurring?

As Grady came to, he realized he couldn't hear the usual electrical hum coming from the corner of the room. Glancing over, he saw the red light on the camera was black. Blaylock followed Grady's gaze and smirked.

"Just you and me now, sunshine."

The sound of cracked knuckles echoed in the room as loud as a rock crusher. Grady's vision doubled when his head was knocked sideways, and his eyelids fluttered like moth's wings.

In the corner behind Blaylock, sapphire eyes glowed above gleaming white fangs. The form of a large black cat stalked from the shadows, staring at their aggressor and licking its lips.

This must be a dream. His burning face begged to differ.

Grady lifted his heavy hands, finding his wrists were zip-tied to the arms of the metal chair. The back of his left-hand throbbed underneath a cheap, plastic bandage.

"Wha' da fugg?" he slurred. His tongue was swollen and mostly numb. He looked around the room, head teetering like a bobblehead doll. The air tasted like sweetened chlorine bleach.

If this wasn't a dream, something very wrong was happening. Grady tried to connect with his panther counterpart, but the cat was detached, like a kite pleading for more freedom to play with the wind.

"Now that you've had a little somethin' to loosen your tongue, I figured it was time you and I had a little chat. Man to man."

Metal scraped against the floor like a soured trumpet note. The Sheriff sat in the chair backwards, arms folded over the top as if they were chums shooting the breeze over a poker game. He was close enough that Grady could smell the steak and potatoes the man had for lunch. His mouth was as dry as the Sahara, but it tingled with anticipation. When his stomach grumbled and twisted into painful knots, Blaylock's upper lip twitched.

"Before we begin, how's about a bite to eat? Can't starve our inmates. That'd just be inhumane."

Come again? Grady kept his mouth shut. The Sheriff's new game sent a shiver to his toes. The man stared, waiting for an answer, so Grady nodded. He hoped his poker face had improved.

"Be back in a jiffy." Blaylock stood, righting his chair across from Grady. Before he left, he called over his shoulder, "Don't go anywhere."

As if he *could* leave.

Grady took this opportunity to study his surroundings. This room looked like the 'VIP' room, but he could hear ringing telephones and murmuring voices. Listening closely, the sounds became words, some he almost understood if it weren't for his water-clogged ears.

His gaze came back to the door. The sliver of light caused his chest to thump.

Every pore seemed to sweat at the same time, leaving Grady shivering from the cold AC blowing directly on him. If he could get his hands loose quickly, he could be free.

Grady had just enough reach to snap the plastic with his panther claws if he could keep everything from doubling every half second. He squeezed his eyes shut for a three count. After opening them and waiting for the images to align, he summoned his claws.

Nothing came.

Panic chose the form of a forceful grunt. Grady breathed out through his mouth, praying for grounding, and tried again.

And again, nothing.

Come on! He implored his counterpart, who lounged in the corner grooming itself. The frustration he felt at being ignored bordered on mania. He wouldn't get another chance like this to escape.

Abandoning hope that his beast would help, Grady pulled against his restraints. The plastic dug into his wrists, cutting into the already bruised flesh, but they wouldn't budge.

Fuck, fuck, fuck.

Grady's heart hammered against his chest. The Sheriff would be back anytime now. A dose of calm would be nice, so he thought of Beth. She was his Northern Star, his compass. If they were at the Grove right now, he'd be showing her all the additions to the cabin. Her eyes would sparkle with joy, and he'd pull her into his arms, confessing his undying love and presenting his heart on a silver platter.

Peace washed over him. He'd only experienced it to this degree during those fleeting moments when her beaming smile was aimed at him or their hug lasted longer than usual.

The click-clack of men's dress shoes and scent of sauteed garlic and onions signaled the end of his repose. Blaylock entered, baring his too white teeth with a leering smile. In his hands were a covered paper plate and a glass of water.

Grady's hunger awoke with a vengeance. His stomach rumbled long and loud. He struggled not to seem eager, but his tongue darted out to moisten his lips, little good when his mouth was suffering from draught.

"Didn't have anyone available to run out, so I had to make do." Blaylock sat the food and drink under Grady's nose. While tearing the paper off the straw, he added, "I know it's not much, but you know what they say: Don't look a gift horse in the mouth."

He dropped the straw in the glass of water. When he lifted the lid, steam chased the greasy smell wafting toward Grady. The plate had a heaping helping of what looked like week-old liver and onions. The onions looked slimy, and the meat was gray with bits of fuzzy green mold.

"Well? What're you waiting for? Eat up."

The Sheriff shoved the plate to the edge of the table, so Grady could reach it with his mouth...if he was willing to eat it like a dog.

No fucking way.

Grady's head wobbled back against the chair to look up at the sadistic SOB testing his resolve. They resumed their staring game from yesterday.

"No thank you." The words flowed like molasses, but they were clear enough.

Blaylock's jaw ticked and his face reddened. "No? Beggars can't be choosers, and you'll need your strength."

He gripped Grady's chin as a picnic spoon appeared in front of his face. Blaylock forced his mouth open and shoved the rotten food inside. The texture set off his gag reflex. There was nowhere else for the spoilage to go but onto those nicely pressed slacks.

"Stupid son of a bastard," the Sheriff hissed, grabbing a handful of napkins to wipe the fabric clean. When he was finished, he tossed the soiled paper towels onto the table, and slumped down in the opposite chair, studying Grady like a lab specimen. "I'm adding my dry-cleaning bill to your bail bond when it's set."

Grady couldn't give two fucks about this man's laundry or the supposed bail bond. It took everything he had to keep cool while whatever drug he'd been given worked its way out of his system. He glanced at the corner where the panther sat on its haunches, watching their exchange. It was disorienting having been cut off from his animal counterpart. The magic had a musky scent he could still detect, but it wasn't as strong.

"Tell me, *Grady*, have you ever killed a man?"

The hair on the back of Grady's neck bristled. The large cat hissed and swiped, its claws slicing through the Sheriff like smoke.

"I can tell, you know?" The Sheriff pointed at Grady's face and sneered. He pressed it between his eyes hard enough Grady's head rolled back. Blaylock jerked his hand back and huffed a dark chuckle. "You have that glint in your eyes. The one of a man who's watched the life of another human fade like a dying flashlight."

The bastard knew, somehow. Grady didn't have the strength to ponder how. Blaylock's gaze shifted past him, hardening again.

"Don't look surprised, kid. Your daddy wasn't my friend, but he was the only person I trusted. Keep your enemies closer an' all that. I suppose I have you to thank for getting him outta my way. Bit tricky for someone in my position to make someone disappear. But for you? Poetic, don't ya think?"

"What da fuck you prattlin' 'bout, old man?" Good. His tongue worked better this time, but his celebration was cut short.

The blow came in a blur. Grady's jaw exploded with pain. His chair teetered on two legs. Blood pooled in his mouth. Swallowing it was out of the question—not on an empty stomach.

Grady spat it straight out...right in Blaylock's face.

"Oh, ho, ho." The deep rumble of angry laughter sent chills down Grady's spine. Blaylock's face matched the blood he wiped away. "You're gonna regret that."

Another hit rocked Grady's head in the opposite direction. The detonation of pain was as intense as the ringing in his ears. He blinked rapidly, trying to dispel one of the two glowering devils.

Next thing he knew, Grady's arms were loose at his side and he was yanked by the collar. He was hoisted on unsteady feet as the room spun like a Tilt-A-Whirl.

The blow to Grady's midsection expelled every bit of air he needed for today, taking tomorrow's rent, too. The next punch landed with a sinister crack.

Involuntary coughs sent heated whiplashes across his ribcage. His mouth opened, gasping for air like a fish out of water. His swollen face felt hot enough to fry an egg. The sheriff finally released his hold, and Grady collapsed in a heap. His groan of pain sucked in a desperate sip of oxygen—but it was hardly enough.

If he survived and made it back to Beth, she'd heal him. And that was a pretty big 'if.'

"Since you won't be leaving this room today except in a black bag, I'll let you in on secret. The rumors about my father are true." Blaylock knelt, his iron grip locking onto Grady's chin, leaning in so close Grady could count his nose hairs. "I was fourteen when I killed the monster who called himself my sperm donor. Everybody in this stupid town called him a hero, but he was a coward who liked to take his pain out on little boys."

A fresh coat of spit hit Grady's face. His skin crawled, and he closed his eyes in disgust.

"Why you tellin' me?" he croaked, every word a challenge.

"Because you know what it's like to live with a monster. You know what it's like to see worse ones in your nightmares, don't you?"

Blaylock's fingers dug into the hollows of Grady's cheeks. He leaned close enough Grady could count the veins in the whites of the Sheriff's eyes.

"You've seen him. He comes to us in our dreams; shows us all kinds of ungodly awful things. Now that Curtis Putnam is dead, you think Ja'azul is twiddling his thumbs? Think again."

Thorny black worms skirted the milky surface around Blaylock's irises before retreating again. Grady's hands went limp, his shoulders drooped. He felt his throat pulsing faster and faster. Ja'azul would never stop—not until he was either banished or had destroyed everything.

"I have one more thing to do for the master, and lucky for me, it also fulfills a promise. Two birds with one stone." Sheriff Blaylock tossed Grady's head back and rose to full height. "I promised your old man I'd take care of you when he was gone. I intend to do that right now."

The tip of Blaylock's steel-toed boot struck Grady's stomach. Stars swam in his vision, causing the edges to darken. He fought to maintain consciousness, imagining Beth's gorgeous smile and easy laughter. Her silky skin and soft hair the color of sorghum syrup. The way she beamed when she was the only one to catch fish on their many trips. The woman who brightened his days and sweetened his dreams. Every memory he had packed into his personal photo album replayed on loop, rebuilding his will.

The snap and rustle of a leather strap broke his concentration. The swish of sharp metal being pulled against leather set off alarm bells. Grady rolled enough to look up from the floor. The room dimmed around the edges, filling with the smell of burnt mustard.

He tensed, trying not to cough, which caused a flare of napalm to sear his insides. A fresh layer of sweat broke out all over his body. Cold. He was so cold that his body convulsed.

"When I finish with you, I'm gonna pay another visit to Miss Harper. I'll bet that pretty little thing is lonely. First, her husband dies, then her lover. I'll make sure your little whore is well taken care of."

"Don't you dare touch her," he growled through gritted teeth. Whatever the asshole had drugged him with was beginning to wear off, but not fast enough.

Grady willed his panther to rejoin him, tugging on the kite string to coax it back. The animal was an extension of him—not only part of his magic, but a conduit for the more brutal tasks to be carried out. They both demanded the sheriff's blood in repentance, but an unseen barrier kept them apart.

"And what are you gonna do about it if I do, boy?"

The lights overhead flickered. Frantic and harsh whispers rose from the encroaching darkness. It couldn't end like this.

"Looks to me like you're in no fit shape to protect your girlfriend. Hell, you can't even sit up."

"I'll kill you if you lay a single finger on her head." Grady's voice was hoarse. He pushed his shaking body to a sitting position, just to prove the bastard wrong. His bravado cost him, paid in the currency of blood-mixed sweat dripping onto the cold tile floors.

Blaylock's laughter turned darker, crawling across his skin.

"Y'ai naflfhtagn 'ng'ngah, Ja'azul h'ee, s'uhn-ngh athg li'hee orr'e syha'h uaaah."

The words slithered across his body like acid, licking his wounds as fire devours gasoline. They spilled into the cracks of his bones, dragging razors across the exposed marrow, and crept past his chest toward his mind. Delirious laughter bubbled from Grady when he reached for his counterpart to have the panther snap at his fingers.

No one in the station knew what was going on in this room, and no one gave a fuck. Their boss pulled all the strings. If Grady was going to make it out alive and back to Beth, he had to get his ass off this floor and stop the ritual.

Grady focused every bit of whatever kept him ticking to get to his feet. With Herculean effort, he managed to pull himself to his knees but it drained his oxygen. Better than the alternative. He liked breathing when it didn't hurt like a son of a bitch.

Blaylock's voice had deepened, morphing into something inhuman. The ancient language of the old gods wasn't meant to be uttered on human tongues. Intent counted for enough. The room grew smaller as the coldness of space filled it in.

He raised a knife above his head, his gaze fixed on Grady as the ritual's chants dwindled. Blaylock's eyes had gone solid black. Grady's sweat froze into crystals as his muscles shriveled from the cold. Getting out of the way in time would be next to impossible.

Beth would find a way.

In a last-ditch effort, Grady grabbed the feet of the metal chair and pulled the chair between them. Blaylock kicked it out of the way as Grady scooted along the wall. His body was shutting down, limb by limb, but there was nothing he could do.

I need to say goodbye. Warn Beth about Blaylock.

His fingers grasped the chain of his necklace, but before he could yank it, the door to the interrogation room slammed open. Deputy Stanton burst in—wide-eyed—with his gun drawn. "Drop the knife, Blaylock."

The Sheriff wasn't home anymore. He was occupied by Ja'azul or his spirit—Grady had never bothered to learn the particulars. Not that the knowledge helped him. The man ignored his deputy's command.

"Move it, Cooper!"

Stanton's barked command jumpstarted Grady's survival instincts. He rolled to the side, away from the table and Blaylock, right as a shot rang out.

His eardrums rang like church bells, but he crawled toward the door. Each inch felt like fighting with a runaway diesel train—a fight he was losing. Every second he stayed in this room was a chance of losing himself entirely.

The deputy's mouth moved, but Grady's hearing was toast. A hand grabbed his leg and yanked. Before he could pull it away, a line of heat went down his calf muscle, almost to the bone. Grady opened his mouth, deaf to his screams. Blaylock pulled his knife free and reared back to stab again.

Madness danced in Blaylock's eyes. A twisted grin was glued to his face, too wide for normal lips to achieve. In slow motion, the tip of the metal plunged downward.

The Sheriff's body jerked, and the knife flew behind him. He recoiled, babying his hand as blood oozed from the open wound. Grady's vision blurred. Tiredness seized his muscles. He fought for control, scrabbling at the need to survive when a hand snatched his collar and dragged him into the hallway.

"Hey!"

Dark stars twinkled in his peripheral, turning white. There was a light tapping on his swollen cheek.

"Don't pass out on me now." Stanton's muffled voice finally broke through the ringing.

Grady wanted to ask, 'Why the hell not?' But a niggling told him to *get up*. Get to Beth and then sleep. That's all he needed to heal. At least his hearing returned.

"I need..."

Grady's arm was thrown across a set of broad shoulders. The deputy slipped his arm behind Grady's back, lifting him with a grunt and a curse.

"You need a doctor, but we've gotta get outta here first."

Stanton led him down the hall. Officers were on phones, their wide eyes darting around as they looked for someone to dispatch. As uniforms hurried past, the faces either frowned or seemed to look through them. Somewhere, a coffee pot had been forgotten. The stench of the cheap brew clung to the air like a bad rash.

Grady's thoughts were fuzzy, but he was lucid enough to know things had gone to hell in a handbasket. He wasn't sure if the ringing in his ears was from his hearing complaining or that of several sirens strung into one wail.

The angry-looking young deputy who helped Stanton arrest Grady stormed over, answering his riddle.

"Stanton! Where the hell you going with him?"

"Back down, Nelson. This man needs a doctor."

Nelson drew his weapon, pointing it at the center of Rich's chest. "I can't let you leave with him. Sheriff gave his orders."

"Put that away before you do something you're gonna regret."

"You know I can't do that." The young deputy inched forward, but Rich matched him

"Serve and protect, *partner*. It's in the job description. You should try it sometime."

Nelson's jaw ticked. "Blaylock will have your badge—"

"He can have it." Rich jerked the nylon string around his neck overhead and threw it at the young man.

Nelson aimed his firearm at the ceiling and caught Rich's badge with his other hand.

"Consider this my resignation."

A lady dispatcher pulled Nelson by the arm, dividing his attention. Grady's head lolled as Stanton readjusted his hold. They were moving again, shuffling faster than Grady's leaden legs could keep up.

"Hold on Cooper."

Suddenly, the sun.

Blinding, beautiful and hot, energizing sunlight.

Grady's lungs took a greedy gulp of fresh air, as much as his constrained chest would allow. It cost him dearly.

He barely registered the squeaky leather seat or the stale cigarette smoke. The same brand his dad used to buy. An engine turned, and the lights went out.

Chapter 12

BETH

Fennick sat across the table in the window booth. His hair glistened in the sunlight in autumn's rich shades. Conversation had slowed to short answers or nods in favor of consuming their food like ravenous dogs. At least, that's how Beth imagined she looked, wolfing down her burger and fries.

She sat back in her seat, full and content for the moment.

"I know it's a strange question, but I have to know." Beth wiped her mouth with a napkin. "What shampoo do you use?"

"I cannot tell you the name, but it has something to do with herbs."

The pronunciation of herbs with an 'h' brought a smile to Beth's face. She was pleased by Fen's stellar behavior this afternoon. He'd been a perfect gentleman, seeming serious about the restart to their friendship. She would almost say she felt relaxed in his company. Having a good night's sleep and a full stomach helped in that regard.

Beth's peace was quickly doused by her phone alarm. She silenced the reminder to call the lawyer's office again and waved the waitress over.

"Sorry about that, but I have an important phone call to make." She reached into her purse for her wallet.

"Elizabeth."

Hearing her full name brought her to a shaky stop. Only her mother used Elizabeth, and it was in formal situations.

"Don't call me that."

"Apologies. Need I remind you that the meal is on me?"

The waitress placed the plastic tray on the table with a sweet grin. "Thank y'all for coming."

"It has been our pleasure, Denise." Fen's megawatt smile painted a blush over their waitress's cheeks. He tossed three twenty-dollar bills onto the tray, giving her a forty-percent tip.

"I'll be right back with your change," Denise said as she took the tray.

"Please, my dear. Keep the change."

"Are you sure?" Fen nodded and Denise placed her hand over her heart. Her eyes glittered as she whispered, "Thank you so much."

Beth waited until Denise was out of earshot and stood, draping her purse strap over her shoulder. "Does your flirtation meter have an off-switch or is it permanently on?"

Fen stood, his cheeks tinged to match Denise's. It was cute, but he wasn't a contender for her affection. The man who filled that role was the one she was currently trying to break out of jail on a weekend.

"When you are as well-traveled as I, you learn how short life truly is. Plus, a little harmless fun is good for the soul." His wink seemed innocent, but the twinkle in his eye suggested more.

"Perhaps I'll get the chance to travel one day," Beth mused wistfully, but her chest tightened when hit with a pulse of excited energy from her dining companion. She brushed it off and continued, "Thank you for lunch, Fen. Now, if you will excuse me, I really need to make that phone call."

She felt a twinge of guilt for spending so much time with Fen while her best friend was probably having a rough night. If only he'd call her or tell her *something*. She needed to hear his voice.

"Allow me to walk you out." He glided to Beth's side. His hand hovered over her lower back close enough she felt his heat. "After you."

Dizzying. This was the effect Fennick Rayon had on women. Between his panty-melting smile, well-fitted black jeans, and spicy cologne—which reminded Beth of a strong chai tea—Fen made basic thought as difficult as trapping fog with your bare hands while inebriated.

She pushed the metal bar on the glass door and a wave of heat rushed past her legs, overcoming the coolness of the air conditioning. It banished the goosebumps and cleared her head a smidgeon while the scent of petrichor offered a healthy serotonin boost.

"I have treasured your company, dear Beth. We must do this again soon."

Fennick stood inside her personal bubble, his hand came to rest below her shoulder. When his thumb brushed over the bruise he'd left last night, it left a gentle volt of electricity. Every time her skin connected with Fennick's, she felt the same zing as with Grady's touch. It wasn't as potent, but it was there and confusing as hell.

Beth stepped back and resisted the urge to rub her arm. She used the space to dig around in her purse. Usually, her car keys stayed on top. Today, the pests decided to fall to the bottom.

"We'll see."

When Fen's face fell, Beth amended, "It depends on how this phone call goes. I've had a lot on my plate lately, so I appreciate the distraction."

She crossed the short distance to her vehicle, hoping Fen would take the hint and go. He jogged ahead and put his hand on the driver's side door handle.

"Any time you need a distraction, Beth, I offer my services." Fen positioned himself between Beth and her escape. He placed his long, soft fingers underneath her chin and tilted her head. Half-hearted static sparks skimmed the area where they touched. "I meant it when I said I enjoy your company."

He was going to kiss her. A part of her magic recognized him, tentatively reaching out. *Curious.* Beth didn't need more complications. Fennick was the definition of complicated.

"Fen," she whispered, grasping his wrist and lowering his hand. "Your friendship is welcome, but that's where it ends. I'm already involved with someone."

"Ah." He pursed his lips and took a step back, keeping his hand on the door handle. "You cannot blame me for making my intentions known. Until such a time you have a change of heart, I shall endeavor to control my desires."

"I'll keep that in mind if things don't work out."

A small part of Beth meant it. Fennick was growing on her. He was exotic and interesting, an exciting contrast to her small-town life. Not to mention conversation flowed easily between them. Had things been different—and if he'd not shaken her trust last night—she may have been open to his advances.

However, her life was messy and full of other potential adventures. Running away with a stranger wasn't part of her destiny. Living the rest of this life with Grady was, and she wanted him by her side again more than anything.

Fen grinned and pulled the door open, casting his gaze over the roof of her hatchback as she got in. His forearm rested across the open window as he bent to eye level. Gentle drops of rain heralded another of the summertime scattered showers Georgia and Tennessee were known for.

"Thank you, again, for the tour of your hometown."

"It was my pleasure." Beth nodded, her lips pursed in a tight smile. "Be seeing you around, Fen."

As he backed away, his hands in his front pockets, the weighted gaze of his dark hazel eyes held her captive past the point of comfort. Before Beth broke eye contact, Fennick turned around. It was sprinkling in earnest, but he didn't seem the least bit concerned. Dispelling nervous energy with a shake of her head, she brought up the lawyer's number.

The line rang for ages, ending with an abrupt click. The telltale 'beep,' 'beep,' 'beep' of a dead line prickled the corners of her eyes. She hadn't expected anyone to answer, but the voicemail hadn't picked up either.

"Shit," she groaned with a sniffle. Her throat was clogged with disappointment. "We'll just go to the house and keep trying."

It was the weakest pep talk in the history of pep talks, but Beth had kept the bar low since Tom's death. With Curtis gone, the only worry she had was clearing Grady's name so they could figure out how to banish Ja'azul.

After being their nemesis for so long, time was finally a friend.

The drive across town to her parents' house flew by in a blink. It was a beautiful second

Saturday in June in her childhood neighborhood. Too bad she brought the storm with her.

Despite the dark clouds crowding her rearview, families were out on lawns tending to smoking grills or spraying kids with hoses. Squeals of children and hearty laughter barged into the open windows. Her smile was more of a grimace, longing for what could have been with Tom. Hell, it still could be except the romantic interest had changed.

As Beth turned onto the street she grew up on, she envisioned a little girl running around in a field of wildflowers chasing butterflies. Her halo of long, bouncing black curls were as soft as down feathers and eyes a crystalline blue with flecks of lavender hidden in fractals around her iris. Beth's contribution was in the form of the little one's smile. Full, pink lips that, once unleashed, had her father wrapped around her tiny pinkie.

The biggest hurdle for that future was coming up with the money for bail and a lawyer, if they'd answer their damned phone. It was as if they had her number blocked. Maybe she'd have more luck calling from the neighbor's phone.

When she put her blinker on, it took her brain a few seconds to register the sheriff's vehicle pulling in beside her. A wave of pins and needles shot up her neck and across her face in a heatwave unrelated to the humid temperature outside. There were a few reasons for a personal visit, and none of them were pleasant.

Were they here to question her again?

Did they have news about Grady?

Had something happened to her parents?

Beth begged her limbs to stop shaking while she put her hatchback in park. It was no use. Her anxiety was through the roof after lunch with Mr. Flirtypants.

"Nervous wreck it is," she sighed, exiting her Outback. She rounded the front of her car, shielding her eyes from the flash of sunlight reflecting off the cruiser's opening door. "Afternoon, officer."

A man with dark umber skin and salt peppering his temples got out of the driver's side. He was one of the arresting officers from last night. His partner didn't bother getting out. She couldn't make heads or tails whether this was a good or bad thing, the situation had her off-kilter. Her stomach tightened as if she'd swallowed a marble-sized ball of gravity.

"Afternoon, Ms. Har—er, Newman."

That voice. It was a blast from the past. How had she missed it last night? "Mr. Rich?"

He turned to face her and nodded deeply. The corner of his lip lifted the tiniest bit. Those dark brown eyes used to hold fierce joy and kindness. Now, they poorly hid the sorrow of a broken man.

"How ya doin', kiddo?"

"Been better. How about you?" Beth took the cautiously friendly route. She wasn't sure how well it was going because Rich's gaze continued to dart around.

Rain tap-danced on the roof of her vehicle.

"I know this is gonna sound like an odd request"—Rich scrubbed his face with his hand. Frowning, he rubbed the sweat on his trousers—"but would it be alright if we parked in the garage?"

"I, uh," Beth scrambled to find a polite way to decline, but the longer she waited, the heavier the pressure pushing against her chest became. "I'm not—"

"I wouldn't ask if it weren't an *emergency*." He jerked his head in the direction of his squad car a couple of times. Beth ducked to see inside the passenger seat. Instead of Rich's partner, there was a man slumped against the door. His face was swollen and red, but she recognized that sweaty mop of black curls anywhere.

"Grady?" she choked in a raw whisper. Tears clouded her vision as she clapped her hand over her mouth.

When she couldn't see the rise and fall of his chest, her feet carried her forward.

"Not here," Rich hissed, catching her across the clavicle with his arm. "Like I said, it's an emergency."

She wiped away the tears and nodded, unable to tear her gaze away. Rich snapped his fingers in front of her face.

"I was gonna take him to the hospital, but I was worried the department would send someone to your place."

"What—" Beth stopped herself. She'd get answers later.

She pressed the button to engage the garage door. Damn thing needed to be replaced, but her dad said it was a waste of money since they barely used it. Thankfully, the door rolled up without a hitch.

Beth eased her vehicle forward, lowering the garage door after Rich parked. Usually, it shuddered about the halfway mark, but today it closed like new.

Rich climbed out about the time Beth opened Grady's door. She knelt on the cold concrete pad and placed her hand on his. Beneath his feverish skin, weak flickers of magic reacted to her touch. She thanked the goddess they were still connected.

Though it was obvious someone had beat Grady within an inch of his life, he should have been able to heal it. So, why hadn't he yet?

"What happened to him?" she asked, not taking her eyes off her best friend. If she put him in the category of 'future' or 'lover,' there was no guarantee her sense of calm wouldn't shatter.

"I don't know what the hell was going on, but it was against every protocol in the book." Rich's eyes were wide as the memory of whatever happened played on an invisible screen. "Help me get him inside, and I'll tell you what I know."

Hauling Grady's limp, heavier-than-a-bushel-of-potatoes form out of the vehicle without dropping him required an engineering degree. Neither of them had one. Beth straddled the console and held him by the arms while Rich basically did the front half of a suplex. She carried Grady's legs the rest of the way.

Once they got him in the sitting room and laid him on the expensive oatmeal-colored sectional, Rich's face was two shades darker and looked like he'd run a marathon.

Beth collapsed at Grady's side. She ran her hands through his damp locks, clearing the hair from his face. Shades of blues and purples formed around the angry welts marring his handsome face. His left eye was swollen shut and his right cheek looked like it was filled with a fistful of cotton balls.

Beth placed a kiss on the only space without a scratch, his forehead. As soon as her lips touched his boiling skin, she pulled back. She straightened her spine, summoning the strength to stay seated and not put the fear of god in whoever harmed the man she loved. Her calm had been sufficiently smashed.

"Like I said, I was going to take him to the hospital, but they'd be looking for us there. Went by your apartment, but it's still taped off." Rich lowered to the matching armchair, resting his elbows on his knees. He kept his gaze on the carpet. "So, I came here, hoping the address was the same as when you ran track with... Bought us some time anyway."

He tapered off, but Beth was too worked up over Grady's rough treatment to ask about her high school teammate, Deena. If she hadn't been so focused on checking every inch, she'd have missed the bandage on the back of his hand. She lifted it enough to see the pinprick of a needle.

"He was drugged." The rage-induced buzzing surrounding her brain had started as a low hum. It was now a full-on freight train running on hellfire as it circled her calm. "Who did this, Rich?"

"The Sheriff, Eric Blaylock. I opened the door, and he was standing over Grady with a knife. He spoke some weird language. Whatever it was made my skin crawl, like there were maggots wriggling below the surface." Rich paused to rub the back of his neck. "Then I shot him. I shot my boss because he wouldn't stop. It was fucking evil."

Beth's carefully constructed bubble of hope popped. What Rich described was the same as when Paul tried to sacrifice her. The room became stuffy, hot. Beth had trouble breathing past the tightness in her chest.

It didn't matter that Curtis was dead because evil kept spawning more evil. She was no closer to protecting everyone than she was before Tom died.

Rich had this faraway look on his face. Not disbelief, but a mix of wonder and terror. Beth vaguely remembered the rumor that he was kicked off the force for his occult hobbies. Maybe he'd be open to what she had to tell him, but Grady needed healing first.

"Look, he's burning up so I can't wait. I'm a witch, a healer. I can fix him," Beth's brows were pulled tight, pleading. "But I need you to trust me. Can you do that?"

"When you say witch, do you mean a Wiccan?" Rich raised his eyebrow.

It was not the reaction Beth expected, but he wasn't screaming for help, so maybe the rumors were true. She counted it as a win.

"Wiccan adjacent. I haven't been practicing long, but it's nature-based." Beth hoped her weak explanation would suffice because she felt the sand running out on Grady's hourglass.

He narrowed his eyes, nodding slowly. "Can I do anything to help?"

"Keep a watch on the door and don't let anyone interrupt."

Rich studied her like a science project before he stood. "Okay. I'll keep post."

Beth put her hand on his arm and gave him a warm smile. "Thank you."

Rich pursed his lips but gave Beth a curt nod and took his place next to the door.

She knelt by her beloved's side and whispered in his ear, "Come back to me."

Beth placed her hands on either side of Grady's head. His skin was a blistering furnace.

She closed her eyes and focused on her magic. The pool of energy she had collected this morning awaited her command.

Another of Beth's gifts was the ability to convert this energy into whatever she needed. So far, she had learned each type was tied to a specific color. Protection magic burned orange, fire turned blue, and things dealing with plants were green. When she used her magic for healing or for opening doors keyed to guardians and blasting bad guys to kingdom come, it was white.

Beth opened her eyes, watching it flow through her fingers and surround Grady's head like soft, shimmery organza. There was more resistance than she was used to, but little by little the lesions on his face knitted together and the swelling reduced. He was back to his normal handsomeness, but it had taken a toll on her.

Using the couch arm, Beth hauled herself to her feet. The way her legs wobbled wasn't a good sign she could make it to the kitchen for a snack.

"Rich?"

Her old friend jogged back into the room, but he stopped as soon as he saw Grady. Rich's wide eyes blinked as he did a double take. "What in the name of all that is good...you fixed him. With magic."

"Yes, but just his head." She held her hand level, showing Rich the shaking. "Whatever the Sheriff dosed him with is making it harder. Can you grab me something to eat from the kitchen? It'll help."

"Sure, sure." Rich looked both ways, as if he had forgotten where anything was.

"To the right, Rich."

"Right, I mean, thanks."

She couldn't blame him for being flustered. Seven years and working for an evil son of a bitch will do that to a person. She should thank him for saving Grady when he came back with food.

Worry was a magnet, pulling her gaze to Grady. His breaths still sputtered. When his face twitched into a pained wince, it was a knife to her heart.

What happened to you, love?

Beth ran her fingers through his soft curls at his temples, being mindful of the worst tangles. Her gaze assessed for more surface injuries while she waited.

Grady wore the same filthy clothes he showed up in, which were covered in more than just blood. A spark of anger conjured up more than a few hurtful ways she could repay the sheriff department's 'hospitality.'

The bulk of fresh blood was centered around his right calf. Beth slid to the carpeted floor and crawled nearer. Carefully, Beth raised his leg. If it weren't for the thick hem at the ankles, the back of his pants would be split wide open. At first glance, it looked like someone had taken a filet knife, sliced down the middle of his calf, and splashed black ink into the cracks.

Using the hem of her shirt, she wiped the blood away from around one side and the color drained from her face. Green gunk oozed from the center, sinking of rot, and there were thin black root-like veins growing from the center.

"No. He can't...Rich!" Her heart had turned into a battering ram, trying to break through her chest.

"Sorry. There's not much—" Rich placed a sleeve of crackers and jar peanut butter on the coffee table, but the jar rolled to the floor. "Why does it look like that?"

Beth's fears were confirmed. She didn't want to believe that Blaylock was able to perform the sacrificial ritual, but he damn well had tried...and almost succeeded.

"It's infected with whatever Blaylock was doing. I need you to sit with Grady."

"What? Where are you going?"

"I need to go outside and replenish my magic."

"Can't you do it from inside?"

"Probably, but it'll be slower. Why?"

"I'm not comfortable with you going outside by yourself. Can't you just open a window?"

Beth fought her panic back enough to think. If the window was open, she could keep a line open, drawing what she needed while feeding it to Grady.

Like intravenous magical healing.

"Actually, yes."

She cracked open the nearest window. It faced the neighbor's house, but the privacy fence gave them enough cover. When Beth returned to Grady's side, Rich handed her a plate.

"Not yet. I need—"

"You're still shaking. You shouldn't do anymore healing until you've eaten," Rich insisted, practically putting the plate in her hands.

"You sound like Grady," she murmured, looking down at the snack despite her stomach threatening to eject anything she fed it.

"Y'all are close," Rich said. His voice was neutral, but she caught the question he was too polite to ask.

"Yes. He's my best friend. I'd have never made it through Tom's death without him." Beth shoved a cracker in her mouth, chewing while she thought about how to broach the subject. "He and Tom were like brothers, so, when Tom and I married, we integrated into a happy triangle-ish friendship."

"The way you look at Grady, though..." Rich's tone had taken a softer edge.

Beth had to look, to see if there was scorn or pity. She found neither. Fatherly concern was all she saw. She gave a one-shoulder shrug and said, "I love him."

There wasn't any need for further explanation. That would come later. Rich tucked his chin in acknowledgement, coming to the same conclusion.

"Then you'd better do your thing." Rich stood, dusted his pants, and took her empty plate. "I'm going back on watch. Call me if you need anything."

"Thank you, Rich." Tears pricked her eyes. "For saving Grady, and for everything else."

He tipped his head with a warm smile before disappearing toward the kitchen.

Beth sat cross-legged by the couch and closed her eyes. She focused on the gentle breeze, followed it outside to the grassy backyard where it gently swayed. Sinking into their roots,

Beth pulled on the lifeforce of the plant life connected to that patch of turf. When she had a steady flow filling her magical well, she opened her eyes and extended—what she called—her aura.

Converting the energy into the healing white, she made it settle over his body like a blanket. She needed to fix the rest before tackling the toxins Blaylock left, so Grady's immune system would be strong enough to fight it with her.

Beth felt his splintered bones snapping back into place, wincing when his fists balled at his side. "Hang in there, Grady. I've got you."

When the last of his ribs knit back together, Grady's fists relaxed. Beth exhaled a slow, relieved breath. *Easy part done.*

Closing her eyes, Beth expanded her source outside to include her parents' backyard and the three neighboring properties. Better to be safe than sorry. With one last glance at Grady, she moved her healing wave to his legs.

Her patient startled awake, crying out with wild eyes.

Chapter 13

GRADY

The last thing Grady remembered was traveling at breakneck speeds down a dark tunnel before being slammed into a brick wall.

Wait. That wasn't right.

His body hurt in places he didn't know could ache. He also felt as though he was roasting over a campfire on a pit. Things moved beyond the heat.

Grady focused on the wavering images. As they cleared, he wished he could stuff them back: Blaylock practicing his kickboxing skills on Grady, punching his lights out, pulling a knife...

The ritual.

The bastard had tried to give Grady's soul to Ja'azul. He'd almost succeeded, too. Blaylock had said the words; he'd plunged the knife into Grady's leg. If Grady had died from his injuries, Blaylock would have won. Game over.

But he'd survived...*Unless I'm still in that room.*

His broken ribs were on fire, hotter than anything he'd ever experienced. Instinctively, he fought past the pain, gritting his teeth and balling his fists.

How long is this fucker going to torture me?

The discomfort faded and whatever pinched Grady's lungs magically disappeared. His chest felt whole again, enough that he took a deep breath. It was laced with the sweet tang of death, but at least it was fresh. *Did Blaylock heal my injuries just so he could give me new ones?*

It didn't make sense.

Unease spilled into his gut and a maddening itch moved to his leg. As the feeling closed in on his stab wound, the itching turned to napalm in his veins. This was it. The moment he died.

Reflexively, Grady's eyes flew open, and he sat bolt upright. A roaring scream like a hell bat rushed from his throat. He raised his fist, but an invisible force around Grady's wrist kept him from striking Blaylock.

"Grady!" Beth's strained voice broke the illusion, but the intense scorching eating his leg remained.

Grady blinked the sweat from his eyes. First, the invisible force around his wrist was a man's hand. The dark skin filled in the missing blanks. *Rich. He helped me.*

He blinked some more and turned to the wall. Instead of the flat-white concrete room, a familiar dusty blue wallpaper with busy floral designs greeted him. The Harpers always had expensive tastes. It seemed nothing had changed since Beth moved out.

His gaze found Beth's. Loose hairs were plastered to her pale face. Though her brows were tight in concentration, relief softened her features when their gazes met. Her smile was weak and short, turning into a chin wobble. She quickly redirected her attention to his leg.

"Nearly there," Beth said, her voice wavering from the effort.

"It's okay, Rich. You can let go of my arm now," Grady said through clenched teeth.

Rich frowned but released his grip. Grady laid back down in case the little white dots in his vision meant he was going to pass out again. The thought was barely formed when his leg went numb. An unholy growl knocked Beth over and caused Rich to stumble backward. Black smoke rose above the couch, then winked out of existence with a wheeze.

Grady slid to the floor and crawled to Beth, pulling her into a tight hug. She wrapped her arms around his neck as he buried his face in the crook of hers. Inhaling his favorite scent, he brushed his lips against her shoulder.

The past two days and a near-death experience had gotten to Grady more than he realized. They'd left him craving physical touch that didn't involve pain, and Beth was the cure-all for what ailed him. He was finally home with the love of his life wrapped in his arms. The urge to grab her face and kiss her until her lungs cried for oxygen was thwarted only because they weren't alone.

"I was worried I'd never see you again." His words were muffled, raw with emotion, but she heard them. Her quiet heartbeat suddenly thudded wildly against his chest. "The Sheriff, Beth, he nearly had me."

"I know. But he didn't, thanks to Rich." She whispered, rubbing small circles on his back.

Reluctance held Grady in place for a few heartbeats longer. When he pulled away from Beth, his gaze roamed every inch of her face, committing her to memory. When she tilted her head, brows furrowed, he gave her the lopsided smile that always made her blush.

It was worth it.

"Thank you, Deputy Stanton." Grady tore his gaze from Beth's to address the man who had the best timing in the world. He got on his feet, bringing Beth with him. He held his hand out for a handshake.

"Just Rich." Rich accepted it, awe still gleaming in his eyes as his gaze flittered to Beth and back. "I'm sure firing on your superior officer counts as immediate termination."

There was bitterness in his chuckle.

"I'm not sorry you did, but I hate that it cost you your job." Grady hooked his pinkie finger with Beth's. The physical touch seemed to help. His poor brain was convinced this was all some trick, that he was back in that room losing his fight for survival.

"Eh. I was a year away from retirement and close to closing a case." He wiped his hand down his face, seeming to age a decade as his shoulders fell. Rich dropped onto the beige settee. "Nothing y'all need to worry about."

Suddenly, the man's shields fell into place, and he sat straight. Grady recognized it for what it was. Slapping a new bandage on his wound without removing the old one. At some point, it would fester. Rich hadn't gotten there yet, but he looked near the point of having to rip them off to deal with the issue. If they didn't have bigger concerns demanding their attention, Grady would pry and do what he could to help the man. Seemed only fitting after Rich put his career on the line to save his life.

"What are you talking about?" Beth pressed. Clearly, she did not share Grady's caution sense. "What case?"

Rich's frown lines deepened as if he were stuck inside a painful memory. Grady recognized that look; the least he could do was change the subject.

"Beth, we can't lose sight of the larger issue." Grady crossed his arms over his chest, making his muscles flex. Beth's cheeks tinged pink. "Blaylock performing the ritual means Ja'azul has more dirtbags on his payroll."

"Right." She bit her bottom lip as her hands pulled at the hem of her shirt. "Were there any clues in your dad's journal?"

Grady dropped his gaze. "I haven't had time to read much."

That was part of the truth. The biggest reason was because he was too busy grieving the loss of his best friend. The Grove and woodworking had been his constant companions. Inanimate objects were good at listening; not so good at giving advice.

"Somebody wanna fill me in on this journal, seeing as we're all neck deep together in shit?" Rich laced his fingers, propping his elbows on his knees. He was all business now. "And who the hell is this Ya-zool?"

"Short answer: Ja'azul is why Blaylock and a whole bunch of screwed up dads in town ended up in a death cult." Grady dropped his arms to rub his now sweaty palms on his jeans. The sour smell of days' worth of body odor, sweat, and blood was mighty. Gods, he didn't know how Beth could stand to be near him. "I have information that, with your help, we can use to stop what is coming."

"Shit. Let's put a pin in the death cult thing for now. Something tells me there's a lot to unpack and we're sitting ducks." Rich wiped his hand down his face. "Speaking of, you do know Blaylock has your house under constant surveillance? There's no way we can get around town without his knowing it."

Grady glanced at Beth, who gripped the moonstone in her pocket through the fabric. "We have ways of getting around unnoticed."

"Magic?" Rich asked, studying them in turn like a college professor handing out test results.

"Yes," Grady confirmed. He was about to ask Rich for his moonstone when Beth spoke.

"How many people in your department does Blaylock control?" Beth asked, her free hand going above her chest, as though she had difficulty breathing. Grady rubbed small, soothing circles across her lower back.

"As far as I can tell, I'm the only one *not* in his pocket."

Call it a hunch, but Stanton didn't seem keen on explaining why he stayed off Blaylock's team. Not that Grady was looking a gift horse in the mouth or anything. It was difficult to trust a stranger, even one who had saved his life. He figured it had something to do with the mysterious case that was gonna end up unsolved.

"Then we need to move fast." Beth broke the long silence and began pacing the room. "Non-perishable food items, extra clothes, toiletries."

Grady knew it was best to let her get through her mental list before interrupting, but it was refreshing to see her in her element. His brain's panic mode downgraded to a code yellow.

"Where will we stay that will be off the radar?"

Rich's question engaged Beth's pause button. She looked to Grady for guidance.

"We have two options. My dad's shop. It's in the middle of town, but we might be able to get away with it if the sheriff expects us to run. Or the Larson farm. It's remote and we have the best chance of hearing company before they get there."

Rich furrowed his brows and rested his chin on his hand. Beth wrung her hands while studying Grady. The question was in her eyes: *Why not go to the Grove?*

There were a few reasons why Grady didn't want Rich at the Grove. The biggest being privacy. Was it selfish of him to want to be with Beth in the same way she was in his dreams for years? If he'd have been asked this question before his overnight stay in Cell Hell Hotel, the answer would have been yes. Funny how being close to losing everything you love broadens your perspective.

"Is there anything in your dad's shop that would be helpful?" Rich stood and smoothed his pants legs as if he were getting ready to leave.

"Perhaps. Like I said, he spent most of his time there. Who knows what we'll find in his office."

"We could split up. Rich can go to the welding shop, you can grab whatever spell books from your house, and I can grab food from my apartment. Divide and conquer."

"I don't like the idea of splitting up, but it may be our only option." Grady added. "Problem is, I don't have my moon stone."

"You can use mine." She pulled her portal stone from her pocket and held it out to Grady.

He covered her hand with both of his, closing her fingers over the smooth rock. "Keep it for now. I need you to be able to get out of here fast if the sheriff comes looking."

"But he hasn't bothered me since your arrest. I feel like I can safely drive around town."

"No, that was before I escaped with Rich's help. I don't want you to go anywhere alone."

"Grady."

"I can't, Beth. He's trying to finish it. If the sheriff gets to you, you'll die and I–that's unacceptable." The thought of losing the woman he loved more than anything caused his ribcage to tighten. His heart and lungs squeezed like someone wringing out a sponge. "I'm not letting you out of my sight."

"Beth can tag along with me. Blaylock will assume you'll go to her after escaping." Rich put his hands on his hips the way cops do when they're thinking things through. "I won't hesitate to shoot if Blaylock decides to get handsy with a knife again. Plus, if there's magic stuff going on, I'd like to stay alive long enough to enjoy retirement."

"What makes you think the sheriff will come for you, Rich?" Beth's face scrunched in a frown.

"I put a couple of holes in him, remember? Albeit he was in the middle of some dark ritualistic shit. Jury won't care that they weren't killing blows. I'll be lucky if I end up with a prison sentence under fifteen years."

"But Grady was in danger. The camera footage will show the truth."

"Not if someone turned it off." Grady countered. Even if they hadn't shut them off, the footage would have been scrubbed. "As far as everyone knows, nothing happened in that room."

"But that's illegal."

"Exactly. Like Rich said, everyone else is in Blaylock's pocket. The only reason I'm putting my trust in this man right here"—Grady pointed at Rich—"is because he saved my life, and you personally know him."

"There's one sure fire way to figure it out, though." Beth nodded, the cogs spinning behind her fern eyes.

Grady begged her to leave it alone, to not say it. But he should have known better. She was a people's champion, always looking for ways to help anyone in need. It's one of her attributes that found a chink in his armor.

"The Grove."

"What's 'the Grove'?" Rich asked, naturally.

"It's complicated." Grady rubbed a hand down his face and cringed at his rancid onion breath. "Look, I'll explain later. I look and feel like I've been rolling around in a fast-food dumpster. I'd appreciate it if we get moving. I need shower."

Beth opened her mouth to ask more questions, but she closed it. Her gaze softened with pity. "You can shower in the guest bathroom. My dad might have something that will fit."

"Thank you, Beth."

She stopped halfway up the stairs and half-turned to us. "You two should exchange numbers."

"I don't have a phone, Beth. My cell was in my truck when it was impounded." The thought irked him. That truck held a lot of memories.

"Give Rich my number, then." She peered at him over her shoulder, her hand on the stair railing. "I'll have some clothes for you by the time you're finished."

Grady watched her bounce up the stairs and disappear. Common sense told him she'd be back, but the panic from earlier reared its ugly head.

Rich cleared his throat. "So, what's the deal with you two?"

He considered how best to answer, unsure as to whether the man was interrogating him or simply curious. Rich's neutral tone didn't clue him in.

"Beth is my best friend."

"I thought Tom Newman was your best friend?"

Aha. There it is.

"He was. You can have more than one."

"I bet it was awkward. Being the third wheel like that."

Annoyance prickled his skin. Grady's nice guy was stepping back. He narrowed his eyes at Rich. "They never made me feel awkward."

"Just making conversation." Rich raised his palms and raised his eyebrows. "It seems like you care for Beth a lot."

"Of course I do." Grady's left eye twitched. He expected his panther's hackles to rise at the man's innuendo, but it didn't. If he couldn't tell the difference between casual conversation and a stab for information, they were in trouble. "Tom made me promise to watch over her if anything happened to him. I'm taking that promise seriously."

"Because you love her."

"Bingo, again."

"What are your intentions with Beth now that she is a widow?"

"Why does it matter to you?"

"Humor me."

"No." Grady deadpanned. Rich's fucked up version of a 'dad talk' rubbed Grady the wrong way. He glanced at the stairway, wishing Beth would save him from whatever *this* was.

"Did you ever meet my daughter, Deena? She'd be about your age. Graduated around the same time." The older man stumped him with a change of topic. He was familiar with the tactic. Louis Cooper used it almost daily.

"No, I don't believe so."

"She ran track and field with Beth. They weren't close; Beth's parents were very strict about her free time. If the Harpers weren't so restrictive, Beth and Deena could have been good friends."

"Sounds about right." Grady wanted to ask what the point of the story was but left it alone. At least he wasn't sniffing around too close to the truth.

"Mr. and Mrs. Harper weren't around for most of her meets, but I was. I made sure the girls on that team had water and snacks and were protected from their pervy coach. The other girls treated my Deena with kindness and respect, so I treated them like they were family. That protective streak didn't end when after they graduated."

"So, you're saying you've got Beth's back?" When Rich nodded, the stress keeping Grady's shoulders around his ears fizzled, and his muscles lowered like a tire with a slow leak. "Good to know."

"I'm not gonna warn you what will happen should you break her heart, because something tells me you already know." Rich reached into his pants pocket and brought out his cell phone.

"May I?" Grady gestured for the rectangle object. He entered Beth's number from memory before handing it back. "I want Beth to come with me, but I'm glad to know she's safe if she decides to go with you."

"Smart man."

Grady almost disagreed, but he didn't. Loving Beth up close was a learning curve. He'd found out the hard way what happens when you tell Beth what she's going to do rather than ask. Her stubborn streak would bite you in the ass.

Chapter 14

FENNICK

Ja'azul's power raked against Fennick's skull like shards of broken glass, cutting a path to the control centers of his brain.

Despite the spent summer rain reaching for the heavens, he broke out into cold sweats. Stumbling around to the back of a brick building, his fingernails scraped against the rough stone as he grasped for support.

Every crashing thump against his ribcage caused Fennick's self-governance to fade further as the foul breath of the predator seeped through the cracks of his subconscious. He feared not only for his safety should the master gain domination, but for Beth's.

"Leave me be. This body is mine and mine alone." Fennick beat the words into his chest with his fist until he was left gasping.

Rough peaks of compressed stone imprinted his forehead with miniature crags as he rested against the building to catch his breath. Though Fennick claimed victory over this battle, the landscape had been left in ruins. It was only a matter of time before the last tower fell.

Until then, Ja'azul would continue to reign supreme in his twisted dream dimension where nightmares were the waking reality and lesser monsters trudged among colossus beings made of spite and cruelty. During Fennick's travels, the brave and cowardly alike named these terrors 'cosmic horrors.' Too right they were, for he had peered into the mouth of such madness, practically inviting the darkness beyond human comprehension to dig its talons deep into his psyche. The holes pulsed with unearthly malice at the acknowledgement, chilling his soul to the bone. Had he been a lesser man, it would have brought him to his knees. However, Fennick's fall from godhood at the hand of his beloved had caused hatred to fester in his heart, burning it to ash. His only solace was his ability to function without a heart.

And then Beth happened.

Her awakening had called to Fennick across time and space. Since then, every innocent touch caused his guardian magic to flare to life, instilling the hope of a second chance. She was well worth the cost of temporary mortality. In a few months, Fennick's magic would be replenished to its full resplendence; she would see that he was the better choice. Once they were bonded, they would be unstoppable, and he would be free. They could travel the galaxy, uncovering the secrets of the universe for however long Beth desired.

His only obstacle was romancing a taken woman before she completed her guardian bond...and before he lost all his faculties.

The shiver that came with the thrill of a challenge was almost strong enough to push his master's unwanted influence back to the gates of Hell. However, after last night's blackout, Fennick did not indulge in half-measures. He needed an hour—two at most—to distance himself from Beth until he was sure he had control of his mental wherewithal. He knew exactly where to go, too. The place where he went to muddle through his problems while enjoying the best homemade apple pie.

Fennick rocked his head back and forth, stretching his tight neck. His long fingers curled until joints popped. Loosening his muscles was a necessary evil for the transformation, one that seemed more difficult than usual.

He took off in a brisk walk up the street where rural houses were spread haphazardly like children's toys along the hill. Once out of sight of town, he sprinted a ways before flinging himself into the air with his arms cast out at his sides.

Wings spread from his fingertips as he became weightless on the wind. Fennick relished the blissful moment when the warm breeze cut through his obsidian wings, and the sunlight bounced off jeweled tones of amethyst and sapphire. At certain angles, his feathers glittered like silver starlight. Flying was a freedom he had never dreamed would be his. The goddess, Circe, had gifted Fennick with fox form. Knowledge of the raven form had come from his predecessor, Barton Cooper, after forcing him to perform the Ritual of Passing.

The name was not nearly as foreign as his father's or mother's. Theirs had been lost in the sands of time, forgotten in the farthest corners of his memory while Barton's became a part of him.

Fennick wondered if his and Beth's love would be like Barton and Myrtle's. Would her kisses spark new life within the husk of what he had become? Beth's magic was a flame, and he was the moth, willing to burn for a fleeting moment of passion and being wanted...being loved.

Would Beth be able to love me despite the poisonous seed I harbor within?

A thick, briar-like rope whipped around his lungs and tightened. His vision wavered, growing dark around the edges. He had sold his soul in exchange for revenge outside of possibility, spending the majority of his life exacting souls for the enemy *he* was meant to vanquish. In doing so, he had unwittingly doomed Beth's soul to oblivion.

And robbed myself of redemption or happiness.

The walls of his chest crumpled under the weight of his failures, sending a spasm through his wings to the tips. His feathered arms curled inward, sending him on a downward spiral.

Fennick contemplated letting the earth swallow the fragile form. He was a shadow of his former glory, unworthy of love or devotion. A pockmark on the good name of magic and of humanity.

Perhaps it was his predecessor's bravery that righted his wings, swooping him toward the sky on a course above the treetops at the last minute. Or perhaps it was the scent of cinnamon and baked meat calling to his hunger. Food always boosted Fennick's strength, and the Bridges family cooked with love. It was a magic all their own.

Once he was well fed and had rebuilt his mental defenses, he would return to Beth's side before nightfall. Ja'azul's hold on him seemed stronger after the sun had set.

Inadvertently, Fennick's last thought had invoked the rule of three. The proverbial mallet struck the spike poised at the seam of his skull. Thick and oily, like rancid molasses, Ja'azul's essence spilled into the crack.

"I grow weary of your defiance. It will gain you nothing but suffering." Ja'azul's raspy voice was like a jagged saw, hacking haphazardly at Fennick's mind.

His vision vibrated, dimming around the edges. His master often spoke to him in dreams, but not like this. Somehow, Ja'azul took over his mind and body, incapacitating him in such a way that his bird form could not withstand the magnitude of power being forced into this small body.

Wingtips flickered between feathers and fingertips. Fennick aimed for a shorter fall should he lose control, descending until he was panting with effort to hold shape. Several feet above the ground, the raven form abandoned him. He had enough time to tuck his head underneath his arms before hitting the dirt and rolling to a stop on his back.

In that split second of lax control, Ja'azul's chaotic force consumed Fennick.

Agonizing pain glued him to the ground. His arms were pinned to his sides, knuckles white as he squeezed his fists to keep from crying out. Every muscle Fennick knew and those he didn't jerked uncontrollably as his eyes rolled to the back of his head.

A fiery tempest swarmed beneath trapped flesh. Rivers of sweat fell in heavy curtains down his blanched face. His long, auburn hair clung to his skin. Loose, wet strands whipped his body with each convulsion. He feared losing his teeth, having them clenched tighter than a coyote in winter fighting for the last carcass.

Ja'azul had never incapacitated him in such a way.

No matter how strong Fennick thought he was or how hard he fought, he was losing this battle of wills.

"Aaaah!" he cried out as the searing across the inside of his skull intensified. He half expected his brain to bubble and melt and ooze from his orifices.

"Poor, pathetic human. Try as you might, you cannot outrun the monster you have become." Ja'azul's voice, as cold as the void between the stars, made his skin crawl as it peeled away from his bones. "You belong to me for eternity, to torment as I please."

If Fennick opened his mouth to respond, his hellish screams would be unleashed upon this damned place, drawing mobs of zealots to snuff out the hounds of hell with their religion.

Instead, he let the pain pass through him, becoming one with it, for this was his doing. For countless years the whispers had been his only connection to anything. Their sweet promises of revenge had blinded him into this hellish servitude. Ja'azul had become his shadow, his end. For Fennick, there was no escape.

As disparity seeped into his heart, his affliction eased enough to grind out, "Master, I am your deliverer."

At Fennick's admittance, Ja'azul released him. Greedily, his lungs sucked in the air he had been denied. He shuddered, laying still against the mossy forest floor while the world righted itself. Leaves came into focus, breathing became less of a struggle, and one by one his muscles quit jerking.

Fennick blinked the sweat from his stinging eyes as the pounding inside his skull became a simple heartbeat. For a long while after his body went still, he basked in the dancing rays of sunlight that made it past the tops of proud pines. As the sun warmed his bones, nature carried on as normal, but despondency kept him from getting up.

Ja'azul called him a monster. There were many times Fennick wondered the same thing. After centuries of serving this dark entity, Fennick had become that which he was designed to protect humanity from. He *was* a monster.

He was also a fool.

Beth could never love someone as unpure as him.

The proverbial dagger he'd plunged into his chest to the hilt twisted. Fennick had to make a choice. His salvation or her life?

Deep in his core, a spark ignited before fizzling as quickly as it had come. He knew his choice even before he asked the question.

Beth's nature was to protect. He would do the same for her. In doing so, he could share in the success of Ja'azul's defeat.

Imagining her smiling face was enough to give Fennick the courage to get moving. Slowly, he sat up with a groan, joints popping as his body adjusted to being human again.

His clothes were a wrinkled mess and his hair stuck up all over. In his periphery, black feathers protruded from his long locks. He yanked them free and dropped them to the ground, where they swirled and flitted into the forest beyond.

Fennick had a quick fix for this issue, but traveling through time to get to Beth had taken a toll on his magic. Transforming had taken even more, leaving his well drier than usual.

He placed his hand on the nearest tree root. Taking the lifeforce of another living thing used to rankle him. After so many years, siphoning power had left him numb. In this case, the situation was dire. If he had any hope of protecting Beth, one tree would not be missed.

As he greedily leeched power from the proud sycamore, the trunk withered, shedding weak branches. It took on a skinny sickness before turning gray. When the tree had been sucked dry, the remaining branches curled in on themselves. Any leaves left blew away with the breeze to fertilize the forest.

Fennick stood and waved his hands over his tattered fabric, mending them to pristine condition. Running his hands through his hair, he combed his mahogany locks free of leaves, twigs, and tangles. The action left him dizzy and weak-kneed.

"Peculiar," Fennick surmised aloud as he searched for the magic he had renewed. Oddly, his well was bone dry. What he had collected should have lasted days.

His skin tingled with a surge of guardian power. Its ascent into stellar fire itching at his chest was rapid. Beth was in danger and he had foolishly fallen into another trap.

The edges of his vision were cast in shadow. A laugh as unpleasant as rusted hinges echoed in his head. Too late, realization washed over Fennick like a tidal wave. In his haste to flee from Beth's certain doom, he had shown his hand.

It would appear he had chosen the Bridges family's destruction over Beth's. He was indeed cursed to live a life of solitude and loneliness.

Chapter 15

RICH

He couldn't get a good read on the Cooper boy at first, but his gut told him he was not a threat. If anything, Rich was happy the young man was so protective of Beth. It made his job easier.

"Sorry it took me so long. The door to my parents' room is locked. Luckily, Dad keeps some of his extra clothes in the guest bedroom closet." The subject of their discussion stood at the top of the stairs with an armful of clothes.

"I'll take those." Grady took the stairs two at a time and relieved her of the garments.

Beth's cheeks were pink when she came down the stairs to join him.

"Have you decided yet if you're staying with Grady or coming with me?" Rich asked, noting how Grady's poker face was on point. In his time as a deputy in Mayes Hill, Rich had learned to never play card games with a Cooper. It seemed Louis's son had picked up a few things after all.

"I'm staying with Grady. He'll need someone to keep watch while he gets cleaned up." She put her free hand on her hip and tried to be nonchalant. Rich wasn't fooled, but he wasn't keen on poking at the state of their relationship anymore today. They'd already overstayed at this location.

"Then I'll head to Cooper's welding shop and lay low. Keep y'all posted if I hear anything over the radio."

Rich also wanted to look around for clues to Louis Cooper's connection with Eric Blaylock. After Louis's death, Rich had tried to reopen the file to find they had been flagged as Classified. Had it been a coincidence or was he reading into something that wasn't there? No better way to make a kid want the candy jar than to tell them they can't have any.

"Cool." Beth walked with him to the door to the garage where an extra remote hung on the wall. She took it off the hook and held it out to Rich. "Here, take this in case your location gets hot, and you need a backup. I'll leave this door unlocked for you."

"Thanks." Rich slipped the gray plastic remote into his pants pocket. "You kids be careful."

"You, as well." Grady came downstairs to clap him on the back.

Beth hugged him around the neck like she hugged her father-in-law. "Be safe. We'll call you when we're done."

Rich saluted the two as he climbed into his cruiser. Once he was on the street, heading toward town, a weird feeling fluttered behind his ribcage. He glanced in the rearview back at Beth's house. It was quiet, but that wasn't what bothered him.

Clarity struck when he passed a man walking his dog.

"Shit."

He'd forgotten about Zeus. Thankfully, he had enough food this morning to last him the day. At some point, Rich would need to stop by his house for his faithful companion, but Blaylock would have put an APB out on him by now. The welding shop was his best bet.

Rich continued down the street, his paranoia growing into a ball of anxiety in the pit of his stomach. By the time he made it to the main road, his stomach was in knots and sweat beaded his forehead. He glanced in the rearview mirror for the umpteenth time. The air conditioner seemed to be on the fritz again.

Loosening the vice grip he had on the steering wheel, he felt around the console for a napkin to wipe the sweat from his brow, dotting his face while keeping his gaze focused on the road. When he finished, a freezing chill rushed through his veins.

I must be coming down with a cold or the flu.

Rich wasn't fully convinced, but he wasn't sure he'd gotten his flu shot this year. Either way, he couldn't sit at the stop sign forever.

The metal building was in sight a few blocks away, gleaming in the afternoon sun like a grungy beacon. After checking one last time, he pulled onto Main Street, then hooked a left. There was a shaded parking area on the right-hand side of the building with room for two. He eased into the space as far forward as possible.

When he got out of his cruiser, an icy breeze crept along the back of his neck. Someone's gaze bore into the back of his head. He turned on his hip and snapped his head to the side, eyes narrowed as he surveyed the streets. Downtown Mayes Hill was a quaint, mountain tourist town, and it was late Saturday afternoon. The sidewalks should be bustling with activity, not deserted.

Rich closed the door to his cruiser. He'd have to double his efforts to keep frosty despite the overwhelming feeling of helplessness and cold shivers ravaging his bones. The last time he'd felt this awful was the night Deena didn't make it home.

Rich pushed onward. He couldn't afford to fall apart. Beth and Grady said they needed his help. By God, he was going to do his damnedest not to let them down like he'd done with his own family.

Before more crushing guilt could damage his diminishing health, he set out to look for something to hide his vehicle. It wasn't long before he found a piece of crumpled tarp that had been discarded next to the building. It wasn't large enough to conceal his entire vehicle, but there was enough to give camouflage. He spread it out, using broken pieces of cinderblocks on the hood and trunk to hold it in place. He brought out his flashlight and unsnapped the strap of his holster. He didn't anticipate needing his Glock, it was out of habit.

The side doors of the metal building were secured by a half-rusted chain running through the set of metal bars. The padlock had been looped through two chain links, but the shackle had missed the locking mechanism.

Rich smirked and lifted it free of the links. The steel chain fell through the handles, pooling at his feet with a satisfying slink. He pulled one of the doors open enough to enter, tossing a quick look toward the main road before slipping inside.

The dark was alarming at first. No windows in the back and paranoia on the forefront of his brain. He closed his eyes, slowed his breathing, and focused on slowing his heart rate.

After a few moments, he opened his partially adjusted eyes and clicked his flashlight on. The illuminated area was a large, open space with two metal tables in the center. Along the walls hung open shelves with various pieces of welding materials and tools.

He shined his flashlight in a steady swoop as he scanned the shop. Nothing living here besides him.

To his left, a stair rail came into view.

Offices.

Rich turned his radio on low as he headed that way. Voices called codes between the static; mostly domestic disputes, armed robbery. Nothing indicated they were being pursued yet.

Resistance met Rich halfway up the steps, causing him to yelp. His hands were on automatic, flying up to protect his face. He swatted at the sticky, silvery strands clinging to whatever gained purchase. His hand hit a big, heavy lump that skittered up the wall away from the ruckus. An involuntary shiver rocked him from head to toe.

"Damn spiders."

Rich returned the sticky webs, rubbing his fingers against the rough concrete wall. He resumed his careful march up the staircase clinging to the railing. He didn't want to disturb any other eight-legged residents. The clanking of his boots on the metal staircase echoed throughout the bay.

When he came to a shallow landing, Rich found the door to Louis Cooper's office at the top of the next flight of stairs.

He bound up the steps two at a time until he was standing in front of the smooth metal door. His chest pulsed with adrenaline. The other side held possibilities he'd been denied. Files that could hold groundbreaking proof of what he'd feared for the past week. If Rich was right and Louis was bribing his boss—*ex* boss, he could find proof to crack the case that had plagued him for two years. He'd finally find out what happened to Deena.

Rich gripped the doorknob and turned.

The overhead fluorescent lights flickered on with a jarring buzz. One of the tubes struggled to stay lit, long past the point of being useful. Between the light's dirge and the spotty lighting, heaviness built behind his ribcage. Rich rubbed his chest over the ball of apprehension as he looked for a place to start.

The modest office was musty with the lingering scent of burnt coffee. In the middle stood a medium-sized metal desk and a well-worn leather swivel chair, while guests were given a single rusty metal folding chair to share. A tall filing cabinet was tucked into the back corner. The narrow wood-veneered table hugging the wall next to the filing cabinet was home to a well-used coffee machine. Not one of those fancy pod ones, but one with a glass carafe. Beside it was a basket filled with sugar packets and various creamers, and a fake potted plant.

Rich slipped between the table and desk to sit in Louis's office chair. It creaked with his weight. The metal desk had three drawers on each side and one locked pocket drawer in the center. He hooked his finger under the lip of the drawer in the center and pulled.

Locked.

The top left drawer opened with ease. Searching through the mess, Rich found several loose papers—invoices from the looks of it—and pens. No key.

Closing it, Rich moved on to the next two drawers. The middle contained a stapler, box of staples, metal rulers, a calculator, more pens, paper clips, and binder clips. The bottom drawer held a single item: a well-worn, black leather-bound Bible. Rich scoffed.

"Owning a Bible doesn't cancel your sins if you don't use what's in it, asshole."

Using his left shoulder and cheek to hold the flashlight, he flipped through the pages. Several passages had been scribbled over with black ink. Others had been circled in bright yellow. As he flipped, he found a small hollowed out rectangle in the middle. A keyring with two small silver keys sat in the recesses. He tipped the book and they fell into his waiting palm.

Rich set the Bible on the top of the desk, so he could use the first key on the locked drawer. It turned easily with a satisfying click. The only item in this drawer was a ledger. At first glance, it read like a typical checkbook, until he read the names of State Senators, representatives, and other politicians from the Tri-State area.

"I knew it." Rich's stomach somersaulted as a wide grin formed.

Whatever Louis Cooper was up to was above Rich's paygrade, but he was certain he'd find Blaylock's name printed here. The next issue was finding someone higher up the chain that he could trust with this information.

He stacked the ledger on top of the Bible and eased the center drawer shut. The clank of a metal can falling over came from downstairs. Rich paused for a three-count before sliding the chair away from the desk, grimacing when it squeaked. He stood quickly and snuck over to the door. A rush of cool air skimmed across his bare arms.

"It's just the air conditioning kicking on." Rich chuckled as he wiped his sweaty hands down his pants legs.

Returning to the desk, he sat back in the chair and looked through the drawers on the right side. Rich found an expensive bottle of Lion and Fox whiskey and several opened envelopes with Louis Cooper's name printed on the outside. The handwriting belonged to a man he'd been taking orders from the past decade: Eric Blaylock.

Choosing one toward the middle, he opened the flap to find a single piece of paper folded neatly inside and removed it.

Rich read the brief, hand-written letter:

"We have the girl. Dropoff at 1:43 am."

"What the hell is this?" He flipped it over, but it was blank. "Some kind of kidnapping ring?"

He wanted to believe 'the girl' was Deena, but that was sloppy. He had no evidence, only a gut instinct. Since the note wasn't signed, he'd needed to prove this was, in fact, the Sheriff's penmanship, which meant he'd be paying a visit to Blaylock's office.

He opened another letter, skimming over line after line with similar wording to the first. He stuffed it back inside, opening another. Again and again, the same wording but with different times. No dates, only the varied yellowing of the envelopes to indicate passage of time.

Rich bound them with a rubber band that barely fit, putting them with the Bible and ledger. Excitement bubbled in his brain like a fizzy soda, urging him to find more proof. His next quest sat in the corner near the plastic plant.

When Rich stood to check the filing cabinet, he shivered from the cold. If he was going to continue working, he'd need to find and adjust the thermostat. He pivoted toward the door and jumped about a foot off the ground when a shadow crossed the open doorway. A gust of freezing air filtered into the room with the faint scent of rotten eggs. Rich put his left hand over his thumping heart. His right hand hovered above his firearm. He strained to listen for the faintest of noises, counting the seconds.

Silence.

"Forget going back downstairs. I ain't cold enough for whatever ghosts are lurking 'round here." Rich decided to check this last cabinet before calling Beth. Staying here wasn't worth a heart attack.

He backed away from the door, keeping his left arm extended behind to feel his way around. He wasn't easily spooked, not since academy. The heebie-jeebies wouldn't let him look away from the doorway.

"Get it together, man," Rich urged himself while the sweat on his face formed into ice particles.

He squeezed his eyes shut, breaking whatever hold the shadows outside Cooper's office held. Once the freight train in his chest slowed, he opened his eyes again. The stillness and quiet were unchanged.

"Paranoid son of a…" he trailed off and inserted the second key into the lock on the top drawer. It popped open with ease. Drawer number one was basic. Hanging folders with manilla folders containing inventory lists, shipping manifests, and older ledgers.

He pulled the drawer until the safety latch caught. Pulling all the files to the front, he checked the back of the drawer for anything.

Nada.

Drawers number two through four were the same. Nothing hiding in the back and nothing of consequence in any of the folders.

When he pulled the bottom drawer all the way to check the back like the others, the latch stopped halfway, piquing his interest. Bringing the files to the front, he shined the light along the edges and noticed a gap between the metal backing at the exact same spot on either side.

"What do we have here?" he whispered with a glance toward the door.

Rich felt around the gaps and located small buttons just on the inside of the lips. Pressing them in unison, the false metal backing came free, and the drawer came the rest of the way out. Rich nearly choked on his excitement. It was short-lived when he found another locked metal box.

He was all out of keys.

Rich found a half-empty bankers box underneath the table and placed the metal lockbox inside, along with the ledgers and creepy Bible. He was one step closer to getting justice for his daughter's disappearance. Rich knew she was alive; she had to be. If she had been kidnapped and sold in some human trafficking scandal, he'd disassemble each and every one until he found Deena.

He closed the bottom drawer and put the lid on tight, leaving everything the way he found it. Rich picked up his prize and turned to head out the office door.

A hideous creature wearing a wispy and tattered black hooded robe blocked his exit. The scent of rotten eggs was strong enough to singe his nostrils. Its robe pulled at the shadows around them, as if they were a part of its body. Red-hot embers burned where its eyes should have been. Below the eye sockets was a roundish, lipless mouth with circular rows of needle-like teeth that was curved into a sinister grin.

"Aw, hell."

Chapter 16

BETH

As soon as Rich was gone, Beth closed the garage door and turned to find Grady where she'd left him, standing near the foot of the stairs. He held her dad's shirt up with a frown.

"What's wrong?" she asked.

"I doubt these will fit." He pointed his chin at one of his huge biceps and Beth's cheeks warmed.

Grady's arms weren't the only parts that had filled out since the funeral. His t-shirt stretched across his chest so tightly she could trace his muscles all the way down—

"Ahem." She cleared her throat, banishing her vivid imagination to the time-out corner. "Apparently not."

Grady tossed the clothes onto the couch. He tucked his thumbs into the front pockets of his jeans, shoulders slouching enough that it gave him that sad, just-lost-his-puppy look. Normally, Beth would offer a hug, but Grady seemed closed off. Things hadn't been this awkward before Rich left, but maybe she was too distracted to notice.

The accompanying silence had Beth shifting on her feet. She'd rather count the fibers in the carpet than it linger.

"If you're not comfortable showering here, we can go to the Grove instead. I'm sure you have clothes stashed there." Beth tucked an invisible hair behind her ear and bit her bottom lip.

"Yeah. I do." Grady reached into his pocket. His frown was replaced by a sigh and an eyeroll.

"Here." Beth pulled her portal stone free, rotating the warm moonstone in her palm. "Take mine. I'll use Tom's until we find yours."

He stared at her hand as a flurry of emotions passed across his face, like he was afraid to touch it. Or was it because she would be using Tom's? Before she could decide whether putting the moonstone back in her pocket was a good idea or not, Grady placed his hand over the top of hers. A pleasant surge of energy tickled the edges of her palm. When she looked at Grady, his lips were slightly parted as he stared at their hands. Raising his smoldering gaze to hers, the heat of their touch matched, akin to a roaring fire in the dead of winter. He closed his eyes and took a shuddering breath before swiping the stone from her hand.

Beth exhaled long and slow to calm her erratic heart. She'd asked him to give her time. He had. He *was*.

Her resolve wavered.

"Grady," she whispered, not knowing what she wanted to say, if anything. That simple touch had sparked the magic inside her, something she'd smothered when Tom died. She was lucky it came to her aid when Curtis broke into her apartment.

Grady raised his hand toward her. He paused inches from her cheek and balled it into a fist, letting it drop to his side. A disgusted grimace marred his handsome features.

"Let's get your bags. I'll feel better after showering."

He turned around and bolted up the stairs without waiting for her. Whatever happened between them just now left her more confused. Her head, stomach, and heart were all tangled together in a solo game of Twister. She could either fight to keep upright or crumble and reset. She was tired of crumbling.

Jogging up the stairs, she saw Grady sniff the hallway outside her room. His shoulders tensed, but he disappeared inside before she could ask.

When she remembered Tom's keepsakes box was left open on her comforter, Beth's face was full of pins and needles. She rushed to her door to find Grady kneeling by her suitcase. He flipped any clothes hanging over the edge to the inside.

"I didn't see or touch anything else." He mumbled from his place on the floor.

The tightness across his shoulders and his low tone made her chest ache. Beth eased into her childhood room as though he was a wild animal she would spook. "It's okay if you did."

Grady zipped her suitcase with a rough jerk, making Beth flinch. In a fluid motion, he stood, bringing her bag with him. His whole body was stoicism carved in marble, unmoving and terribly beautiful. The only emotion he couldn't hide was the sorrow rimming his eyes in red.

"Is this everything?"

"I have another bag in the bathroom. Toiletries and such." Beth wrung her hands and Grady nodded.

As she crossed the room, the intensity of his watchful gaze were like firm hands on her skin, keeping her grounded. How loudly was she projecting the fragility of her pity tower?

Or is he fighting what's growing between us as fiercely as I am?

Whatever the answer, for the first time in days, she didn't feel invisible. Admitting she liked his attention felt shallow, but dammit, she was lonely.

As a predator seeks injured prey, guilt nipped at the first sign of happiness or positivity.

This time Beth let it. She was too damn tired to fight the trivial emotional drains when there was heavier stuff in the next room.

She stuffed her toiletries into her duffel bag, adding an extra toothbrush and a fresh tube of toothpaste in case Grady needed them. Once it was full and zipped, she joined him.

"This is it," Beth said, stopping when she realized the room was empty. The pinching in her chest pricked her eyes.

Grady left because I can't commit to him. But I can't betray Tom if he's not alive, can I?

"Good. Let's go." Before her eyes welled with tears, Grady popped his head back inside. He frowned and stepped inside, glancing over his shoulder as he did. "What's wrong?"

"Nothing."

"It doesn't look like nothing, Beth."

Beth didn't have anything left in her to argue, so she went with the truth. "I thought you had left, okay?"

Grady's hardened edges softened as he studied her face like she was a work of fine art. "I'm not leaving you, Beth. Not now, not ever."

His words struck a chord in her soul, making it sing again. She held onto the steadiness of his voice and the promise of his words like a life vest.

"Good," Beth whispered, wiping away the evidence of her vulnerability. She tucked the flaps on Tom's keepsakes box and secured it in her arms. "I'm ready."

Grady's lip ticked upward a fraction before he turned and pointed the portal stone at her bedroom door. "Exgradi."

The space filled with a *whoosh* as it took on a white pearlescent sheen. Beth was always impressed by the simple spell. Connecting two doorways via an interdimensional bridge was something she'd never dreamed of doing a week ago.

So was the thought of finally being alone with Grady. At the Grove. Undisturbed by the outside world, which moved at a fraction of the pace. They could spend an entire day at there, and only an hour passed outside of its magical bubble.

The last time she had been here was to lay Tom to rest. Returning would be a bittersweet homecoming.

Beth wanted to be excited, but the weight pressing on her shoulders sprinkled doubts of what to expect once they were there. She could read the passages Tom marked for her in Myrtle's journal. He wouldn't have mentioned them if they weren't important.

Grady hefted the bag, hesitating for a heartbeat. "I, uh, I made some changes. You'll see." He didn't wait for her to respond and stepped through.

Beth's steps faltered with his words, and her chest grew uncomfortably tight. She should have been there with him. Spending time with Grady could have helped her mourn Tom, potentially speeding up the healing process. Instead, she had left him alone to process the loss of his best friend. She was a shit person for being so selfish.

What was done, was done. She could make it up to Grady by being there for him now.

The smooth, dry substance that made up the portal caressed her skin like the finest organza. Darkness surrounded the tunnel bridge, but this time the faint whispers beyond were eerily silent.

Beth pushed onward, coming out into the radiance of the midday sun. Her eyes took a moment to adjust, and when they did, she was greeted by a field of poppies, cornflowers, and various other wildflowers whose names she had yet to learn. The warm sunlight bathed her in its golden rays. Beth rolled her shoulders back, her head following suit while her eyes fell asleep. Here, the perpetual spring held an abundance of life and magic. As she drew a deep breath, it seeped into her pores.

She filled herself to the brim with the peace that was the Grove. As she exhaled, the excess weight of her troubles went with it. For the first time in days, she could breathe without it hurting so damn badly.

Her eyelids fluttered open, and her gaze found Grady. He stepped up onto a newly built front porch. Beth jogged the short distance to catch up, but he disappeared inside. She didn't blame him for hurrying. The thought of what kind of ick lingered after his stint in jail made her skin itch.

The closer she got, the more the picture changed. Crisp white chinking mud filled the cracks between the logs on his cabin and English ivy climbed lattices on the sides. Across the front of the cabin, he'd built a modest log porch to match the rest of the house. It was wide enough for a porch swing or two rocking chairs and had hooks between the two columns for hanging baskets. The boards gleamed with a coat of fresh varnish. Her stomach flipped, causing the corners of her mouth to curl upward.

"Grady," Beth called from the front yard. Her smile widened into a huge grin. "The cabin looks amazing. And this porch!"

Grady pushed the new screen door open, causing the hinges to screech like a prehistoric chicken. A towel and clean clothes were draped over one arm. Despite his earlier grumpiness, he gifted Beth with a tired grin.

"I'm glad you like it, beautiful." He descended the two steps and held out his free hand, stirring the butterflies in her stomach again. "Come. I'll show you how to work the shower out back."

"You built a shower?" Beth asked, hooking her pinkie with his. The sparks were stronger here in the Grove. She struggled to keep herself from falling into peacefulness too quickly, otherwise her grief would be cheapened. "You've been busy."

"Had to be, or I'd have never left you alone like you asked."

Beth stopped in her tracks. When her pinkie slipped from his hand, Grady slowed and turned, his face blank. She cursed the damned necklaces for working too well. She didn't have a clue what he was thinking. Some reassurance he wasn't pissed at her for kicking him to the curb would have been nice.

"Grady, I'm sorry."

She raised her hand to place it on his cheek, but gravity used her hesitation to stay the distance.

Grady's warm hand gripped her wrist, making the decision for her. "Wait."

The lines between his eyebrows deepened. He rubbed his thumb along her skin as his gaze conveyed a hundred thoughts fighting for dominance. Finally, he turned his head and sighed. "I need five—ten minutes, max—to scrub all this shit off so I can feel human again. Then we can talk."

Beth swallowed the lump in her throat and nodded. She could only imagine what horrors Grady went through at the city jail. Of course, the words 'we can talk' were never a good thing. "Of course. Do what you need to do."

When Grady released her wrist, Beth missed the feel of his thick, calloused hand. His touch was soothing to her soul, allowing her to breathe without feeling like her lungs were full of poison. But she couldn't follow him now, not when embarrassment paralyzed her limbs.

Beth chastised herself for being selfish and headed inside the cabin. She couldn't have her cake *and* eat it, too. There were steadfast rules after becoming a widow. Jumping straight into bed with your husband's best friend wasn't on the list.

Her feet carried her to the sink overlooking the backyard. Grady's head bobbed past the window. As he stepped behind the wooden enclosure, his broad shoulders held the weight of the world. He flung his clean towel and clothes over the side. When he gripped the back of his shirt and tugged it overhead, Beth brought her fist to her lips.

She'd never seen Grady naked, but she had a vivid imagination and plenty of fantasies after his first shift from panther to human. He'd had a single cloth covering his loins, but his chiseled chest with its smattering of dark, curly hair was on full display along with his bulging biceps and large-as-logs-legs. Grady's body was a work of art, earned by hard labor rather than spending hours in a gym.

Conjuring the image turned the Grove's perpetual Spring into a sweltering Georgia Summer.

Beth swiveled around, putting her back to her wanton needs. Her gaze fell to the table where a lace-bound journal sat. The cover was made of pressed wood pulp, inset with dried flowers. Two cornflower ribbons peeked out from the bottom, holding the reader's place.

Is this the journal Tom told me about?

She crossed the short distance. When Grady groaned deeply as if he'd found an oasis after being in the desert for days, her body's heat migrated to her southern regions. Beth picked up the journal with shaking hands, panting and sweating like she'd run a marathon. She opened it to the first bookmark. Myrtle's handwriting filled the page with her sharp, neat script. A single passage caught Beth's attention.

"After our rather adventurous picnic, Barton broke terrible news to me. His father's company is set to leave on the morrow for Savannah, Georgia. He has requested—in no certain words—for Barton to accompany them. They will leave at dawn and return in a fortnight. Though our courtship bloomed in as many days, my soul cries for Barton in a way it never for sweet Josiah. My widow's cross seemed permanent until my beloved brought sunshine and love into my heart. I pray for strength to see us through and for the fortunes to bring my Barton home safely."

Beth re-read it twice before closing the journal and placing it back where she found it. A strange buzzing started in her head and heart. The dream she couldn't remember her first night at the Grove resurfaced. Myrtle and Barton's adventurous picnic in the wildflower field had been a lesson in passion. The unfathomable love conveyed in a single look, their all-consuming lovemaking... How could they have achieved this level of completeness in two weeks?

Deep down, the answer waited patiently. It was as clear as the nose on her face. Beth looked up to find herself back at the sink, watching Grady rinse his hair. He shook his tresses, then flung his hair back. His eyes were closed but pure bliss smoothed his worry lines. His Adam's apple bobbed just before his head tilted to the side. He opened one eye, aimed at her as if some force in the universe alerted him to her creeping on him.

Beth whipped back around, her cheeks burning. Myrtle and Barton may have just met, but she'd practically grown up with Grady. Their case wasn't as simple as boy meets girl and falls head over heels. Theirs had complications and the potential for fatal emotional wounds that would never get the chance to heal. They had pulled through in the end, but the scars were still fresh. The only way to fix them was together.

One last doubt niggled at her gray matter: Did she love Grady because of the magic?

She surveyed the room, taking stock of each little nuance Grady had added to make the space more welcoming to her. A vase filled with her favorite flowers—dark blue bachelor's buttons, white Shasta daisies, and pink and purple larkspur—sat on the center of the table. The cot in the corner had been converted into a corner reading nook complete with a bookshelf, which also held a few crossword puzzle books with a pencil, sharpener, and an extra eraser.

Her chest was full of love, and it wasn't because of magic. It was solely because of the man who had always considered others before himself.

In response to her internal musings, the Grove pulsed with magic, encouraging her to let go of her remaining fears. Fear that she wouldn't be enough to save everyone. Fear that after all her training, she would crumble when coming face to face with Ja'azul. Fear of moving on with her deceased husband's best friend.

Going forward with her future didn't mean she'd cherish the memories of her first love any less. It was simply a closed chapter of her life. Her chapter with Grady would be new and exciting. It waited to be written, only this time the monsters from her nightmares would be flesh and blood. Thankfully, she wouldn't have to battle them alone. She trusted Grady. If he believed in her, by gods, she could believe in herself.

The screen door creaked, and in walked the object of her internal debate. Grady had toweled off, but his soft black curls were still dripping. She traced the droplets to his set jaw, following the beads as they traveled down his chiseled chest. When she finished her journey, they locked gazes. The way his hungry blue eyes looked at her through his lock of hair was almost predatory.

Grady had crept closer until they stood almost nose to nose. One hand kept the towel firmly in place, the other gently brushed her cheek.

Beth could feel the heat from his body, pulling her in like a magnet. While she had her existential crisis, things had been set in motion the moment they stepped foot in the Grove. The air was thick with guardian energy, peeling away the unnecessary layers keeping them from completing their bond.

"Don't keep me at arm's length anymore, Beth. Please." His voice was strained, deep with need. An intense longing and wild heat burned in Grady's gaze. "I thought I was going to die without being able to tell you how I feel about you—"

"I know—"

"Please. Let me finish."

His interruption coincided with her stomach sinking. Lead-filled boats would have sunk slower.

"I'm sorry. Go ahead." She finally cupped the roughness she'd been itching to touch. Grady leaned into her hand, covering it with his.

Beth's bunched shoulders found release in the still waters of his serenity. A contented sigh broke through the shoddy emotional walls she had built, leaving her emotions raw.

Grady closed his eyes for a breath. He pressed a kiss into her palm, setting fire to her skin. Her whole body craved that same burn. "My leaving taught me a few things. One, I am not as strong without you by my side. Two, I need you, Beth, or breathing ain't worth it. Hell, *living* ain't worth it. I could do it, but it'd be like limping around without half of my organs."

Grady moved their laced hands over his erratically thumping heart. The only thing containing it was his hot-to-the-touch skin.

"*This* beats for you. Every smile you pass my way, every touch, every laugh, keeps it going. You make me *want* to be a better man. Not just for you, but for the world and for our children. I want to be the one who fills your days with happiness and your nights with passion. To be your confidant and shoulder to cry on." Grady pressed his body into hers and slipped his free hand around her waist. If they separated, the towel would fall, making Beth's heart race. Heat pooled in her nethers.

"I want to hold you knowing I did everything I could to deserve that moment, and I will fight each day to earn it again and again until the day we draw our last breath. If that doesn't tell you how much I love you, then dammit, I don't know what will."

Tears pricked the corners of her eyes. She was tired of fighting her feelings and battling loneliness. Grady seemed to be teetering on the edge of patience and wild abandon. It was in the hardness of his muscled body pressed against hers. It was there in his hungry gaze; the way he stood firm and confident, waiting for her to jump in with both feet and join him.

Desires she'd hidden way, tucked beneath her grief and social respectability, awoke and arose like a lioness waking from a nap. Her guardian magic stretched and flared to life.

What good had come from arguing with fate anyway?

She squeezed his hand and whispered in a voice that was hoarse like she'd swallowed sandpaper, "I love you, too, Grady."

Grady wrapped his other arm around her waist and snugged her tight. When Beth wrapped her other arm around his neck, the thread between them cinched in the middle, pulling them impossibly close.

"I really want to kiss you right now," his chest rumbled as he spoke.

Her body surged with feverish desire. Beth gulped, letting her apprehensions fall to the wayside. A spurt of bravery pushed the words waiting on the tip of her tongue, "Then, kiss me."

Grady's lips were on hers with a low growl. She surrendered herself to the kiss. Soft and warm lips contrasted deliciously with his rough, short beard. Beneath the clean soap smell, his familiar woodsy musk reminded her of cold nights by the fireplace. When she opened her mouth, the taste of spearmint coated her tongue.

The world melted away, leaving them suspended in a pocket of air. Most of her needs were met with every scrape of his stubble, every swallowed sigh releasing pent up anxiety. She still throbbed in neglected lower places, but she wasn't ready to leap that far. Not yet. When they broke for air, Beth was dizzy with a drunken smile plastered on her face.

"Wow," Grady whispered, eyes half-lidded and lips swollen.

"You can say that again," Beth murmured.

Grady's hugs had always rendered her troubles to dust, but his kisses made her forget they ever existed. What would the next step would cure?

Chapter 17

GRADY

Grady's whole body still buzzed like the Fourth of July. Gods, his skin ached for more. The intenseness of it could only be described as wholly consuming. Beth was still here in his arms, timidly waiting. A contrast to the desire burning in those fern eyes, and the heady scent of her interest.

Whatever blood hadn't already migrated south followed.

Every atom that made up his entirety was drawn to Beth. He slowed his breathing to keep control over his southernmost faculties. Knowing the only barriers between them were a towel and a few clothes made it difficult. A metaphorical finger hovered over the 'shut down' button for his brain.

"Does this mean our connection is complete?" Beth smoothed her hands down his biceps.

She waved her hands at the thick golden glitter saturating the air. Everything shimmered electric with the magic he'd practiced for nearly a decade, but he didn't feel different. Better? Yes. He felt closer to Beth and much less stressed. The hardest issue to address was still trapped between their bodies, waiting for release.

"Maybe." His voice was husky and maple syrup thick. Unable to keep the grin off his face, he added, "We can make out some more, just in case."

Beth playfully punched his chest, pursing her lips to hide her smile. "We'd better not. I'm a teacher. I'm supposed to discourage incorrigible behavior, not encourage it."

Grady chuckled darkly. He was in danger of losing control of said release prematurely. Her teasing snark only made matters worse. Plus, it had been a while.

"How will we know for sure?" She swallowed, her widened doe-eyes staring into his.

One of her hands lowered to his chest, warm and soft. Fingers flexed over his skin, feeling the firmness.

Yes. More.

"I have a few ideas," he murmured, hyper focusing on her touch. He locked his muscles into place for fear of spooking her. If this was another dream, he didn't want to wake up yet.

Please, if anyone in the universe can hear me, let this all be real.

"Oh yeah?" she asked, her breathy voice tickling his chin. She leaned closer, rubbing her cheek along his jaw like a cat. "Like what?"

Grady took it back. This was torture, not a dream.

As if the gods heard his plea, the air turned heady and sweet like honeysuckles soaked in whiskey. Butterflies swarmed in his stomach. This was finally happening.

Lifting her chin, he whispered, "For starters..."

Grady drew a line from her chin to between her breasts, making her breath hitch. He continued his journey along her waist, before moving his hand across her back. Tenderly, he rubbed up and down her spine with his fingertips, ending above her supple ass. "I don't want any half-measures between us. I want to be with you in every possible way."

Beth closed her eyes and shivered. He wanted so badly to smooth the lines between her eyebrows, but he kept a firm hold. Not because he was afraid she'd pull away, but because it felt natural. As sure as the sky is blue and the sun would rise, they were supposed to be together.

"I'm scared."

Those two words were like dunking a hot glass in cold water. Through the cracks, his doubts chanted their litany, *'she doesn't love you,'* and *'it's the magic forcing y'all together.'* For a moment, he believed them, halting the happy fluttering in his midsection. Deep down, Grady believed if she didn't want this, too, she wouldn't be here.

"Beth." The firmness in his tone made her eyes open. The uncertainty swimming behind them was heart-stopping. "Please don't be afraid of us."

"It's not *us* that scares me, Grady. I think it's pretty damn clear what we want. I'm worried about how fast we're getting there. And there are questions that need answers. Are we forcing things because the world is in danger?" Her frown lines deepened as opened her glistening green eyes. "Isn't there a rule somewhere that says, 'widows must wait X days before moving on?'"

There it is. The bitter truth was out.

Grady knew better than to argue, but Angry Beth shuts shit down. They weren't forcing anything. He'd already done his part, spending two months sawing, sanding, hammering away at his grief. It was her turn to sort through the issue, to work past giving a shit about what others thought.

"I don't know about any rules, but you're already my best friend. The way I figure, most of the leg work is done. The rest is up to us." Grady tried for the lopsided smile she was so fond of, but it felt more like a grimace. He'd be taking a cold-water bath in the pond after this.

The creases between Beth's eyes deepened as she studied his truth. "But what if people talk?"

"That's what people do." Beth glared at his non-answer. Grady squeezed her ass and amended, "If you'd have asked me a couple of days ago, I would have cared. Now, I don't. We are the masters of our happiness, Beth, not anyone else."

Beth turned her head, breaking eye contact to gaze at the ground past his shoulder. If he could hear her thoughts, maybe he'd understand why she still held back. He should have suggested taking their necklaces off as soon as they arrived.

While he made wishes, she laid her head on his shoulder. "I'm sorry to be such a pain, Grady. This place...makes letting go seem so simple, but I'm twisted up in knots over what's right and how it all reconciles with what I want. I feel like no matter whatever we decide, people are gonna make the worst of it."

"They probably will, but does their opinion *really* matter?" Grady shrugged, nuzzling the top of her head with his cheek. "I say fuck the gossipers. We have Tom's blessing. Who cares what they think? You're the only one that matters to me, Beth."

"You're right." Beth sniffled, snuggling so close it was almost painful below the belt.

Grady's chest extended with certainty while his skin vibrated with adrenaline. Blue sparks popped nearby as energy built like pressure before a rainstorm.

"Fuck the gossipers," she whispered, pulling back far enough to look into his eyes. Her lips brushed against his scruffy chin, causing his breath to shudder. "I'm still afraid of the cost when I let go."

"Do you trust me, Beth?"

"Always."

"Then do it. Let go."

"What if I fall?"

"I'm hoping you do, because I'll be here to catch you." Grady dropped the towel to cup her face in his hands and whispered, "I'll always catch you."

Grady teased his nose along Beth's, lighting sparklers everywhere their skin touched. Brushing his lips against hers, she shuddered and slipped her fingers behind his neck. The scratch of her nails against his nape awoke a ravenous craving he'd put off for too long.

He pressed their mouths together in a scorching kiss. Feverish chills flashed from head to toe. Beth was more addictive than any fine whiskey. Making out with her was the top of his 'favorite things to do' list.

When he broke for air, green sparks had joined the blue, swirling around their heads like fairies on ice skates. It was a brilliant sight but paled in comparison to the joy in Beth's intoxicated smile.

"Pretty."

"Yeah, but it doesn't hold a candle to you, beautiful."

"Smooth talker." Her fern-colored eyes were painted with dew drops.

Goosebumps covered his body when Beth smoothed her hands down his chest, past his matching fluorite necklace, and across his shoulders, ending at his rough hands. He loved the way her appreciative gaze swept over his muscles. Grady's guardian magic pulsed in rhythm with his heart, pervading his whole self. The heady rush of power activated his self-subdued dominance. The need to be with this woman went beyond desire. It was a life-or-death issue.

Grady raised her hands to his lips. His bearded chin prickled her knuckles, making Beth shiver. This attraction was feral, and he wanted nothing more than to ravage her. "Do you want to take this upstairs?"

"Actually, I think the wildflower field would be more appropriate." Beth squeezed his hands for confirmation.

Her first introduction to the world of magic had been a dream about their predecessors, Myrtle and Barton. It seemed only fitting to carry on tradition.

"Sounds perfect," he murmured, capturing a quick kiss on his way to scoop his towel off the floor.

Beth's lips parted and her face burned beet red. A wolfish grin formed on his face. This was the first time Beth had seen him completely naked. It certainly wouldn't be the last.

"You're so beautiful." She clasped her hands over her mouth, eyes wide in embarrassment. "I mean, handsome. Gorgeous? Gods, Grady. I'm rambling."

"I'm glad you like what you see, beautiful. It's all yours." For added effect, he flexed his pecks. "But if you keep giving me that come hither gaze, we aren't making it to the field."

Beth released a long breath and rolled her bottom lip between her teeth. The look she gave him said, 'Damn, he's hot.' He resisted doing a fist pump, lacing their fingers instead.

She dragged him past the new arch he'd made to the top of the hill. They cut a path through the thickened magic. It swirled and twisted into golden threads, chasing the sapphire and emerald trails in a swirling vortex that tightened with each turn.

Grabbing the hem of her shirt, she said, "I feel overdressed."

"We can fix that." Grady helped her bring the tee overhead and dropped it to the ground.

Perfect mounds of soft flesh begged to be freed. Grady's chest spiked in excitement at the possibilities, at all the things he'd dreamt of doing with Beth. It was all finally happening.

Beth molded herself to his body, wrapping her arms around his neck. His hips moved instinctually against her core. The friction was enough to make her moan. "I'm gonna lose my damn mind if you don't take make love to me right now."

Grady dipped his nose to the sensitive spot below her ear and placed a kiss. "Yes, ma'am."

Using the towel as a blanket, he laid it on the ground and dropped to his knees. Grady kept eye contact with Beth as his fingers worked the button of her jeans. The zipper came next, teeth parting at a painfully slow pace.

"Grady," Beth begged, sucking in her stomach when he pressed his lips above her belly button.

"Patience," he drawled, effectively ruining her pants. She wasn't the only one affected. Grady was painfully hard, like petrified wood.

Beth whimpered and gripped his shoulders. As he slipped her legs from the denim, he made sure his fingers grazed her soft-as-silk skin before tossing them somewhere in the grass. Grady took a moment to appreciate her soft curves and firmness. While he ogled Beth, her bra fell loose, joining her other clothes.

"Gods be praised." He cupped her breasts with his large hands. They fit perfectly, like they were made to. He gently squeezed, causing her breaths to quicken. Beth panted wildly when he took a taste. He promised, "I'm going to make you mine now, Beth."

"All talk so far," she chuckled with a hoarse whisper, causing a low growl to resonate in his chest.

Grady tugged Beth to the ground, laying her on her back. Her soft hair feathered around her head like a halo of honey. The sight of her, glowing around the edges with a fey-like glamor, stole his breath. She leaned up for another kiss, but he blocked her lips with his finger.

"Wait," he commanded softly, despite her frown. Dragging his finger past her pouty bottom lip, he hooked the fluorite stone resting between her breasts. "We're gonna want to lose these."

Grady pulled her necklace overhead and dropped it near her jeans. Beth's emotions burst into him like the river rapids after a hard rain in summer, hard, cold, refreshing, everywhere all at once.

Eagerly, he gripped the chain around his neck and yanked. It found its home among the flowers as he stared into the eyes of the only woman he'd ever loved. Beth's gaze never broke from his as he laid his soul bare. Breathing became less laborious, but his heart pounded like war drums.

Her arms snaked around his neck, pulling him down to cover her body with his. Grady propped up on his arms to keep his full weight from crushing Beth. He was hyper aware of the vicinity of their pelvises, especially when Beth wrapped her legs around his waist and kissed him firmly.

Grunting, Grady fought the urge to sink inside Beth. He was a gentleman, and a gentleman made sure their woman was warmed up first. He broke their kiss to trail more down her neck, stopping to nip at the curve of her shoulder.

As Grady touched her most intimate parts, he paid close attention to which elicited more excited responses and cycled between them until her hips bucked and her head rocked back. His name on Beth's lips as she lost all control was his new favorite song.

"Please," Beth begged as she came down from her high.

Her legs were shaking as Grady drank in the sight of the radiant goddess he finally had in his arms.

"Tell me what you want, love."

The moment his brain registered the endearment, his heart stuttered with uncertainty. He had already confessed his love, but this was the first time he'd said it naked and vulnerable.

Beth released his hair to hold his face in her hands. Uncertainty melted away at her loving gaze. "I want you, Grady. All of you."

Suddenly, she was straddling him, squeezing his pecs. His attention was drawn to the heat simmering below the belt where they were almost locked together.

"Is this okay? I don't know what you like yet." She tugged her bottom lip between her teeth, snapping the last of his control.

In a blink, Grady flipped them again, so his hands were beside her head in a plank position. "It was a nice view, but I want this one first."

The magic that had built and swirled, danced in a choreographed frenzy. Grady lined up with his destined one. "It's always been you, Beth."

With a single thrust, their universes collided and the world righted itself. His instincts combined with Beth's needs, creating a rhythm that brought her to ecstasy within seconds. Grady gritted his teeth against her tightening muscles. He'd not been with anyone in over a year. His first time with Beth wouldn't be cheapened by his inability to last.

Her hands locked around the back of his neck; fingers tangled in the wet curls at the nape of his neck. She pulled him down for a kiss while Grady freed a hand to explore the curves of her body. His journey ended at her ass cheek. When he squeezed, her lips parted with a moan, allowing his tongue to lazily caress hers. He savored her taste, which reminded him of the snow ice cream from his youth. Sweet vanilla and cream.

As they made love, they became a mess of hot breaths and wild magic. The dazzling outdoor lightshow surrounded the thread connecting them, weaving in and around it, pulling tighter and tighter. Lava flowed through his veins, but there was no pain, only pure bliss.

"I can't hold on." Grady grunted as his body shuddered, breaking his stride. He slowed, dropping his sweaty forehead to her shoulder.

"Let go, love. Don't ever hold back."

On Beth's command, Grady released his restraints, giving her everything. Her fingers dug into his back, clinging to him as they crested the hill together into paradise. Pure white light burst from behind his eyelids in speckles. The rush of power as their bond snapped into place made him think of exploding stars, locking them in a limbo of passion.

Their climax continued until they were both gasping for air. Finally, the thumping of the world quieted, leaving his throat raw and his heart full. No matter where Beth went, he now carried a part of her and she a part of him. They would never be alone again.

Grady's arms wobbled, he fell on his side and pulled Beth on top of him. She settled onto his chest with a sigh, playing with his patch of hair.

"Gods, Grady. That was..." Beth trailed off as a yawn stole her words.

"Amazing, beautiful, satisfying." He filled in for her, running his hand in a lazy path from her back to her thigh and back again. *Perfect.*

"Yes. Perfect," Beth murmured, kissing his neck.

When her lips brushed against his chin, his whole body spasmed. Unsurprisingly, it sent a 'ready' signal southward. Of course he wanted more. He'd never tire of spending every second with his perfect partner, his soulmate.

"You know," he murmured, tucking his chin to study Beth. Her hair was well-tousled, cheeks flushed a powdery rose, and lips properly plump. *Again, perfect.* "If you're still the least bit worried our bond isn't fully complete, we can have another go at it."

"Grady Alan Cooper." Beth poked his ribs. His retaliation involved playing her ribcage like a xylophone, causing her to snort with laughter.

This was his Beth, not the uppity girl he grew up with. The humble woman who found laughter often but would also burn someone in righteous fire with a single look if they threatened what was precious to her. The brat from school, his best friend, the other half of his soul.

Where she saw herself as broken and flawed, he saw strength and a brilliant beauty. He would happily spend lifetimes reminding her. He hadn't realized it until the day he truly *saw* her, but his heart had always belonged to Beth. Now, she had gifted him with hers. For the first time in a long time, Grady was whole. Even his stress over the coming battle seemed manageable. It was a pretty damn good feeling.

"For years I dreamed of this moment, and for years I was convinced we would never be more than friends." Grady lowered his face to brush his nose against her cheek. "I'm glad I was wrong."

"I am, too." Beth's dazzling smile lit a flame in his chest.

She threw her leg over his and sighed. The woman he had yearned after for so long, who had tattooed her name permanently on his tongue, his heart, his mind, was finally his. Contentment flowed through their bond, luring Grady into sleep mode.

"Hey," Beth whispered after a long moment.

Grady kissed the top of her head. "Yeah?"

"Are you *really* ready to go another round already? You don't need time to recover?"

He smirked, reached for her hand, then placed it around his very attentive friend. Beth wiggled against his side before straddling him again.

"Are you sure you don't like this view?"

Beth didn't wait for an answer before taking charge, but Grady's answer was he liked *any* view of her.

Chapter 18

FENNICK

THE BELL OVER THE door of the roadside diner jingled when Fennick pushed it open. There was a young woman in her mid-twenties behind the register.

"Good afternoon, Ms. Elsie."

"Good afternoon, Mr. Rayon. Haven't seen you in these parts for some time." Elsie pronounced his name 'Ray-yen' with her charming southern drawl. She smiled and nodded toward the modest dining area. "You here for some supper or just passing through?"

Elsie Bridges was sunshine incarnate. The woman's southern drawl was one of the most endearing things about this tiny store in the middle of nowhere.

"I am *ravenous*, darling. What are your specials today?" Fennick laid on his British accent thick, loving the way it flustered the sweet girl.

"We've got Marvin's Famous Meatloaf with bacon green beans, mashed 'taters, and gravy or Nana's White Chicken chili with grilled cheese."

"I will have the meatloaf special, please, with a cup of coffee." Fennick looked past Elsie toward the cabinet case where fresh apple pies were still steaming. He raised his chin. "Add a slice of pie, if you will. It smells marvelous."

"Sure thing, hon." She finished scribbling his order, tucking the pencil behind her right ear. "Let me put your order in, and I'll be right back with that coffee."

"Thank you, my dear."

Her swift departure summoned the scent of meatloaf wafting from the kitchen. His mouth-watered and melancholy dimmed with the promise of a home-cooked meal.

Fennick glanced around the room, stopping when his gaze met the framed photo behind the counter. Elsie's grandparents stood on either side of Fennick wearing proud grins. They were some of the first people he met when he traveled back to 1918 to sow his American oats.

When Marvin and Billie Bridges first bought the building, it was old and in dire need of repairs. Three years later, the young couple were struggling. The alternative survival plan for most folks on this side of the mountain was coal mining. Plenty of positions available if you did not care to slowly poison yourself. Healthcare in poverty-stricken areas was unavailable, but if inhalation did not kill the workers, faulty equipment or collapsed mines did the work.

However, Fennick had accumulated wealth from across the globe in his travels. He donated a healthy sum to cover renovations, hence the photograph. Ever since, he and his 'family' were valued guests and ate for half price. The Bridges' always marveled at Fennick's likeness to his namesake.

"Here's your coffee, Mr. Rayen," Elsie placed the mug of black coffee in front of Fennick. "Your food'll be ready in a few."

"Wonderful." He beamed, flashing his pearly whites.

Elsie wandered off, leaving him to his thoughts. He raised the cup to his lips and sipped the dark brew. As the liquid ran down his throat, it left a warmth all the way to his stomach. A jolt of energy shocked him.

"This is good coffee," he murmured and took another sip.

This time there was not only a jolt, but a full-bodied tingle. The hairs on Fennick's arms raised.

Whatever this was, it wasn't the caffeinated brew. It was guardian-related but different from the power surge he'd felt earlier. This burst tingled the base of his spine, which could only mean one thing: Grady and Beth were completing the bond.

How the young guardian had gotten out of jail already, Fennick did not know. All he knew was he had been denied the love and happiness the Goddess had promised not once, but twice. An unbearable pressure sunk in his chest, crushing his soul.

He banged his fist above where his heart should be, hoping to knock the pain back. Instead, flashes of Heliotta's porcelain skin merged with Beth's bright, warm tones. Their beauty lashed at him like whips, cutting him to the quick. When his control slipped, the memory of Heliotta's first visit wormed its way through the crack, torturing him with its reminder that he was good enough for greatness, but not for love.

"It is only for a short time, my love. I promise we will be together again after you are well." Heliotta rushed forward and placed her hand on his cheek.

Fennick shrank away from her touch as if struck. "I am well."

"You are a changed man. Surely you can see this?"

"I only see that the woman I adore is terrified of the man sworn to protect and love her for eternity." Fennick turned his back, fists promising to rend the fabric of his tunic should he witness pity swimming in her eyes. "Perhaps I am not the only one who has changed, Helly."

Her soft gasp was accompanied by the tell-tale gust of wind signaling her departure.

Yes, Fennick had returned from his travels a different man, but he was a *better* man. The sights he had seen, learning of mysticisms and rituals outside of their culture had formed his practice into something beautiful. Fennick had been so certain his place was by Heliotta's side. He wanted to share all these new things with his wife...but she was terrified of his hunger for more power. She had lost faith in him.

It was all moot now. After Ja'azul helped to free him, the first person Fennick looked for was his predecessor. He performed the rite that Circe had created, to pass magical knowledge down the line of guardians. The Ritual of Passing. It was the fastest way to cram centuries of lost history and to find his betrayer. However, when Fennick located Barton Cooper, the man knew nothing of Heliotta, only of his lover, Myrtle. The vengeance he sought was unattainable. Fennick's only consolation was to help burn the world which had scorned him, so he fed Ja'azul souls.

Eventually, his carefree life came to an abrupt end when he found Beth. She had raised his hopes, only to dash them against the stones when she bonded with her fated one. Yet again, he was being punished for wanting to be more than mundane. Happiness was never his to have, not even with his own fated lover.

Who would want a cursed man anyway?

Despair tore at the husk of his heart, causing it to weep. What miniscule well of life Beth had cultivated vanished, leaving him in the throes of despair once again. Fennick had believed things with Beth would be different. When would he learn that the debt he owed to the universe was too great to repay?

Another jolt, much stronger than the other, caused his jaw to tighten. His teeth crunched under the pressure. The line between guardians frayed like a rope, tested beyond its capacity. Each fiber held strong while the others snapped until resistance was naught.

The ceramic cup in his hand shattered. Somewhere, a yelp sounded with urgent assurances they were grabbing a mop.

Fennick did not flinch at the scorching liquid nor the slips of tiny cuts that stung like the devil. Emptiness filled the void in his chest, taking the space reserved for oxygen. The otherworldly sickness nesting in his gut festered with its poison. Ja'azul's influence oozed from the spillover, seizing the scant amount of control Fennick had remaining. An unnatural frost coated his insides with evil intent, and Fennick was powerless to stop it. His senses were numb of anything positive.

"Sorry it took so long, hon!"

Elsie's sweet voice helped Fennick claw his way to the forefront of his mind, only to be dragged back to the dark recesses of his mind by some abyssal ghoul he could not see. She made quick work of cleaning up the mess. However, the seed of destruction had taken root, holding his body hostage. His lips would not part, though he screamed at her to run, to take her family as far from him as possible.

"I'll take this back and wash up. Marvin said yer food was fixed." She flashed him the signature Bridge's family smile, leaving him to his demise.

A teardrop rolled down Fennick's cheek as he fought one last time to save his only friends. The only family he had left, even if they were chosen and not blood relatives.

Sweat beaded on his brow, his breath stilling as drifted farther from consciousness.

Inside his head, the whispers grew, speaking of the awful things they were planning to do to the ones he loved. The visuals they planted in his brain caused him to fight harder. He focused on the plastic veneer tabletop. Tracing the fake woodgrains with his gaze, he looked for patterns to help sharpen his mind. Finally, he pushed them back enough to wiggle his index finger. One by one, he regained his faculties.

"Here ya go, hon." Elsie's voice was muffled as she placed his plate of steaming food on the table along with a new cup of coffee.

The woman's warm smile was the lighthouse amid the night, but it was too late for Fennick. The shadows inside the restaurant had grown darker, larger. His course had been set and the rudders locked into place. The biggest regret he had was not telling Beth the truth. Had he but warned her first, rather than prolong the inevitable, she may have had a chance of surviving what was to come.

Had you played your cards right, you would have been forgiven for so many of your transgressions, too, old boy.

The bite of anger was enough to loosen his tongue, though his jaw fought to move. "Thank you, my dear."

If he had any sense, he should have run to the edge of the world, away from anyone he cared for. But he was a fool. Ja'azul would make this planet suffer. Nothing of Earth would be left except a cindering rock floating among the stars. A cursed place, a memorial to humankind...a warning to future travelers who found seeking other life among the stars.

Tentacles of black smoke rose from the floor, caressing his legs with the coldness of space and death. It burned through the denim. He would have hissed in pain, but he took it as penance for the sins he was about to commit.

Knowing this would be his last meal, Fennick savored every bite. As he faded into oblivion, the tears he kept behind the dam became a river. At least he would not hear the screams this time.

FENNICK GASPED, SLOWLY RISING to sit like Dracula waking up in his coffin. Only Fennick was covered in blood and lying outside in a field atop a hill only goddess knew where. The sun balanced on the horizon.

Images of viscera strewn across tabletops and linoleum floors, of masterfully painted glass covered in red came in shutter flashes behind his eyelids. Thorny whips made of shadows shredding flesh to ribbons. Screams echoed between his ears, and—dear gods—the pitiful cries, the begging.

One memory had his gut plummeting with a sharp twist and sweat covering his body.

A large pentagram drawn in blood with ancient symbols took up most of the restaurant's dining floor. Laid in the center was Elsie Bridges. Her blank stare would be forever burned into his brain; eyes wide in surprise, lips frozen before the words 'why' could form. But the question was there, as was the truth behind his most heinous act.

Ja'azul had been freed by Fennick's hand. The damnation of his soul was complete.

His hands frantically swatted the air as if they had somehow become things he could grasp and rip from his memory. Tears ran down his face, each one a prayer to the goddess to take them away since they were not tangible things, but tools of torment. The motion roiled his stomach. Heat sprung across his face as he rolled to his hands and knees in time to empty his stomach in the grass.

When Fennick's dry heaving stopped, he spat the remaining chunks in the grass, pushing himself to stand with shaky limbs. Dismembering an entire family was a deed fit for someone of a more muscular build or with more of a cardiovascular acumen. His body would ache for days, but he would never eat again.

A sudden crack thundered overhead, causing tree limbs and leaves to spasm like a seizure. It was the kind of boom prefaced by lightning but echoed as if the world were encased in a glass globe.

An aurora of oily greens and blistery reds spread across the early evening sky. In the center, stretching past his field of vision, a jagged black line divided the colors. Thin and pulsing, the center of this ribbon opened enough to see a night sky full of twinkling stars.

As Fennick studied the phenomenon, the air grew thin and chilly. He rubbed the goosebumps raised on his arms. His breaths came out in white puffs. A staticky black ball fell from the maw tainting the heavens. It hurtled through the air toward the thicket of pines between him and the tiny town below and struck the ground with enough force to make him stumble. Flocks of birds took to the sky, fleeing this unknown danger.

"Bloody hell," Fennick swore, casting a wary gaze at the thing in the sky. He would investigate whatever had fallen, preferably from an aerial point of view, before it made its way to the populace.

Fennick's legs were wobbly as he jogged down the hillside. As he gained speed with the decline, his stride strengthened. It did not take much to transform, and normally, it came to him as smoothly as running your fingers through silk sheets. But, when it was time to jump and shift mid-air, the jumping came easy. It was the fall that was perplexing.

He tumbled through the air like a ragdoll being juggled by a child, though the ground yielded nothing. Fennick's chest took the brunt of the impact, leaving his feet dangling by his ears for a breath while his cheek rested on a mound of dirt. Fennick twisted and rolled to his back, planting his feet firmly on the ground so he was reclined with gravity pointed in the right direction.

As he lay there, Fennick searched for the familiar magic he'd been gifted almost a thousand years prior. An emptiness deeper and more despondent than before sat where his well of energy should be.

The universe was against him, yet again. What had he done to deserve such ill comings?

Panic drug its jagged fingers along Fennick's insides until every atom thrummed with loss. Without the use of his magic, he was useless. Not even his multitude of sins were redeemable, not when the sky bled with the cry of the stars.

Fennick's fingernails burned as soil was forced to the quick. His chin dropped to his chest as his tangled hair fell limp around his face. "I am nothing. A wretch. A worthless mortal who is undeserving of life and too ruined for death to be a just punishment."

His entire life had been a farce for the gods. How utterly pitiful.

At the edge of despair, something in Fennick's brain shifted. He sucked in a quick breath the moment everything went silent. As he exhaled, fury raced through the gap, lighting fire his veins. He scrambled away from the edge.

Getting to his feet, Fennick rounded his shoulders. Ja'azul may have used him like a puppet, but he was more than his magic. His talent for alchemical concoctions predated his ascension as a guardian. The ever-present voices told him he was useless. He had almost believed them.

With a smug grin, he shouted at the top of his lungs, "You were right not to trust me! Mark my words, Ja'azul, you will meet your doom, and I pray to the gods that I am there to see it!"

After Fennick dusted himself with a quick pat, he jogged in the direction of the fallen enemy. His chances of defeating the creature hand to hand were nil. Getting to his lab outside of town would be the smarter choice, but there was something pressing he must tend to first.

He must warn Beth and Grady.

Humanity's survival rested in the hands of the two new guardians. He only hoped they would listen to what he had to say before striking him down.

Chapter 19

RICH

THE CREATURE FLOATED ABOVE the ground outside of Louis Cooper's office like the wraiths he'd read about in his books on occult creatures, but this fucker didn't look like the renditions on those pages. There's no way to capture that amount of pure evil in *print*.

"What the fuck are you?"

With a snarl, it brandished a gnarled hand with razor talons at the end of long, thin, black bony fingers. The thing floated above the ground, propelled by a wind Rich couldn't feel. It raced forward and swiped at Rich.

He jumped back, dropping the bankers box as he withdrew his firearm in one swift motion. He aimed at the creature's chest and fired four shots, all solid hits.

The creature howled and scratched at its torso. Blackish green blood oozed from the wounds, coating the metal floor. The stench made Rich cough and gag. Whatever the substance was it burned his eyes and lungs.

While he used his free hand to wipe his stinging eyes, the creature glided toward him. Its eyes glowed with a hatred that set his teeth on edge and activated his fight or flight radar. As Rich backed away, the creature swung wildly. The movements were slower, like it was moving through runny mud.

Rich refocused his aim and squeezed the trigger. Before the bullet fired, one of the creature's claws finally made contact. The glass window shattered behind them, and a piercing pain shot through his forearm.

"Dammit!"

Sweat poured down Rich's forehead. The deep gashes in his skin pulsed and stung like he'd been branded with a hot iron. His hand shook.

His movements were further hindered by deep regrets and limited space to maneuver.

The only thing between him and the creature was Louis's desk. Rich moved in a slow circle toward the door. The creature mimicked his movements. Unless he found a way out of here, survival didn't look like it was in Rich's cards.

When his back was to the door, he reared his foot and shoved the metal desk. The metal floor screamed in protest. It barely budged.

The creature flew toward Rich, and the metal desk regained the distance he'd gained and more. Claws passed centimeters from his face. By the grace of a higher power, it continued to miss. Rich wasn't ready to die, but he was fading fast from an abnormal amount of blood loss.

He bellowed, activating his second wind as he crouch-lunged at the desk like a linebacker driving the quarterback on a tackle. The sound of ripping cloth and cool air across his back barely registered as the metal desk glided over the floor like a bobcat scraping asphalt. It got the job done, pinning the creature against the wall.

The thing screeched a god-awful sound that made his ears throb until there was one long whistling noise. He straightened and rolled his shoulders. His back was stiff and felt the bad kind of odd.

"Not today, motherfucker." He drew a slow breath and steadied his still shaking hand. He squeezed the trigger, putting the last two rounds into the creature's head. The chamber clicked a few more times before he realized the clip was empty.

A gurgle came from its mouth as more greenish-black blood spewed from the hole. The creature shuddered twice before the embers of its eyes fizzled to lumps of coal, and it slumped against the desk.

Rich's head became a slow-motion top spinning on the vertical side. He reached for one of the three walls dancing in front of him but grabbed the wrong one.

The floor met his face halfway as the office shrank and wavered. He could feel his heartbeat in his right arm and across his back. His left hand wasn't obeying, so he had to use his shaky right to fish his cell phone from the front left pocket of his pants. Took damn near forever.

Rich managed to get it in front of his face, blinking several times to clear the sweat burning his eyeballs. All the while, his hand convulsed and the phone slipped from his hand. The throbbing in his arm had numbed. That couldn't be good.

"God dammit."

The edges of his sight turned dark. Through sheer force of will, Rich picked up his phone and pressed the blurred numbers, hoping it was the correct pattern or else he was fucked.

His effort was rewarded with a vibration. Two tries left.

Using his shoulder to clear his vision, he tried again. Rich's victory was short-lived when the light dimmed to the size of a keyhole. He pulled up the last number dialed and hoped to God this was the right one before pressing send.

Darkness swallowed him before the second ring, but he was still somewhat aware. Rich couldn't hear anything, but his back burned as though he had been doused with napalm. Gradually, the air surrounding him became a blast furnace, threatening to blister his skin.

A pair of smoldering eyes the size of archery targets wavered above him in the pitch. As they came into focus, black smoke curled in the center where the iris should be.

Rich's muscles had seized up. When the alien eyes turned on him, his feet were plunged into a pool of tar. The sticky substance ate at his flesh like a school of rabid piranha. His cries begging for mercy were muffled by whatever had commandeered his body.

The acidic goop gurgled and stretched toward his calves. He was going to die...in his sleep or whatever *this* place was. The weight of failure crushed his chest. He would never find his daughter. His family would never be whole again. The thought devastated him enough that he almost gave up hope. When he couldn't feel anything below the knees, he let it go.

What good can a cop on the brink of retirement do anyway?

If you survive, you have no job to return to, no family besides your dog, Zeus.

Rich nearly choked. He heard these thoughts in his head, in his own voice, but they weren't *his*.

The fiery orbs above him intensified, becoming mini suns. Rich tried to turn his face, to protect his eyes, but he couldn't. He closed his eyes and drew on his training to keep his head straight.

If Rich gave up now, he'd be letting his wife and son down. He'd be giving up on finding Deena.

He'd be abandoning Beth. While she had lived a sheltered life, Beth always kept his daughter company on away meets when the other girls ignored 'the outsiders.' He'd be damned to stand by and let the world clip her wings before she could fly now that Beth was free to live her own life.

As if thinking about her had summoned Beth, her voice cut through the nothingness, "Rich!"

The enemy's eyes rippled. Rich's neck twitched and the substance devouring him slowed at his thigh. His fingers on one hand were like a flower bud opening in reverse, curling in slow motion to form a fist. He concentrated on doing the same with his other hand, but the whoosh of flames and the smell of burnt hair broke it. His lungs had been robbed of oxygen.

Through the haze, Rich heard Grady's urgent voice say, "You're losing him, Beth."

"Not yet, I'm not."

The determination in her voice gave Rich a burst of strength. He gulped for air, despite it feeling like he had swallowed volcanic ash. Rich made a fist with his other hand. When he lifted them against the invisible restraints, the evil entity roared. The tar reacted, covering Rich to his hips.

"Beth. *Please.* You've been at it for hours."

"I can't let him die. He saved your life at the cost of his job, then we sent him to hide in your dad's shop."

"I didn't know there'd be an Ungenth there," Grady countered heatedly.

"I'm not blaming you. Neither of us knew, Grady. I'm just not ready to give up." Beth's tone had softened but held firm.

There's a long pause and soft curse. "Tell me what I can do to help."

"Funnel energy into me. I need *more*. Ja'azul keeps pushing back, and pausing to refill lets him undo some of my healing."

"Alright. But if I think you're gonna pass out, I'm ending this. Losing you is non-negotiable."

Smart man.

Rich felt a cooling sensation cover his body. His singed nerves sighed in relief as the sweltering heat was knocked back. The floating eyes didn't like that. They rippled again, widening as another heated blast rolled over his body. This time, Rich screamed.

Memories flashed behind his eyes. The hard knock on the door... him leaving Bea on the couch with a box of tissues to answer it. Greeting two grim-faced co-workers as they delivered the news. Bea's screams when she heard they found Deena's abandoned car. Randy's bedroom door slamming shut. His world falling apart around him.

Stop struggling, and I can help you end the suffering. I will erase the memories and take away the pain.

"Don't let him win, Rich. Fight him with me," Beth shouted.

Clearly, he was vocal outside of whatever hellscape he'd tumbled into. There was pressure on his chest, like two hands pushing down.

"I will not stop fighting," Rich ground through clenched teeth as Beth's power flowed into him.

Above, the glowing orbs turned into white supernovas on the verge of exploding. Growling and snarling filled his ears before a roaring wind swept away everything into what Rich could only describe as a void vacuum. The roaring rose in pitch, whining like a balloon losing air before ending with a *pop*.

Suddenly, Rich's eyelids fluttered open to bright sunlight and the smell of clean air. Seems his one-way ticket to the afterlife was thwarted by the Uno 'skip' card he didn't know he had in his arsenal. He tried to sit upright, but a small hand pressed into his shoulder.

"Don't move. You're lying on a bed of healing herbs. Your back will be numb until we clean it out." Beth gave him a tired grin.

There were deep lines on her forehead and her eyelids drooped. Earlier, it didn't seem to take anything for her to fix Grady. Now, she looked like she needed a week's worth of sleep.

"I'll be the model patient," Rich promised, swallowing the lump in his throat. "Thank my lucky stars I hit the right number."

"Yeah," Grady replied distractedly, watching Beth like a hawk. "The longer you stay on the salve Beth made, the better. Some of those gashes hit the bone."

Rich winced, remembering how numb he had been while trying to slay the beast. He turned to Beth. "Thank you. I owe you both my life."

"You're practically family, Rich. You would've done the same for us," Beth murmured, dismissing his apology as if it weren't needed. Sweat beaded her forehead, and her skin looked paler than usual. Her face was screwed into one of concentration. "The infection on his arm isn't normal, Grady. The one you got from the first Ungenth we fought wasn't half this bad."

"I had my panther to help me heal."

Panther? Rich thought. The question froze on his tongue when Beth's hair lifted on the breeze. A pulse of something heavy and warm pushed into the slash marks on his forearm. The meat and muscle tingled with uncomfortable prickles that made him hiss.

"Sorry," she whispered with a thin voice.

"It's okay." Rich grit his teeth as he sucked in a deep breath. He let it out slowly, trying not to tense his arm while Beth worked. "Hurt worse getting cut up."

One second, Beth stood next to him, the next her eyes rolled to the back of her head. Rich reached for her, but he couldn't leave the table. Thankfully, Grady scooped her in his arms before she could even fall. His downturned lips were pressed together tightly while he looked her over.

Beth's eyes fluttered open and her hands gripped his forearms. "I'm sorry, I don't know how that happened."

"I do," Grady grumbled. Some seriously deep frown lines had formed above his brows. "As always, you do too much."

She opened her mouth to protest, but Grady's raised eyebrow had her keeping it zipped.

The prickles faded but it still felt wet. Rich raised his head enough to watch the skin knit together. Thick black gunk was mixed with his dried blood, but the pain was gone. He flexed his fingers, expecting resistance and tightness where the creature had slashed to the bone and severed nerves, but there was nothing.

"I think you also healed my arthritis," Rich murmured as he lifted his arm and turned it side to side.

"Good." Beth leaned on Grady, who scooped her up bridal style. When he had them situated on a chair next to Rich, she snuggled into his chest and closed her eyes. "Y'all don't mind me. I'm just gonna rest my eyes for a bit."

"I've got you, beautiful," Grady murmured, pressing a kiss to her head. "Rest."

Beth released a happy sigh and rested her palm over his heart.

Rich's heart squeezed. He and Bea were in love like that once. Maybe one day, his wife would forgive him for failing their family.

Grady cleared his throat, diverting Rich's attention from the well of dark thoughts he'd often dipped into. "Now that you're awake, I'm sure you have questions."

"Lots." Rich rolled his head to the side so he could see Grady better. "We can start with what you meant by panther. Is it your familiar or something?"

The smirk on Grady's face made Rich feel like he was the only one not in on a secret. He ignored the pinch in his gut and waited for the young man to answer.

"No, not my familiar, but my form."

It was Rich's turn to frown. "So, you can shape change?"

Grady nodded, but Rich blurted his next question, "Can you change into anything else?"

"Nope. Each guardian is given a special ability. Mine is changing into a panther."

Rich's chest swelled with excitement. Reading about these things was fun, but being able to witness it firsthand would be the pinnacle of his research on supernatural beings. "Can you show me?"

"Later," Grady answered before his gaze dropped to Beth.

She not only looked like she was sleeping soundly, but the color had returned to her cheeks. Rich did a double take when he noticed what looked like glittering emerald dust flowing from Grady into Beth.

"Are you doing that? Healing Beth?"

"Sort of. I'm giving her energy so she can convert it into healing. That's part of her gift."

"Ah." Rich was still trying to reconcile teenage Beth with this grown-up version. The one he watched growing up was so unsure. Adult Beth was grounded, and the earth moved when she did.

While he pondered this, Rich studied his surroundings. They were in a field of wild daisies and cornflowers surrounded by a ring of thin, ghostly white trees with black eyes. Birches, if he remembered correctly. The sky was a brilliant blue with fluffy white clouds crossing over them on a lazy spring breeze. It was the most peaceful place he'd ever visited.

"We call this place the Grove. It's a magical sanctuary where I practice my craft and where we'll train for the coming war."

"War?" Rich snapped his head back around to stare at Grady. "What are you talking about?"

Even as the words left Rich's lips, his brain connected the dots. "You mean against those creatures."

"Yes. The Ungenth was the weaker of Ja'azul's creatures that we've faced. There are bigger and faster ones called Agnazar." Grady closed his eyes and sighed heavily. When he reopened them, his gaze went to Beth. "There will be an army of them if we don't figure out how to stop them from getting loose."

"And by stopping them, you mean by magic."

"Yes. Guns are effective in a pinch, but Beth and I were gifted the tools to destroy them much quicker. Think of our magic being like holy water to a vampire."

"Ah. So, you guys do white magic." Rich rubbed his chin in thought. "Was Blaylock using some sort of black magic for his ritual."

"Not exactly." Grady met Rich's gaze with a wisdom he didn't expect anyone under the age of thirty to have. "Both white magic and dark magic use natural elements and ingredients in their workings. Herbs, bones, blood, you get the idea. Blaylock is toying with something unnatural, something not native to this planet. It's old and twisted, not even of this universe. But, to understand, you have to know the whole story from the beginning."

"The only thing I have is time." Rich paused, remembering his faithful dog, who was either worried or sleeping. "And Zeus. I'll need to go to my house."

"Who's Zeus?" Grady asked.

"About fifty pounds of muscle and slobber but has a heart of gold." Rich smiled, remembering the day Deena and Randy picked him out. "Adopted him from the animal shelter when he was barely older than a pup. He's not used to being alone for too long."

"We'll fetch Zeus after Beth wakes up and we eat. Until then, I'll catch you up on the untoward happenings this town had hidden for centuries."

Grady's grim grin didn't match the youth of his face. Rich shuddered at thought, but underneath his interest piqued. By the end of Grady's explanation of Ja'azul and his death cult, the father's and how he, Tom, and Beth fit into the puzzle, Rich's eyebrows were in his hairline. If what Grady said was true, he'd bet his left lung there were clues in the banker's box that would solve crimes going back decades.

"Y'all didn't happen to grab the banker's box next to my dying ass, did ya?"

"Afraid not. It took both of us to get you through the portal. Why?" Grady idly rubbed up and down Beth's arm.

"It had a boatload of evidence I found while in your dad's shop. I'm sure there are more than a handful of families who would benefit from the closure in that box," Rich said, burying his face in his hands. He was so tired. If he didn't need to get to Zeus pronto, he'd take a nap, too. "When can I get up from here? Half the day has gone. I'm worried about my dog."

What Rich didn't voice was how much *he* needed Zeus. The old boy had been his constant companion after Bea and Randy moved to middle Georgia, to her momma's. He groaned, sitting up slowly. His back was like one big scab, tight and itchy.

"Please lay back down, Rich," Beth complained, opening one eye to peer at him. "Time moves differently here. In the Grove, when an entire day passes, only an hour has gone by on the outside. Take advantage and heal while you can."

"Of course it does. Next thing you'll be telling me is that fairies exist."

Rich laid back down and closed his eyes. He couldn't sleep knowing that his faithful dog had been left alone with nightmarish creatures like the Ungenth on the loose. He also couldn't just up and leave because he didn't know where the hell 'the Grove' was.

Resigned to his post, Rich ignored the rumble in his gut and crossed his ankles. For once, he'd wait on the young'uns to steer the ship. *I'm getting too damn old to deal with this nonsense.*

Chapter 20

BETH

EXHAUSTED, BETH PLOPPED INTO the dining chair. Grady lumbered around the kitchen, checking the cupboards for food. His tight blue t-shirt stretched across his wide shoulders and highlighted the years of hard labor rippling beneath. Beth had never considered backs to be so sexy, but Grady's was.

I bet his back looks even sexier with the nail marks I left this morning.

Grabbing three bowls, he divided a near empty bag of trail mix equally between them. When he turned around, the smirk he wore was a reminder that her thoughts were not her own anymore. Beth's fingers grazed the empty space where the fluorite pendant used to hang. She blushed despite being the happiest she had ever been.

"I love how much I affect you, just by doing normal stuff." Grady placed their bowls on the table to cup her face with his warm, firm hands. "You're welcome to mark me as yours any way you want. I like the reminder. But I need you to stop overdoing it with the healing."

Heat spread to her whole face. She knew Grady was right, but being called out about wearing herself out again wasn't fun. At least he wasn't scowling. The lines in his face were worn with worry. "I'll do my best."

"That's all I ask." As he pressed his lips against hers, a zing of heat passed through her veins, making her gasp. Grady took the opportunity to explore her mouth in slow, curious strokes. Beth always loved his hugs, but his kisses were ten times better. They'd practiced those—and other things—all night.

He pulled away first, making Beth whine with disappointment. "Eat, beautiful. You need your strength."

Grady dropped a kiss on Beth's forehead, settling into the chair next to hers. He turned his body toward hers as they picked at the piles of fruit and nuts. Hers, she noticed, had a lot more.

"Here, take some of mine. I won't finish it." Beth scooped a modest handful and passed the bowl to Grady, who shook his head.

"If healing Rich's arm took so much out of you, imagine what healing his back is gonna do." Grady squeezed her hand. "Eat what you can, love, and I'll fill in for the rest."

Beth left the bowl between them, eating from it when her palm was empty. She usually liked trail mix, but the lack of variety had her forcibly swallowing down her meal. While the cottage's vegetable garden was lush with fresh fruits and vegetables, there were only so many meals you could make from tomatoes, wild onions, and squash. Vegetarian cuisine was fine, but Beth favored an omnivore's diet. Meat made it a meal.

"I can't possibly eat another bite."

"You feel any better?" Grady cocked an eyebrow before downing the rest.

"Mm-hm."

Grady stood and deposited their empty dishes in the sink. Beth followed, wrapping her arms around his waist from behind. His muscular back was warm against her cheek.

"Thank you for taking care of me."

His rough hands felt good against hers. Safe.

"Always." He whispered before his soft lips pressed against their entwined fingers.

Despite the peace of the moment, unease gathered in her chest like the beginnings of heartburn. She tried to play it off as concern for Rich, but it wasn't that. Something else, something bigger was happening. They couldn't hide in their sanctuary forever.

They had the whole of humanity to save.

"Why do I feel like this is the calm before the storm?" Beth clung to Grady as though he was the last island of peace in a war-torn world.

"Because it is." Grady turned in her arms, resting his large hands on either side of her neck while he studied her face. As his fingers brushed down her arms and laced behind her back, calmness coated her panicked mind. Her frown fell away, and he gifted her with his signature lop-sided smile. "Much better."

Beth's chest warmed. Her love for Grady swelled from her center and threatened to burst free, but you can't cover a hornet's nest with smoke and expect the swarm to be okay with it. The dull warning pain gathered in the middle of her chest, growing with every second. "Hold me for a little bit longer."

Without a word, Grady drew her closer. She nestled her head against his chest, tilting her face so the scruff of his beard tickled her nose. It was easy to forget everything else while wrapped in his embrace. Eventually, all good things come to an end. She hoped theirs didn't come too soon.

"Let's take some food to Rich. I'm sure he's ready to get going." Grady rested his lips on her temple with a sigh before letting her go.

She shivered from the loss of his heat and smoothed her hair. Grady waited by the open door with the extra bowl in hand. The way he stood, having every bit of confidence that they would succeed, made her heart flip.

As she passed, Grady winked and she legit swooned.

Yeah, this is going to take some getting used to, she thought while the 'team Tom' side of her softened a bit more.

RICH WAS LAID OUT like he was sunbathing. His ankles were crossed, and his hands clasped on his stomach. When they approached, he opened one eye.

"We come bearing gifts," Beth chimed as Grady lifted the bowl to Rich's eye level.

"A room with a view as well as room service? Y'all spoil me." Rich chuckled.

"It's not much, but it's what we had. When we go out for Zeus, we'll grab what we can find." Grady set the bowl on the wooden log stool before stepping around Rich opposite Beth.

"I'm grateful nonetheless," Rich answered, lifting his arms. Beth grabbed one and Grady grabbed the other. "Let's do this before I change my mind."

"One, two, three."

Rich sat up straight as a board as he rose like Frankenstein. "Huh. I expected that to sting like a son of a bitch."

Beth skimmed over Rich's back, her chest swelling with pride. The herbs were working wonders. She'd need to replenish the cottage's supply as soon as they had time. Thankfully, Myrtle had left a detailed process on how to properly dry and store herbs as well as what each was good for. Her sketches would also be helpful when Beth went harvesting from the garden.

"Hold still," Beth instructed, smoothing more of the healing paste over the reddest areas around the gashes. Her patient jumped a few times, but for the most part stayed still while she worked.

"I still feel like I'm gonna wake up and this will all be some weird dream." Rich held his healed arm up and flexed the muscles. His fingers played over the pink scarring like he thought it would smear. "I know I said it before, but I appreciate the two of you taking care of this old man."

"We're glad you're here, Rich." Beth wiped her hands on a rag and stepped around to face him. "You know, if you stay here another day or two, your back would be completely healed."

"Can't. 'Sides you two, Zeus is the only family I got." Rich shook his head. His stare was cast beyond the trees, looking at something she couldn't see. His hand darted to his chin, swiping at his tears like a thief. "You got an extra shirt or something? I apologize in advance 'cause Imma 'bout to ruin it with this magical mud."

"I'm sure Grady can find something," Beth replied softly.

The antsy feeling returned with the reminder they were going back outside, into unknown territory. Again, she wrote it off as concern for Rich's well-being. She didn't want to rush, but if something happened to Zeus, it would be her fault.

Grady jogged back with a t-shirt in hand. "When we get back, you should read my father's little black book of incrimination. You'll be surprised at the caliber of names you find in there. Might have some answers you're looking for."

"I'm sure it will," Rich scoffed as he put his arms through the armholes. "Um, would you two be so kind?"

While Rich was a few inches taller than Grady, he was a little softer around the middle. It was a tight fit, but they managed to get the shirt in place and his back covered in the medicinal paste.

"How far away is your car parked?" Rich stretched his arms and rolled his shoulders.

Beth swallowed a laugh, biting the inside of her cheek for good measure. "That's a loaded question, Rich."

Grady grinned and pulled the moonstone from his pocket. "Where we're going, we don't need roads."

"Did you just quote 'Back to the Future?'" Rich chuckled.

"Yea. Only we're not travelling through time and we're not using cars. We're using this." Grady held the stone between his thumb and fingers up toward the sun. The smooth surface glinted proudly, but Rich's unimpressed stare broke the spell.

"I have one of those in my pocket." Beth glanced at Grady as Rich rummaged around. He frowned, pulling a handful of rubble free. "Well, I *did*."

Beth studied the pieces. The familiar magic emanated from them like lost spirits. "Where did you find it?"

"My partner had it in the car the other night. I thought it was a worry stone. Didn't occur to me it came from Grady when Wilson patted him down." He let the pieces fall into her open hands. "Sorry about that. Must've broken when I fought the Ungenth. Was it important?"

Beth bit her bottom lip and winced. "Kinda. There were only three. Tom, Grady, and I made them. If we've been to a place before and visualize it, we can connect the doorways. Grady was the brilliant mind behind the design."

Rich's excitement deflated. His shoulders slumped and his face was drawn in pain. "I'm so sorry. It didn't look like much. Guess that was the point."

"What's done is done. Forget about it." Grady grumbled, taking the crumbs from Beth. "We'll put it to rest in the garden later. For now, I'll wrap it in a rag."

Beth tossed him the cloth she had used earlier. Grady carefully laid the pieces in the center. He folded the edges over one another and left it on the table where Rich had been laying.

"C'mon." Grady laced their fingers, leading them to the field to a wide archway made from a tree.

"This is new." Beth still hadn't had the official tour. She blushed when she remembered what they'd done instead.

Grady patted the arch. "It's easier to get large stuff like lumber or furniture back and forth. The cabins only have so much room."

"You mean to tell us that *this*"—Rich hooked his thumb at the opening—"is a portal?"

Rich stopped just outside of the arch and stuck his hand through. When it didn't do anything, he turned his skepticism on Grady. "Or are y'all messing with the old timer?"

"I promise it is." Grady smirked, slinging an arm around Beth's shoulders. "But it only works with the stones."

Rich's mouth was parted and his eyes sparkling with wonder as he stalked around the archway. Beth enjoyed Grady's closeness. It took the edge off the ever-mounting dread that had taken residence in her chest.

"Is there anything you haven't thought of?" Beth kidded, but she was in awe as always.

"Nope." Grady winked, melting her insides.

When he stepped up to the archway, the unease tugged at Beth's stomach again. Rich was fine, Grady was fine. Perhaps the worry was because her boyfriend was a wanted man.

Boyfriend, she snorted internally at the label. It didn't fit what they had.

"Do you have a photograph of the inside of your house," Grady addressed Rich, who shook his head. "Then we'll go back to my dad's shop and take your car." Grady aimed the stone at the opening and said, "Exgradi."

Rich startled at the 'whoosh,' but his apprehension was short-lived. Tentatively, he prodded the film with his fingers, letting them sink into the vertical pool before pulling them free. He examined his dry fingers with childlike amazement.

"This is incredible." Rich turned to Beth, his face alight. "It should be wet, but it isn't."

"While in the tunnel, keep your arms and legs inside the walls. We don't know what's past them." Grady clarified before stepping through.

Rich grabbed Beth's arm, worry lining his brow. "You've done this before?"

"Many times," she replied, placing her hand on his arm in comfort, clicking her tongue. "Technically, *you* have, too. Once. Does it still count if you were passed out?"

That pulled a relieved chuckle from Rich. "Sure. If we're counting technicalities. How long does it stay open if y'all don't close it?"

Beth tilted her head and drew her lips into an exaggerated frown. "Not sure. We've always closed it in case someone—or something—tries to follow."

"Fair enough." Rich rubbed his hands together so hard, Beth thought she saw smoke. "Here goes nothin'."

Beth's stomach was a knotted ball of yarn, twisting tighter and pulling at the lining. She rubbed her midsection, willing it to unravel. She'd spent the afternoon ignoring it, coming up with excuses.

Something was seriously wrong.

"Beth, come quick." Grady's shaky voice sent a chill down her spine. In the eight years she's known the man, he's only been this scared once, when his mother died.

"On my way."

The knots had worked their way to her chest as she stepped through the portal. Scenarios of a brutal battle between her loved ones against a hoard of Ungenth and

Agnazar played through her mind. Swiftly, she moved to the other side, noting that the whispers that once occupied the space beyond were silent.

Her throat constricted as ghostly strings pulled it shut. Beth stumbled through the doorway with her hand outstretched, searching for relief.

Grady grabbed her by the arms. She was warm but not safe. The shadowy corners pressed against the waning light, seeking to steal away the rest and leave only the night and all the terrors it would bring.

"Beth, breathe."

He gently shook her, eyes wild. When Grady swallowed hard and touched foreheads, she remembered who she was, and what power ran through her veins.

She shouldn't be afraid of the darkness, it should be afraid of *her*.

A faint, white glow emanated from her skin and sweet oxygen was hers again. Grady rubbed her biceps, up and down in a rhythm that grounded her.

When she felt like she wasn't breathing through a straw anymore, Beth pulled back. "Show me."

Grady's lips formed a line. His nod was curt, and his clammy hands shook as he laced their fingers, keeping her tight to his side. They descended the stairs with the weight of reluctance surrounding their feet. Green light the shade of vomit clashed and wavered against angry reds along the walls and workbenches.

Rich stood by the bay windows, staring at the sky. She would say he was mesmerized by the display, except his body trembled. Beth knew what it was before looking...why they were so afraid.

In the center of the sky, an awful bruise. Across the middle stretched an obsidian crack, spilling its dreadful aura into the crevices of anyone who dared look upon it.

This could mean only one thing...

Ja'azul was coming.

Chapter 21

GRADY

"He's free," Beth whispered.

Grady broke out in cold sweats. His lungs struggled to keep up with the oxygen his beating heart demanded. For years, the pressure of responsibility and defending his corner of the world had been a faraway thing, a preparation. The possibility of losing everything was now a tangible thing. The meditation techniques he'd practiced for years weren't doing jack shit because *they weren't ready*.

Beth squeezed his hand. Grady inhaled deeply. Somehow, she was pushing her stubborn determination through their link. Damned if it didn't ground him and give him strength to kick his panic attack to the curb.

When he turned to Beth, she sent him one word that bolstered his confidence, *"Together."*

"Always," Grady replied aloud, bringing his hand to cup her face.

He pressed a kiss to her forehead. Returning his gaze to the stain above their hometown, he expected some giant monstrosity to step through the charcoal-colored crack. Something resembling a ball of staticky black wire fell from the blackness.

"Did you see that?" Rich asked.

"Yeah." Grady followed its trajectory to the woods outside of town, further into Tennessee where the copper mines had long been stripped. Right where there were sprawling underground mines and hills of slag. "Fell somewhere near Potato Hill."

"That's not far from here, Grady." Beth's brows drew together, but her jaw was set. His girl was ready to do what she could. "What about the townsfolk?"

"It's like the Purge out there." Rich murmured, doing the slow turn until his eyes could no longer focus on the thing in the sky. He pointed to a window showing the streets.

"Look. We've become the nightmares."

Some layer of Hell had descended upon Mayes Hill.

Across the road, an axe-wielding man wearing overalls chased a group of teenagers down the sidewalk. Seconds later, a man limped past the shop, eyes wide and lips pulled back in a scream. He was the owner of the local hardware store. On his heels was his wife of thirty years carrying a crimson-colored chainsaw. Her face matched his except her eyes had gone full white.

A stream of chaos continued to play before their eyes, neighbor against neighbor in bloody fist to cuffs to the death. It didn't seem to be slowing.

"Can you still get to your cruiser?" Grady's priorities shifted. Chances were, his place was already compromised, but judging by the current state of town, it was worth a shot. The only things he'd left were extra clothes and his photo albums. The latter were most likely gone, but they could raid the kitchen.

"I could, but with this many civvies ready to turn Mayes Hill into the Thunderdome, it's gonna be tricky." Rich paced the front of the shop, hands on his hips, murmuring, "Where are the uniforms? There's not a single deputy or officer out there."

Grady peeked outside, looking for anyone resembling the law. No sign of them anywhere.

"You're right. For whatever reason, Blaylock is keeping his crew on lockdown." Grady wasn't holding out hope that the bastard had died from a ricocheted bullet. "I say we make use of the distraction; portal over to my house."

"I *need* to make sure my dog is okay first," Rich countered, his face resembling a cartoon bomb about to go off.

"We can do both," Beth promised, placing her hands on her hips and pursing her lips. "The portal will get us around faster without being seen."

"Then let's not dawdle." Rich rubbed his hands together, eyeing the top of the stairs before taking them two at a time.

Beth tucked a lock of hair behind her ear, then hooked her pinkie with his. "After you."

Grady led the way back upstairs, kicking himself when he saw the pearlescent sheen still open in the doorway. "Claudere."

Nothing of Ja'azul's could breach the Grove, but the next portal wouldn't be connected to its defensive magic. They couldn't afford him being sloppy.

"I'll head through first, to make sure the coast is clear." Grady touched his forehead to Beth's. "If you don't hear from me in five minutes, close the portal and get Rich back to the Grove."

"Not without you." She fisted the front of his shirt in both hands and shook her head. Her eyes glistened with a fresh coat of fear. "I won't lose you, too, Grady."

"You won't." He sealed his hollow promise with a quick kiss, then pulled free of her grip. He pressed her hands against his lips, mumbling, "Five minutes."

Grady stepped up to the gate. He nodded at Rich before gazing at Beth. She gave him a weak grin. His heart flipped. If he didn't go now, leaving Beth would only get harder. Dropping his gaze, he disappeared into the unknown.

GRADY POPPED OUT INTO the hallway outside his bedroom on light feet. He concentrated on his heightened senses, using them like sonar to read the house. Faint traces of overlaying footprints, gunpowder, and mud were found in every room. The strongest of which was where he stood. There was no other indication of life.

Taking a deeper breath, he also found no traces of sulfur.

Anxious to get check the state of his house—especially his bedroom—Grady called to Beth through the thread, "*All clear, beautiful.*"

"*On our way.*"

When Beth came through, she threw her arms around his neck. He hadn't realized how tense he was until his body loosened, and he had full use of his lungs again.

"From now on, we check things out together," Beth scolded as Grady carried her down the hall, making room for Rich.

He planted Beth's feet firmly on the ground before lowering his gaze to her eye level. He smoothed his finger down the frown lines above her nose. "I can't promise *not* to keep you safe, Beth, especially if it's within my power."

The portal whooshed, and Rich stepped in behind them. Grady closed it immediately. Rich whipped around to face the portal, but it was just Grady's bedroom door. When Rich turned back to study the hallway, his mouth was slightly ajar.

"Reminds me of my momma's old house." The former deputy shared, smoothing his hand down the 70's style wood paneling. Abruptly, Rich yanked his hand back and wiped it on his jeans.

Grady pursed his lips, knowing all too well what clung to the walls. Once upon a time, the wood was a lovely shade of oak. Years of neglect and heavy cigarette smoke had taken the shine. Even before that, the spark of joy the house held was snuffed out the day he found his momma lying dead on the kitchen floor.

"I can see Blaylock has been here already." Rich gestured to the cluttered ground.

"Not sure what he's taken yet, but they were all over the house." Grady tapped the side of his nose. "Their scents are everywhere."

Beth tangled and wrapped both of her hands with his free one. Along the thread connecting them, Grady sensed Beth's calm like the waves at the lake lapping upon the shore. He'd like to share in it, let it ease the ache in his chest, but some tasks needed sharp focus. This was one of them.

"I'll go to the kitchen; see what kind of food I can pack up." Beth squeezed his hand, then cupped his cheek. He placed a kiss on her palm.

"Thank you. I'll come help when I finish in here."

"Don't be too long."

"I won't."

"Where were most of your books?" Rich asked.

"The ones that matter are already at the Grove." Grady downwardly wiped his face. It didn't reset the frown lines, only made Grady realize how tired he still was. "I'm mostly here for food, clothes, and whatever else can help us live off-grid."

"Where's your camping gear?"

"In the garage. Door is through the kitchen."

The deputy was cautious as he turned the corner. Grady hoped it was enough to distract Rich from worrying about Zeus.

Grady turned to face what was waiting in his bedroom. At first glance, he thought of 'Poltergeist'. Papers strewn all over, framed photos on the wall either missing or askew, his dresser with drawers hanging out.

As expected, the modest bookshelf at the foot of his bed was empty. No photo albums. His only consolation was that someone would have to pour through books on birdwatching to find the witchcraft for which he was accused. They were right, but Grady didn't care. The whole department was corrupt, and as far as he was concerned, Rich was the only decent officer in the county.

Grady stepped over the rabble to his closet. His trusty backpack remained, albeit on the outside of its designated space and upside down. He picked it up, dusted it off, and placed it on his bed. It took several minutes of searching through the mess to find enough outfits for the next few days. The bastards had shredded half the clothes in his closet.

He zipped his backpack and slung it over one arm. Stepping out into the hallway, he stared at his parents' bedroom across the way. The normal amount of clutter showed that little had been disturbed.

Sentimentality pulled Grady into the room. He took a ragged breath, nostalgia hitting his chest like a ton of bricks. He knelt next to the antique trunk at the foot of his parents' bed. Inside held a treasure his mother would have passed to him, as it was passed to her.

Dust bunnies hid in the cold, dark corners when he lifted the lid. Despite being tucked away for years, if he closed his eyes, he could still scent his mother's magnolia perfume. Grady brought the quilt to his face and breathed deeply. On the surface, his old man's brand of two packs a day stole front and center. It clung to the fibers with a permanency his father's love was never capable of.

Beth's lavender vanilla lotion announced her arrival. She slipped her arms around his middle and rested her cheek against his back. He didn't want to cry in front of her right now. Too much was at stake for him to have a breakdown.

"You know, crying doesn't make you weak. Think of it as letting your worries leak out of your face rather than holding them inside to weigh you down."

"We can't afford to let me have a moment, Beth, not until we get you to the Grove and train up. I've fucked up so bad already, wasted too much time. He's coming, and we're not ready."

Grady's tear ducts burned, and his face heated as he clenched his teeth. He'd made decisions *for* them rather than deciding together, and now they were royally screwed. At the time, he thought he was doing the right thing, but even the best intentions can be futile.

He missed Beth's touch when she pulled away, but he didn't deserve it right now.

"Fine. Suck it up, so we can get outta here." Her tone was all business, but it was the uncharacteristic harshness that did the trick.

"You're right, as usual."

Tucking the family quilt underneath his other arm, Grady rounded on Beth, expecting her to be frowning. Instead, concern was written all over her face.

"I'm not trying to be harsh or mean, Grady. I need us to be on the same page, 'cause that *thing* out there in the sky...it scares the ever-living shit out of me."

"I know, love. I'm sorry."

She shook her head as if trying to dispel a bee looking for nectar.

"Don't apologize. It's not your fault. If you want to blame anyone, blame Ja'azul. He's the one who came to Earth, who wanted to swallow the soul of humanity for whatever the hell he plans to do."

"I should have stayed with you that night, but I panicked."

For days, he'd been there, letting her grieve Tom's death while he kept his bottled up. She never asked him to stay, but that time had brought them closer. As always, he'd fucked it up by pushing her away when she begged him not to leave. Grady had beaten himself up a million times over his stupidity.

"Do you honestly believe I would have let you? I told you the truth, that I needed to know I could be on my own for once. I have always had someone there to guide my decisions or tell me what was best." Beth wiped the tears from her cheeks. "Tom's death seemed like a good time to start but being alone with all that grief... it was too much. Bottom line, I was wrong to send you away, but it had to happen for me to realize how much we need each other."

When Beth's glassy gaze met Grady's, he dropped the bag and quilt on the trunk lid and pulled her against his chest. Their embrace lasted a handful of heartbeats, but it was long enough to close the gaping holes between them.

Grady followed Beth to the kitchen, his steps lighter than they had any right to be, given the circumstances. Rich was stacking Grady's campfire cooking set on top of sleeping bags.

Outside the kitchen window, the darkening sky was hidden behind Ja'azul's monstrosity, but the stovetop clock said it was almost dusk. The thought of being out after dark gave Grady the shivers and a tightness in his gut. Best not tempt fate more than they had already.

"Let's get what we've packed to the Grove so we can go to Rich's before we lose what little daylight we have."

"Sounds good. I didn't find much that looked useful."

"Unsurprising. Most of what I needed was in my room. They cleared it out."

Rich paused, an idea coming to light by the way his face went from deep concentration to 'aha' over seconds. "If there's more of those Ungenth out there, we'll need guns and ammunition. While we're here, we should go to the precinct. May can hit the evidence locker for your things, too."

"Possibly." Grady chewed on the idea. Another loss would dampen their spirits, but getting his photo albums and truck back would even things out. There were a lot of good memories tied up in that hunk of metal. "Is the impound still in the back lot?"

"Yep." The corner of Rich's lip twitched, and he added, "The key to the padlock is yours if we go by my house first."

"Tempting, but we know if getting Zeus means a fight, we'll be better off armed to the teeth." Grady's gaze darted to Beth's retreating form. She hadn't used defensive magic around him since they'd completed their connection, but her power wavered like a desert sun above her skin. When she finally believed in herself and let go, 'armed to the teeth' would be an understatement.

Chapter 22

RICH

RICH CROUCHED BEHIND A shrub in the Gilberts' backyard with Grady and Beth huddled beside him. The neighboring house sat in a pool of night. All of the white curtains were pulled closed, but he swore one of them moved.

When nothing else seemed out of sorts, Rich declared, "Coast is clear."

His knees did not appreciate the treatment, popping when he walked with a stoop. But he kept moving because the creepy lightshow in the sky gave him major heebie-jeebies.

As Rich approached his quaint back deck, the automatic floodlights kicked on. Typically, this was Zeus's cue to frighten the intruders, but Rich's dark house was too quiet for his liking.

Kneeling next to the bottom step, Rich hooked his hand underneath the decking for the hidden box holding the spare key. Bea had wanted to keep it underneath a flowerpot in the front of the house. He'd argued it was too cliché.

"Uh, Rich? The back door is open," Beth whispered, pointing.

No, God. He peered over the porch to see for himself. The silver trim at the closure was doubled, as though someone had tried to close the sliding door too hard, and it bounced open out of spite.

His old boy loved to be outside, but he was very territorial. Rich found out the hard way that not every dog owner adhered to leash laws. Rich wouldn't find his faithful dog inside.

"Someone let him out. There's no telling where Zeus went." Rich hung his head as he used the steps as a crutch to stand.

First Deena, then Bea and their son, now Zeus. Everyone Rich ever cared about had left him. There was a black hole the size of Texas in his heart.

"What kind of dog is he? There's a chance someone locked him in a room." Grady started up the steps, his ear pointed toward the house.

Rich swore the young man's nose was twitching like a hound dog. "Not likely. Zeus is a bulldog; we've had him since he was a pup."

He snapped his mouth shut, for fear the other possibility would manifest. Those words pushed at the back of teeth. He scraped them to the back of his throat and swallowed.

Grady slid the glass door open. When it was wide enough to fit, he stepped inside. Beth tugged on Rich's shirt sleeve and pointed her chin at the house.

"C'mon," she whispered, her attention momentarily flitting to the sky.

Inside the house, things were relatively untouched. Open files and pages were still scattered in organized chaos across his dining table. He caught a glimpse of the name on the case file, causing another flashback. A missing person case opened two years ago. Rich—being the lead investigator despite his personal connection—had been the recipient of pity rather than of hope. No trace of Elladine Stanton was ever found.

But he never stopped looking.

"Dad! I told you to call me Elle." She rolled her eyes, trying to look annoyed, but his princess would always be Elladine.

"I know, I know," Rich pulled his daughter into a hug. "Last time, I promise. You may be turning twenty-two in a few weeks, but you'll always be my baby girl."

"Love you, too," she replied, her serious face softening. "No matter how old I am, I will always need my dad. Thanks for always having my back."

He hugged his daughter once more before she protested. His baby was moving to Ashe, North Carolina. Elle's recent breakup had been a bad one. Rather than wait for summer, her roommate invited Elle to move in that weekend. While it wasn't ideal having four hours between them, he had to let his daughter live her own life. He was damn proud of her.

Elle had gone for a walk that night and never returned.

Rich startled from his stroll down memory lane when Beth placed her hand on his shoulder. Wiping the tears from his cheeks, he stood and stretched, looking for a distraction.

The Jenga tower of unopened mail had finally tipped, leaving last week's newspaper and past due bills scattered on the floor. He knelt to pick up the envelopes when the front-page headline of the paper caught his eye, 'Local Teacher Survives Shooting, Dies Days Later.'

When he opened the spread, front and center was a photograph of Beth, a blonde man, and Grady. The caption said he was Tom Newman, late husband of Beth Harper-Newman.

"Damn."

"When we get back to the Grove, we'll swap stories."

Beth's voice was thick as tar. When Rich looked at Beth, her eyes were glossy and rimmed in pink, matching her downturned lips. She reached for one of the case folders, tracing Deena's name with her fingers.

"I'm sorry for your loss, Rich. I-I didn't know."

"We lose people every day. Sometimes, those people can be found; sometimes they can't. Don't mean I won't stop looking for my daughter."

"Grady and I are here for you, too, Rich. We'll work through our losses together." Beth sniffled, putting on a brave smile.

Too many loved ones in this town had gone missing or found dead since he'd uprooted his family and moved to Mayes Hill. After Bea left, Rich appointed himself as gumshoe for the deceased, investigating the box of unsolved mysteries stuffed in the back corner to gather dust. After years of dead ends, Rich was tired of digging up more cases than he could solve. Seemed sadness was the only thing holding up the walls of this town nowadays.

"All clear," Grady announced as he skulked into the room, his gaze immediately finding Beth. "Are you okay?"

Beth nodded, leaning against the dining table. "Did you find Zeus?"

"No." Grady sighed, rubbing his chin. "Are there any friendly neighbors he could have visited?"

Rich's shoulders were laden with his failures. He shook his head. "Just Theresa and Charles next door, but they were murdered last night."

"What?" Beth covered her mouth with both hands.

"Same protocol as Beth's place." Grady moved closer to Beth, placing his hand on the small of her back. "Pack any food, guns, ammo, or any other supplies you think would be helpful, like blankets, sleeping bags, and tents. We're not sure what the state of things will be hours from now."

"We should hit the precinct. Normal circumstances, the night shift runs a skeleton crew." Rich ran a hand through his short hair, finding a stray spiderweb. "We'll go in through the back door and you two can magic the armory guard to sleep. Might be able to bust your truck outta impound while we're at it."

"Sounds like a plan, man."

They say dogs are man's best friend. Well, seeing how Grady's face brightened, his was his truck. Rich suppressed a smile.

"I've got a bookshelf in the master. Might have something useful."

Rich stalked toward his room, hearing Grady's boots behind him. When Rich pushed the door open, his hopeful meter dropped to zero.

"Oh, shit," Grady hissed over his shoulder.

It looked like Edward Scissorhands had tried to read Rich's books but gave up and decided to make confetti instead. He didn't expect to find his personal firearms in the closet, but a sliver of hope foolishly remained.

"Check underneath the bed. There are a few boxes of shotgun shells and some clips for the 9mil, if they didn't take those."

"On it."

Rich opened the closet bifold door the rest of the way. His clothes were luckier than his books. Only a small portion of them were shredded. Nothing he couldn't live without.

"Found somethin' in the back." Grady grunted and something rattled. The shoe box landed on the side of Rich's bed as Grady stood. Inside, there were a pair of clips and twice as many shells. "Better than nothing."

"Yeah," Rich agreed, wiping his hand down his face. If he kept this up, he'd be looking like a cartoon character with melting eyes and exaggerated jowls. "I'd feel better if we had more ammo. I emptied most of a clip into that Ungenth before it stopped."

Grady closed the box lid and held it out. Rich tucked it underneath his lock-picking set. "Let's help Beth."

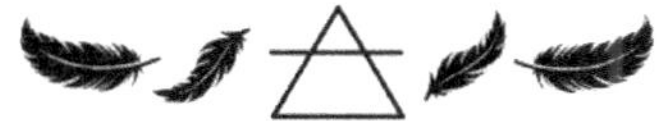

BETH HAD HER HEAD in the pantry, her hands on her hips. She turned to greet them with a disapproving frown on her face. "Slim pickins, Rich."

"S'posed to go grocery shopping today or tomorrow. Weekend off and all. Y'all see how that turned out."

"I packed what I could find, mostly canned soups, some tuna. If we're creative, we can come up with ways to stretch what we've got." Beth pointed to the half-full bag of Zeus's kibble. "While I'm not keen on eating it, we have the dog food as a last resort."

"I don't think we'll be that bad off, Beth." Grady crossed his arms, turning his nose up at her suggestion. "I can go hunting when we need meat."

"I have no doubt you can, but what happens when the animals are gone? I'm betting they'll either flee from the area or Ja'azul's army will eat them."

"You have a fair point."

Rich watched the young couple play volleyball with their words. Beth had a valid concern, but there was a question still burning a hole in his tongue. "How far do you think this Ja'azul's influence has spread?"

That got their attention.

"Good question." Grady leaned against the wall, his thinking cap whistling like a hot kettle. Suddenly, the young man raked a hand through his messy curls. "I don't know. I just...I don't know."

"If the craziness is centered in Mayes Hill, we can drive my cruiser to Ridgeville." Rich offered.

"And if it's not?" Beth's voice broke at the end. Her composure crumbled as she gazed into Grady's eyes.

Rich was left in the dark, wondering what had shaken her so suddenly. "I'll make a few phone calls. Check to see if anyone else is affected."

"You don't understand. My parents..." Beth fisted Grady's shirt as he enveloped her in his large arms.

"Do you have the number to the cruise ship or line—whatever—they're on?" Grady asked, his jaw ticked while he consoled Beth.

Rich figured his nerves weren't the only ones Beth's parents had stepped on. They never seemed the loving type of parents, not to him anyway.

"It's on my refrigerator, at the apartment." She sniffled, hope shining through the wall of tears.

"Why don't you two get that number while I make a quick phone call?" Rich held his cell up and wiggled it.

"But what about you? We can't leave you stranded here. What if something comes after you?" Beth pulled away from Grady's arms. Unsurprisingly, the young man stayed close by her side.

"You'll pop in and pop back. Two seconds." Rich wouldn't dare tell Beth that with nighttime so near and the bruise in the sky, being alone terrified him. He pursed his lips and put on his bravest mask. "Divide and conquer."

"Okay." She straightened her back like a soldier getting ready to begin training. "Be back in a jiffy."

Beth had her phone ready as Grady opened the portal. They stepped through without looking back this time.

Rich peeked out the window over the sink, the heaviness in his stomach sinking with the sun. Nary a cricket could be heard, nor the booming bass of the Impala who drove by his house around this time every night.

The silence was broken by the garbage can on the curb being violently knocked over. He locked the back sliding door and flicked open the holster clip on his belt. His hand hovered over the butt of his standard issue in a move that came as easily as breathing.

Easing past the portal, Rich hustled to the front door. There was shuffling coming up the sidewalk, making its way to the front.

Rich's hand went to the lower knob first. It was the quietest, but that didn't matter. It was still locked from earlier. When it rattled, Rich slid the deadbolt in place, hoping the noise covered the sliding metal. It did not. Whoever was on the other side stopped trying to open the door via knob and fully assaulted the solid oak door.

"Fuck this."

Rich turned on his heel and ran straight for the portal. His dried shirt crinkled and scraped the open wounds on his back like stinging nettles, but there was no force in this universe that would keep him from getting the hell outta dodge.

Behind him, the sound of splintering wood and vinegar-heavy, garlic-pickled eggs were incentive to move his injured and tired old ass. He'd had enough near-death experiences today.

Chapter 23

FENNICK

THE PINE THICKET WAS greedy, hogging any ray of light attempting to pass its needles. Covering the ground were the unlucky ones, dry and useless to the tree, but to anyone traversing the fallen spindly leaves they were a nuisance. Keeping your footing while trekking over these slippery devils was tricky business, which made quietly maneuvering the forest even more of a struggle. Without magic, Fennick's legs worked as effectively as a newborn deer's. Spoiled, was he, swallowing his grunts and surprised yelps. Cursing was not allowed in a game of cat and mouse, especially when the mouse was unaware it was being stalked.

Charred sulfur and brimstone hung heavy in the air, growing more pungent the closer Fennick got to the landing area. He had been fortunate not to run into whatever evil creature Ja'azul had sent. If Fennick was a betting man—and he was—it would be an Agnazar, one of the clever and cunning scouts on the *master's* force...sent to test the waters.

Normally, the shady forest would be a reprieve from the summer heat. The impact crater countered it, sending a line of sweat rolling down the center of his back. Fennick pulled at the collar of his black cotton V-neck tee.

Twigs to his left snapped.

Fennick went as still as the dead.

He counted the heartbeats pulsing in his neck as he eyed the tree line. A rush of cold air ran across Fennick's skin, causing goosebumps to race up his spine. It smelled faintly of burnt boiled eggs. His gaze flitted into the further dark.

Suddenly, a beast lumbered past a patch of giant wood ferns, stopping when it saw Fennick. Loose skin drooped like heavy tapestries laden with muddy water. A line of drool hung from its jowls. Eyes with above-animal intelligence watched him, waiting for him to make a move. Warmth permeated his torso as the memory of a family pet wavered between the lines of caution tape he had wound around his exterior.

Fennick cast another glance into the woods before whispering, "These woods are not safe for the likes of us."

The large bulldog replied with a deep and somewhat annoyed 'woof.'

A large pink tongue swept over its nose. When he dipped his head and gave it a shake, metal jingled. A collar perhaps.

Fennick's gaze quickly swept over the area as he crouched slowly, resting his wrists on his knees so his hands dangled. "Come here, boy. I will not harm you."

The large brown eyes studied him before the dog shuffled to his side. He nudged Fennick's hand with his nose, as if to say, 'there are scarier things lurking about.' Fennick scratched behind the dog's ears with his free hand, hooking the tag between his fingers.

"Well, Zeus, it is lucky we ran into each other and not the foul beast wandering these woods, though I fear it is nearby still." Zeus licked the hand he had nudged. Whining, he looked over his shoulder.

"Yes, I agree. As Beth would say, let us get a move on."

Fennick's fondness for dogs would not allow him to endanger his new friend. He stood and headed in the opposite direction of the smell, lamenting not having confirmation of which monster Ja'azul had sent. Alas, the universe had sent him a companion. Perhaps someone, somewhere, had finally taken pity upon him.

Outside the pines, the sky had grown darker, but light pollution from the small town was enough to thwart most of the stars. The rest were hidden by Ja'azul's gaudy exit route.

The heavy chain of servitude around Fennick's neck tightened like a noose. His master—the interdimensional monster—had *allowed* him to continue his meager existence. For whatever reason, it was not yet clear.

"When we get to town, there is a friend I would like you to meet. Unfortunately, I have not been entirely honest with her, so I expect you to help me into her good graces."

Zeus chuffed, brushing against Fennick's leg.

As soon as Fennick's hand lowered for some behind the ear scratches, the dog's hackles rose. The chill and rotten egg smell Fennick had been traveling against was suddenly in front of them, clouding his senses.

An Agnazar hovered a stone's throw away. Its body resembled a long trench coat hovering over a thick, black fog. Its lipless mouth was pulled back to reveal rows of needle-thin teeth. Fennick always compared it to a leech's mouth, which was applicable in almost every way. The only difference was, instead of sucking blood, they sucked souls.

It slowly drew its scimitar without breaking eye contact. Ja'azul's lightshow caused the edge of the curved black blade to glow neon green. The substance coating the blade was the equivalent to battery acid. One cut against mortal flesh was fatal.

"Our Master sends his regards," the creature hissed with its wet smacking voice, raising the sword to strike.

I suppose I spoke too soon. The vice grip around his chest loosened. Death was knocking at his door. *Finally.*

"He is no Master of mine, not any longer." Fennick's lip curled in disgust, hands balling into fists.

He reached into his well of power, but thorns lashed out like whips. Fennick cried out as metaphorical cuts manifested in blisters across his forearms.

The Agnazar lunged forward, swinging the blade at Fennick's head. He ducked at the last minute and rolled out of the way, landing in a crouch. Long strands of auburn hair floated to the ground. The unwelcome haircut left an acrid taste in his mouth. If by some miracle he survived this encounter, growing it back the natural, human way would take years.

Zeus growled and barked, stalking the creature. The Agnazar turned its malice on the bulldog.

While Zeus's vicious snarls grew more frantic, Fennick searched for some semblance of a weapon among nature. His choices were a sizeable rock and some loose dirt. No matter who you were, a fistful of dust in your face burns like the devil.

The rock barely fit in his hands, rough against his long fingers. Grabbing a handful of soil, Fennick jumped to his feet.

"Leave the poor beast alone. It is I whom your master wants."

The Agnazar ignored Fennick. It swiped a claw at Zeus as if swatting at a gnat. When it connected with Zeus's solid body, he barked a high-pitched yelp at the contact. Fennick's world moved in slow-motion while the bulldog's body hurtled through the air. Zeus landed several feet away in an unmoving heap.

Fennick roared, hurling the stone with enough force to cause his rotator cuff to burn. He launched forward, the dirt in his hand leaving a misty trail. The sick-wet crunch of the rock hitting its mark gave Fennick the split second he needed for the creature to turn around. He let loose the microscopic minerals. Tiny particles of sand mixed with slag covered the Agnazar's face. It screeched in the universal sound of pain. Loud and long, like a prehistoric beast, setting his teeth on edge.

The Agnazar's arms flailed wildly, its sword cut random swaths in the air. Fennick could not squander this chance to run, but he also could not leave Zeus. He bolted to the left, but it was a false opening. A line of napalm ignited across his left shoulder. The sudden pain caused the muscles in his entire side to seize, slamming him onto his backside with jaw-jarring speed. A sweeping cold sweat began at his head and moved down to his toes. No human survived the poison from an Agnazar's blade.

"I am sorry," Fennick whispered as he crawled to Zeus's side. If he were to die this day, he would do so next to the only friend he had.

The Agnazar's screeching ceased, replaced by labored breaths. Fennick kept his gaze on the stalking creature. The hatred in its eyes burned hot enough to melt a diamond.

He blindly reached for the bulldog as he dragged himself along the ground at a snail's pace. Each inch gained was met by the sadistic enemy toying with his fragility. It was enjoying Fennick's fear, which was thick on his tongue. The taste, he knew, was mingled with cowardice.

Part of him eagerly awaited to be freed of his mortal coil. Then again, he wasn't entirely certain he *could* die. He had never fully understood where his extended life came from, only that he had never slowed or aged like others. He had assumed it was something Circe gifted him with when appointing him as a guardian. His hypothesis would be put to the test.

His hand found the soft underbelly of warm fur. When he felt Zeus's shallow breaths and steady heartbeat, Fennick thanked the Universe.

The flame within Fennick, the part of him that called to the goddess Circe so long ago, flickered and grew. Magic or no magic, Zeus was not the only one who needed Fennick. Beth and Grady would not succeed in saving this world without his help. He would not give up.

Fennick's injured arm had gone numb, but he pushed himself to stand, keeping himself between Zeus and the Agnazar. The creature flexed its chest and gripped the hilt of its scimitar with both hands. Its head tilted sideways in a jerking motion like how a clockwork doll would move.

"Tell your mas—"

Before he could finish, the Agnazar turned on a dime and bolted toward town. Confusion paused Fennick's brain function long enough for realization to surface. Why else would Ja'azul's scout leave without finishing the job?

The answer was not pretty. Fennick was a dead-man walking. And without his magic, he posed no threat. It was a hard pill to swallow.

"Zeus."

Fennick shambled to the dog's side with what equated to two left feet. Zeus gazed up at him with sad brown eyes, but there was a glimmer of hope. Fennick squatted and scooped the big boy in his arms. His left arm spasmed so strongly he lost his grip. Luckily, Zeus wasn't too far off the ground, but his high-pitched whine had Fennick's chest caving.

Am I cursed to never be righteous again?

Fennick ignored the pain of his lament and cleared his throat. He patted the dog's side. It was a meager excuse for atonement, but his body warred between scalding or arctic. The profuse sweating did little to appease either temperature.

"Apologies, old boy. Seems I am worse for the wear. Can you walk?"

Zeus lowered his gaze and took a few limping steps toward town, looking back at Fennick.

"You really are an extraordinary animal, Zeus." Fennick smiled. "Let us continue our search for Elizabeth, only this time we shall skip the fighting."

Zeus replied with a wheezy 'woof.'

They must have looked like a motley pair, dragging their broken bodies toward Mayes Hill. The sentiment would have made him smile had he not been fighting to survive. Once he found Grady, he could pass along his magic, as was tradition, and inquire as to why Beth had not yet completed the Ritual of Passing.

If they ever made it to town, that is.

Moving as fast as a drunken cat was new to Fennick, but learning patience was on his list of redemptive practices. He just hoped he lived long enough to check off the boxes.

Chapter 24

BETH

BETH STEPPED THROUGH THE portal into her living room with Grady on her heels.

In the living room, the orange and green paisley curtains—gifted by her mother—blew inward with the early evening breeze.

In the foyer, the police tape joined in the dance. The place wasn't as barren as the day she and Tom moved in, but it was damn near close. Looters had come and gone during the night, relieving her of any unbroken furniture.

The carpet crunched beneath her sneakers as she made her way to the refrigerator. The doors were wide open with half the food spilled onto the floor. What a shame. Wasting food when there were starving children in her county grated on her nerves.

Beth stepped over the mess and closed both doors. She scanned the top freezer door for the slip of paper with her parents' cruise info. Her fingers traced the empty space between the Benny's Pizza magnet and the one from Walden Creek, TN.

Figures.

She turned to find Grady's face set in a worried frown. He raised his hand and wiped her cheek. She hadn't felt the tears.

"I'm so sorry, Beth." Grady's free hand squeezed her shoulder. "Tell me what I can do to make it better."

Beth looked around at the broken table and shattered glass. Aside from the new coat of paint, nothing in this space felt like *hers*. A sense of detachment settled in her brain, comfy and cozy and ready for the next new adventure. Her future no longer fit between these walls, but by Grady's side.

"I've always hated those curtains." Beth turned and placed her hands over his heart. "I have everything I need right here. The rest is just stuff."

Beth's heart skipped a beat when Grady's hand covered her hers. His eyes sparkled with joy as he pulled her into a warm embrace. She nuzzled into his chest, finally able to let this place go.

"You've always been my home, Beth. Even when I fought against fate for Tom's sake, it was always you." Grady's rumbling voice filled her with so much happiness it spilled down her cheeks. "Thank you for giving us a chance."

"Not gonna lie. I'm still scared. Scared that now, after we've accepted our relationship—took it to the next level—that something else is gonna come and fuck it up."

Grady pulled back and cupped her face in his large hands, his jaw twitching. "Not gonna happen. You know why?"

"Why?" Beth whispered hoarsely while Grady's intense blue-eyed gaze held her captive.

"Because our love is a fortress. Every brick was forged by years of friendship; the mortar was mixed with the magic of our ancestry. Our love was written in the stars and our souls made from the same stardust. The moment we accepted each other was the moment we won. Nothing and no one can take that away from us." Grady's thumbs traced her jaw as he leaned in to brush his lips against hers. "You are my person, Beth. My ride or die."

Beth's brain lost the signal to her tongue or she'd forgotten how to speak. Thank goodness her hands and lips still worked. She gripped Grady's shirt and erased the gap between them. As with every time they kissed, their magic charged the space surrounding them like sparklers on the fourth of July. She'd never tire of the sensations.

"Rich is probably wondering where we are." Grady was first to pull away, petting the back of her head and smoothing her hair. He whispered, "And I hear more people moving around outside. We should get going."

Despite having to cut things short, her frayed nerves were soothed. Beth strained her ears, but the loudest sound was the rapid thumping in her chest. Rather than say anything, she nodded against his chest before turning toward the portal. Beth took a step and grabbed Grady's hand, pulling him along.

They were about to step through the portal when the surface wavered, and Rich raced through, screaming, "Shut it down!"

His eyes were wide, face glistening with sweat. Grady pointed the stone at the portal, and chanted, "Claudere."

As it disappeared, Rich fell to his knees, panting. When his breathing was under control, he bounced his spooked gaze between Beth and Grady. "Something broke through my front door."

"Shit." Grady went to the window and peeked between the curtains. "Godsdammit."

"Did you see what it was?" Beth asked Rich as she joined Grady to peek through a crack in the curtains.

There were a few people on the street checking on the ones asleep on the sidewalk. In Beth's mind, 'sleep' was the easier denial. The twist in her gut suggested otherwise.

"Hell no. As soon as it started banging on the door, I hightailed it to youns." Rich stood and wiped his face on his shoulder sleeves. He hissed a soft curse.

"Your back. It's hurting again." Beth left the window to check on Rich. Fresh blood spotted the shirt. "We need to get Rich to the Grove."

"We should go to the precinct," Grady said at the same time. "I see curtains moving in multiple windows where the people hunkered down are checking on things. We won't get another chance like this."

"Grady," Beth pleaded. She knew once they were in the safety of their bubble, they would lose the chance to stock up without much interference, but Rich was like family. She would heal him, dammit.

"The calm before the storm?" Rich's deep voice sounded like a rock tumbler.

"Exactly." Grady glanced at her before giving his attention to Rich.

Beth pressed her lips in a line and crossed her arms. "Fine. Your way. But if Rich's back worsens, we go back so I can heal him again. If it means we miss out on an easy arms run, I will personally come back and magic the shit outta whoever gets in the way."

"That's my girl." Grady nodded in approval.

She gave him a wry smile.

Rich cleared his throat. "After what happened at my house, I don't wanna be anywhere near town when dark falls." Rich grunted when he walked forward. Beth opened her mouth to protest, but he waved her off. "I can keep going a little while longer."

Beth rolled her eyes and raised her hands in defeat. *Stubborn men.*

"What's the closest building to the sheriff's station we can portal to?" Beth followed the line of the street to the IGA's parking lot. From there, it was a five-block hike plus a river crossing. The bridge would leave them too open. "The bank is across the road. I've been there a couple of times."

"We don't have to go to the closest building." Grady's intense gaze pinned her in place. "I can take us inside."

Beth shivered, but not from being cold. Grady had kept his jail time experience close to the chest. Other than the firsthand knowledge of how awful the death ritual is, Beth only had Grady's bad feelings to fill in the gaps. "You don't have to. We can try somewhere else."

"I'll do it." Grady rolled the smooth, gray rock in his palm. "Having the element of surprise is better than being arrested for walking through the door."

"Guys," Rich interrupted. He held her living room curtain between his first two fingers just wide enough to peer through. "I think we're being hunted."

Beth's face flushed with pins and needles. Grady's warm hand went to the small of her back as they tip-toed to Rich's side. Beth squinted, searching for whatever Rich saw. A solid, larger than human black figure zipped from shadow to shadow. It avoided the remaining pockets of light.

"How can you be sure it's headed our way? Maybe it's scouting the area?" Beth asked as the tattered cloak got too close to the sun and started to smoke. "What do you think, Grady?"

"I think that man and his dog are gonna find out before we do."

"Who?" Beth asked. Grady gently gripped her chin and turned her face. Sure enough, a man with long hair shambled beside a limping dog. "Do you think they're good guys or bad guys?"

Rich leaned in, and whispered, "Looks like they're hurt. My money is on unfortunate travelers."

Beth's gaze shot between the two sights. The man and his dog were on a collision course with disaster if they continued. But if they intervened, Rich could be injured worse than he already was. They needed a diversion.

"If they keep coming this way, they're dead," Beth said aloud. Suddenly, a thought occurred. Rich said he was attacked at his house. They were only gone for a few minutes and now a creature was coming for them. What if Ja'azul's minions could sense their magic? "Grady, I think they're following us when we portal."

He pinched the bridge of his nose and closed his eyes. "What do you propose?"

"I portal to my parent's house on the other side of town. If I'm right, it'll draw the monster away. You two can grab Rich's vehicle and pick me up."

"Beth." Grady's warning tone had her shaking her head.

"Your dad's shop is a few blocks away. Wait until the coast is clear then make a run for it." Beth hugged him around the middle, pressing her cheek into Grady's chest until his woodsy scent was all she could smell. "This will work, it has to."

For a long moment, Grady was silent. Finally, he heaved a sigh and kissed the side of her head. "I don't like it, but I trust you."

The swarm of butterflies in her gut were happy at his admission.

He dropped his arms to her waist and stepped back. The pain in his eyes was almost unbearable as she backed away, but he'd said he trusted her. Letting Grady down wasn't an option.

"Stay safe." Beth opened the portal to her bedroom and stepped through before she could change her mind.

Grady's words, "you, too," followed her through.

Chapter 25

GRADY

Letting Beth go alone went against his baser instincts. Grady knew she could protect herself, it was the aftereffects of his brush with death at the hands of Eric Blaylock that had him rattled.

The portal Beth had opened disappeared, leaving her bedroom door open once again. The emptiness echoed in his soul like a phantom limb.

"It worked. The monster changed direction. It's headed in the direction of the Harper residence." Rich grabbed Grady's shoulder and squeezed.

They waited until the creature was out of sight before they shuffled down Beth's apartment stairs. Rich started in the direction of the man and his dog.

"Let's move."

"Wait," Grady whisper-yelled. "Car first, then the injured. They'll only slow us down."

Rich's mouth opened to argue but snapped shut with a curt nod. Grady sighed internally with relief. What he said was the truth, getting the car would be faster without covering the distance with two limping people. His main goal was getting to Beth before unwanted company.

As the men jogged the distance, the sun loomed over the horizon. If nothing slowed them down, they'd make it to his dad's shop and grab a few passengers well before sunset.

"Nearly there," Rich huffed; the sound of his steps was becoming more and more heavy.

Grady gazed over his shoulder. The older man sweated profusely while breathing heavily through his open mouth. The healing herbs must have lost their potency again.

"That's right. We've got this." Grady doubled his efforts to scent or hear for aggressors before any surprise attacks. The streets were as quiet as a graveyard. Normally, he liked the silent stillness cemeteries offered, but not like this. Too many familiar faces laid on the sidewalk for him to find any peace. "Where's your car?"

"Side of the building."

Grady looked toward the sky, to where the sun dipped into the mountain peaks. His skin prickled at the thought of a false dusk. Parts of the valley—namely downtown Mayes Hill—would be dark while the rest waited on true night to fall much later. The thought stabbed into Grady's right temple like an ice pick.

Out of his periphery, a portly man in overalls stumbled into view. He spotted Grady and lumbered in his direction.

"Incoming," Grady growled in warning.

Rich shot a look over his shoulder and picked up the pace.

When ol' Al in the overalls passed a dark alleyway, a woman's blood-curdling scream echoed. Grady peeked between the brick walls to see a purple-haired woman running straight toward them. Her hands were above her head, and it looked like she wielded knitting needles.

"Run!"

Grady sprinted across the road to Cooper's Welding Shop. The top of his head pounded in time with his pulse. *They should have listened.*

Rich pointed to the holey tarp, causing his keys to jangle softly. "Grab that corner. I'll take this one."

Grady grabbed his corner, but it smelled of rat droppings and piss. The old plastic came off quick and easy as it crinkled and popped with the movement. They tossed it on the ground in front of the hood and hopped inside.

Rich turned over the engine with a smooth purr. Gravel crunched beneath the tires as he backed onto the asphalt. A thunderous metal clank on the trunk of the cruiser had Grady jumping out of his skin.

"Shit." Rich floored it, leaving a black rubber line.

Grady looked in the rearview to see the man in overalls and crazy knitting lady giving chase.

Rich didn't stop at the four-way. The car's tires screeched as they slid around the left turn. "Do you think the man and dog are still alive?"

Grady shook his head. "I dunno. Probably not. We should go pick Beth up."

The car skidded to a stop, and Rich jumped out, mumbling something about 'Zeus.'

"Wait," Grady whispered harshly as he followed. Beth would never forgive him if anything happened to Rich. The man only had an inkling of how high the stakes were.

The streets were quiet again, save for the quick shuffle of a dog who wasn't moving well and of a man who was worse off. When Grady got a good look at the face hidden behind long, matted wavy brown hair, his jaw clenched.

"You."

"Please," the man wheezed before falling to his knees.

"Who is he?" Rich nodded toward the man as he loved on his best friend. Zeus's floppy tongue kissed his human's hands and face.

"I saw him at Beth's apartment the night I was arrested." Jealousy was a fickle thing, creeping up when you had other shit to worry about.

"My name...is Fennick." He pushed his hair back with one arm and winced.

Grady grimaced at the oozing black and green injury across his left bicep. Agnazar blade. Fennick stunk of the creature, but how the hell had he survived?

"Can you make it to the car?" Rich asked as he stood, breathing a little too heavily for Grady's liking. Sweat soaked the front of the man's shirt.

"Possibly." Fennick pushed the ground for leverage. His whole body shook with the effort, but the man didn't make it to his feet.

What would Beth do? He groaned silently and rolled his internal eyes.

"Here." Grady jumped to Fennick's right side and slid his arm around his waist.

Faint tingles—like the ones he felt every time Beth and he touched—played along his skin. He spasmed, nearly jerking away from Fennick like he'd been zapped by static electricity. Fennick's body tensed.

"Apologies, friend. Dry weather, I suppose." Fennick ground out, his voice barely above a whisper.

"Yeah. Dry weather." Grady parroted and readjusted his grip. Fennick's injured arm flopped uselessly at his side.

Grady knew better. Summers in the southeast were prone to pop-up showers, and they'd just had one. Fennick was hiding something. Grady thought it best to keep this one close, better to learn more about his new 'friend.'

"On the count of three." Grady braced, lifting Fennick with his knees. The stranger's chest heaved with effort.

The longer Grady chewed on Fennick's name, the more it held a hint of something familiar. He could almost grasp it, like trying to figure out which wood stain he'd used on a repair project when he only had vague colors to go by.

Suddenly, the wind shifted, bringing with it a cold current.

Rich opened the back door of his cruiser and ushered Zeus inside. The three of them—Fennick grunting with effort—lifted their chins, gazing at the ugly bruise in the sky.

Another of the blackened plasma balls fell from the crack. This one zipped across the sky like a Plinko chip, darting this way and that, until it fell somewhere around the copper mining plant. The earth beneath their feet vibrated. Glass windows rattled at the impact, sending car alarms into havoc. Too close to town for comfort.

A pit settled at the bottom of Grady's stomach. Sweat beaded his forehead. His wide eyes met Rich's with a wordless understanding. Rich nodded and rushed to help Grady get Fennick in the back seat next to Zeus.

"Where is...Beth?" The air rushed from Fennick as he struggled to sit upright.

"We're goin' to her right now," Rich replied, hopping into the driver's seat while Grady took the front passenger.

Grady turned to face the man in the back seat as Rich drove, the engine whining and tears squalling with each curve. Wet hair stuck to Fennick's face, sweat and blood soaked his clothes, but the unmistakable spicy aroma of cardamom and cinnamon were there below the surface, forcing a memory forward.

He remembered where he had heard the name Fennick Rayon...Fen... Curtis Putnam's attack on Beth. Grady and Tom had been at the Grove saying their goodbyes and laying ground rules for the future when it happened. *He* should have been there to protect Beth, not this stranger.

"I know who you are."

The quiet words left Grady's mouth before he could stop them. Stuffing them back inside was fruitless because Fennick raised his uncovered eye to meet Grady's gaze. Despite his injuries there was a threatening nature about the man that broke the stillness to Grady's inner peace. For the first time since being drugged, his panther counterpart paced in his inner mind, unsure whether Fennick was predator or prey. The air in the car became stale, heavy with their intense staring game that dragged on past the point of friendly.

"Two minutes out," Rich said, breaking their stalemate. His tires whined when he turned right at the stop sign.

Grady looked away first, uncaring if Fen took the win when Beth's safety mattered more. He counted the homes until the Harper's two-story Georgian-style house came into view. White, unchipped siding with navy shutters and meticulously landscaped yard. His heart skipped two beats when Beth slipped out the front door.

Rich eased his cruiser toward the curb, but Grady was out of the passenger door before it halted. He jogged to Beth, meeting her halfway. His arms wound around his safe place like a lock and key clicking together, burying his face in her hair.

"Where were you?"

"Sorry we're late."

They said at the same time.

Grady pulled back enough to cup Beth's face, searching her face for any sign of trouble. "We found them; found Zeus."

"And the man?" Beth's gaze went to the cruiser. Recognition passed over her face, but a frown tugged at her brows.

Grady's instincts wanted to keep Fennick far away from Beth, but not because of jealousy. "I know he saved you from Curtis. It's the only reason I couldn't leave him in the streets." Grady pursed his lips. "But that's where we're even. There's something off about him, Beth. He's dangerous."

"I dunno, Grady." Beth's frown deepened as she glanced back. "He seems...lost."

"I'm not making it up. The tingly feeling when we touch." Grady motioned between them. "I felt it when I helped him stand."

"That's strange. I felt the same tingles when he brushed my hand." Beth appraised Fen again before returning her attention.

"I think he's a guardian," Grady whispered, watching her face for a reaction.

Beth frowned, her lips going into line. "You may be right. Do you think we can trust him?"

Grady had chewed on that same question on the way over. "Short answer: No, but it doesn't matter. His arm is in bad shape. Agnazar blade."

Determination coated her eyes in glass. He knew the words were coming before she even opened her mouth.

"Let me see him."

"Beth." Grady's grip tightened around her waist. They didn't have time to stand around and check on injuries, especially with an Agnazar and possibly an Ungenth after them. But he couldn't bring himself to let this go. Too many unanswered questions; too many variables.

"Please, Grady." She firmly pressed her lips against his, effectively swallowing any argument he had. The heat radiating from his face cooled as his tight shoulders loosened. "I'm a healer. It's my *gift*. I can do this."

"I know, but we should find out who he is first."

"It's an Agnazar blade. What if he doesn't have that much time?" Her steely gaze challenged him, unyielding. Gods, he loved her fire, but not when he thought she was being reckless.

"Fine." Grady kissed Beth's forehead, pulling back to make firm eye contact. "But I'm watching him like a hawk. He pulls something, all bets are off."

"I expect no less from you, love."

She hooked their pinkies before departing with a confident stride. Grady followed close behind. The sooner they returned to the Grove, the better. Guns and ammo are great, but Beth needed to tap into her potential, hone her skills. When things came down to the nitty-gritty, firearms weren't what would stop what was coming.

Chapter 26

BETH

THE COOL AIR OUTSIDE coupled with the perpetual sepia made her nostalgic for fall. Beth hoped they'd be able to see the leaves change.

She eased the back passenger door open, bracing for bad but getting a lot worse. The stench of decaying flesh, that sweet, sickly scent that puts your senses on alert, saying, 'stay away because predators are going to finish off this dying creature' hit her full in the face.

The deep, festering slash across Fen's arm oozed with yellow pus, mixing with ribbons of blood as well as the black substance she knew well. Aberratious ichor.

The light smattering of freckles across Fen's skin was more prominent due to his pallidness. His chest rose in fits of short, quick breaths. Swallowing seemed to be an arduous task but happened often.

Zeus rested his head in Fen's lap, casting worried brown glances up at Beth. The sight would have been endearing except for the blood and rot.

Placing her hand on Fennick's forehead was like putting her hand on a red stovetop burner. She jerked her hand away, waving off the heat.

"Goddess, you're on fire. How are your insides not boiling?"

Fennick rasped what sounded like an attempt at a laugh, but it turned into a long, wheezing cough.

"Sorry. Try not to talk." She backed out of the backseat and straightened. One hand went to her hip, the other palmed her forehead. Her brain wasn't braining. She could really use some coffee right now. "Grady, we need someplace safe so I can heal Fen."

Grady gave Fen a good, hard look, lips pursed. After a long think session, he sighed, running his hand through his too-long black curls. "There's no safe place as long as shit's falling from the sky. We either leave him here—"

"We're not—" Beth argued along with Rich's echo.

Grady raised his hands, silencing them both. Beth never understood how he was able to command people like that. A natural talent, perhaps.

"He's not gonna make it, and using magic will draw more creatures." Grady splayed his hands open; a gesture Beth had seen many times before. He was at his wits end. "Unless somebody else has a better idea, I say we get him inside Beth's house where he's comfortable, then get outta dodge."

Beth didn't hate the idea. At least Fen wouldn't be left on the side of the road in some strange town to fend for himself. "Right. We deal with the threats and check on him later."

Fennick groaned, then fell across the seat and grabbed Grady's arm. His voice hoarse as he muttered three words that sent warning bells clanging inside Beth's mind "Must...perform...Ritual."

Grady hissed, 'Jesus,' as he jerked away from Fen's grip. "Ritual?" His gaze snapped to Beth's. "Who the fuck is this guy?"

His red-faced frown had Beth hugging herself.

"I have no idea," she answered quietly as the clues were laid on the table.

The tingles when they touched, not immediately dying after being attacked by an Agnazar. Both were guardian attributes, but the ritual part stumped her. The only one they knew was Ja'azul's.

Shivers rolled down Beth's spine as her feet carried her away from the cruiser. She had opened her home to Fen, broke bread with him. Had Fen been in league with the enemy this whole time?

"We need to figure shit out and fast, 'cause we've got company," Rich added, pointing to the road behind them with the raise of his chin.

Beth turned her head, and her blood ran cold. Barely two blocks away, an Agnazar waited, staring them down. The only reason it hadn't come closer was the river of golden sunlight in its path. Hatred pressed toward them like a prickly wave. Her muscles ignored her brain's demands, exactly the way Tom's had on her birthday hike. She couldn't look away, couldn't make her legs *move*.

As the seconds ticked away, the luminous orb giving them a buffer finally dipped below the mountaintop. A veil of shadow fell over the neighborhood, swallowing the pockets of sunlight like the rising tide.

Grady's strong arms wrapped around her middle and her feet left the ground. The moment she lost eye contact, the Agnazar's hold on Beth was broken. She sucked in air when her lungs remembered how to function. Grady made sure she was seated inside the vehicle before shutting her door.

"Floor it," Grady commanded at the same time the Agnazar sped toward them.

Rich slammed his foot on the pedal. The engine roared; car lurched forward. Grady's back passenger door slammed shut as they sped down the rural streets.

Grady's warm hand rested on her shoulder, squeezing gently in support. She placed her hand atop his and exhaled slowly. The hopelessness coating her insides with its oily viscosity sloughed away the further from the Agnazar they drove.

"I've never felt anything like that before." She swallowed the dry lump in her throat. "It was as if my will to live vanished, leaving a pit of nothingness so deep, that if I fell inside, I'd never stop falling. And it was cold...so cold."

Beth shuddered at the not-so-distant memory, tightening her hold on Grady's anchoring hand. Suddenly, her skin prickled with heat and the hairs on her arms raised. When looked in the rearview mirror, Fennick's gaze was trained on her, filled with pain. With longing. It was the same look Grady wore after her magic awakened, back when Tom was still alive. She tucked her chin against her shoulder, letting Grady's arm block Fen from view.

"Just keep driving," Grady instructed Rich, his voice thick. Shit. Their connection was wide open. She projected everything loudly.

"Where are we going?" Rich ground out between clenched teeth as he swerved to miss an oncoming car.

The tires squealed when Rich straightened his cruiser. Beth white-knuckled the grip-bar. The near collision had made her chest attempt to invert itself.

"Careful!" Grady barked, eyes so wide that his blues were swimming in white.

"I am *trying*." Rich blew out a harsh breath. "Didn't figure anyone else would be on the road. Hasn't been another car in hours."

In the rearview mirror, Fen's head lolled like a ragdoll. Zeus licked his hand, whining when he didn't respond.

"Grady, Fen needs help now or we're gonna lose him." Though they weren't sure *who* he actually was, Beth wasn't inclined to let him die yet, not until her debt was paid.

"Lion and Fox," Fen murmured, his voice like molasses. "Distillery. Go there."

Rich glanced at Fen, then Grady in the rearview mirror, waiting for the go-ahead. Grady studied her.

Beth raised a shoulder in indifference. "It's on the outskirts of town."

"And it's a fortified steel structure," Rich said, adding with a shrug, "I've been there a few times."

Grady closed his eyes for a beat, something he did when he needed to think on the fly without distraction. When he opened them again, he stared straight through the front windshield, and grumbled, "Do it."

New growth trees barely older than her passed by in a green blur. She remembered a time when there was no green except in the water. Toxins from the mining facility. Beth was eight when she first witnessed the devastating effects of acid rain. She couldn't let Ja'azul destroy her home, not when conservation efforts had come so far to restore the soil to her small, mountain town.

The world slowed as Rich turned down a newly paved two-lane road. In the distance, white steam rose from two silver smokestacks. As they neared, the rest of the two-story building came into view. The white walls with black trim looked like they were made of wood. Glass walls lined the front like the fragile sentries they were.

Beth's shoulders deflated along with her optimism. "I thought you said it was a steel building?"

At least the parking lot was barren and large enough for half the city to park trunk to hood.

"Looks can be deceiving." Fen's words tunneled underneath her skin like a parasite.

Damn right. Beth didn't have the energy to point out he was calling the kettle black.

"I'll find a side door; pick the lock," Rich offered, driving alongside the building.

Beth gnawed on her nails, watching as the glass walls ended where the wood walls began. When her teeth scraped to the quick, she winced.

"What is it?" Grady asked, his head poking between the headrests.

"Nothing, just bit my nail back too far."

He reached for it, turning the bleeding finger around for a better look. When he kissed it, her insides turned to goo. "Try not to do that anymore."

"Okay," she whispered, her cheeks warming.

Grady continued to hold her hand, letting his lips rest on the top of her knuckles. His gaze was trained straight ahead. Beth redoubled her efforts to watch for trouble, but her mind had become a foggy landscape. When had she last eaten a full meal or fed her caffeine addiction?

"Damn." Rich stopped beside a plain metal door with a keypad entry and beat his fist against the steering wheel. "This is the only access point besides the front door."

"8-9-6-5." Fen's frail voice broke the silence.

"What?" Beth turned in her seat, but Fen's eyes were closed.

"The code. 8-9-6-5." His Adam's apple bobbed when he swallowed. The effort of doing so seemed to take a lot of concentration. "Try it."

Rich put the car in park and jumped out before anyone could protest or ask questions. Beth was thankful. Fen's condition was deteriorating too fast, and her brain struggled to keep up.

"I want ya'll to go straight inside." Grady was close enough to Beth that the vibration of his voice plucked the thread connecting them. The low thrum sent a wave of calm through her, pulling a heavy sigh from her lungs.

"Wait. Why aren't you coming in with us?" Beth rotated in her seat, so she was face to face with her love. She ignored the hazel eyes in the passenger seat watching her every move.

"I'm going to put up some protective wards." Grady sealed her argument by placing his finger across her lips. "Five minutes. I promise."

Dangling Grady like a sitting duck created a vacuum in her chest. In the corner of her eye, every shadow became an agent of Ja'azul. If he used his magic, he'd be broadcasting to every creature in the vicinity.

"But—" she mumbled against his thick digit, making the corner of his mouth tick upward.

"Rich and Fennick are injured. Taking care of them is your job." Grady lowered his finger to her chin, hooking it underneath. "Protecting you is mine."

His words had her fluttering heart doing cartwheels. He leaned forward, sealing his promise with a chaste kiss.

"Be done in a jiffy." Grady hopped out before another argument could form. His hand was on the door when Fen raised his arm and called out, "Wait."

Grady's grip on the door tightened, but he paused. "What?"

"Building protected. Runes," Fen slurred before passing out.

"Fuck." Grady ran both hands through his curls and tugged. "Watch my back."

"I will." Beth joined Grady's side, watching the shadows with distrust.

"I'll get Fennick inside," Rich chimed as he ducked into the back seat and hoisted the man, tossing Fen's good arm across his shoulders. "Come, Zeus."

The dog whined when his paws landed on the pavement. Beth wanted to check and make sure they made it safely inside, but Grady raised his arms. He chanted something in a low voice that Beth couldn't make out. In a matter of seconds, the trees in her field of vision took on an orange glow.

"I'll be damned," Grady whispered.

"Orange means protection, right?" Beth asked, the urge to peek warred with her need to be vigilant.

"Yeah, and these are the same runes I learned. The same ones I use to protect my house."

Beth's insides squirmed with worry. "Does this mean what I think it does?"

"Afraid so." Grady put his hand on her shoulder, his face grave and stern. "You need to stabilize Fen, so we can get some answers."

Chapter 27

FENNICK

His world was plunged into a lake of fire and ice. Fennick's skin blistered internally while his body was wracked by shivers so intense, he was sure his teeth would shatter.

"Fen? Can you hear me?"

The voice of an angel pierced through the echoes of his screams.

His eyelashes fluttered, revealing the face in his dreams of late. The way Beth's brow was scrunched in worry made the place where his heart should reside ache. He lifted his chin and brought it back down with a wince.

"Good. As soon as I'm finished stabilizing you, we're going to a place called the Grove."

"N-not...safe," Fen stuttered through his chattering teeth.

"I promise it is. The monsters can't—"

"For...m-me," Fen finished in time for his body to convulse. Zeus whined and jumped off the couch. He squeezed his eyes shut, riding the waves of agony.

Cool small hands held his head in place. Tiny zaps flooded his synapsis like electric fireflies. The icy waters turned into a comforting gel, creating a protective layer against the Agnazar's poison. Breathing became a less arduous task, *thank the gods*, but the gash in his arm still had a vendetta against his mobility. He was certain he would lose the limb, a thought which served to put him on a downward spiral. Many of his alchemical creations required two hands. He would never be able to work again.

"How's your patient?" Grady asked, towering over him with a look of someone who had *caught* the cat drinking the cream.

The baby guardian thought he was intimidating. Codswallop. Amusing? Yes. Delectable? Absolutely. Attainable? Sadly, no. If—by some miracle—he survived this day, Fennick doubted his charm would assuage Grady.

"Well enough we can move him after you're done." Beth replied, her inflection ending with a higher pitch. Her movements seemed slower, more purposeful as she heavily leaned against the desk.

"I'm sensing a 'but.'" Grady dropped his arms to place his hands on his hips.

"Look at his arm, Grady."

Fennick braved a glance. She was right. His arm looked ghastly. Most of his shoulder and arm were caked in dried blood. Where the flesh of his bicep was split wide, the skin had turned black, leaking away from the injury like fine roots. In the valley between, yellowish-green pus pulsed in time with his rapid heartbeats. The attention caused it to ache more fiercely. He prodded the flesh beside the wound and gagged. It smelled of spoiled vinegar and cat food.

"His arm needs to be drained before that shit gets into his blood stream," Rich mumbled behind his hand, pinching his nose shut.

He dug into his pocket and pulled something out. In the palm of his upturned hand sat a pocketknife. "Sorry, kids, but I'm only human. I ain't touchin' that."

"I'll do it." Beth took the knife and hefted it, checking its weight. Under her breath, she whispered, "You can do this."

Fennick took a calming breath. Beth's gentle nature would transfer to her tender care. There was nothing to worry about.

Grady dragged a plastic trashcan around the desk to Fennick's side. "Here. A bucket."

"Thanks." Beth gulped, her eyes wide beneath her shimmering forehead. "Okay."

She studied the wound and winced. Whatever she saw caused her to hesitate. Glancing at Fennick, she asked, "Do we have something for the pain?"

"Just do it," Fennick quickly answered. The sooner they got the vile substance out of his body, the better.

"This is gonna hurt," Beth warned as she got into position. "Ready?"

"Ready." Fennick gritted his teeth, holding as still as the dead.

The anticipation chewed at his nerves like a dog with a fresh bone, insistent and methodical. His stomach bubbled and turned, sending bile up his esophagus.

"Here we go," Beth whispered, pressing the knife's edge against the side of the wound.

When she added her fingers to the other side, pushing against the blade, Fennick groaned. Vomit swelled up his throat, but he kept it down. His face was slick with sweat. Heat radiated from his body despite the blood in his veins freezing.

Beth pressed harder. The pinching coaxed a pitiful whine, but he held firm as she moved along the gash at a snail's pace.

A glob of pus hit the bottom of the empty trash bin with a wet plop. The air thickened with the pungent odor, causing the room to groan. Fennick turned his face, adding the contents of his stomach to the bucket.

"Fen?"

"Don't." He waved Beth off. They had to finish.

"If you want me to stop"

"Keep...going." No matter that it felt like Beth was rending his arm from its socket, he would take this torment. He deserved it for failing the goddess for so many years.

Beth's furrowed gaze shot across to Grady, who shrugged. With a puff of air to clear the lock of hair over her eye, she continued her treatment.

As the poison was expunged, his screams filled the room. He barely noticed Grady's pacing or that, at some point, Rich had left the room with Zeus.

Fennick shut his eyes so tightly there was only whiteness. His throat was well worn to the sinew. When his hoarse voice was no more than mousy squeaks, he threw in the towel.

"Please," Fennick begged, his merciful plea frail as an old man staring into the face of death. He hated it. Hated how weakness had robbed him of his virility.

"Finished," Grady announced at the tale of his thoughts. "Beth drained all she could."

Fennick heaved a slow sigh. He engaged the muscles, commanding his arm to raise. Despite the stiffness, the lightness was immediately apparent. Strength returned in small doses, first straightening his back.

He peered into the wastebasket. Ribbons of brownish-yellow floated amidst blackish-red fluid like oil in water. Fennick was certain half of his bodily fluids filled the receptacle.

The edges of his sight wavered. Raised voices became muffled behind the glass wall surrounding him. Oxygen became scarce. His brain commanded him to sleep...so he obliged.

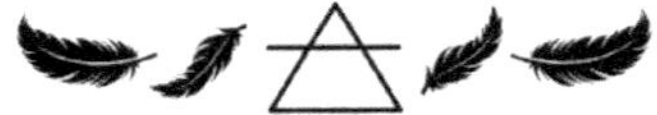

"We both recognize what he is, Beth. We aren't taking him to the Grove until he's awake. We need answers."

Pragmatic. That would be Grady.

"Restraining him will only aggravate his injuries. He's already lost too much blood. I don't care who he is, I won't let him die when I can prevent it."

Noble and righteous. Elizabeth.

"What did he say?"

Deep baritone... Zeus's owner.

"Fennick? Did you call for me?"

Oops. Did I say these things aloud?

"Yes, you did." Beth stifled a relieved laugh. "How are you feeling?"

Fennick's arm itched like an incessant mosquito bite. His fingers twitched, looking to appease the spot, but he knew better than to aggravate the sore. He opened his eyes against the bright sunny sky. No, these were soft LED lights. The ones that have the low hum that drives him mad.

Dark lumpy forms stood above him, surrounding his head. The one closest to him smelled of lavender and vanilla. Her mere presence made his chest swell with warmth.

"Eliza—" He caught himself, remembering how upset she had been when he called her by her formal name. "Beth, please, forgive me."

"See? I told you he was hiding shit." Grady's hulking shape came closer, drawing Beth away. They continued their heated discussion outside of earshot.

"Hey. Fen, right?" The dark-skinned man wearing a crown of wisdom gave him a stern eye. "Look, whatever it is you're hiding, better to get it out in the open. These kids are good folks, but they can do things I had only dreamed of seeing until recently."

"What is your name, sir?" Fennick asked, noting the man's hesitation before he averted his gaze to Zeus, who was curled into a ball in the corner. His big brown glossy eyes watched Fennick with concern.

"Rich." The older gentleman wiped a hand down his face and put it on his hip. "I didn't get a chance to thank you for saving Zeus. So, yeah. Thanks for keeping an eye out for my boy."

"The pleasure was mine." Fennick's sight gained focus. He studied the dog with fondness before bringing his attention back to Rich. "He is most intelligent and very loyal."

"Heh, yeah. That he is." Rich chuckled half-heartedly. "Listen, these two are dealing with enough trouble without you puttin' more on 'em."

Rich thumbed over his shoulder where Grady hung his head low while Beth rubbed his arms. The sight pricked Fennick's chest with regret. By the time the universe finished with him, he would be little more than a pincushion.

"I will reveal all." Fennick tore his gaze away from the couple's embrace. "Please, tell Beth and Grady I am ready to talk."

Fennick mustered the courage to sit upright. It came easier than he had hoped and he wondered how much energy Beth had wasted on him. He did not have time to ponder long, for the one in question stopped a few feet from where he lay, on an uncomfortable couch bolstered with every throw pillow in the building.

"Okay, pretty boy. Talk." Grady crossed his large biceps over his chest.

The handsome young man was a morsel, but there was no getting past his tough exterior. No doubt it was born of a long line of toxic masculinity. Fennick preferred his partners to be of a softer nature anyway.

Taking a deep breath, Fennick began at the end.

"I have fulfilled my dire purpose, to remind you of what happens when you put your faith in false gods who fell from distant stars, whose constellations have never been touched by humanity, and whose planets are named as such as those our tongues are unable to utter let alone understand. The master, Ja'azul, manipulated my need for vengeance and my thirst for knowledge and power, to gain his freedom. Now, I fear, you all are doomed to pay the price, for I am his deliverer...his Harbinger."

He poured forth the words, swaddling them in the sorrow he had carried for the past century. He hoped to appeal to their good-naturedness, their willingness to forgive. Neither gave him a clue. Both wore blank masks as his proclamation wormed into the thinking center of their brains. They could not hide the fear seeping through their pores. It was a taste all too familiar to Fennick.

"This is the part where you become angry or despair." Fennick scoffed, bowing his head in defeat.

He expected Grady to throw fists, for violence to be put upon him. He did not expect Beth to lay a hand on his unharmed shoulder.

"You are a victim, Fen. Ja'azul used you just as he's used humanity for a millennia." Beth smiled but wore pity in the creases.

Fennick did not want her sympathy. He wanted her love, her companionship. But she was meant for another, just as he was meant for Heliotta. He had lost his heart, his magic, *everything*. And to what purpose?

"No. I am not a victim, Beth. I am a fool. The world was at my fingertips, but I could not see for the wool over my eyes."

He curled into a ball and gasped at the sensation, the stinging in his eyes. He had not cried in centuries, but here he was, trembling like a terrified child. Broken into so many pieces, he dared not to breathe around them, lest he lose another part of his humanity.

Suddenly, Beth wrapped her arms around his shoulders, but he could not bring himself to reciprocate. Grady's heavy sigh was followed by a large hand on his back, then another. Zeus's wet nose found his cheek, and he licked the tears.

Salvation lay at his feet, surrounding him by people he barely knew. They were the only ones who gave a damn about him, who cared an ounce. Even Grady's compassion—which was no doubt moved only by Beth's—was something. A crumb.

He would take it. Not only for himself, but for Beth, for Grady, for Zeus and his human, Rich and all the other people of this planet he had hastily damned in the name of revenge.

There, in the bottomless pits where the husk of Fennick's soul slumbered, a fire lit. It burned, consumed him from the inside out. He was not going down without a fight. Not this time.

"Please, let me stand."

They did more than let him stand, these people, his friends, raised him up. When on his feet, he stood tall and...humbled.

"Shall we unearth such unpleasantries in the employee lounge? There is a considerable amount of information I must relay before we dare attempt to defeat the enemy."

Fennick did not miss the way Beth and Grady studied each other before answering. The love conveyed in the way Grady slid his arm around her waist and kissed the side of her head. Her trusting gaze as she closed her eyes with a soft smile.

"Lets. I have a feeling whatever you have to say will go down better with food," Beth offered.

"Right this way." Fennick nodded, stuffing his insecurities back inside his skeleton closet.

As he led the way to his uncertain future, he held his head high. Dignity was something he had taken for granted in the past. No longer.

Chapter 28

GRADY

GRADY SAW THE WAY Fennick watched Beth, tracking her every move. The man practically had cartoon hearts in his eyes. Grady couldn't blame him. Not when he'd done the same while his best friend was alive.

Is this what he did to Tom? Probably. At least Beth hadn't responded to Fen's advances in any way to say she'd kept her options open.

"Can you not feel how alone he is? According to Myrtle's teachings, guardians weren't meant to serve the goddess alone. He's obviously hurting. Just think of how happy he'll be when we reunite him with Heliotta?" Beth had said moments before Fennick's breakdown.

Grady stared at the back of the mystery man's head as he navigated the halls as if he owned the place. Even slightly hunched with his injured arm cradled close to his chest, Fennick had the natural gait of a king. Graceful movements filled with purpose and strength. A man who got things done no matter what was in his way.

Zeus whined and ran past the group. He sniffed around until he found a potted plant, and lifted his leg.

"Down, boy! Don't piss that!" Rich huffed as he jogged past Grady.

The second round of herbal paste had colored the back of his clean gray shirt an earthy brown. At least the bleeding had stopped.

Fennick let out a hearty belly laugh that caused Grady's face to warm.

Of course he has a great laugh to go with his perfect hair. Grady grumbled to himself.

"This door leads to an enclosed garden. Zeus will be safe to do his business here." Fennick pushed on the horizontal metal bar. The door opened to a grassy courtyard with a glass dome.

Zeus didn't wait for Rich, zipping outside as fast as his four paws would allow.

Beth followed Rich, pausing to admire the greenery. Like always, Grady followed the pull of the thread connecting them to her side.

Fennick stopped him before he stepped through. "You should know, many times, I have attempted to sway the affections of your young beauty."

Grady pinned Fennick with a frown, unhappy with the man's power play. "She—"

"Not to worry." Fennick halted his argument with a raised hand, adding hastily, "for Beth is completely enamored by your rugged handsomeness and beguiling charm."

"Are you making fun of me?" Grady's face flushed with heat. He wasn't a brawler, but he also wouldn't stand for someone blatantly insulting him.

"On the contrary," Fennick chuckled before flashing him a seductive grin. "I find there is no harm in casual flirtations."

"Why?" Grady's frown deepened.

He had no issues with men liking men, or women liking women. Love is love. He just didn't bat for the home team. Never had. He'd also never had another man hit on him. Fennick's advances tickled untouched corners of his brain, confusing the hell out of him.

"Because it is *fun*, and I have not allowed myself the simple pleasures in life for so long." After a long pause, Fennick added, "Much to my chagrin, you are also a fruitless endeavor. Who could compete with the likes of such a pure soul as hers?"

Fennick raised his chin toward Beth. Her hands were on her hips, and she wore a smile brighter than the sun. She leaned back as one hand went to her mouth, covering her chime-like giggle as Rich lectured Zeus on what was considered a proper 'marking' spot.

The fire fueling Grady's hot-headedness fizzled. Joy surrounded her like an invitingly bright beacon. He wanted every day with the love of his life to be filled with this kind of carefree happiness, and he would fight until his last breath for this future. Perhaps Fennick would have some useful information to help them achieve it.

"Please tell me there's food in the lounge." Beth hooked her pinkie finger with Grady's, gifting him with her brilliant smile. His heart fluttered.

Grady glanced at Fennick, who gave him a toothy grin and a wink, causing Grady's cheeks to heat.

"Did I miss something or is Fen trying to woo you now?" Beth teased through their mind-link.

Grady slipped his free hand around the nape of her neck and pulled her flush against him. Pressing his forehead against hers, he stared deep into her eyes. Placing a tender kiss on her lips, he whispered, "Absolutely not."

He would never tire of that playful twinkle in Beth's eyes, nor the way she molded perfectly into his embrace. There were no doubts he and Beth were made for each other.

Fennick closed the garden door and proceeded down the hallway. "If you will follow me, the lounge is this way."

They passed two more doorways before Fennick turned right and disappeared through a pair of double push doors. Grady peeked through the tall rectangle window and raised his eyebrow. Pushing the door open, he couldn't help but smile when Beth squealed in glee.

The employee breakroom was more of an industrial chic cafeteria. Along one wall was a long countertop with a modest breakfast bar and commercial coffee station. A few vending machines with various drinks and quick bites lined the next wall, leading to a U-shaped kitchenette with an extra-large refrigerator. A lush sectional hugged the opposite corner around a square coffee table littered with magazines. The center space was filled with round tables and chairs fitting four to six people at each. When full, the space could easily hold thirty people.

"Please, everyone, help yourself." Fennick gestured widely to the room once they were all inside.

"Dibs on the coffee machine," Beth claimed, kissing Grady's cheek before taking off.

Love welled behind his ribcage, squeezing the air from his lungs. *That woman and her coffee.*

"You should replenish as well."

Grady tore his gaze away from Beth to look at Fennick. The man studied him as though he was a puzzle to solve. He didn't like to be under scrutiny, so he changed the subject. "Won't the owner be upset about us stealing?"

Fennick's smile added an amused glint to his eyes. "Not if you have permission, which I have given."

"Hot damn," Rich whispered, his face bright like a child on Christmas morning. "I knew I liked you, Fen."

"When people learn who I am, they usually do." Fennick's dry comment grabbed Grady's attention.

"Are you for real?" Grady prodded, cocking an eyebrow. "You're the owner?"

Fennick tipped his head in a nod. "There is much you do not know. For now, please indulge, and I will divulge more."

Grady's stomach growled when the scent of ground beans filled the cafeteria. Knowing Fen wasn't all uppity about his wealth earned him a point in Grady's respect book. The more he learned about this stranger, the more Fennick became a curiosity, albeit a dangerous one.

"Thanks," Grady said with a nod, adding, "You and me might be able to get along some day."

"I look forward to the day." Fennick's grin reached his eyes. "Please. Eat."

Grady made his way to Beth's side. She handed him a steaming cup of aromatic black coffee and a plate with a microwaveable meal. He popped it in the second microwave and punched the buttons. While they waited, he sipped the heady brew. Fennick sure didn't skimp when it came to coffee beans.

"I think this was ground fresh this morning." Beth pointed to an air-tight glass jar with a spoon slot. Beside them were bags of roasted coffee beans and a grinder. "We should get our own coffee grinder, 'cause this brew has me spoiled after one cup."

Grady's chest warmed at the thought as it morphed into cool nights by the fireplace, bringing Beth a cup of the world's best coffee. They'd cuddle together and talk about the day, maybe see if they can winterize the Grove so they can watch the snow fall.

"I'd like that very much," Beth whispered over her cup. The faraway look on her face and the slight grin told Grady she was already there with him.

The microwaves beeped, signaling the end of a happy thought in exchange for full stomachs. Soon, everyone was settled around the table, and Fennick cleared his throat.

"If you do not mind, I would prefer to get straight to the thick of things."

"By all means." Grady waved his hand across the table, giving Fennick the floor.

Beth and Rich nodded their agreement.

Giddiness sapping the air from Grady's brain. If he was right and Fennick was a guardian, he had so many questions. Learning new things—especially anything dealing with occult practices—was more than a hobby. It had become Grady's obsession. His practices with Myrtle over the years only magnified his desire to learn. When he discovered his destiny, he sought to become the best possible guardian.

Fennick stood, rolling his shoulders back and paced. He cleared his throat again.

"For what I share today, I pray you keep an open mind," Fennick began, casting furtive glances at he and Beth. "I am what you are."

"You're the first," Grady added, and Beth gripped Grady's leg beneath the table.

"First what?" Rich asked while chewing his burger.

"The first lightbringer guardian," Beth supplied, studying Grady.

"Yes." Fennick tucked his chin, hiding his face behind his mahogany locks.

"This is good news, right?" Rich straightened in his seat, his brows dipping in confusion. "Three magic users are better than two, no offense."

"None taken," Grady said as his emotions bounced between caution and what ifs.

"I have no magic." Fennick's declaration burst Grady's bubble.

"What do you mean you don't have magic?" Beth asked. Grady placed his hand over hers, keeping it on his knee.

"It is a long story, one which I will regale you with shortly." Fennick faced away from them, rocking on his heels as he studied the ceiling. "About a thousand years ago, magic was bountiful and used by all. Then Ja'azul crash-landed on our planet."

*This is old news...*Grady thought, biting his peeled boiled egg in half. Beth looked at him, scrunched her nose, and gave a little shake of the head. His lips ticked up, imagining her admonishing her students the same way.

Fennick whirled back around and paced beside the table. Beads of sweat gathered above his upper lip.

"The devastation he caused left a scar on the land large enough to put the power in flux. The goddess, Circe, heard the cries of her people and found Ja'azul siphoning the souls of those who were in his path." Fen paused to study each one in turn. When he got to Grady, he didn't linger like he did with Beth and Rich. He averted his eyes.

"A great battle ensued. Circe grew weak, unable to single-handedly defeat Ja'azul, for he has regenerative powers. So, she did the only thing she could to ensure victory: she took every drop of magic from the earth. With her renewed strength, Circe locked Ja'azul away until a time in which he could be banished."

Grady's hand paused. His black coffee sloshed over the side of the cup and onto the plastic table top. He hadn't learned anything about regenerative powers or draining all magic.

No wonder Circe was the one to imbue guardians with power. It's all that's left.

Grady's coffee mug lowered to the table, forgotten as he gave Fennick his undivided attention.

"Over the next three hundred years, the world forgot the tales of space rocks and catastrophe. Magic became myth, fantastical bedtime stories meant to lull children to sweet slumber. Meanwhile," Fen said, stopping to hold up his pointer finger before continuing, "Ja'azul spent this time fooling lesser-minded humans into servitude, therefore, gaining power. When he was on the verge of breaking free, Circe came to Heliotta and I. She imbued us with a portion of her magic, thus creating the first lightbringer guardians."

"Wait." Beth stretched her neck, cocking her head as if she hadn't heard right. "I thought the first battle with Ja'azul was between the guardians? Myrtle didn't say anything about a battle before that."

"Exactly." Grady nodded. His question basically came straight from her mouth. "How come we weren't taught this part of our history?"

Fennick's eyes widened. His mouth opened to reply, but he snapped it shut. He blinked away the shocked expression from his face. "The Ritual of Passing. It should have revealed this information."

"Let's table the rest of your history lesson so you can explain the Ritual of Passing." Grady wasn't sure if he should be pissed or not. Based on Fennick's reaction, he was leaning toward a hard 'yes.'

"It—it is the *Ritual of Passing*...given to us by Circe." Fennick had his palms splayed out before him as if he were explaining how water boils or how rain came from clouds.

Grady shook his head, fighting off the sinking feeling in his stomach.

"The Ritual ensures there is no gap in knowledge." Fennick's frown deepened when he saw Beth's blank stare. Grady shrugged. "It is performed before a guardian perishes...to-to preserve the magical learnings of the previous guardian. Surely, you have heard of such a thing?"

"Nope." Grady glanced at Beth. It was her turn to shrug.

"Then how in the bloody hells did you learn magic?" Fennick's voice rose as he raised his arms in frustration, hissing when his injured arm went too far.

"We have the archives. A cave containing all written knowledge of the previous guardians," Grady answered. Until now, he'd never questioned why they spent years going through the journals. He'd assumed it was the reason time worked differently in the Grove.

Fennick cursed under his breath. He placed his palms on the tabletop. "Heliotta's writings, do you have them so that I may read what came after...after my absence?"

"We do, they're in the archives. But..." Beth trailed off, her eyebrows raised as she questioned Grady.

He wasn't shy enough not to rip the bandage off the touchy subject. "You can talk to

Heliotta. She's still there."

You could hear a pin drop in the room.

The next thing Grady knew, Fennick was falling. He leapt out of his seat and grabbed Fen underneath his arms from behind. Fen's head rolled from side to side while Grady dragged him to the sofa. While he fitted Fen's upper half, Beth draped his long legs over the armrest on the opposite end.

"Is fainting a habit of Fennick's?" Rich asked, biting another chunk off his dinner roll.

"I haven't known him very long. The times I have been around him he didn't faint." Beth wrung her hands. Worry seeped into their bond.

Grady clasped her hands in his. "We should talk to Myrtle and Heliotta. See what their side of the story is."

"Grady, how do we tell who's giving us the truth?"

He took a moment to consider. "I can hear when people's heartrates increase. Unless Fennick is really good at hiding his pulse rate, he wasn't lying. I'll do the same with Myrtle and Heliotta."

"What then? Fight Myrtle and Heliotta if they turn hostile? According to Fennick, both guardians are needed to perform the Ritual of Passing, and I have *two* predecessors. We can't kill them, or I won't be powerful enough to fight Ja'azul or his armies with you. And we can't die without it dooming the rest of humanity."

"Fennick and I will do our Ritual before we call on them." He turned his attention to Fennick, who was still sound asleep.

Embracing his inner asshole, Grady slapped Fennick across the cheek. The man was still out like a light. "Never mind."

"Grady!" Beth gasped, her eyes cartoonishly round as she gazed at him behind her hands.

"What?" Grady shrugged, pretending he didn't feel a smidge of satisfaction at his cheap shot. "It always works in the movies."

"This isn't a movie," Beth replied with a slight chuckle. "Gods, Grady. I'm gonna go find an ice pack."

With an eyeroll and a kiss on the cheek, Beth left Grady to figure out the next step.

"Honesty is always the best policy," Rich chimed in, wiping his hands on his pants legs. "Tell them the truth, that Fennick wandered into town and mentioned the Ritual. If they're supposed to be the good guys, they'll understand."

Grady dropped his chin to his chest. It wasn't as simple as that, but there wasn't enough time to explain. They'd wasted enough already.

After this next obstacle, I'll explain the rest to Rich.

"Rich, can you stay with Fennick while we meet with the elder guardians?"

"Of course." Rich's eyebrows crinkled. "How much do you trust him?"

That was an excellent question. Normally, Grady had a good sense of a person's character. Fen confused his people-radar. As far as Grady could tell, Fennick believed his story to be truth.

"As far as I can throw him." Grady studied for any sign he was awake. They were talking at normal volume, and Fen was unmoving outside of the normal chest rise or the occasional quick rolling behind his eyelids. "Just keep an eye on him and trust your instincts."

"Can do. Y'all be careful." Rich clapped Grady on the back.

Beth passed them and knelt to balance the paper towel-wrapped ice pack on Fen's cheek. When she stood, Grady held his hand out to Beth. She laced their fingers without hesitation.

"Ready to do this?"

"As I'll ever be."

Things had to work out, because if shit went sideways with the elder guardians, Grady didn't have a backup plan.

Chapter 29

BETH

"Are you seeing what I am?" Beth moved closer, her hand hovering in front of the opaque outline of the archive's door.

Every other time they visited, revealing the way required her to use magic. Not today.

"I am. I'm betting it's because our magic has changed." Grady raised his chin, eyes sparkling with his sly grin. "Go ahead."

Beth pressed her hand flat against the center of the door, and the image wavered. It hardened under her palm then continued spreading until it was completely solidified.

"Cool."

Grady gave her his signature lopsided grin and opened the door. "Ladies first."

As soon as they were inside the archives, the sound of two pairs of feet scampering toward them echoed in the chambers.

"Beth? Grady?" Myrtle's voice came seconds ahead of her. Heliotta appeared right behind her. Both looked frazzled. "Thank the goddess!"

Myrtle nearly stumbled as she hugged them the moment they came within arm's reach. Beth's chest tightened. She focused on breathing normally, watching Grady for cues.

"What's going on?" Grady asked as his gaze passed over the room. Beth's shoulders loosened when he pulled away from the hug, giving her an out to do the same.

"Much, I'm afraid. But we will get to that in a moment." Myrtle stepped back, smoothing invisible wrinkles on her dress skirt. Her gaze darted to Beth before averting to some speck on the wall. She clasped her hands in front and walked to the nearest bookshelf. "I see you two have completed the connection. Which also means—"

"We have no idea how much time has passed since we last saw you," Heliotta interrupted, appearing beside Myrtle. "The walls of Ja'azul's prison are weakening. His influence is leaking into the world like a poison. If you two are to be ready, you cannot delay."

"About that." Beth glanced at Grady before continuing. "A portal opened over town today. There are creatures falling from it, but it's sporadic and not often."

"There must be forces muddying the waters." Heliotta's eyes widened as she paced. "I should have *seen* this coming."

Myrtle shot them an apologetic glance before grasping Heliotta by the shoulders. "We cannot change what has transpired. Whether Ja'azul is free or not, the younglings still need our guidance."

Heliotta's face paled. She stared past Myrtle at nothing. Beth thought she had zoned out, but Heliotta whirled on her, intense blue eyes keenly studied her. Without warning, she placed her palms against Beth's temples. The mad-woman's eyes turned milky white.

"What—" Myrtle started, but Heliotta dropped her head back, staring at the ceiling without viewing it.

Beth tensed, afraid to move even when Heliotta's nails pressed into her scalp. She didn't want to interrupt the elder, but Beth had never been a fan of movies like 'The Ring' or 'The Grudge.' And Heliotta was giving her the major jitters, making her heart gallop like a race horse.

She implored Grady to help with her wide-eyed gaze and plucked the thread tying their fates together. Myrtle placed her hand on his arm and stopped him from interfering with a small shake of her head.

Heliotta gasped. Beth's attention snapped back to the woman holding her hostage. She wished she'd gathered power before visiting, but how was she to know the eccentric witch had lost more marbles?

"I see a vast, calm ocean. It stretches on and on without end." The raven-haired woman's face scrunched in pain. She sputtered nonsensical words as her shoulders and head jerked around like she was possessed.

Beth's blood ran cold. She didn't want Heliotta to touch her anymore, but her arms were stuck to her side by some immobile force. *"Grady, help!"*

Heliotta's fingernails dug deeper into Beth's scalp, making her whimper. The woman's raven-colored hair levitated like puppet strings, making Beth's skin crawl. Microscopic scratches inside of Beth's skull caused her mouth to open in a soundless scream as pain coated her brain like an oil slick.

Grady's heavy hands landed on Beth's shoulders and pulled her backward. She fell against his chest, clawing at his arms for warmth. Heliotta drew in a long, sharp breath. Her eyes rolled to the back of her head. For half a heartbeat, time paused. Suddenly, she dropped to the ground like a ragdoll with a thump.

Myrtle fell to Heliotta's side, cradling her head in her lap. Myrtle's whispers were too quiet to understand as she caressed Heliotta's cheek.

"What the hell happened?" Grady asked in their secret way, staring with a frown at the elder guardian.

Beth turned into his chest, gripping the soft fabric of his shirt. She took a shuddered breath. She felt violated, but Grady's earthy cedarwood scent helped to take the edge off. Myrtle checking on Heliotta first only deepened the wound. *I don't think she was supposed to peek inside my brain like that. It felt wrong.*

"I won't let her touch you again. Not without permission."

"What about the Ritual? Fennick didn't give us specifics on how it's done. What if we need to be touching to transfer magical knowledge?"

"We'll cross that bridge when we get there." Grady lifted one hand to caress the back of her head, the other tightened around her waist. The security of his embrace, the love radiating from his self like a comforting hum...Beth wished she could bottle the feeling of contentment for emergencies.

Heliotta gasped and her eyelids flew open. Her icy blue and penetrating gaze caused Beth to look away. The woman sat abruptly, pushing Myrtle away to scramble to her feet. "I must check on something."

The skirt of her simple garnet-colored dress swirled when she stormed out of the sitting area.

"Wait!" Myrtle called out, but to no avail. Turning to the others, she sighed. "Apologies. When Heely gets a notion to study something, she delves deeply into it. Shall we catch up?"

Grady unwound his arms but kept Beth's hand tucked firmly in his. He steered them to the loveseat while Myrtle took the chair closest to them.

"Why don't you start where things left off? What's going on in the outside world?" Myrtle propped her elbow on the arm of the chair, resting her jaw on her fist.

Beth's brain still itched from whatever Heliotta had done. She wasn't in the mood for conversational catch-up, so Grady filled Myrtle in with all that had happened since their last visit, beginning with Tom's death. He left out Fennick's version of history. They also opted to keep his being a fellow guardian close to the chest.

"When we left, Fen was passed out at his distillery, but he's tough. He survived an Agnazar blade long enough to get help." Grady leaned back to put his arm around Beth's shoulder. She snuggled into his side, resting her head above his heart.

Myrtle leaned as far forward as possible, enraptured by their news. She addressed Beth with pinched brows, "What is your take on this Fen fellow?"

"Same as Grady. Fennick is resilient to have held out as long as the walk back to town." She tucked a loose hair behind her ear. "He's not done anything to warrant concern outside of his odd behavior."

Beth locked down her not-so-fun encounter with Fennick. Grady getting angry over slight bruising would only sow mistrust, and Fen had already apologized.

"Interesting," Myrtle responded quietly as she reclined. "What is his surname?"

"Rayon. Fennick Rayon," Beth answered, studying her mentor closely.

Myrtle's face was a rollercoaster of emotions. Her frown deepened. After a heartbeat, her mouth slackened, and her eyes widened. She snapped her jaw shut and straightened in her chair, regaining a mask of composure though her hands shook as she placed them in her lap.

Movement in the doorway caught Beth's attention. "Yes, Myrtle." Heliotta stood in the frame with a dark cloud hanging overhead. Her eyes shimmered with unshed tears. "Fennick was...*is* my beloved," she whispered.

After how Heliotta terrified her earlier, Beth had every right to be a petty person, but that wasn't her nature. "If you want to be reunited, we can bring him here."

"No. He cannot pass." Heliotta shook her head, knocking the welled tears loose. "Goddess, forgive me, for I have made a grave mistake."

Myrtle rose to her feet, her back ramrod straight. "What have you done, Heliotta?"

"I have doomed us all." Heliotta felt her way past stacks of books, bumping into an end table on the other side of the room before slumping haphazardly into a reading chair.

"How is this possible?" Myrtle demanded; her fists balled at her side. "There have only been three male guardians and three female guardians in existence and the former must pass on before the next is chosen. So, again I ask, how is this possible?"

"It is a long and weary story." Heliotta's watery gaze hovered on Grady before lingering on Beth as if she were to blame. The woman tapped the side of her head with such force Beth thought she'd leave a dent. "But you already know, do you not? *He* told you."

Heliotta jumped to her feet and stomped across the room. Grady picked Beth up by the waist and deposited her behind the couch. Myrtle moved to stand beside him, effectively shielding Beth. The air was charged with dangerous, crackling energy.

"Don't come any closer," Grady warned, voice deeper and gravelly like a growl.

Heliotta stopped short of where Grady stood and thrust her hand into the folds of her skirt. Her wild eyes held his challenging gaze without flinching. Carefully, she withdrew her hand. Clutched between her fingers was a roll of faded parchment. She held the other end out to Grady.

"Take it," she insisted, wiggling it when Grady hesitated.

"What is written on the scroll?" Myrtle demanded.

"If it is not too late, the salvation of humankind." Heliotta's hoarse whisper was strained.

Grady wrapped his hand around the proffered paper tube. As soon as his grip was secure, Heliotta's arm flopped at her side.

"Will someone tell me what the hell is going on?" Myrtle's confusion sounded genuine. Beth trusted her gut. It told her Myrtle knew less than they did.

"It's the Ritual of Passing. Given to the first guardians by Circe to pass their accumulated knowledge to the next in line. She hoped, by doing this, we'd eventually figure out a way to either banish or defeat Ja'azul," Beth answered, making her way around the couch. "Does the previous guardian need to be alive—or whatever state you two are in—to perform this ritual?"

"I honestly cannot tell you." Heliotta closed her eyes, as if to hide herself from further shame. "We would need to study the ritual."

"Fine. Let's get to it." Grady broke the wax seal with a hooked finger and more gusto than needed. He unrolled the scroll and held it away from his chest.

Beth read silently over his bicep, while Myrtle did the same opposite her. Beth ignored

Heliotta's fidgeting as she absorbed the neat handwriting.

The Ritual of Passing looked simple enough: light some candles, bless some herbs with the athame—

"What's that?" Beth asked, pointing to the word.

"An athame is knife dedicated to the sole purpose of being used during rituals or magic workings," Grady explained, his gruff voice faltered as he rubbed his eye socket with the ball of his hand. Guilt gleamed in his beautiful blues as he mouthed, *"I'm sorry."*

"There's nothing to be sorry about." She wrapped her arm around his waist, adding, "I may be stubborn, but I'm also a fast learner."

Grady pressed his forehead against hers and kissed her nose. "I know you are, love."

Beth reread the ritual and made a mental note of the ingredients. Her lack of magical knowledge was glaringly obvious, but she made up for it with determination. Beth was a pro at cramming for exams the night before a test. She'd treat this the same.

"What will happen to Beth if the ritual fails?" Grady's frown deepened, brows almost touching when he added, "What happens to you two afterward?"

Heliotta scoffed, crossing her arms over her chest. "As with any spell, you light some candles and chant some words. Should you succeed, the candles go out and life resumes. This is all I know on the matter."

Beth's grip on the parchment tightened, hands shaking. If Heliotta hadn't hidden the Ritual in the first place, they wouldn't be in this mess.

Myrtle glared at her consort. "If you had read the scroll, you would know how complex the spell is, Heliotta."

"Should they fail at such a simple task, there are greater things to worry about, Myrtle. For instance, how little Beth knows about her destiny. Failure is not an option."

"That's it," Grady barked, his face red. He marched over to Heliotta and held the spell inches from her face. "Do your damned job so we *don't* fail."

Heliotta's poker face was scary good. She didn't look the least bit ruffled by Grady's outburst, and that worried Beth more than anything.

The eldest guardian took the paper between her fingers and pulled it free. "Myrtle and I will make the preparations. I suggest you do *your job* and make sure your destined one is up to the task."

Heliotta's skirt ruffled as she whirled and marched out of the room. Beth shot daggers at the woman's back as she left the room, but it didn't make her feel better. It wasn't Grady's fault she fought against her magical nature. Rather than embracing her fate, Beth denied it all.

She just hoped her stubbornness hadn't cost them the turn of the war.

"Are you sure about this?" Grady asked for the fiftieth time as he rubbed her arms. "We should do them one at a time."

Beth chewed on her cheek. There wasn't anything in the Ritual saying you *couldn't* do two at a time.

"Think about it, if Heliotta had performed the ritual for Myrtle, when Myrtle performed it for me, I would have their combined knowledge anyway. The quicker we do this, the quicker I can train. It'll be fine." Beth kissed Grady for good measure, taking her time to make it last. They'd not had a quiet moment in what felt like ages, which was another reason for the 'two birds, one stone' approach.

It *totally* had nothing to do with her being stubborn and trying to make up for it.

Besides, if she kept worrying, she'd lose her nerve. The time for doubting had passed. She needed to be battle ready *yesterday*.

"Beth," Grady murmured admonishingly as he broke the kiss too soon. Guess he caught onto what she was doing. "Have you ever made jelly?"

"No." Beth pulled away to see his whole face. Worry lines creased his forehead. "Why?"

"Well, I used to make jelly with my mom back when I was a tween," Grady explained. "There was this one time we made a batch of jalapeno jelly. I suggested we double the recipe, so we didn't have to measure everything out twice. Mom agreed."

"What does jelly making have to do with our situation?"

"When we doubled the recipe, we didn't use a bigger pot. The jelly boiled over, essentially ruining the eye on our gas stove."

Grady's words were punctuated by his direct gaze, as if he was trying to put the answer in her mind. Slowly, her brain knitted two and two together.

"Are you saying my pot isn't big enough to hold two guardians' magics?"

"Basically. What's more concerning to me is what happens afterward. I don't want you to be ruined."

The sincerity shining in his dark sapphire eyes almost broke her heart. He had voiced the thing bothering her most. Their relationship was still new, still blossoming. The last thing she wanted was for it to lose the spark that made their love unique, or having someone else's mistakes ruin it. She couldn't let that happen.

Beth sniffled, putting her hands on either side of his scruffy face. The pricks of his short hairs tickled her palms. When things settled down, she was asking Grady to keep the beard.

"I'm not going to be ruined. You heard Heliotta, the well holding my magic is larger than the Pacific Ocean. Don't fret, love. I'll be fine," Beth promised, bringing her lips to his again.

This time, the kiss was slow and sweet. Beth savored the softness of his mouth, the way she melted into his arms as if the gods had molded them from the same clay. She clung to the immense joy flooding every fiber of her being, knowing this man loved her as fiercely as the sun and as deeply as the farthest reaches of the universe, because she felt the same for him.

When they broke for air, Grady murmured, "I can't *help* but worry when your safety is involved."

He rubbed his nose along hers, nibbling her bottom lip before leaving a kiss on her jaw.

"Grady," Beth whimpered as his lips left a hot trail to her neck, to the sweet spot behind her ear. His arms went around her waist. She couldn't lose *this*. The way he made her heart race or how he stole her breath when they worshipped each other's bodies the few nights they'd been given together.

"I wish we had time to make love before..." Grady trailed off, ending his kisses too soon at the crook of her neck. He tightened his grip, as if he could absorb her into his body.

"I know." Beth's hands wound in his soft curls as she nestled her cheek against his. "Tonight. After."

The perfectly rational questions plaguing her mind escaped the box she'd stuffed them in, endangering her calm. Would she be the same person afterward? How much of Heliotta's crazy would transfer to her? Would Myrtle's cold detachment more than rub off on her? They'd skipped over the part regarding what happened if the Ritual failed. Heliotta had gone for Beth's jugular instead.

"I hate to break up your love fest, but we are ready." Myrtle's firm voice broke their bubble. Reality rushed inside.

"Coming." Grady released his hold on Beth, grabbing one last quick kiss before following Myrtle and Heliotta to the chamber.

Beth *was* nervous, but not as much as Grady. His misty eyes were almost enough to change her mind. Would it matter much if she went through the ritual twice rather than all at once?

They were on the brink of destruction, so yes. By now, the rest of the world should have caught on to the happenings in Mayes Hill, Tennessee. But, by the time the military figured out what they were up against, it would be too late. She and Grady had been chosen for this task. There was no other choice.

"You'll stay by my side?" Beth's voice wavered. She needed to be strong for Grady, but *damn*. The crushing weight on her chest made it difficult.

"Always." He kissed her hand and helped her step inside the circle.

Beth's crash course in candle correspondence explained the significance of the five candles. White for cleansing and renewal, green for nature and success, black for protection, purple for knowledge, intuition, and manifestation, and indigo for wisdom and acceptance. They had been placed evenly on the outside of their circle of salt. Her task was to light each candle to begin the blessing of the area.

"Use your inner flame to light the wicks, beginning with cleansing and ending with spirit," Myrtle commanded as she laid her implements on a wooden plank.

Beth called to her signature blue flame. Her left palm heated, and a tiny spark grew into a baseball-sized ball of warm fire. As always, her flesh was unscathed. The only difference this time was how her whole body felt lighter as if she was one with the flame and the air touching her skin seemed denser.

She approached the white candle. The fire danced with the movement. Beth touched it to the twisted twine, silently asking for the Goddess's blessing and for the success of the ritual. She did this for the rest, lighting the black candle last. The flame in her palm was now half the size, but still warm.

Beth made her way to where the other two guardians sat. Heliotta held a bundle of cured sandalwood chips, dried sage, and dried spearmint above Beth's flame. At first, it shied away from her, but fire's nature is to consume. The flames licked the sandalwood until it caught. Heliotta let it burn until all the elements had ignited. She blew it out and waved the smoke around each candle.

Back at the center, Heliotta purified the ritual knife in the same manner, repeating the process to purify Myrtle. After Myrtle bathed Beth in the smoke, Beth did the same for Heliotta, who took the remains, and placed them inside the small cauldron next to the blade.

"Join me, sisters, around the sacred space," Heliotta commanded, picking up the ritual knife and holding it over the cauldron. "Since we are expediting the process, Beth will receive a cut across both her left and right palms."

Beth caught the impatient tone in Heliotta's voice and glanced at Grady. *"What is her problem? She's been even weirder after finding out about Fennick."*

Grady studied Heliotta with a slight frown before answering, *"I dunno, but you're right. She's been off, but we don't know her very well. I promise I'll keep an eye on her. I won't leave your side. When y'all are done, I'll pull Myrtle aside, see what I can find out."*

His promise didn't do much to alleviate the twist of distrust growing in her gut, but at least he was there if things went wrong.

"Thank you, love."

"Myrtle, yours will be on your left, mine will be on the right. As the blade of the blessed athame passes over our skin, we must chant the words we practiced earlier. Are you ready?"

"Yes," Beth and Myrtle replied in unison.

"May this Ritual of Passing be blessed by our Triple Goddess! So mote it be," the three chanted in harmony.

"Let us begin." Heliotta placed the edge of the blade against her palm. "I pass my knowledge to the one who wears the mantle when my work is done. Blessed be, Elizabeth Marie Harper."

Heliotta held her hand over the cauldron. In a clean, downward sweep, she drew the knife across her palm without wincing or a peep of discomfort. She squeezed her hand, and a thin stream of blood flowed into the basin.

The power gathering in the cave crept along Beth's skin like pins and needles. She resisted the urge to wipe away the goosebumps, focusing on the others.

Heliotta passed the blade to Myrtle, who repeated the process. Again, magic rushed into the space, giving the air a spicy cinnamon flavor. It permeated Beth's lungs like smoke from a burning building. She held in a cough.

The thread connecting her to Grady thrummed. She was able to take a gulp of the heady oxygen without struggling as much. Her gaze connected with his. Sweat formed above his upper lip, but he nodded.

She turned back to the ritual and the athame was in her face.

Heliotta's face was half-hidden in shadows. The flickering candlelight gave her small grin a sinister quality. Dread balled its fist and pounded her chest. "It is your turn, Elizabeth."

Beth swallowed her apprehension like a child swallows a spoonful of bad medicine. She wouldn't let this woman keep her from doing what was right. If Heliotta's madness were somehow passed down to her, Beth had a superpower at her disposal. Her stubbornness would serve as a shield against any changes she disapproved of.

Instead of Beth taking the knife, Heliotta and Myrtle each had one hand on the hilt. Beth positioned her palms on either side of the blade and took a deep breath. As the knife made a swift slice down both palms, Beth hissed.

She powered through the throbbing sting, speaking the final phrase of the ritual, "I, Elizabeth Marie Harper, receive the knowledge from the ones before me and pledge my life to the goddess's work, to protect all life, and to only do harm to those who harbor evil in their hearts."

Time stilled and the cave hummed. Beth's muscles tingled with the fight or flight response. It was as if she were being given the choice: bow out now or stay and accept your fate. The clock was ticking. She clenched her jaw and forced her legs to stay in place. The Ritual approved her agreement and time resumed, making her eardrums pop.

Heliotta placed the athame in the bowl of the cauldron. They pressed their palms together and laced their fingers. A soft purple glow came from where their hands met.

"So mote it be."

A gust of howling wind whirled through the chamber, pulling at the candle flames as it circled the three women. Beth's head grew heavy. A low pain started at the base of her head.

"You must relax, Elizabeth! Do not fight it." Heliotta shouted above the roaring. "Let the knowledge flow."

Beth tried to relax, but the deafening wind threatened to tear her to pieces. She panicked, reaching out to the one person she trusted with her life.

"Grady!"

"Root yourself. Feel the ground beneath your feet." Grady's pinched voice came from inside her head. She grasped his familiar voice and entwined his thoughts with her own, praying to the goddess to come out the other side whole.

Beth squeezed Myrtle's and Heliotta's hands. Rooting herself as Grady had instructed her at the beginning of her magical journey, her bare feet flattened against the cold earth. The raging storm stilled, allowing her a window of clarity. She had time to suck in a quick, shuddered breath before it kicked back in and the funnel widened.

The magic was a vortex, rushing through so violently that Beth gritted her teeth. Combined memories from the past thousand years and all of Circe's magical knowledge crammed inside the too small space. At her awakening, Beth had swallowed a lake. This time, she expected an ocean, but this was much, much more.

Thrust into the darkness of her inner mind's eye, a dim figure emerged. The longer she focused, the clearer the image. Beth saw herself suspended in the middle of a vast, dark sea, her body bowed, arms, legs, and hair spread out. Her mouth was open in a scream, eyes blown white, wide and unblinking. From her observation post, Beth's chest rose and fell like overworked bellows, while the image in the water was motionless, unbreathing.

The juxtaposition was so jarring, so *real*, that panic closed her windpipe. Tears pricked her eyes. Beth scraped her nails down her neck. If only she could break through and create a hole, the air would flow.

Unseen hands tugged at her wrists, pulling them free of their frantic task. Beth thrashed her legs and head, trying to break their hold. If she didn't get air now, she would die.

Her ankles were pinned in place. She pulled at her binds, needing to be free, but a weight was placed over her waist and chest, keeping her from moving.

She cried out, the sobs robbing her of precious oxygen.

More hands, this time holding her face, warm and tingling like honeysuckles in a summer rain. The feeling spread to her lips. For half a heartbeat, she willed it away and tried bucking her hips. A whiff of cedar and pine laced with wood stain calmed her.

Grady.

His distraction allowed Beth to recenter.

A loud 'pop' echoed in her mental space, and her inner eye opened.

Finally, Beth *understood*. She realized the complexity of her mistake; the failsafe Circe had written into the ritual. It was meant for one-on-one, to be processed before consuming and not presented raw from the source. As it was, there was *too* much and no way for Beth to reverse the process.

She stared at the near-incomprehensible learnings that spanned lifetimes, spread out in her mind as unlabeled boxes to be sorted. The knowledge was like several football fields worth of rowdy people waiting outside the department store on Black Friday. Once the door was opened, they would rush inside, demanding her attention.

Her heart sank like the Titanic at the thought.

Seemed her pot had been too small after all.

Chapter 30

GRADY

Shortly after Beth rooted herself, she collapsed. No matter how much Grady screamed at them to help her, the elder guardians wouldn't touch Beth until the candles snuffed out. By then, the delicate skin of Beth's neck had bloody grooves from where she had raked it with her nails.

Myrtle tackled Beth's arms. Heliotta grabbed her ankles. Beth's mournful scream was a knife to Grady's heart. He jumped over the candles and straddled her body, trying to touch as much of her as he could. It wasn't until he pressed his lips to her that she relaxed.

The break was short-lived.

Beth's unseeing eyes opened for a long blink before shutting tight. When her limbs fell loose on a long sigh, he waited for her to draw another. He put his ear to her chest, but there was no heartbeat.

Grady's soul left his body.

"No. I'm not losing you."

He climbed off Beth and tilted her head back. Doubling his hands into a stacked fist, he placed his palm at the center of her chest and pumped five times. He tilted her chin slightly and gave her the kiss of life. Each time he repeated the process, her head lolled to the side.

This was the second time Beth had died in his arms. She *had* to come back to him again, otherwise, how was he expected to *live* without her? He'd tasted how sweet life could be with Beth's love. It was everything he'd dreamed of and so much more.

"Please, Beth. Please don't leave me," Grady begged between sets.

Guilt gnawed at his efforts. He'd known better than to let Beth go through with a combined ritual. He should have put his foot down. As with most occult things, there is a price to be paid. But the scales were unbalanced, because he certainly didn't believe her life was a fair bargain.

A niggling in his brain implored him to stop. He'd been at this for who knew how long. He could have bruised her chest or broken a rib. He wouldn't know it either, because she still hadn't responded to his efforts.

Grady's arms were heavy. His movements became sloppy. It was time to face the ugly truth.

Beth was gone.

His heart imploded, tearing a gaping hole in his chest. It was hard to swallow, and his lungs rejected oxygen. There wouldn't be any more long strolls in the moonlight, no more laughter or fishing trips. The picture of his future, of curly-haired children with fern green eyes and their mother's radiant smile faded with his hope of surviving Ja'azul's invasion without Beth. He could simply lie here and wither away to nothing. Death was coming for him one way or another. He imagined his broken body being crushed beneath the army of unearthly creatures; his bones would be ground to nothing, mixed with those of people who were a blip in his short life. He'd rather have his final resting place next to Beth.

For once in his life, Grady chose to be selfish. He chose her.

He scooped Beth's limp body in his arms and crushed her against his chest. With his free arm, he dragged them to the nearest wall and propped his back along the flattest part. Here, he had a clear view of the cavern. His and Beth's tomb.

Heliotta and Myrtle were nowhere to be seen. They had probably left him to grieve in peace. It was for the best. If he never saw Heliotta again, it would be too soon.

For a fleeting moment, Grady considered calling Rich, to explain what had happened and that they were on their own. He just didn't have it in him to pick up the phone. He wanted to spend his last hours reminiscing over his past with Beth and mourning the life they could have had.

"Remember Tom's twenty-first birthday? We were gonna hit all the bars and go club hopping in the city, but he was sick as a dog. Instead of letting him go without celebrating, you organized a last-minute get together for the three of us." Grady nuzzled her head with his face, letting the tears fall where they lay. "You had a movie theater buffet with our favorite candies and popcorn and made Tom chicken soup."

Grady was stopped by a hiccupping sob when he remembered how he'd given her shit for putting on the wrong Russel Crowe movie. Tom's favorite was 'Gladiator.' Beth put on 'Master and Commander.' Grady had been such an asshole, but Tom didn't care. The man was convinced Beth hung the moon that day. He wouldn't stop talking about it for *weeks*. It was the beginning of their weekly movie night Fridays.

"I think the reason I was so damn mean was because I was jealous. No matter how hard I tried to not fall in love with the girl my best friend was crazy about, I did. I fell *hard* and continued to fall even harder after our first kiss." He sniffled and paused to lower her so he could see her peaceful facade. She looked as if she were in a deep sleep. "I swear, I'll find you in our next lives and we'll find the happiness that was stolen from us."

He swept the hair on her face to the sides, chin quivering as he traced her smooth skin with his fingertips. A trick of the light made it seem like her chest rose. Her warm skin helped with his delusion.

"I love you, so much, Beth. I'm sorry we didn't have more time. I'm sorry I…" He hugged her again, pressing his lips against her temple.

Her hair tangled with his damp cheeks and caught in his beard. He broke, bawling loud and long until the glass bottles on the shelves above shook and rattled. Beth hadn't said it aloud, but every time she touched his scruff, her eyes lit up and she cracked a fond smile. Beards were itchy and took a lot to tame, but he'd have grown his out for her. And if she got tired of it, he would've shaved it off without complaint. He could've used this opportunity to show his son how to shave.

Tears blinded him. Grady flicked them away with trembling fingers. His heart was tired, ready to let go. Limbs became heavy with gravity leaving. Beth lowered to his lap as his head eased backward; the stone wall his pillow.

Grady's puffy eyes were so tired. He wanted to close them, but it might be for the last time. Instead, he lowered his gaze to his sleeping beauty, memorizing Beth's face so it was the last image he saw before slipping away.

He frowned. Her honey-brown hair had already lost its luster. His illusion was falling away before his eyes. Soon, her limbs would stiffen with rigor mortis, and she would be as cold as the stone walls surrounding them.

Grady sighed at the revelation, tightening his hold as his body became numb to the sorrow. "I won't leave you, Beth. Never."

A glimmering sheet of gold formed over Beth's front, like see-through silk.

This is it. Her soul is leaving to rest among the wildflowers.

Grady readied himself, pushing back the grief enough to watch, to make sure she was free. Instead of turning into a glittering orb, Beth absorbed the golden sparkles. His attention was drawn to the lock of hair above her right eye. Color leaked from the strands, starting at the roots and spreading the way colored syrup does in shaved ice, but in reverse. When it reached the ends of her hair, Beth had a stripe of white that shimmered like sunshine on newly fallen snow.

Did this mean what he thought it did? Had they succeeded and this was an outer physical manifestation of Beth's power? The possibilities sent a thrill down his spine.

"Is this normal? What's happening?" he asked aloud in case Myrtle and Heliotta were nearby. He was unable to pry his gaze from his beloved because the claw marks on her neck closed, leaving smooth skin behind.

Almost imperceptibly, her chest began to rise. His heart thumped in response. When her mouth opened, taking in a long draw of oxygen, he breathed with her.

Thump, thump. As life returned to her body, so did his energy. The thread connecting them rang like a percussion band.

"Gods, Beth. Can you hear me, love?"

Grady kissed her cheeks, the tip of her nose, her forehead. When he reached her lips, her response was like lightning. Fierce, raw, *needy.*

Her hand was on the nape of his neck, fingers winding in the curls and pulling him closer. She opened her mouth, stealing his breath in a sacred kiss that caused stars to burst behind his eyelids. Her other hand painfully fisted his shirt.

Grady didn't care. He held on for dear life, consumed by the flames of the only woman he'd ever loved.

She came back for him.

When Beth broke for air, her raspy, whispered voice was music to his ears, "I was so scared, Grady."

"It's over now, beautiful." Grady hugged her to his chest, afraid if he let go, she'd disappear. "I've got you."

She tensed before snuggling into his chest. "Things are far from over, my love."

Beth's ominousness tone gave Grady instant heartburn. He figured she meant the impending doom looming over Mayes Hill, but he was too often reminded of the age-old saying about assuming things.

"Have Myrtle and Heliotta gone?"

Grady opened his eyes and scanned the empty area. They were still alone. If the others were nearby, they'd have heard the commotion. "Dunno. Don't care."

Worry lines formed across her forehead.

He was being an idiot again. They needed answers to what had just happened.

"We'll go look for them. Can you stand?" Grady leaned back so he was kneeling. He still held Beth's hands in his, untrusting. This could be a fever dream for all he knew.

"Maybe?" Beth wiggled her toes.

Grady kissed her forehead, gently tugging her up as he stood. Beth's limbs shook, but her footing seemed solid enough. She didn't take her eyes off Grady and gave him a breathy chuckle.

"Try taking a step," he urged.

"Okay." She gave him a curt nod. Her lips formed a line, brows furrowed in determination.

Beth had always been tough. She was one of those people who would finish a 5K race after spraining her ankle. With everything that happened in the archives, he believed she could do anything.

She adjusted her grasp to hold onto his biceps and looked down. Her frown deepened. "Grady? Whose blood is on my hands?"

"Um," he cleared his throat. "Yours. You were scratching at your neck. We had to hold you down."

"Oh." Beth's stare went beyond the blood on her fingers to his shirt. She was stuck in remembrance but snapped out of it with a flutter of her eyelashes. "Sorry about that."

"It's just a shirt, Beth. You didn't hurt anyone."

"Still. I didn't mean to be so much trouble." She tucked the lock of white hair behind her ear, leaving a streak of red. If Beth noticed her new hairstyle, she didn't say anything.

"I'm going to try on my own." She let go of Grady, and her knees wobbled. "Don't go anywhere."

"Wouldn't dream of it," Grady replied with a wink. If he had his way, they'd never leave each other's sight again.

Beth's pink tongue stuck between her lips as her arms held balance. A sheen of sweat covered her forehead. The moment her foot left the floor, she tumbled forward into Grady's waiting arms.

"Okay, so maybe I *do* need help," Beth pouted with her nose scrunched up. It was so damn cute.

"I've got you, babe." Grady winked and scooped her bridal style into his arms.

Beth yelped; her cheeks flushed red. She slapped one hand against his chest but her other went around his neck. He'd dreamed of doing this for so long. The *rightness* of her being in his arms like this was everything. Next time it would be after making things official.

"Warn a girl before you sweep her off her feet." Her forehead wrinkled and her lips turned down like she'd eaten something sour. "Also, not a fan of the pet-name 'babe.' Feels disingenuous."

"Noted." Grady chuckled, gripping her closer to his chest. Gods, he wasn't sure he could contain the happiness at having Beth back. The way they slipped right back into their natural groove cemented his confidence. The Ritual worked. Beth was going to be okay. "For the record, I was quoting Sonny and Cher."

The song was also from one of his favorite movies. Two people meant to be together, stuck in a time loop until he got it right. He was hooked the first time he watched it.

She rolled her eyes, but Grady was elated to see one corner of her lips lift into a semi-smile. "Sometimes, I forget you're an old soul in a young man's body."

"If you're feeling up to it tonight, I can remind you how beneficial it is to have both wisdom and virility."

"I'll hold you to it." Beth kissed his jaw before nuzzling her head into the crook of his neck and murmured, "Don't forget the basket."

The action welded the fractured pieces of his heart into place. Their connection held steady, stronger than before. Had he not been so damn devastated earlier, he'd have noticed the low thrum never wavered. When the woman you love nearly dies in your arms twice, sometimes logic flies out the window.

Basket? Damn, his focus was shot.

"You need to think quieter, love. My brain is on the verge of a small meltdown," Beth said, squeezing her eyes shut. She'd also put up a shield. "I think I feel a migraine coming on."

"Apologies, beautiful." Grady kissed the top of her head. As he passed the basket, he hooked his finger under the handle, and lumbered toward the front library.

As Grady passed rooms full of books, the eerie quiet formed a lump in his gut. There should be the sound of pages turning or pen scratching on paper. By the time they reached the front sitting room, a pit had engulfed the lump, leaving a bad feeling in its place.

"Where are they?" Grady turned in a circle to survey the room. Everything was as they'd left it before the ritual.

He placed Beth on the red chaise in the corner. He knelt to cup her cheek, setting the basket on the couch beside him. Her skin was cool to the touch, and her blinks slowed.

"I'm gonna pop my head into the hallway and check again. You'll be okay? I promise I won't leave the room."

Grady didn't like Beth's frail smile as she gazed at him pityingly. She placed her small hand on his shoulder. "You won't find them."

A shiver ran down his spine. "What do you mean?"

Beth took a labored breath, like she was trying not to yawn. "What I mean is they have become one with the goddess, same as Tom. By design."

"Wait. You mean..." Grady trailed off when Beth nodded. A terrible thought slid into his 'Free Parking' space. "What'll happen to the archives?"

There was so much knowledge here, thousands of years of it. If they returned to the Grove, would the archives still be standing? With the elder guardians gone, would the Grove remain intact?

"We are the keepers of the Grove now, Grady." Beth's voice was wispy and soft. Her eyes closed. "The archives will remain as long as they are needed."

"You mean, the archives will cease to be after Fennick and I...but that—" Grady swept a hand down his face. What if there were things written in those books that didn't exist anywhere else? The knowledge would be lost forever.

Another thought pounced into the tumultuous fray, weighing on his already tired shoulders. "It would put us another man down."

"Yes, but Fen will wreak what havoc he can on Ja'azul before that happens."

Grady didn't care much for Fennick, and now the man stood between them and success. "What good is he without his magic?"

"Before Heliotta locked him away, Fennick was an alchemical genius. Just imagine what he's learned since. Given a proper lab, he could do great and terrible things." Beth's eyes took on a playful twinkle as a sleepy grin settled on her dusty-rose lips. "Kinda reminds me of a certain dark-haired magic man with gorgeous blue eyes. Who is brilliant, eager...excitable."

Her compliment sent a zing of warmth straight to the center of his chest and to his cheeks. "Sounds like a pretty cool guy. We should hang out after we save the world."

"I was talking about you," Beth chuckled as he bent and wrapped his free arm around her waist. Her arms came around his neck, and when they stood, she pressed her lips against his with a smacking kiss. "Are you gonna carry me again?"

Grady's arm tightened around her. "I was thinkin' about it."

"Later, then. I think I can walk now." Her gaze went to the door. "And I need to be outside."

"Of course." Grady pressed a kiss to Beth's forehead, threading his fingers through hers.

At the door, he cast a forlorn glance over the room. Knowledge, especially of the occult, was his thing. It felt wrong leaving all of it sitting here, unread. But that's what the Ritual was for, wasn't it?

Grady expelled his worries with a breath and stepped outside.

As soon as they stepped through the archives into the woods, the door faded into invisibility again. Grady placed his hand on the space, sighing when the door wavered and solidified. He dropped his hand and turned back to Beth.

She lay on the forest floor on her stomach. Her arms were stretched above her, bare feet pointed, and her cheek against a patch of moss. She was surrounded by a faint iridescent light, like she wore a Beth-shaped bubble suit. The way she shimmered in the dappled sunlight took Grady's breath away.

"Just a minute, love," Beth murmured.

Grady wanted to touch the energy, but he wasn't sure if it would disrupt her. Instead, he opted to sit at her side and observe. The longer he studied the dazzling display covering Beth, the more he noticed the enchanted threads were woven into a kaleidoscope tapestry. His hand hovered above her body, skirting the edge of curiosity and want. With the amount of restraint Grady demonstrated, his mother would have called him a saint, and they weren't even religious.

"You can touch me, Grady." One of her eyes opened. She smirked as best she could with her face smushed to the ground. "I know you want to."

Grady's face turned fifty shades of red before he finally threw his head back in a burst of laughter. The load on his shoulders was lighter, freer.

"You are trouble, woman," he chuckled, wiping the tears from his eyes as he knelt on the ground next to Beth.

His hand hovered over Beth's back. Miniscule zaps of electricity skimmed across his flesh like minnows nipping at skin, giving him instant goosebumps.

Grady closed his eyes to concentrate and recognized the signature immediately. The magic covering Beth was the same as what housed the Grove.

As Grady studied further, he noticed the shield was being strengthened as Beth's power ebbed and flowed like the tides. Essentially, she pulled power from the earth, feeding it back to the Grove, while it gave it back. They had created a superb, symbiotic circle.

"Holy shit, Beth." Grady's body vibrated, and his mind raced. What other snippets of knowledge were tucked away in Beth's beautiful mind? "Is this something you just learned?"

Breathe, or you'll hyperventilate.

"Yes." Beth drew out the word until the buzzing shimmery blanket dispersed. "Done."

She popped up off the ground with a spring in her step. Grady counted to three before he was on her, cupping her cheeks in his hands and kissing the shit out of her. Her hands slid around his waist fisting the back of his shirt.

Grady basked in the afterglow of Beth's magic. He felt so *alive*. The tension he clung to after Beth's heart stopped sloughed away like winter's transition to spring.

"I've said it before, and I mean it every single time. You are the most remarkable person I have ever met." Grady stared into her eyes...the eyes that captivated him daily—*moved* him. The eyes of his past, present, and future; they glistened with love. "I thank the gods every damn day to have you in my life, Beth."

"I don't know what I'd do without you," Beth whispered with a smile that sent his soul soaring to the heavens and made her green eyes glitter. "I love you, so freaking much, Grady."

"I love you, too, beautiful." Grady sealed his words with a chaste kiss, resting his forehead against Beth's.

Never again. No more dying in my arms.

"Let's go relieve Rich of sitter duties."

WHEN GRADY AND BETH came through the portal into the distillery, they stepped into the middle of story time. Fennick held Rich captive as he told a grim tale about who knows what. The flamboyant man's face was dark, while his hands and body moved like liquid, adding another level. He reminded Grady of a Shakespearian actor dialed up to an eleven.

"...but the husband had rehung the duck painting, saying it was a good luck charm. That same night, the woman heard the whisperings, calling her name. When she tiptoed into the living room, the duck painting was awash with red."

Fennick's gaze flickered their way, but he didn't break character, continuing in his deep voice.

"She watched in horror as the canvas stretched outward, in the shape of a long-fingered hand with sharp tips. When the painting could take no more, it ripped, revealing another hand. The demon in his fire-kissed skin the shade of molten lava pushed his way through the hole in the fabric until he stood over the woman."

Yeah, right. Grady rolled his eyes and crossed his arms. Beth nudged him in the side with her elbow.

"The woman could not scream, though she longed to. The demon's devilish grin widened. He leaned as close as lovers and commanded, 'Kill them. Kill them all, or I will rip them to pieces, fingertip to toenail, flaying the flesh into ribbons to make braided ropes from which they will hang for an eternity.'"

Fennick straightened, light stretching over his face to hold back the darkness. "I'll spare you the gory details, but suffice it to say, she murdered her husband and their children, before finally ending her own life."

"Goddamn, Fennick." Rich wiped his hand down his face, leaving his mouth ajar and eyes wide. "I thought you were gonna tell me more about Ja'azul's creatures, not give me more fucking nightmare fuel."

"Heed this cautionary tale, for it is one of the many ways Ja'azul inflicts pain and sows fear upon humanity. His essence exists in the dreamlands, where he hunts, creating terror so he can feast upon it like a decadent dessert. I told you this tale to prepare you for what is to come. Terrors beyond belief are what we will face. You must stand strong, or Ja'azul will unravel the fabric of your being."

"Sounds like a charmer. Does he at least buy you dinner *before* the mind-fuck?" Beth's comment oozed with sarcasm.

Grady was temporarily taken aback by her newfound confidence for two seconds. Not that *he* didn't have any. He did. Or so he thought.

Is this why Fennick also exudes self-confidence in spades? Opening your mind to the universe for an endless supply of conviction?

Beth's thoughts floated effortlessly into his mind as she squeezed his hand. *"My love, park your insecurities at the door. You are more than enough, with or without the passing ritual."*

Grady's cheeks flushed. As long as Beth kept loving him this way, he'd be a happy man. However, when he looked back at Fennick, the warm fuzzies buzzed off. Fennick's clothes were pristine, and he glided around like someone who hadn't been knocking on death's door less than an hour ago.

"You're looking awfully healthy for someone who was dying." Grady pointed out, narrowing his eyes as he took in the man's appearance. The scent of cardamom and spice was strong to Grady's sensitive nose. Which also made him wary of the day Fennick had supposedly 'saved' Beth from Curtis. Her apartment wreaked of it. What kind of magic did he have then?

"Between Beth's care," Fen said, his gaze flicked to her on a blink, quickly returning to him. "And the potion I whipped up, I am well."

Grady called bullshit. He'd only dabbled with making a few potions, but they took more time than Fennick had to make one. No. Fennick replenished his energy in the courtyard. Unfortunately, Grady had no evidence to back his suspicion. Even if he was correct and the creatures could sense when they used magic, they'd already be on their way with the portal usage.

Grady trusted Fennick as much as he trusted a rattlesnake in tall grass.

"What the hell happened to your hair, Beth?" Rich was on his feet, making his way to her side.

"What's wrong with my hair?" She gathered her locks in one hand and brought them over her left shoulder. When she didn't see anything, her gaze slid to him. "Grady?"

"Other side, love." Grady pulled the white streak free, letting the silky strands run through his fingers. "It happened after you–after the ritual."

"So, it is finished." Fennick came to his feet and ran his hand through his hair. His gaze darted around the ground at their feet. An array of muscles on his face twitched and twisted, landing on agony. "She–Heliotta, is she..."

Was it possible Fen still loved Heliotta? The woman had been scared shitless at the mention of *his* name.

An unexpected wave of pity hit Grady square in the chest. For once, he didn't want to rub salt in Fennick's wounds. He wasn't sure what to say, not that he could say anything to comfort Fen.

Fortunately, Beth came to the rescue.

"I'm sorry, Fen, but she has returned to Mother Earth in the way we all do eventually." Beth let go of Grady's hand to take hold of Fennick's. Grady hated the momentary sting of rejection, but Beth didn't mean anything by it. In her eyes, she was helping to comfort a friend.

"Take this as a consolation, Heliotta wasn't the woman you remember." Fennick huffed and dropped his gaze, but Beth dipped to maintain eye contact. "Her mind was fractured and broken. It was a wonder I was able to absorb anything coherent. But, in the end, she upheld her sworn duty."

What? This was news to Grady. They hadn't had time to talk about what it was like, to have a millennium of history and magic shoved into your brain space all at once. He forced himself to focus on them before he lost himself to a journey of philosophical logic.

Fennick stared at Beth for a long time, his jaw working back and forth while his lips were pressed together so forcefully, there was no line. When a tear slipped down his cheek, Grady placed his hand on the mourning man's shoulder with a gentle squeeze.

"We're here for you." Grady wasn't sure what else to say. He felt he had to say *something*...and Beth had already gone the typical sympathy route.

Fen's eyelids slammed shut and a pained sob burst from his barely parted lips. He shook his head with a bitter chuckle. "Fate may be a cruel mistress." When he opened his bloodshot and red-rimmed eyes, they studied him and Beth in turn. "But she also soothes the ache with an unconventional balm her own making."

The brokenness of the man smoothed over like reclaimed glass. It wasn't as perfect as it was before, but was a new, beautiful creation, nonetheless.

Envy was not a feeling Grady was accustomed to feeling outside of when Tom was alive. How a person could compartmentalize such heavy feelings the same way a child forgets about a scrape after the first lick of ice cream perplexed him.

"I appreciate your sentiments, Grady. However, the difficulties in knowing I shall never shed my mortal coil are lessened significantly by the promise of our newfound friendship."

Fennick said the word 'friendship' with pause. Grady didn't put too much thought into its implication. There were plenty of other more pressing things to discuss than double meanings. And, goddess knew, he was still reeling with all the sudden changes Beth may have gone through.

"Hold up. Are you saying you're immortal?" Beth's surprised tone piqued Grady's curiosity, bringing him away from the distracting thoughts.

"It is true." Fennick pulled away, a frown creasing the edges of his eyes and mouth. "But I fear it is not a gift from Circe."

"Wait, is Fennick saying he's gonna live *forever*?" Rich asked, his eyes wide as if he'd puzzled out something significant.

Grady hadn't considered the implications, but he wondered how long guardians lived typically.

His cocked eyebrows and ajar mouth must have been broadcasted as confusion because

Rich added defensively, "What? I may be Agnostic, but my parents made me read the Christian Bible—King James Translation—every Sunday until I graduated. Hell, they even led the church study group Wednesday nights."

Fennick turned his back on Grady and Beth and strode forward. He paused and whirled back around. "To answer your questions"—He pointed to Rich—"yes." Looking to Grady. "Hundreds of years."

"I didn't say anything aloud."

"No, but you wear your thoughts on the outside."

Grady drew his brows together. Fennick's answer sparked another question. Had people been able to harness magic at the beginning of the Common Era or even before? Grady peeked at Fennick, and the man gave him a subtle nod. His brain tingled with wanting to know more.

"Okay, regarding the history of magic, how did you come upon the knowledge if Beth doesn't know?" Grady looked at Beth for confirmation, but she had her lips pursed. "Oh."

"In due time, my friend." Fennick pointed the pity compass on Grady, squeezing his large shoulder before facing everyone.

Not for the first time, Grady was out of the loop. Fennick and Beth shared secrets, they knew important things about saving the world Grady wouldn't understand, not until he and Fennick performed the Ritual.

The feeling of falling set Grady's mood into a tailspin. He needed something familiar, something comforting to keep him from spiraling out of control. Beth put her arm around his waist. She graced him with one of her brilliant smiles as she snuggled into his side, giving him partial relief.

Fennick cleared his throat and wound his hands behind his back. "As I was saying, while Circe blessed us with longer than human lives, being bound to an interdimensional god has its own set of *rewards*."

"Wait." Beth tensed, but she didn't try to pull away. "What does that mean for the Ritual of Passing between you guys?"

Fennick grimaced. Grady's heart sank.

"This is where things become muddled." Fen took a calming breath and smoothed his hair before continuing, "The way I see it, we have three possible outcomes. One, the ritual will carry on as intended." He inclined his head. There was no need to elaborate. They all knew the end result.

"Two, we complete the ritual and my connection to *him* will keep me alive. Which, given the state of affairs, is the most amicable result."

"Thirdly," Fen paused to study Grady. "It is possible the stain I carry—Ja'azul's black mark—is transferred in part or in whole."

Chapter 31

FENNICK

Listening to two people decide his fate without asking his opinion made Fennick feel like a child again. While he understood their caution, the Grove had been his home long before he was championed by the Goddess. He and Heliotta had built the cottage together, brick by brick, mixing the mud and thatching the roof.

Patience was a virtue in which he was lacking, so Fennick chalked this exercise as a positive thing. He also wished to yank his hair out.

"We'll save so much time returning to the Grove, Grady."

"I agree, Beth, but I'm also trying to take your safety into account."

"We still have magic and *his* is locked away. I hardly think Fennick is a threat."

Grady's face hardened. He wrapped his large hand around the back of Beth's neck and drew her near, whispering in her ear. The way her eyes widened, and her gaze shot to Fennick told him all he needed. The young guardian was pleading his case.

"You have a valid point. Just, please, let him in so we can figure out why these headaches keep coming back."

Should I supply my opinion or leave them to muddle things out? He knew, roughly, what the headaches meant. It was the magic trying to fix itself. Without being able to peer inside her mind, all Fennick had were educated guesses.

"Fine, but I don't want you to be alone with him."

"Done." Beth kissed Grady with such tenderness, it caused a deep, dull twinge in Fennick's chest.

Even from several feet away, Fennick could see her magic. Golden shimmers danced around her like dust caught in a ray of sunshine. It still called to him as it had when she first awakened.

Whatever gifts the Goddess had given Beth, they far surpassed what he and Heliotta had been given. Case in point, when Beth held his hands earlier, Fennick touched the forcefield keeping his powers at bay. There was a moment he could taste the heady spice as his magic pushed against the wall like sparklers in a balloon. If only he could penetrate Ja'azul's barrier or find a weakness. With Beth's help, Fennick may find a way.

"Are you ready?" Beth asked, pulling Grady along, her pinkie finger hooked with his.

The sunken spot between his ribs spasmed. He rubbed the center of his chest as if working out a muscle cramp. *What on earth is wrong with me?*

"Yes," Fennick replied, unable to speak past the panic blocking his airways.

"Let's do this." Grady pulled the familiar grey stone from his pocket, its smoothness gleaming from the LEDs above. He pointed it at the cafeteria doorway. "Exgradi."

A pool of pearl-colored liquid filled the arch between the metal posts with a 'whoosh.' It shifted like fine sands by way of a phantom current. When Fennick touched it, he expected his finger to be wet. The portal was dry and had the softness of Egyptian cotton.

"Extraordinary," Fennick whispered. Without warning, the pleasantness turned to coarse sandpaper. He pulled his hand back and rubbed his fingers together. "Well, that was short-lived."

"I'll go first," Beth offered, planting a quick kiss on Grady's cheek before stepping through.

Giddiness bubbled in Fennick's gut. He had been eager to try passage since first witnessing the portals. Alas, crossing promised discomfort...and not just from the portal. Grady's pursed lips and tightened jaw dared him to follow Beth. He almost did.

"Rich, would you take Zeus through? Make sure you keep him on a tight leash. We don't know what's beyond the tunnel walls."

"Can do." Rich picked up Zeus and rested the dog on his shoulder. Over his other shoulder he added, "See you on the other side."

The man left in a hurry; his shoes squeaking on the spotless floor. Grady stepped forward, bringing his nose level with Fennick's chest. He put on his most brilliant smile and directed it at the young guardian. If he were to steal a kiss from Grady, would the man blush and stutter or would he give Fennick a painful souvenir on his jaw?

Grady jabbed a finger against his chest. The gaping hole over his heart pulsed with life. *Interesting.*

"Don't give me your bullshit." Grady lowered his voice. "I know what you did. Ain't no way you concocted a potion in the little time Beth and I were gone. I know you used magic to heal yourself."

Fennick reined in his smile. "And how would I have accomplished such a task when I am still unable to touch my well?" Grabbing Grady's hand, Fennick placed it on his chest. Grady's eyes widened, but the spark of curiosity in his eyes stayed his hand. Grady's teeth pulled his bottom lip under. "Can you read me as well as I can read your open book? I dare you to peer inside my black heart, into the pit where despair reflects only pain and misery."

"Fennick."

"Read. Me," he demanded, letting the shields he kept so tightly bound slide away.

Grady's strong hand was hot to the touch, even through a layer of cloth. Fennick's pulse raced from the contact. People of these times called it being touch starved. Fennick was ravenous.

Grady closed his eyes and brought his brows together. A trickle of his wild power flowed toward Fennick's center. He detected a hint of cedarwood, freshly dug earth, and heady amber. Grady's scent was amazing, taking Fennick back into the deep woods where he often found solace. *No wonder Beth cannot get enough.*

"It's...Shit, Fennick." Grady withdrew his hand, nursing it as though he had been injured. "I don't know what to say. I'm sorry."

"See? Ja'azul has somehow bound my connection so viciously that to even touch upon it causes pain." Fennick sighed heavily. There was something else he should say, to ensure his trustworthiness. "I must implore you, if at any time I appear out of sorts—"

"No man, I was wrong. I'll try to keep a more open mind." Grady tugged at the back of his curls. He would not look Fennick in the eye.

"I appreciate your understanding, but the enemy may use me against you."

Grady stilled, finally bringing his gaze to Fennick's. "Use you? In what way?"

The images of the Bridges family slaughter at his hands flashed into mind. Instead of confessing his most recent egregious sin, Fennick took the coward's route.

"He once took hold of my faculties while in Beth's presence," he admitted, quickly adding, "but I was able to regain control. I would never willingly allow her to be in danger."

Grady's scrutiny was fierce enough to stay the bite of a hungry lion. Finally, he dropped his head into his hands and bit back a curse. "Fuck."

When he appraised Fennick once again, Grady narrowed his gaze. "For some reason beyond me, I believe you. Godsdammit."

"Thank you. Your acceptance means more to me than you will ever know." Fennick braved touching Grady's bicep. The man tensed at the touch, but he did not shy away. "For the record, I *did* drink a healing potion. It was one I had tucked away in my office desk for over fifty years."

Grady's lips quirked into a sly grin, which turned into a laugh. Fennick could not recall a melody that soothed his soul until it glowed, not since he first met Beth face to face. He dared not push his luck and wish for more than a platonic relationship. Beth and Grady's love was still in bloom. Perhaps once the roots were more established, they would be willing to explore voyeurism.

"Let's go before the others get worried." Grady clapped Fennick on the back and gently nudged him toward the portal.

Fennick paused at the edge. His feet were glued in place, weighed down with sudden fear. "Will you be right behind me?"

"Of course." Grady's hand squeezed his shoulder. "We can go at the same time, if you like?"

"Please and thank you," Fennick replied breathily, glad to be light-footed again.

So as not to lose his nerve, Fennick balled his fists, releasing them with a breath, and stepped into the unknown.

Fennick came out the other side. His skin itched like he had run through a healthy bramble patch and was being wrapped in a thorny quilt. Otherwise, he was unharmed.

His eyes squinted against the bright sunny sky, but he basked in the warmth he had been denied for so long. The air here had a pure sweetness he had forgotten, making his chest twinge. He placed his fist over his heart, lips parted in wonder. The gaping hole where his heart should be carried a lump. Perhaps it was because of Beth and Grady.

"You made it. How was the trip?" Beth asked, receiving Grady in a hug. He held her as if they'd been apart for months.

"Expectedly unpleasant, but tolerable nonetheless." Fennick's smile came easier.

Still, there was a question burning on the tip of his tongue. He took the opportunity to wade through Beth's walls. Fennick wondered if Beth realized how deep in the proverbial *shit* she was.

"The greater question is how are you feeling?"

On cue with his question, Beth yawned.

"Tired," she chuckled, "but okay."

Fennick turned away the moment Grady leaned back to check on his lady love. He told himself it was to give them privacy, but he knew it was to stay the sting of loneliness to his newly grown heart.

Instead, he recalled when he performed the ritual with Barton Cooper. Fennick's mental muscle had bulked up the same way your muscles do when consistently working them. They grow to meet the demands put upon them. Magical abilities were the same.

Fennick had felt the growth from his head to the tips of his toes. It was as if he'd grown into a giant overnight but retained his smaller physical form. His skin was constantly being stretched over a never-ending explosion. He had spent a short period relearning how to control his magic without blowing things to smithereens, as well as performing basic motor functions.

Beth was not exhibiting any of these. Her hip-swaying walk had a tad more gusto, but this was the only physical change Fennick noted.

Metaphysically? The first description that came to mind was a train wreck where all the cars were filled with balls of yarn. It would take more hours than they had available to untangle and untwist this mess. Fennick could not pinpoint what had gone awry. Either Beth had done things differently, or...

Beth mentioned Heliotta's deteriorated state of mind. Perhaps—

No. He dared not voice such accusations against his late wife.

"Let's get everyone's sleeping quarters set up for the night, then we'll go over the Ritual." Beth announced, breaking Fennick from one set of troublesome thoughts to another.

The possibility of having an expiry date was both terrifying and exciting. He wanted to ensure victory against Ja'azul, but lamented the loss of redemption. Survival ensured his ability to seek knowledge for the sake of knowledge, to practice alchemy to his heart's content.

To aid his new friends in the war against a common enemy.

They trudged up the hill, toward two small cabins. Fennick recognized them as Barton Cooper's handiwork. The man had built one for his mother-in-law, and one for his teenage son, Solomon. His new heart twinged in sadness for his part in their demise. Fear snuck closely behind, though, knowing Grady will have a front seat to his most diabolical acts.

"How sure are we that whatever hold Ja'azul has on you will pass to Grady?" Beth spoke, biting her thumbnail as her gaze cycled between him and Grady. "I bet I can purify it."

"It is uncertain what effect your cleansing will have on the magical transference. However, there is a way to make sure Grady is not tainted." Fennick's gaze leveled with Beth's when he took a shuddering breath. "You can remove Ja'azul's hold on me before I pass my knowledge onto Grady."

"No." Grady shook his head, placing his hands on his hips. "There's a chance it will kill you, Fennick. We'd be screwed."

Fennick swallowed a gasp. For a second, it sounded as if Grady *cared* whether Fennick perished or not. His small heart grew two sizes.

"Well, the only sure-fire way of success is for me to catch it, like with a metaphysical net or something." Beth aimlessly paced as her thinking cap worked. "I can lay it across Grady—"

"Have you done such a thing before?" Fennick's enthusiasm barked out the question before Beth could finish her thought.

Hope was the folly of humanity, but it had been too long since it pierced his horizon. It bloomed in the barren desert of his soul, igniting a fire he had thought was long extinguished.

"Not exactly. But, I'm certain the four of us"—Beth gestured to Rich, who was silently petting Zeus while listening intently—"can put our heads together and come up with something. Besides, what other choice do we have?"

"Lots." Grady hid his face behind his hands. He seemed to be stalling.

Fennick could not blame the young witch. Weighing the uncertain outcome against Beth's well-being put a damper on things, but Fennick had a feeling. Call him a fool, but he took it as the goddess's reassurance. This would work.

"I hate to admit it, but I think Fen and Beth are right," Rich replied, the shadows beneath his eyes darkened, a testament to the man's bone-deep tiredness. "If we had a couple of days to work things out, we could come up with something else."

"Plus"—Rich placed his hand above Beth's shoulder, like he was petting air—"Since y'all got back, Beth is putting out some major vibrations. It's enough to make my skin crawl when I get too close."

Beth's cheeks flushed with embarrassment. She shuffled toward Grady, mumbling, "Sorry."

Grady huffed a sigh and put his arm around her shoulders. "I get it. Her spark is brighter, denser, but I've not trained her like I should have." He played with Beth's snow-white lock of hair and spoke directly to her, "I'm worried you won't know what to look for. What if his essence doesn't pass through your net because it likes you better and stays?"

Beth shifted enough to lay her hand against his chest. "I'll make sure there's nowhere for it to go except where I make it. When you can see the weave above us"—Beth raised her gaze to the sky—"you'll understand why I'm not worried."

"Beth is more than equipped for the task. She has the power and the know-how." Fennick tapped the side of his head, giving them what he hoped was an assuring grin.

Grady dropped his chin, resting his forehead on Beth's. "You're one hundred percent sure this will be okay to do in the Grove? Ja'azul's evil isn't gonna make it go haywire or anything?"

Fennick placed his hand on Grady's shoulder, allowing the tiniest sliver of satisfaction to curl his lip when the young man did not shy away. "I am positive. The Grove was created by the Goddess Circe, and Beth had the forethought to secure the shield before coming to the field. It will be fine."

"So, with that settled." Rich rocked back on his heels. "I just have one last question, what happens if all three of y'all pass out?"

Beth's stomach chose that moment to growl. "We can figure that out over food. Who's up for an early dinner?"

For the umpteenth time that day, Fennick's chest cavity fluttered with warmth. For too long, he had yearned for meaningful companionship. Ja'azul's offer came with loss and a lifetime of giving, more and more, until he was a shell of the person he once was.

He had been gifted a chance for companionship with Beth and Grady, if they would but have him. And, if Rich seemed amicable to the idea, Fennick was sure they could be friends. Zeus certainly enjoyed his company. It had been many, many moons since Fennick had something worth fighting for.

During a modest meal consisting of sauteed fresh vegetables over a bed of creamed chicken and rice, they went over the 'dos' and 'don'ts' with Rich regarding the Ritual. Nerves chased the hunger from his stomach; however, sustenance was needed for what they were about to attempt.

"At no point in time should you enter the circle until *after* the candles are extinguished. This must happen on their own, or else the spell will not be successful." Fennick impressed. The determination on Rich's face told him the man understood.

"Once clear, if I have three unconscious witches, I'll move y'all to the nearby cots."

Rich repeated, the faint aura surrounding him brightened but fuzzy around the edges. Fennick was certain the man's ancestry held a speck of magic.

"Make sure our feet or hands have contact with the ground," Beth reminded, covering a yawn with her hand. "The more of it we're touching, the faster we replenish."

"Of course." Rich scratched Zeus behind the ear. "Speaking of replenishing, you look like you need a long nap before tackling this large of a spell."

Beth waved him off. "I'll be fine after a couple cups of coffee."

"Young lady, you look as if a strong wind would blow you over." Rich crossed his arms over his chest and pursed his lips. The eyebrow raise was a practiced arch, which spurred Fennick to wonder if the man had children or a wife.

The fatherly relationship between Beth and Rich appeared to have deep roots. The older man watched after and protected Beth with a fierce parental pride Fennick had not had the pleasure of experiencing. There was an odd sort of panging twist behind his ribs. Fennick shrugged it off as nerves.

This new friendship group would not last, for he had secrets he was incapable of resolving before the sands in his hourglass ran dry. Soon, Fennick would have no way to hide his indiscretions. If the young witch was the type to tell his lover all, there could be two against him.

However, he was never one to squander an opportunity. "That is a splendid idea. Beth should use the time we prepare to recuperate. There are protections to put into place, and concoctions to be made."

"I agree. You haven't stopped yawning since you–since the Ritual." Grady's hands migrated to Beth's waist.

His ulterior intentions were not as well masked as the regret tinging the strain in voice. Twice, Fennick had noted the direness surrounding his words, piquing his curiosity.

What happened during their time performing the Rituals?

Perhaps they would enlighten him at breakfast.

"Fine. Since y'all are teaming up on me, I suppose I'll sleep." Another yawn betrayed the young beauty. The way her nose crinkled was most endearing, causing the middle of his chest to warm. This seemed to be a common occurrence whenever Beth was involved. "Wake me up when y'all have everything set up. I'm feeling very positive."

Beth's warm smile found Fennick before she turned it to Grady.

"I'll tuck you in." Grady lifted her hand and placed a kiss on her knuckles.

Fennick heaved an internal sigh of relief. Would that he could bottle his tempest of emotions. It would be a potent weapon against the enemy, who knew not of love or the joys of friendship.

The longer he was part of this little group, the more his sense of belonging grew. At least he had this day. Gods be damned if he would waste it.

Chapter 32

GRADY

BETH GAZED INTO HIS eyes as he brought her closer to bliss. Her lips parted, begging to be sucked, caressed, but Grady enjoyed watching her come undone beneath him more than he wanted to kiss her.

She threaded her fingers in the hair at the back of his head while her other hand branded his back with half-moons. When she threw her head back with a sigh, he resisted the urge to languish kisses along the column of her neck. He was close. Beth pulsed around him, but there was no way he was missing out on one of his favorite sights. The pretty rose-colored flush across her cheeks and sheen of sweat coating her silky skin were a work of art.

"Eyes on me, beautiful," Grady murmured, his voice pinched.

She forced her lidded gaze back to his, lost in the euphoria of their lovemaking. The base of his spine tingled right before the built-up pressure released. He fought his heavy eyelids, not wanting to miss the finale.

Finally, Beth's face and neck bloomed rouge as they crested the peak together. Grady didn't just see stars but swirling nebulas, experiencing beyond the spiritual into soul shattering.

"Gods, Grady," she whispered, her lips grazing his in a lazy kiss as her arms slid down his body to the mattress like liquid.

Rendering Beth to a boneless mess was Grady's measure of adequately pleasing his partner. The more they explored each other, the better he made Beth feel. This session, however, left *him* shaking.

Grady trailed featherlight kisses along her jaw. Before the muscles in his arms gave out, he flipped them over. Beth rubbed her cheek on his chest, swinging her leg over his. As she snuggled him, she raked her fingernails through his smattering of chest hair.

"I'm nervous about tomorrow," Beth whispered after a quiet moment.

"I'd be worried if you weren't."

"You don't *sound* worried. How can you be so calm?"

"I hide it well." Grady ran his hand along the smooth skin of her thigh. "Truth is, I'm terrified. Too many things can go wrong. But, we're as ready as we can be. I'd rather focus my fear into something useful."

Beth agreed with a hum. "That makes me feel better."

Grady squeezed Beth's body with his large arms and kissed the top of her head. "I love you so much."

"I love you, too." Beth tilted her head and kissed his jaw.

Nuzzling his neck with her nose, her sigh of contentment tickled. Moving Beth to scratch the itch wasn't worth it. Grady had her right where he wanted her.

They'd settled into a comfortable silence when Beth's breathing slowed, and her hand stilled. He counted her heartbeats until she was well under. As he'd done with Fennick, Grady prodded Beth's shields. He only meant to take a peek, to see what her well looked like, but whatever force she held in place zapped him. He had a second to picture an angry storm pummeling an endless ocean fraught with waves before being bodily ejected and the door slammed in his face.

His erratic heartbeat pounded against his chest with enough force to move Beth's head. Goosebumps broke out over his nakedness, but the covers were still pooled at the foot of the bed.

"Everything is as it should be," Beth whispered, kissing his chest and adding, "Sleep, my love."

When she shifted to hook her leg over his, Grady finally closed his eyes. He hugged Beth tightly, letting her warm body and soft snores pull him under.

"So, we're clear on the plan?" Rich asked as Beth came around the table collecting their dirty breakfast dishes.

"Thanks, love," Grady whispered as she gathered his.

"Yep. Cleanse the circle, put protections in place, begin the ritual." Beth paused as a thought flittered past her features, but she turned toward the kitchen before he could decipher anything. "Before I activate the spell weave, I'll send an extra prayer to the goddess that it'll be enough."

"We are as prepared as humanly possible, given the circumstances and allotment of time," Fennick countered, slightly snippily. He must not have gotten enough beauty rest.

"Funny." Beth leaned back against the kitchen counter and crossed her arms with a sly grin. "Grady said the same thing last night, almost verbatim."

Fen choked on his coffee, scrambling for a napkin while having a coughing fit. Rich was on his feet as quick as Grady to help, but Fennick waved them away.

"For gods' sake, leave me be for one bloody moment."

When regret passed over Fen's face, it occurred to Grady that Fennick must think his chances of survival were nil. It would explain the withdrawal this morning after they all bonded over dinner last night.

"I apologize for my atrocious behavior." Fennick hid his face behind his hands, which was a feat given how hunched his shoulders were. His knuckles almost grazed the tabletop. "Sleep, I fear, was neither restful, nor replenishing." His lithe frame rolled back like an unfurling fiddlehead fern. "Still, my short temper is inexcusable. Please, forgive me."

Grady felt there was more than Fennick's happiness hinging on their forgiveness, but before he could say anything, Beth beat him to the punch.

"It's understandable, Fen." She came up behind Fennick and draped her arms around his shoulders, resting her chin on her arm. Grady shoved the tightness in his chest down into his gut. There wasn't anything to *be* jealous of. "We're all under a lot of stress, so let it out. Go outside and scream, beat on a poor tree, whatever you need to do to get squared away, okay?"

Fennick leaned his head against Beth's for half a breath before abruptly tapping her arm twice. She pulled away and stepped back so Fen could stand.

Grady followed suit, reaching for Beth. She walked backward into his chest, pulling Grady's arms around her waist.

"There is no need for such theatrics. Let us retire outside and begin." Fennick made toward the door. He paused and threw over his shoulder a strained, "Please."

As soon as he disappeared outside, Grady took a deep breath, allowing Beth's lavender vanilla scent to soothe his nerves.

"I guess I stole your calm last night, 'cause y'all are all a big ball of anxiety." Beth turned in Grady's arms to face him. Her brows were drawn, deepening the crease lines that had formed over the past two weeks.

"It's Fennick. Something besides shitty sleep has him in a mood." Grady mirrored Beth's face. He'd worn the mask so often, the edges of his 'normal self' blurred against the seams.

"Well, you'll find out soon enough everything he's ever learned and done." Beth probed his worry lines with the tips of her fingers. As she smoothed his, hers vanished.

"That's what I'm afraid of."

Beth's clenched half-smile unsettled Grady. He frowned deeper, inventing a thousand secrets Fennick could be hiding.

"Stop it." Beth gripped his face firmly between her hands. "We know Fen's done terrible things under Ja'azul's influence, but he's here now, prepared to die so *we* have a chance at living."

"I know." The restful sleep Grady had gotten last night drained from his neck and shoulders.

"Tell me to call off the Ritual and we'll do it." Her fern-colored irises darkened with her conviction.

"Beth," Grady shook his head and tried to pull away, but her grip firmed. "You and I know that's not an option."

"Then we stop messing around and go outside. Figure things out, okay?" She squeezed his cheeks together, so his lips stuck out like a fish. "But, first, I'm gonna kiss your squishy face because it's adorable."

Grady huffed a chuckle as Beth slid her hands down his biceps, giving them a squeeze. She pressed her lips to his, and the ball of tightness in Grady's chest eased enough he could breathe again.

"Thank you," he whispered against her lips.

"I love you," she replied with another peck as her hand slipped into his.

THE SUN TEETERED BELOW the treetops, keeping most of their morning light hostage for the next fifteen minutes or so. Fennick's tall frame stood in the center of the field where it was flattest. His face was tilted toward the morning sun, eyes closed and arms out at his sides. All semblances of the boisterous and confident man they'd grown accustomed to had been traded for a somber man awaiting his last meal on death row.

The thought prickled the corners of Grady's eyes and jabbed a dull knife into his chest.

"Fennick," Grady began, but the words died on his tongue when Fen opened his eyes. Haunted.

"I am ready." Fen's normally smooth voice sounded like scraping a rake over loose gravel. "Beth and Grady, please step into the circle with me."

When Grady's stomach clenched, Beth squeezed his hand. Fennick was currently the smartest guy in the room. He had the most magical knowledge, which meant he was the most qualified person to protect Beth. Grady should have been thankful, but it was a fact that didn't settle well with his pride. He squashed those feelings between the rock of reason and the need to keep Beth safe.

"Please, Beth, take a seat here. Grady, you will stand opposite me." Fennick reached into his pocket and produced two small vials of dark green liquid stoppered with corks, holding them in the palm of his outstretched hand. "This tonic will render our vessels as inhospitable hosts for as long as it takes to complete the ritual."

That's probably why he's in such a bad mood. He stayed up all night making these potions.

"What's in it?" Grady took two from Fennick's hand and gave one to Beth. His, he held aloft to let the streams of sunlight spilling over the treetops illuminate the swirly substance.

"White sage, mugwort, bladderwrack... Too many things to list. You will find all of my transcribed notes in a journal in the cottage." Fennick reached into his other pocket.

He pulled free two small muslin sacks no bigger than a travel-sized bottle of hand sanitizer. The tops were secured by cotton strings that also served as loops. As they swayed, the sweet scent of honeyed jasmine mixed with something akin to eucalyptus and an orange Creamsicle wafted around the area.

"These serve as both protection and to ward off evil spirits. You will wear them throughout the ritual." Fennick handed them to Grady.

Grady placed Beth's over her head, fluffing her hair so the string was secure around her neck. He turned to Fennick, noting the man didn't have a necklace.

"Where's yours?" Beth asked Fennick, stealing the words from Grady's mouth.

Fennick's features twisted into a grimace before he schooled his them. "For this to work properly—and to minimize the amount of negative energy transference—the best place for Ja'azul's influence is to stay inside me."

"But—"

"No." Fennick held his right palm up, touching his heart with left hand. "I thought long and hard about it all night. It is our best chance at success."

"But at what cost?" Grady asked as his stomach sank like an anvil. He'd had similar thoughts, but, as much as he disliked Fennick, Beth's words from before breakfast clung to his compassion organ. Plus, their list of allies was on the short side.

"I do not know. But I am not ready to give up, not when so much is at stake." Fen tied his long locks into a messy bun at the nape of his neck. His smile didn't reach his eyes. "Worry not for me, my dears. Even if this is all in vain, I have lived a *very* long life."

"It's not the same, Fennick. You were in servitude most of the time. I hardly call that living," Beth pleaded, craning her neck. Her eyes were glossy.

"Perhaps," Fennick whispered, his frown not helping the worry raking Grady's gut. The claws dug deeper when Fen pegged him with a mournful stare. "However, you may change your tune once all is revealed. Please know that I can never convey how terribly sorry I am in words. I ask only that you allow my actions to speak what my heart cannot."

Shivers chased the heat wave under Grady's skin. There were precautions against Ja'azul in place, but nothing to shield Grady from Fennick's depravity.

Would he lose himself in exchange for Fennick's vast amount of knowledge? If it meant losing Beth, it was a hard pass. The rock and hard place he was stuck between didn't allow for much wiggle room. Not when the alternative could be losing Beth to the war.

"Let us commence before I lose my nerve." Fennick handed something to Rich. The increased scent of mint, orange, and jasmine told Grady it was another bag. "Fail-safes should Ja'azul's essence seek another host. Zeus is far enough away; he should be fine."

Grady sat in front of Beth, putting him in the middle. He didn't trust this ritual to go much smoother than the first one and wanted a front row seat if things went sideways. Hell, Beth had barely rested and was pretty much going for round three.

"We must switch places," Fennick murmured, ducking his head sideways and spreading his hands. "The flow of energy and what not." A light blush lined the tops of his cheeks and the bridge of his nose, darkening Fen's freckles.

"Alright," Grady grumbled, crawling around Beth.

Her hand brushed his bicep as he passed. Once he was settled on the ground behind her, he twirled the end of her ponytail around his finger.

Grady took a slow, deep breath, exhaling to release his tension and negativity. With a quick pulse of power, he pushed it outside the circle.

Meanwhile, Fennick walked the circle, lighting the candles and sweeping the area with smoke from the sage bundle. He moved with a precision and confidence that helped Grady's tense muscles relax enough to stamp out most of his doubts.

Finally, Fennick took his place in front of Beth. He nodded with pursed lips; the most serious Grady had seen the man. They sat cross-legged and were so close that Fennick's knees almost touched Grady's had Beth not been kneeling between them.

"No matter what, do *not* let go," Fennick ordered before addressing Rich, "or break the circle until I say."

"Other than what we discussed, what can I expect to happen?" Mr. Stanton asked, one eyebrow cocked while his forehead and jaw were set.

"Gusting winds, glowing stuff, maybe some screaming." Beth scratched the side of her neck.

"These are possible, yes. However, I must impress upon you the importance of not interfering. Should you interrupt the ritual, you put all of our lives at risk." Fennick's words sent a cold chill down Grady's spine, followed by angry swarm of hornets inhabiting his insides. "If you feel you must do something, wait until *after* the candles have extinguished by themselves. Only then is it safe."

"I remember." Rich said, taking a seat. "You sure this is necessary? Why can't you just teach them what you know?"

Fennick sighed deeply before answering, "Even within the Grove, time is against us. This is the best course of action to ensure victory."

Grady had asked himself this a hundred times since watching Beth's experience. A thought niggling at the back of his mind burst free. His jaw tightened as he ground out, "Fennick knows because he's done it before."

"Barton Cooper," Beth whispered. Their attention was on Fennick, whose head was tipped forward; rich mahogany hair shielded his face.

"Yes," Fennick's reply was barely audible. He raised his head, letting an eye peek through his wavy, brown curtain. "It is one of my greatest regrets, and there are many."

Grady's sight dimmed as he shook with fury.

"Who was Barton Cooper?" Rich asked, closer than he had been. Grady hadn't even heard the man move.

"He was Grady's great grandpa, *several* times removed," Beth answered as she wrapped her arms around Grady's neck and planted his face above her bosom. As her fingertips deftly massaged his scalp, his rapid pulse slowed. "We knew this was a possibility."

"Then his death shouldn't come as a surprise?" Rich asked. Beth shook her head in answer. "Look, I don't have the particulars, frankly, don't need them, but it sounds like what happened was something the *old* Fen would do. The Fen here and *now* wants to do the right thing. Y'all keep saying we need all the help we can get. Well, this man here is ready to step up and give it, even though he's scared to death he's gonna die."

Rich's words were a bucket of ice to his anger. Grady figured the confirmation that Fennick had murdered Barton hit him so hard was because of Myrtle. She never found out what happened, never had closure. His consolation was knowing their spirits were reunited in the hereafter.

"Rich is right." Grady pulled away from Beth to face Fennick again. This time, he wouldn't let his emotions get the best of him. "I can't hold something that happened before my grandparents were even a thought against you. All is forgiven, Fen."

Fennick's eyes glistened. His lips were pursed into a frown to keep his chin from wobbling. "I appreciate your understanding, as undeserved as it may be."

"We're ready to begin again?" Beth's soft voice brought the moment to a close.

Fennick wiped his nose with a cloth and nodded. "Before we begin, make sure the pouch is secure around your necks, and drink the potion."

Grady slipped his necklace over his head, letting the bag sit over his heart. He popped the cork top and whispered, "Bottoms up."

Beth lifted the vial at the same time as Grady. The cool liquid slid over his tongue, hitting the bitter and tangy taste buds before the spice kicked in. The first potion Beth made was much tastier, but you know what they say about medicine. The more terrible the taste, the more effective.

"May the Triple Goddess bless this Ritual of Passing. So mote it be," Grady followed along with Fennick. Hearing Beth also whisper the words loosened the remaining knots across his shoulders.

Beth handed an athame to Fennick. As he cut a line into his palm, he sucked a quick breath through his teeth. "I pass my knowledge to the one who wears the mantle when I am done. Blessed be, Grady Alan Cooper."

Beth looked over her shoulder at Grady, holding the athame in her hand by the pointy end. Grady gripped the cold iron handle, drawing the blade across his palm as he recited, "I, Grady Alan Cooper receive the knowledge from the ones before me and pledge my life to the goddess's work, to protect all life, and to only do harm to those who harbor evil."

Beth took the knife and placed it on top of the flat rock Fennick had insisted they use. As discussed, Grady placed his left hand on Beth's left shoulder while Fennick placed his left hand on her other one.

Beth's left hand gripped Fennick's. His hazel eyes glowed with specs of lilac. When she tucked her right hand behind, Grady's grasped it and the ground within the circle illuminated with a brilliant white light. The dazzling display shot skyward, encasing them inside a cylinder.

The wind inside their protective circle swirled as if they were caught in a slow-motion tornado. Unlike the wind inside the cave, there wasn't enough force to cause damage, but this tugged at their clothing.

Gradually, grey leached into the white light until it took over, darkening to black. Fear entered Grady's gut for a wink. This was a true black, not Ja'azul's power.

As black faded to silver, then to gold, an itchy warmth wriggled its way into the opening in Grady's palm. He didn't have time to think about what was happening, because the magic surged inside. His body jerked forward. He locked his torso into place to keep from bumping into Beth.

Fennick's magic was unlike any Grady had touched before. It was wild, primordial. Already, he could *feel* the trees breathing. Colors were saturated, deeper and sharper. They looked unreal.

Beth tucked her head forward, resting her chin on her chest. She squeezed his hand. If she was aware enough to give him comfort, things were going well...until the air around them thickened like gravy.

The hairs all over Grady's body rose.

"No," Fennick hoarsely whispered. His eyes were pressed shut, and he gritted his teeth so hard spittle flew from his lips.

"It's okay, Fen. Don't fight it," Beth urged.

"I will not let him have you, too," Fennick choked out, his eyelids flying open.

Grady startled at the shiny black orbs staring back at them. Beth's hand tightened, crushing his fingers, but he ignored the discomfort.

"I'm safe, Fen. He can't infect me; I won't let him."

"Beth," Grady warned, but his voice was too high pitched to carry any weight. She was going to let Ja'azul through, and there wasn't a damn thing he could do about it without endangering all three of them.

"Please, just trust the process. Trust *me*."

She tugged the thread connecting them like an angler checks their creel to make sure the fish are still swimming in there. Beth's thoroughness calmed his racing heart. He swallowed the lump forming in his throat.

"I'll always trust you, Beth." Grady left the other half of that sentence to hang in the air. *I don't trust Fennick, but what choice do we have?*

Time stopped for a fraction of a second before Fennick lowered his walls like a heavy bass drop. Suddenly, Grady's body was charged with the power of an exploding supernova. He was aware of every pore on his person, leaking the excess as if he were a sponge cake drenched in rum.

As Grady rode the intoxicating wave, blood rushed to his ears, drowning out all thoughts. The urge to let go of the tethers keeping him grounded, to experience the world rather than simply existing in it caused his chest to constrict. This urge screamed 'Fennick.' His need to explore and ability to leave Heliotta behind stumped Grady. He could never do that to Beth. Exploring the world would be richer and more fulfilling with her by his side.

Grady wrangled those errant thoughts in time to see their golden circle of light darken to an orange.

Instinctually, he sucked in a quick gulp of oxygen half a second before the air in their space compressed. He felt like he was being dragged underwater to the bottom of the lake.

Grady focused on Beth's solid hand and steady heartbeat. What seemed like hours passed. The oxygen in his lungs pleaded for a refresh. Deep in his memory something stirred, begging him to wait it out, to not take another breath.

Hold on a little longer, the phantom voice insisted.

He squeezed his eyes shut. Grady's heartbeat was in his face. His lungs were on fire. He *couldn't* hold it any longer, not when his chest was going to implode.

A little longer was more like eternity.

Grady's eyes were on the verge of bulging out of his head when the pressure dropped with a whoosh. He expelled the stale air with a pained groan before clean air rushed back in like a decompression chamber.

His tear ducts overcompensated, but he didn't care. Sweet oxygen was his...and so was the power to move not mountains, but continents.

No. Knowledge is the real power, Grady corrected.

Beth's grip on his hand loosened. Her body went limp. Grady reached out, catching her before she keeled. He slipped his arm around to her chest, holding her back to his front while moving their hands to her lap without breaking contact. He thanked the Goddess for Beth's strong and steady heartbeat.

When his gaze met Fennick's, white ribbons swirled in the black pools. Fen's hazel irises peeked at the edges, but his face lacked emotion, save for a single tear on each cheek.

Steadily, the torrent of magical energy slowed to a trickling brook. The orange hue surrounding them faded to brown and flickered. With a hiss, the candle's flames went out one by one.

"It is finished," Fennick croaked, jerking his hands away from Beth as if she were infected.

Grady expected the new memories to be automatically imprinted onto his own, not floating in a parade around his brain until absorbed. He drifted between blissful ignorance and wanting to know Fennick's dirty secrets.

"Is she okay?" Rich asked as he knelt by them. He placed the backs of his fingers on her forehead. Whatever he found softened his frown.

"I think so. Her heartbeat hasn't changed." Grady sat back on his heels, pulling Beth onto his lap.

With some finagling, he was able to sit cross-legged so Beth was more comfortable, resting her cheek against his stomach. Her body temperature had risen as if she'd been sunbathing, but that wasn't what had Grady's stomach turning sour. The muslin sack around her neck was black. The greasy substance had soaked through the fabric and bled onto her shirt.

"The talisman did its job well." Fennick snatched it up and broke the string loop. Once it was free from her neck, his Adam's apple bobbing for the tenth time, he deposited it on the rock next to the athame.

Grady scanned the former guardian, searching for clues to what the man hid, but Fen wouldn't look at him. The sourness in Grady's stomach festered and burned his insides.

Chapter 33

BETH

WHEN FENNICK LET LOOSE, the torrent of magic jolted Beth's memory. There was this one time Tom had borrowed his dad's bass boat to take her fishing in Padena, Georgia. About the time Tom anchored, a freak thunderstorm hit with tornado-force winds and skull-vibrating thunder.

They'd had no time to pull anchor and were forced to hold onto the sides of the fiberglass vessel. As the rain pelted her face like rubber bullets, Beth's grip slipped. The next thing she knew, her body was flung over the boat, lungs taking in water.

She remembered the listlessness of her shocked system, the panic of drowning. For the briefest of moments, Beth thought she was going to die. Her heart had jumped so violently, she thought it was trying to break through her chest.

Beth kicked with all her might, barreling through the choppy water until the surface broke. Oxygen didn't come like she'd expected, though. She needed to expel the water first.

Tom's strong arms had snaked around her waist. He dragged her to the boat and somehow got them to shore. Her vision darkened. She opened her mouth, and her airways cleared on their own.

"Breathe, Beth."

She didn't remember passing out.

"Come on, love. Stay with me."

When she came to, Grady's warmth surrounded her, as did his familiar woodsy scent. She expected the memory of Tom to tear her up, not give her peace.

However, it was short-lived.

Ja'azul's oily essence crowded the mental tank she had created to contain the poison.

Better than letting it run unchecked. So far, it had worked, but she was unsure what had transpired in the split second of unconsciousness. Beth had to trust Fennick's protection spells did their job.

Fennick's words, 'it is finished,' floated through her haze. She had no time to celebrate, because her metal container groaned from the pressure. Before she was ready, it burst, spilling gods knows what inside her.

A sick, tangy heat bubbled in her stomach, working its way up her throat. Beth clamped her mouth shut. She pushed against Grady and rolled to her hands and knees. Thick, black vomit jetted onto the grass. The way the mid-morning sunlight hit the slick pool, highlighting rainbowed ribbons throughout the gunk, made her think of burnt motor oil. It *smelled* like it.

Beth's knees and elbows wobbled. She heaved again until her eyes blurred. Her chest cavity was bruised from the forcefulness of her retching, head pounding with as much fury as the asshole who drives down the street at midnight on a weekday, blasting his subwoofers so loud the windows rattle.

She had a split second to inhale before a final wave of nausea hit her. Expelling the last of the vile substance, her limbs finally gave out. Strong arms wrapped around her midsection, thwarting her inevitable face-first crash into the puddle of muck.

"I've got you, love." Grady's voice was soft despite cracking at the end.

"Thank you," Beth rasped though her throat was raw.

Her heart ached for her beloved. She had put him through the ringer with all the near-death experiences. Not that this was one of them, but puking a stream of black junk certainly didn't inspire confidence in the 'living to see the next day' category.

Grady had been her rock between Tom's death and funeral, but who'd been there for him? He had no one else. She made a silent promise to step up and be there for him more often.

"Here."

A cloth was thrust in her face. She lifted her hand, but her arms had been replaced with wet noodles.

Grady lifted her away from the puddle of yuck. "Let me."

His chest vibrated against her back before he settled her head in his lap. Grady wiped her face and chin with tender, careful strokes as everything around them melted away. His handsome face was scrunched in concentration, eyes twinkling like stars reflecting on a smooth as glass blue lake. If possible, Beth fell even deeper in love.

"There," Grady said, tossing the cloth over his shoulder. He tightened his hold a fraction. "How are you feeling?"

A slow smile spread as she tried lifting her arm again. This time, she was able to raise it enough to lay it over the hand Grady had on her midsection. "Right as rain, just can't get my muscles to listen."

Beth's smile fell when she was betrayed by a yawn that nearly dislocated her jaw. A week-long nap wouldn't be so bad, and they could get away with it while here in the Grove.

Grady frowned but closed his mouth. He took a deep breath and exhaled slowly. "How long do you need until you can be up and battle ready?"

"Because we're supposed to raid the armory at the sheriff's station?" Beth guessed, trying to piece together what they'd already discussed.

She couldn't concentrate on more than a single thought at a time. Her brain was still jumbled by the Ja'azul ick, and there was already a lot going upstairs. The globes of knowledge circling the mile-high fence she'd erected around her mind were a constant reminder. Occasionally, one or two would jump it or slip through the cracks. Those fragments were pieces to a ten-thousand-piece puzzle with no picture to go by and none were the same size or shape.

"Exactly. We'll need as much artillery and ammo as we can get our hands on." Grady diverted his attention to the former deputy. "Rich can get us inside, but once the portal is open, we'll need to haul ass."

Beth rolled her lips inward as she considered the least amount of sleep she could get while still helping the guys. "A solid ten should do it."

"You also need sustenance, to keep your strength." Fennick's voice caused an instant reaction in Beth.

Her heart skipped a beat, and her stomach flipped. He *hadn't* disappeared after the ritual. Warmth bloomed in her chest, only to recede when she saw Grady's hardened gaze. Hurt passed over his eyes as his fingers curled, biting into her hip.

"Hey," Beth murmured, cupping Grady's cheek using the miniscule strength she'd mustered. "Of course I'm happy Fen's still here. He's my friend and deserves a chance to live his own life for once. When are you going to get it through that beautiful head of yours? I am as much yours as you are mine. Stop looking for trouble where there isn't any, alright?"

"I'll do better," Grady promised, turning his head to kiss her palm.

"Perhaps Rich and I can go ahead on a reconnaissance mission." Fennick offered, his voice brittle.

"Beats sitting here not doing anything. I'm not used to staying idle," Rich agreed, nodding his head with enthusiasm. "We can find out how many big uglies we'll have to face and gather what we can before y'all come through."

"How will you protect yourselves until then? Y'all will be sitting ducks." The somersaults in Beth's stomach didn't stick the landing this time. They fell flat, seizing some of her gusto. She hadn't heard from her parents in weeks, which made Rich the closest thing she had to family.

"I believe that is where I come in," Fennick said behind his curtain of mahogany waves. He wouldn't make eye contact with anyone except Rich. "We shall, first, raid my personal laboratory where I have the inventory and means to cause destruction. It is located beneath my distillery, which also presents the perfect opportunity to draw the enemy away from where we need to be."

"If you lure Ja'azul's baddies to your laboratory, how are you guys gonna get past them on foot?" Beth stomped on the panic filling her gut.

"I also have an underground garage with a few vehicles at my disposal." Fennick's sly grin was softened by the light blushing. "We will be quite alright."

"It's a good plan, Beth." Grady nodded his head as the wheels turned behind those deep blue eyes she loved to get lost in. "Even with time outside our bubble moving at a snail's pace, Ja'azul is still working to move his hoards. It's an efficient use of time and resources."

Beth bit her tongue. She knew Grady and the guys were right. She also knew they were aware of the dangers and were willingly doing what they deemed honorable. It was still a hard pill to swallow. "Fine, we'll eat, and I'll sleep while you guys go do hero stuff."

"If you think I'm gonna leave you here by yourself, you are sorely mistaken." Grady's angry face was charming. Face red, jaw set, and frowning eyebrows. Beth found it almost as endearing as the lopsided grin she liked so much.

"I won't be alone. Zeus will be here with me," Beth argued, though it was futile. Her man wasn't likely to leave her side any time this century.

"Grady will need sustenance and rest as well, Beth. He may not feel like it now, but the fatigue will creep up unannounced." Fennick stared at the ground as he pulled his hair into a low ponytail. "Both of you should stay and rest. As you said, I have a second chance at living. Taking unnecessary risks would be foolish and unwise."

Everyone was against letting Beth go solo. With a sigh, she surrendered. "Fine. Who's on cooking duty? I'm starved."

She looked down at her clothes, noting the black spot over her heart. The protection charm was nowhere to be seen. *Holy shit.*

"Fennick removed it after the Ritual." Grady brushed her hair over her shoulder, pretending to fuss over her when she could practically feel his need for physical contact.

"Ha, good," she chuckled nervously despite the pressure underneath the stain. "I'm gonna burn these clothes and scrub until the top layer of skin is gone."

"Go ahead and get started on that." Grady pressed a kiss to her forehead. "I'll bring you some clean clothes and a towel."

As Beth walked toward the back, Grady's voice chimed in her head, *"But no shenanigans."*

Despite her pout, the warmth that came with Grady's love crowded out any lingering negative feelings.

BETH HAD NEVER CONSIDERED herself a potato connoisseur, but Fennick's bangers and mash were to die for.

"You're *sure* you won't randomly 'poof' out of existence like Myrtle and Heliotta did?" she asked after swallowing the last bite of creamy mashed potatoes.

Fennick nodded, though his ghost of a smile disappeared. "Last night, I had an epiphany. It is the goddess's favor that grants guardians extended lives. In my case, Ja'azul's pact grants me immortality. Should I lose this *gift*," he sneered, "we lose a valuable asset. In fact, despite my skin feeling as though thousands of needles are scraping against the surface, he has not been able to influence me while within the Grove's protection. I did not want to get your hopes up should I be mistaken."

"So, this connection you have with Ja'azul, is it possible it's a two-way street?" Grady propped his elbows on the table and rested his chin at the point where his hands were fisted.

"I believe so." Fennick finally made brief eye contact with Grady before he became obsessively interested in the wood grains on the tabletop. He added quietly, "It is one I plan to walk soon."

Beth's skin crawled at the prospect. There had to be a way to protect Fen, to keep him from losing any more of himself. Unfortunately, the answer was most likely among the knowledge she had not fully absorbed. One thing at a time.

Fennick stood, running his hand through his hair and freeing some strands from one side. "We should get on with it. Please, may I borrow a portal stone?"

Beth's thinking cap winked on. "Will the stones work for you if you've not got, well, you know?"

"There is only one way to find out, dearest." Fennick's charming smile made her stomach flutter. "I promise to take good care of it and return said stone immediately upon usage or lack of effectiveness."

Beth stuck her lips out in thought and rubbed her chin. Reaching into her pocket, Beth gripped the moonstone and handed it to Fennick. "Okay. Make sure she comes back with a full tank."

Grady snickered at her side, pushing against the ground to stand. His legs wobbled like a baby deer walking for the first time. He planted himself back in the chair, doing one of those double yawns where the first wasn't big enough to dislocate your jaw, so your body tries again. "Whoa."

"Let's get you to the cot in the corner before we go." Rich sidled up to Grady and offered his arm.

"I'd rather sleep up in the loft, so maybe, boost me up?"

With several grunts, a string of curses, and a lot of shuffling, the guys managed to get Grady up the ladder. Beth tucked him in, and climbed back down to see the other two off.

"Exgradi," Fennick spoke, holding the stone toward the open door. The moonstone glowed faintly, but there was no whoosh and no pearlescent pool.

"Well, it would appear I am unwo—" Fennick was cut off by a flickering light followed by a faint sigh. The portal's normal opalescent sheen coated the space. "Worthy."

"Cool." Beth smiled, her arms open wide for Rich. "You two be careful." She switched, hugging Fennick and added, "Don't hesitate to call if you get into trouble."

"We will." Fennick released Beth before facing Rich. "Are you ready?"

"As I'll ever be," Rich replied with a grim grin. He stepped up to the portal and turned back to Beth. "We'll be in touch."

Rich disappeared through the mists, and Fennick went to follow. He stopped short and cast a quick glance in Beth's direction. Fen's lips parted. Beth could practically see words perched just beyond, but he snapped his mouth shut and stepped through.

While Beth waited for the portal to close, she sent a silent prayer to the goddess to keep the guys safe...and for Fennick to forgive himself as she had. Maybe, then, he'd finally learn to trust them.

Chapter 34

FENNICK

STEPPING THROUGH A PORTAL unknowing of whether it had materialized properly had to be the stupidest thing Fennick had ever done.

Well, aside from the time he unwittingly wooed the sultan's wife. She had been an exceptionally beautiful woman. Hair the color of spun gold, the most seductive whiskey-colored eyes, and spotless olive skin that sparkled like diamonds in both the light of the sun and of the moon. Back in those days, he pursued only perfection.

Grady would know this once he awoke. He would know everything.

The thought had burrowed into his chest, sowing heavy seeds on its path to his heart. Now, they ached, which brought him back around to the *whys* of his hurried stint of heroism.

The walls of the tunnel were so transparent, he was obligated to test them. His fingers skimmed along the thin veil, thus proving their existence. Furthermore, those damned whispers were no longer haunting him from the shadows beyond.

"Thank the goddess."

"What did you say?" Rich asked over his tensed shoulder.

"The whispers. I can no longer hear them." There was no use hiding truths from this man unless lies would serve to protect him.

"Creepy," Rich countered as his wary gaze probed the blackness beyond. "If I had heard whispers on my first time through, I'd probably have nope'd out."

The men trudged onward, their journey coming to a fast end.

"You wanna go first?" Rich pointed his thumb at the portal, which spoke volumes about the officer's sense of self-preservation.

"Yes." Fennick scooted past Rich, pausing to place his left hand on the shimmering surface. Closing his eyes, he probed the internal well of his power. He figured nothing had changed and was correct. Ja'azul's fortress was locked down tight, albeit a trace flimsier.

Fennick tucked away his disappointment and pushed through into the conference room at the distillery. He had last visited in 1959, leaving the running of the company in the capable hands of a board of directors he had personally appointed. If Fennick survived the coming battle, he was due to assign their successors.

"Have you ever considered corporate work, Rich?"

"No, why?"

"Simply making conversation."

Fennick walked over to his desk phone and dialed Beth's number. The digits had been in his mental vault since the first day they spoke. Coincidentally, it was the same day he had compelled Curtis Putnam to attack her in her own home, all so Fennick could ride in the gallant hero. The memory poisoned his mood further, causing his insides to twist painfully tight.

"Hello?" Beth's melodic voice drifted across the sound waves.

"It is Fennick. The portal was a success. We have both made it safely through."

"That's great! Do you remember the word to close the portal?"

Fennick's smile was so wide, he could practically feel the sparkles in his eyes. "Claudere."

The portal shimmered and fell away like glittery dust, disappearing as though it never existed.

"Beth?"

"Yes, Fennick?"

"Though I have done awful things in the name of revenge." Fennick's free hand trembled. He made a fist and pinned it to his side. "Thank you for believing in me. For seeing me as a person, and not as a monster."

"I should thank you as well."

"Whatever for?"

"For choosing our side and not Ja'azul's."

Fennick's heart was so full, that it could not fit in the space required, for it was whole once more. His cheeks hurt from smiling. "As if you and my new friends gave me much choice."

Beth's giggle released the knots his insides were working to tie. "Sounds like you have a lot of reasons to help keep the world intact and spinning."

"Indeed, I do." Fennick paused to study Rich as he squinted at the photograph on the center of the wall. The man looked to be catching flies.

"Y'all stay safe. I'll sleep better knowing y'all are not in direct way of harm."

"It will be done." Fennick grinned, his life organ turning into a purring fuzzball knowing she cared for his well-being. "We wish you the sweetest dreams. Rest well."

Beth yawned, making a cute mousy noise. "Excuse me. Y'all keep in touch, m-kay?"

"We shall." Fennick held in a laugh when he checked on Rich. The man gestured to the framed photo, an amused bewilderment lighting his face. "And should we require assistance, we will not hesitate to call. Now, sleep, dearest." Fennick was not one to hang up first, so he waited.

"Good. Talk to you later." Beth yawned again, the sound muffled before he heard the click and dial tone.

"This. This is you?" Rich jabbed at the photograph. He practically bounced on the balls of his feet.

"Yes." Fennick's smiles came easier after speaking with Beth. He dipped his head. "Taken on ribbon-cutting day for the Lion and the Fox, home of the finest whiskey in the world."

"You don't look a day older." Rich stopped, his eyebrows tugging in opposite directions. "Which would make you older than me."

Fennick belted in laughter, feeling freer than he had any right. He clapped Rich on the back between his shoulder blades. "Come. My laboratory is in the basement. We must hurry to the elevator before our *'guests'* arrive."

As they strode through the halls, several desks held upright photographs of smiling faces. Fennick hoped his employees had packed their belongings and gotten the hell out of ground zero.

He led Rich down the hall to the main lobby. The floor to ceiling windows up front provided an excellent view, especially if you were expecting company. He breathed a relieved sigh when he spotted nothing.

The elevator dinged and the doors opened. Light jazz music flooded the interior. Rich stepped in first, but Fennick threw one last glance out the front. Not one, but two shadows converged at the far end of the parking lot. One, they could handle. But two? Fennick mentally calculated what he had on hand in his lab. No concoctions other than the last flavor of whiskey came to mind.

"Looks like we've got company." Fennick wasted no time jumping into the lift and pressing the button marked 'B.'

"How many?" Rich rubbed his palms down the thighs of his pants.

"Two."

Rich grimaced. While Fennick sounded cool as a cucumber on the surface, his insides were in full panic mode. Had he had access to his powers, he would not have broken a sweat.

However, promises had been made. Promises he intended to keep.

"Once we arrive at the laboratory, I want you to head straight for the garage. Go to the door opposite the elevator, then turn right. The vehicle bay is at the end. Just inside, keys are stored on the left-hand wall."

"Wait. You're coming with me. I can't leave you knowing there are two nasty creatures heading our way."

Which was precisely the reason Fennick needed Rich out of harm's way. The man was pure hearted and someone Fennick considered a friend. More to the point, Beth would be devastated.

"I will catch up to you by the time you locate a vehicle."

"Fen, I can help."

"Getting an automobile ready *is* helping. I have been away for over fifty years. You and I are on equal footing as to the whereabouts of keys in regard to car locations." Rich's eyebrow raised, so Fennick amended, "I do not remember where anything is parked."

"Ah. Why didn't you just say so?" The man chuckled.

The lights in the elevator flickered as a shudder spread through the building. Fennick and Rich raised their gazes toward the ceiling, then looked at each other.

"Was that what I thought it was?" Rich asked, glancing back at the lift's roof.

"If you think it was my protective wards being triggered, you are correct." Fennick allowed the squeezing around his chest to loosen a fraction. He needed to remain vigilant. With as old as the runes were, there was a slim possibility one or both creatures survived.

The elevator slowed. "If it's all the same, I'll stick around in case there are two really pissed off Agnazar coming after us. Strength in numbers." Rich popped the magazine from his pistol, slammed it back in, and cocked the slide. The safety clicked off. "Plus, Zeus seems to have taken a liking to ya. I'd hate for something bad to happen."

"I appreciate your valor, young man." Fennick jabbed, the corner of his lip ticking up in a grin he tried to hide. Rich was growing on him as well.

A brief silence fell while they waited for the 'ding' to announce their arrival. Double doors parted, and nostalgia took Fennick's breath. It only lasted a heartbeat before he was out of the lift behind Rich.

"So, whatcha gonna brew while we're here?" Rich didn't catch flies this time as his gaze swept the room, noting every detail.

"I am going to whip up a few parting gifts in case we have company." Fennick pointed across the large, rectangular room to a windowless door. "Should anything happen to me, and you need a speedy exit, the parking garage is through those doors, then right."

"Got it." Rich shuffled around before taking post behind one of the long tables. His barrel locked on the door leading to the stairwell. "Do what you need to. I've got you covered, though I'd feel better if there was a way to bar the door."

"I see. Something I shall endeavor to remedy once we return." Fennick replied, hoping his hairbrained idea did not render the lab useless.

He launched into a methodical search through the cabinets. Things were relatively in the same place.

"Aha."

He found a shelf housing six glass jars, grabbed two with the smallest necks, and placed them on the countertop.

Fennick's hand was on a drawer when the room dimmed, and the air conditioning turned to refrigerator cold. His gaze flicked to the stationary elevator before flicking to the stairwell. Nothing as of yet.

Eyeing the Bunsen burners further down the counter, Fennick switched workstations. There was a mini refrigerator built into the cabinet with a clear glass front. A real smile touched his lips as his luck seemed to finally catch up. On the top shelf sat a nearly full jar of test whiskey. He added the fuel to his ingredients. The last thing he needed was a fuse.

"We've got company," Rich warned in a tight voice.

Fennick looked up as twin shadows flittered along the wall of the stairwell. "Damn."

He yanked his shirt sleeve, and the fabric ripped free easily, a testament to the lack of quality made garments in these modern ages. "I need only two minutes."

"Noted," Rich answered gruffly. "If anything happens, promise you'll take care of Zeus."

"On my word," Fennick promised, relieving his other arm of its shirt sleeve. "However, I shall ensure your survival this day, so that I may visit not only Zeus, but my friend."

Fennick divvied up the whiskey between the two glass bottles. He used his sleeves to wipe any spillage before tucking them into the mouths. If only he had a few extra ingredients, he could have made these more potent, more lasting.

"Ungenth, not Agnazar?" Rich asked distractedly. "How did *they* survive?"

Sure enough, when Fennick raised his gaze to the door, the Ungenth stared back. Their wispy 'cloaks' were singed on the edges, but one of them had burns on an entire side. Still, the Universe had showed mercy by sending the lesser beings. Fennick swore he would prove to be worthy of such a gift.

His shaking hands reached out to the gas valve on the side of the burner and gave it a half-turn. The blue flame at the top of the barrel was a beautiful sight.

"There is a sprinkler above the door. Hold your fire until they come further into the room." Fennick commanded, his hands shaking slightly. He could not afford to miss.

When the door opened, sulfur spewed into the lab on the reaper's wings. The world held its breath. The quiet was breached by Rich's finger tightening on the trigger. Fennick held his Molotov cocktails near the flames.

"You are too late, human. Master is coming," ugly number one hissed.

"Surrender now, and he has promised a quick death," ugly number two added.

Their promises were hollow, Fennick saw this now. He would no longer allow the yoke of evil bind him into servitude. His conviction stoked the flames within.

"There was a time when I would have welcomed death's sweet embrace. Unfortunately, for your master, I have finally found something worth living for."

Fennick had to keep them talking. They were advancing too slowly. At least the Ungenth had not split up.

"Nothing on this planet will survive the wrath of Ja'azul." Ugly number one made a phlegmy cough noise, and Fennick's skin crawled.

He tilted forward so the cloth caught on the Bunsen flame.

"Bold words for a lowly drudge." Fennick knew he was poking the bear, as the modern colloquial went, but he was the one with handfuls of explosives...and they were finally standing on the proverbial 'X.'

"Now."

Fennick launched the first bottle. The trajectory was beautiful, landing right in front of the Ungenth. The glass shattered, spraying Ugly Number One with whiskey up to its middle. Fire laced its other side, giving it matching scars. It's high-pitched screams mixed with Rich's gunfire as he emptied an entire clip into Ugly Number Two. It fell to a twitching heap on the floor.

Fennick flung the second cocktail at the retreating form of the other Ungenth. Sadly, the splash lacked the dramaticism of the first. The meager flames only served to further anger the Ungenth.

It charged Fennick with its long, gnarled talons aimed at his chest. A flash of red against a stark white wall grabbed Fennick's attention. The fire extinguisher was a few steps away, and the angry Ungenth had to contend with a long workstation.

The clatter of metal was followed by a sharp, "Shit!"

Fennick wrapped his hands around the apparatus and pulled it free. As he spun, he released the pin and let loose at eye level. His aim was that of a drunkard fighting a mad bull. The Ungenth swore in a language Fennick should not have understood, proving he hit his mark.

As if to mock Fennick, the sprinklers activated, coating the lab in chlorinated rain. He hefted the empty metal cannister in two hands, using it as a battering ram against the head of his adversary. The creature hissed. Foul-smelling spittle the shade of the swamps from Fennick's homeland sprayed from its mouth. The excrement sizzled wherever it landed, including his shirt.

"Can I not have a single victory?" Fennick grunted as it ate through the fibers to the top layer of skin.

Fennick struck the Ungenth in front of him again, coming away with blackish green goo. The sprinklers worked to rinse the vile substance down the drains. He briefly wondered what damage it would cause to the pipes.

Repeatedly smashing a metal cylinder at shoulder height into a tough-as-leather husk had worn Fennick to the bone. He was also *soaked* to the bone and shivering from the innate cold front that followed Ja'azul's minions wherever they went.

Fennick raised his arms, pushing past his screaming muscles.

The Ungenth jerked forward. Its round leech-like mouth made a sucking noise as it sputtered. Something was lodged in its skull.

It jerked again, and the malicious cinders in its eyes darkened as the light snuffed out. It tipped forward, falling to the floor in a puddle of slime. The water washed it toward the grates with the rest of the gods-awful mess.

Rich breathed heavily and blinked the water away. In his hands he held a fireman's ax. "Gun was jammed."

The muscles in Fennick's arms forgot how to work. He dropped the fire extinguisher to the floor with a dull clink, choking on a relieved laugh. Willpower kept his legs from buckling at the knees.

"I admit having underestimated the perseverance of an Ungenth." Fennick tilted his head back, letting the vestiges of filth wash away the stink. When he was clean again, he shook the water free and smiled at his friend. "Thank you, Rich. I owe you my life."

"Think nothing of it. You'd have done the same for me."

"Yes, I believe I would have."

As the sprinklers ceased, errant droplets of water broke the monotony of blanketed quiet. They needed to move to the next part of their plan.

"Let us go before more unfriendly creatures stop by for a social visit." Fennick rolled his shoulders back before shuffling toward the door. As he crossed the lab, he surveyed the minimal amount of damage. Knowing he would be able to return made leaving easier.

"Mind if I keep the axe?" Rich asked as he kept in step beside him.

Fennick studied his companion with a side eye. Rich had the axe slung over his shoulder and the upper body build of a lumberjack.

A sly grin formed on Fennick's lips as he nodded. "It suits you."

"Damn straight."

Laughter bubbled from Fennick's gut. No matter what awaited them at the armory—or the Grove—he was glad to have Rich on his side. It had been a very long time since Fennick had experienced being a part of something, and they made a good team.

Chapter 35

GRADY

Consciousness pulled a reluctant Grady to the surface, courtesy of the classic xylophone tune playing on loop.

One of his arms was around Beth's waist and his leg was thrown over hers, holding her back tight to his front. Strands of her honeyed brown hair tickled his nose, and Beth's warm vanilla and lavender scent surrounded him. Waking up like this was pure bliss.

Except for his damned phone ringing off the hook.

The thought jolted his brain awake, and his eyes popped open. He extricated himself from the angel now dozing at his side. She hadn't even moved.

Grady found his buzzing device on the floor, tucked into the pocket of his jeans. Without looking at the screen, he answered with a hushed, "H'lo?"

"Sorry to wake you, Grady, but it's time to raid the station," Rich's bassy voice rumbled into the receiver.

"Did Fen finish making his explosive concoctions?" Grady wiped his face with his hand, hoping to clear away any leftover sleep, but a yawn caught him unawares.

"There were some complications," Fennick supplied in a louder than necessary yell.

"What kind of complications?" Adrenaline swept the lingering tiredness away in a blink. "Are y'all injured?"

"We're okay," Rich answered quickly. "The two Ungenth that found us weren't so lucky."

"Shit."

"Yeah, shit is right," Rich grumbled. "Our play to lure away any bad guys worked too well. We took care of them, though Fen's lab didn't look so pretty afterwards."

"Suffice it to say," Fennick's voice was tight with frustration, "my lab will need some minor repairs before it is functional again.”

“I’m sorry to hear that.” Grady grimaced at the thought. Alchemy was to Fennick as woodworking was to Grady. “How long have you two been gone anyway?”

There was a long pause before Rich added, “’Bout thirty minutes, give or take.”

So much for a nap.

“Seems like he’s using our need for sleep against us.” Grady sighed, looking over his shoulder at his sleeping beauty. “I’ll wake Beth now and text before we portal over to the side door.”

“Sounds good. We’ll hold down the fort until you get here,” Rich replied.

“See ya.”

The phone line clicked, but the cloud of dread hovering over Grady darkened. Bits of Fennick’s most recent happenings had worked their way into Grady’s memory banks while he slept. The worst so far being the slaughter of the Bridges family. Fennick loved them as his own kin, and he had been forced to murder them while they looked on with hopelessness, wondering why. The images would haunt him for a long while.

Grady needed time to process. He needed Beth.

He climbed back into bed and curled around her, burying his face in her silky hair. The muscles all over his body felt like someone had tied strings to each bundle and had tightened their grip until he was balled up. Each slow inhale and slower exhale eased the tension until he was finally unwound.

“Beth,” he murmured into her neck, running his nose up the slope of skin between her shoulder and ear. “Wake up, beautiful. It’s time to meet up with Rich and Fennick.”

She snuggled deeper into his embrace. He tucked the little whine she made into the vault he kept in his heart, full of the things he loved about this woman.

As usual, her reaction to his affections caused southbound stirrings they didn’t have time to visit. Still, he placed soft kisses on her shoulder and down her arm until his cheek rested on her bicep. Her lips were slightly parted and her breaths were shallow. He hated having to wake her from such a restful slumber, but their friends needed them.

Grady pulled his arms away to shift Beth onto her back. Her instant frown melted as quickly as it came, which left an unsettling in his chest. This was a woman who woke with the slightest temperature change or when the house settled in the middle of the night.

Pins and needles covered his face and torso in a pricking wave. His hands gripped her shoulders as a line of sweat beaded his forehead and upper lip. Grady shook her gently as he fought the lump clawing up his throat.

“Beth, baby, please wake up. Please—” His voice cracked as visions of her lifeless body the day before pressed to the forefront.

He saw her chest rise, saw her eyelids move with REM sleep, *felt* her warm skin, but it was like his brain didn’t register these as signs of life. Instead, his chest caved over his heart, tumbling into the dark chasm.

“Grady?” Beth’s speech was slow, as if her brain was still rebooting after a deep sleep. The feel of her palm pressed against his cheek brought him away from the edge. When he opened his eyes, her gaze burned with concern. “What’s wrong, love?”

He shook his head, unable to speak of the waking nightmare that was still raw enough to make him crumble. Her arms encircled him, pulling him tight. She lightly raked her fingernails along his scalp, causing him to shudder.

"Your sadness woke me. What caused it?" Beth tried asking again.

"I'm okay, darlin'. Just had a moment when you didn't wake up right away." Grady sniffled. His face burned with embarrassment. Clearing his throat, he added, "Rich and Fennick are waiting for us."

Was he a coward for not confessing his issue to Beth? Probably. They'd be fine. *He'd* be fine. He just needed to keep his mind busy with other tasks.

Beth pulled back, her assessing gaze roaming his face. When she didn't find what she was searching for, she moved one of her hands over his heart. "How long were we asleep?"

"Not even an hour."

Beth's eyes went wide. She released him to fall dramatically backwards. With an equally dramatic arm toss, she hid her eyes and groaned. "I know Fennick is good at his job, but now he's just showing off."

"They had company and dealt with it."

Beth slid her arm above her head and leveled him with a frown. "What? Are they okay?"

"They said they're fine."

"Fine." Beth huffed, blowing away the strands of hair that landed on her nose. "Help me up?"

"Gladly." Grady shifted to his knees and took Beth's hands in his. When he pulled, her body collided with his, knocking them to the floor.

"You knocked the wind out of me, brat," Grady wheezed, stuck between stifling his cough or laughing. He did both, but the sparkle in Beth's eyes was worth the oxygen loss.

"Sorry, handsome." She wiggled off of him and stood, offering a hand.

Grady raised an eyebrow, distrusting the olive branch. Ultimately, he accepted. Beth's wide-legged stance rooted her, so he had the leverage to stand.

"Let's get dressed before you start anymore trouble." Grady's voice had gone husky, and just like that, things were back to normal.

Beth winked before questing for her clothes. They'd gone straight to bed, but their outer clothing had been discarded who knows where.

Grady pulled on his other boot and grabbed his phone. "On our way."

His phone dinged immediately.

"Rich said they're parked at the side entrance at the distillery. The one we initially came through."

"Once we portal to the guys, do you think it'll draw more Ungenth?" Beth tucked her upper lip between her teeth, wringing her hands.

"Don't know. Better to expect hostiles and be ready rather than go in with our hands tied behind our backs." Grady placed his hands over hers, stopping her from rubbing them raw. "We'll get a better handle on things once we get on the road."

"Right." Beth's lips formed a line. Her gaze turned steel. "Let's not leave them hanging."

"First things first, we need to commune with nature." Grady raised her hands to his lips, kissing her knuckles a few times before helping her down the loft ladder.

Even as they sat outside his favorite place, Grady's gut churned. He didn't like going into the unknown, and the sheriff's station had a *lot* of unknowns. He made a mental list of things he did know, like how they were four strong, and Rich knew where to go and how to get into the armory. More importantly, while they didn't have ready access to all guardian magic, it was *there* in their minds. When push came to shove, he had no doubt when they needed something, it would present itself.

THE SUMMER SOLSTICE WAS a little over a week away, but the darkness settling over eastern Tennessee gave strong winter vibes. Not the pretty, snow-covered hills kinda winter the tourists flocked to. No. This was more the bleak, shivering cold type of winter where—instead of sticking to the ground—the snow mixed with rain and made mush that turned into black ice.

Grady held Beth's small hand in his as they made their way to the...whatever gorgeous hell-on-four-wheels they were about to get into.

Rich raised his chin toward the bluish-black sky devoid of stars. "Looks like we'll be working against the night shift after all."

"Sucks, but what choice do we have?" Grady patted Rich on the shoulder as he passed, while Beth stopped to hug her father figure.

Fennick leaned against a vintage car with his arms and ankles crossed. When he lifted his chin, Fen's guarded gaze watched them like an abused pup. The flaky bits of black clinging to his now sleeveless shirt didn't help.

"Glad you survived." Grady offered his hand in a truce. "Nice car, by the way."

The worry lines across Fennick's forehead softened as he accepted the handshake. "This lovely thing? It is a 1945 Riley RMA. One of the few four-seaters I happened to collect. Fortune be praised I allowed the pushy salesman to talk me into it."

A low whistle came from behind as Beth and Rich joined them. "Nice ride," she eyed the automobile like it was an expensive designer fishing pole or a dressed out hiking backpack with all the pockets. "How're y'all holding up after taking on two Ungenth at once?"

"Thank you for your concern, but I have fared much worse." Fennick brushed off any concerns with a well-practiced flippancy, waving his hand in dismissal.

"Have y'all seen anymore of Ja'azul's agents?" Grady asked the question that had been burning his tongue since before they left the Grove.

"None. Of course, we were underground for most of the time." Rich scratched the back of his neck, casting a glance over his shoulder. "Hopefully, anything left will find their way here."

"Hope so." Grady opened the back passenger door and gestured for Beth to get inside. She stepped over a fireman's axe and settled into the bucket seat near the middle. While Grady got comfy next to her, Rich hopped in the driver's seat with the biggest grin Grady had ever seen on the man. Fennick struggled to get in the front passenger seat but finally managed.

"You sure you're alright, Fen?" Grady buckled up and placed his hand on Beth's leg. She turned her brilliant smile on him, mouthing, 'Oh my gosh!'

"Of course. Now, buckle up, kids. Depending on the turn of events this evening, this may be your one and only ride in this rare beauty," Fennick said with a wink over his shoulder before turning toward the windshield.

The pleasant and uneventful fifteen-minute cruise to town ended at the bank parking lot across the street from the Sheriff's department. They all quietly exited the fine piece of machinery, making sure the doors quietly clicked shut. Standing at the edge of the road, they studied the pillar of law-and-order they were expected to raid.

A lonely light in the front held vigil while the rest of the building slept in shadows. Two cruisers were parked on the right side nearest the front door.

"It'll be quicker if we go in through the back door," Rich instructed. "Unless they've changed the code, that is."

"Can we break the lock otherwise?" Fennick asked.

The rest of their conversation was drowned by the rowdy gremlins stirring a pot of thick acid soup Grady's mid-section. Part of him, the part tremoring uncontrollably, didn't want to go back so soon. He'd come close to dying in that place, unable to protect himself. Now he was willingly taking his reason for surviving in that awful place.

What if I lock down? What if I can't protect her?

Suddenly, Beth was in front of him, holding his face captive. "This isn't the same situation as before. This time you can freely kick ass without worrying about breaking the law."

"I get it, Beth, it's just... The last time I was here, he did something to disconnect me from my panther."

It was a terrifying experience he had no interest in revisiting.

"Then transform now. Your senses are sharper as a big, cuddly cat, and we can communicate through our bond."

"I dunno, Beth. I haven't tried since before lockup. Haven't really had time."

"Close your eyes, connect with your inner cat, then do the thing."

"You make it sound simple."

"Because it is, dummy." She kissed the tip of his nose. Whispering against his lips, she added, "I believe in you."

Grady's fingers dug into her hips and his heart skipped two beats. Hell, with conviction like that from his woman, Grady figured he could fly if she asked.

"Love you," he whispered back.

Beth took a few steps back and crossed her arms, dipping her head in support, as if to say *'go on.'*

Grady concentrated on the part of his magic tied to his panther form and nudged it. The sleepy cat yawned lazily before getting to its feet. There were two unfamiliar energies next to the feline, but they were out of focus.

His panther cantered forward, gaining speed. Once it was at a full run, its back haunches coiled, and the furry beast leapt, dissipating into a million tiny fragments.

Grady's bones heated from the inside, rearranging and snapping into place. Sleek black hair sprouted all over his body. As his world shrank, his senses magnified. Amid the blanketing songs of tree frogs and crickets, a mouse two blocks away scurried along the barren streets, seeking shelter. He could make out each individual vein running through the whispering leaves of every tree nearby. Their coloration looked as if someone had cranked up the saturation setting to maximum. As it was every time he shifted, the gloriousness of his surroundings invited peace into his being.

Once he was on four paws, panther Grady shook his coat before gliding over to Beth. She smoothed the hairs on his head, causing him to purr. His tongue swept a sloppy kiss on her wrist before he turned to the others. Fennick nodded his head in approval while Rich picked his jaw off the ground.

"He could have done this at any time while he was in lockup, couldn't he?" the former deputy asked.

"Yep. But he was trying to protect himself," Beth answered for Grady.

"Well, I'll be damned."

Panther Grady curled his upper lip and inhaled. The first scent coating his receptors was copper, and lots of it. Underneath, he detected sulfur, gunpowder, and expensive whiskey. The last of which had an accompanying heartbeat.

Revenge was like fire in his veins. He was eager to end the man who had threatened Beth and almost ended his own life.

"All dead, except one. Blaylock." Grady passed the message through the open gateway between him and Beth.

Beth relayed to the others, and he headed across the bank parking lot.

The click and slide of a clip being checked, and a bullet being chambered came from behind. "You good with the axe, Fen?"

"Quite good, though it's been a century, give or take."

Rich gave him a curt nod. "When we get inside, there'll be only one door between us and the hallway. Hang a right and the armory is the last door on the left."

Grady added Rich's directions to the mental map he'd formed during his short stay. The closer they got to the building, the stronger the ground beneath his paws buzzed like a hive of bees. It didn't hurt, instead it felt like a warning. He wasn't sure if it was a guardian thing or not. If it was, he couldn't remember doing it before.

Beth followed on the inside edge of his periphery, shivering when she crossed whatever made his paws itch. The fact that she wasn't going ahead of him meant he could concentrate on what lied ahead. He looked forward to thanking her later.

"After we catch up on sleep, I'm all yours."

Panther Grady peeked over in time to catch Beth's wink.

He crossed the road and veered toward the side of the building where the patrol cars were parked. He couldn't pinpoint where exactly the singular heartbeat came from, but he recognized the pattern. Bump, bump, pause, bump. Eric Blaylock was anxious, same as when he interrogated Grady the second time.

"I think he's expecting us."

"Shit," Beth murmured before relaying Grady's thought.

"Figures." Rich didn't sound surprised in the least. "Blaylock treats vendettas like fine wine. He lets it sit a spell before enjoying a glass."

"And he's had a couple of days to stew over a missing deputy and prisoner," Beth finished with a grimace. Her jaw was set, and her eyes narrowed. "If he thinks he's gonna hurt the people I care about, he's got another thing coming."

Grady stopped at the back door and waited for Rich to enter his code. The process should take seconds but not knowing whether it would work made it seem like an eternity. The panel turned green and the door mechanism clicked open.

Rich had his hand on the knob, when Grady noticed the heartbeat was on the move.

"He knows we're here."

"Blaylock's coming this way," Beth rushed in a loud whisper.

"Let us not leave him waiting." Fennick's knuckles turned white as he tightened his grip.

Rich yanked the door open. Grady slipped inside to blinding darkness. It took a moment for his panther vision to adjust, but eventually the room looked like a slightly grainy black and white movie.

The space was large enough to fit a refrigerator and a round dining table with four chairs on one side. Across the room, a single countertop held a coffee pot and a microwave.

There was a bump and a curse. Something clicked and a beam of light scattered the room as though someone had dropped it on a trampoline. Grady hissed when the light shone in his eyes.

"Sorry." Rich's deep voice mumbled.

Panther Grady shook his head and slunk further into the room. The only way deeper into the lion's den was through the door opposite where they entered. He honed his hearing in on the moving heartbeat. It had stopped...on the other side of the door.

Why isn't he coming through? What's he waiting for?

Beth's hand brushed against his flank. He felt something akin to a static charge but less-sharp zap discharge. Knowing Beth had her magic at the ready loosened the band squeezing his lungs.

He inched forward on silent paws. Blaylock didn't give anything away. The man's heartbeat and breathing were steady. Unchanged. Grady glided in front of the door, turning his head and pulling back his lips to taste the air.

His hackles raised. The spring mechanism holding back their deaths screeched with misuse. He hissed a warning, but it was drowned out by the booming dirge.

Grady did the only thing he could. His panther jumped back sideways, hoping to put as much of his body between Beth and the scatter shot.

A quick flash of light, and the door exploded into projectile murder splinters. His entire left side was engulfed in flame from a multitude of lacerations. He thanked the Gods for the adrenaline rush hiding most of the damage.

Grady landed with a thud, legs sprawled in front of him. His head felt heavy, but he lifted it anyway. He couldn't see Beth or the others amid the thick cloud of dust. His hearing was shot except the loud ringing in his ears.

Movement brought his attention back to the door. A glint of metal poked through the hole, seeking a target. Panic pushed him to his feet. He was close enough in the tight room that, when the barrel slowed to take aim, he was already there. He clamped his panther jaws around the steel barrel and jerked.

The man's grip remained firm.

Before Grady could let go, his tongue was ablaze with the taste of burn bacon. He yelped and dropped his hold on the smoking weapon. The gamey scent of meat cooked on a campfire invaded his nostrils. At least he'd managed to somewhat mangle the barrel.

The smoke cleared for a split second, allowing Grady to catch sight of Blaylock. In place of the man who'd tortured him, an Ungenth-like screen overlaid his body. Over Blaylock's steel gray eyes, flaming embers flickered, and his tattered uniform was saturated in a tacky black substance. The Sheriff's well-styled charcoal gray hair was no longer slicked back, but stuck up in tufts. In several places, clumps of hair were missing...as if they had been ripped from his scalp.

Panthers lacked the mouth parts to gasp properly, so it came out as more of a hiss. Grady backed away, wanting to look for the others, but his gaze was fixated by the change in his would-be executioner.

"'Bout time you cowards showed up," Blaylock's stern voice had lost its brusqueness. It was otherworldly like all Ja'azul's minions, akin to broken shards of glass being dragged in a burlap sack across asphalt. "And you brought a pet."

Grady didn't care much for monologues, ignoring Blaylock's muffled words. The man wasn't bleeding enough for Grady's liking.

Neutralize the threat, then check on Beth and the others.

The door flew open. The still intact bottom half caught him off-guard. Grady had a moment of weightless flight before his body crashed into the wall. The door followed, added insult to injury. His ribs chose to reminisce old wounds when he limped out from behind the mangled door.

Blaylock's boot lowered slowly to the floor, an evil grin plastered on his ugly face. As he sauntered into the room, he cocked the shotgun and said, "Welcome to Hell, kiddies."

Oh, good. I can mostly hear again.

The sheriff made a show of checking around the room by exaggerating looking left and right. The frown of disappointment would have been more enjoyable if Grady knew Beth was safe. "Well, shit. Don't tell me e'rybody's down for the count already. I was expectin' a little more fun."

In the back left corner, a body moved into a crouch. Grady paced in front of Blaylock, hoping to hold the bastard's attention so whoever it was could get the drop on him. The panther's low growl was full of menace as he swiped a heavy claw, pointy side aimed at Blaylock's meaty thigh.

The man hopped backwards out of the way with shocking speed. A memory wiggled to the forefront. Paul had been faster, *stronger* while heavily under Ja'azul's influence, too. In panther form, Grady hadn't been able to best his ex-friend, either.

He blinked and found himself staring down the end of Blaylock's shotgun barrel.

"Now, that was a rude fucking thing to do, wasn't it?" the sheriff sneered. "Then again, I never was a cat person."

There weren't many places Grady could hide that a double-aught buckshot wouldn't find. So, he slunk backward, hoping to draw the man toward him so the tall shadow behind the bastard had room to swing.

Blaylock took a single step forward, zeroing his aim on Grady's head. He was out of ideas except one...changing back to human form so he could use magic.

If only he could slow time.

Grady called his panther to retreat at the same time a ripple pulsed from his body. It parted the air like waves in the ocean.

Wha-?

His neck spasmed, skin tingled and itched as the change took hold. A clatter from somewhere in the room had Blaylock swinging around. While his bones cracked and reverted, Grady forced his head to turn so he could see what was going on.

To his horror, Blaylock had his shotgun aimed at Fennick. Grady fought against the searing pain and pushed off the ground. His body tumbled into the Sheriff, rocking him forward but not off his feet. Grady was not so lucky.

Fennick had used the distraction to make a grab at the firearm. Blaylock gritted his teeth and held on as though he'd affixed it to his hands with superglue.

Fennick's widened gaze met Grady's. Sweat glued the man's hair to his face, making him look like some gorilla-man hybrid. He grunted a hiss, "Quickly."

Grady willed his panther to finish the transformation. Heat coursed underneath his skin in waves as bones popped and rearranged to accommodate his human frame.

Blaylock's face was beet red. He roared and bull-rushed Fennick. His friend smacked into the wall with a painful thud.

Where the fuck are Beth and Rich?

He was almost back to biped status when he blanked out. This had never happened before. He'd also never been drugged. A troublesome thought pinched his airways shut and a death-like chill swept across his mind.

What if I can't change back?

"You are going through...other changes," a voice nowhere spoke. Sensing Grady's rising panic, it added, "Patience, guardian. You will regain your human form. We are nearly done."

The sense of falling into a barren space of nothingness was one of Grady's least favorite experiences. At least the descent was slow. Whenever he reached the bottom, there shouldn't be much damage.

"You are funny. If it makes you feel better, picture a cushion in your mind." The voice had no accent or inflections to place whose it was.

Grady opened his mouth to ask who was speaking to him, when the blackness turned gray. Like a monochrome sunrise on fast-forward, the space lightened to a brilliant white.

His feet were on firm ground when someone whispered, "Open your eyes."

Grady's eyelids fluttered open to pitch dark. After a few blinks, his panther vision kicked back in without him thinking about it. He sat up and rolled his shoulders. The last of the black fur fell to the ground on a shudder. He jumped to his feet, not knowing how much time had passed during his mysterious and untimely reboot.

Blaylock had lost the gun. Instead, his shoulders were hunched forward, elbows locked at his sides. His fists were ready to administer pain.

Fennick was in the corner, bent at the waist and breathing heavily. When their gazes connected, he winked. Quicker than a blink, Fennick smashed his fist into Blaylock's midsection. The man stumbled back half a step, spittle flying from his bared teeth like a rabid dog.

Grady had heard stories of men on drugs, the ones that give them superhuman strength and make them unafraid of anything. This must be what they were like.

And Blaylock was laser-focused on putting Fennick down.

Grady put his hip into the swing, and his balled fist struck the Sheriff's back. If Grady was correct in his anatomy, Blaylock would feel that right in the kidney.

A guttural roar tore from Blaylock as he spun on Grady. The backhand he wasn't expecting exploded Grady's jaw and sent him flying across the room. He greeted the wall before falling to the concrete floor. On his way down, he was lucky enough to crash through the table. A slew of soft curses wasted what oxygen hadn't been knocked out of his lungs. Sharp stabs of heat lined his ribcage with each inhale and exhale.

Unable to let Fennick take on Blaylock by himself, Grady summoned Beth's stubbornness. He planted a hand on the floor and pushed. His body shook, sweat poured down his face and back, his ribcage screamed at him to stop. His vision darkened around the edges.

As he stared ahead to concentrate, Grady's brain made sense of the shifting lumps in the corner. Beth and Rich were waking.

The rapid tiredness sweeping over Grady was overwhelming and unwelcome. He fell to a heap on the floor while the sound of grunts and wet smacks of bone on flesh echoed in the room. His burst of concentrated stubbornness had burned off too quickly. Darkness reclaimed him once again.

Chapter 36

BETH

WHEN THE DOOR EXPLODED, debris flew everywhere, and dust blanketed the room. Beth had thrown up a shield at the last moment, but it drained her mental and physical batteries. She'd loaded for bear before they came. It should have lasted her the whole fight, but she was depleted.

Drowsiness lapped at the distant sounds of a struggle until they morphed into a crackling fireplace, warm and cozy. A long nap sounded nice, especially after having to wake before she was fully rested.

She'd just settled into a comfortable place when there was an odd tugging sensation in her gut. It took her several seconds to realize it was her connection to Grady, warning her of danger. He needed her help. The adrenaline rush gave her the boost she needed to climb out of the metaphorical bed in which she'd fallen.

Whiffs of gun smoke, sweat, and copper slithering into her nostrils were like smelling salts. Grady, Rich, and Fennick. The Sheriff, the explosion. The events slammed against her chest, chasing away her desire to rest.

Beth lay on her side on the dirty concrete floor. It took seconds for her eyes to adjust to the dark. Nearby, she heard the smack of boney knuckles on sticky flesh followed by pained grunts and shuffling feet.

She glanced around the room. Fennick looked like he'd stuck his head in a hornet's nest and a gaggle of kids mistook it for a pinata. Despite this, Fennick's slow movements remained concise.

Blaylock reminded her of a zombie extra from the show her dad watched religiously. Blood soaked his clothes and streaked his face. Lines of rouge ran down his arm, dripping off his elbow. He struck Fennick again in the face with the fierceness of a cobra and the strength of a rhino.

Fennick spat a glob of blood at Blaylock. His exhales were wheezy. He couldn't keep taking hits like this without dying.

There was something wrong with the picture, someone was missing...

Where's Grady?

Beth's chest rattled with the pounding behind her ribs. Her shaking hands pushed against the concrete, but something heavy pinned her from the hips down. Pins and needles had already started at her toes.

Rich.

He hadn't hesitated, jumping in front of her when the door exploded. Her racing heart spared a beat for sentiment. Rich was like a father to her, but he was barely scratched. He'd live. She wasn't so sure about Grady.

Bracing her hands on Rich's shoulders, Beth shoved. After a couple of tries, she managed to pull her legs free. Doing so got a grunt and an incoherent mumble from Rich, but she was a woman on a mission.

Beth's frantic gaze searched her love. A mop of black curls lied among the remnants of the dining table. His eyelids were half-closed while his hand reached for her. Her chest squeezed tight, but she wouldn't let panic take hold. If Grady was dead, she'd know because her heart would stop in that instant.

She crawled to his side, her heart now a battering ram. Blood pumped into her ears with the force of a stormy ocean. Her sight stayed on the man whose love was vaster than the stars in the night sky, and brighter and warmer than the mid-day sun in July.

Beth gripped his hand in hers and scooted next to his shoulder. Her free hand went to his chest. Grady's breaths were the same as his heartbeat, shallow and even.

The last time she needed to save a life, she took Elliott Larson's life force. She summoned the ability and turned her attention to Blaylock. When Beth tried to take his essence to convert like she did before, she was metaphysically kicked out and the door slammed in her face.

Hot tears rolled down Beth's cheeks. She didn't have anything to give to heal him but herself. Grady would complain but at least he'd be alive. She'd sit through a hundred lectures to have another day with him.

Beth dipped into her reserves and pushed healing energy into his center. There wasn't time to check where the damage was or how much. Grady's body would have to figure it out.

He took a deep breath and gently squeezed her hand. Waiting for his eyes to open was like watching sands fall in an hourglass. When his blue eyes focused on her, the tight band around her chest loosened. Beth allowed herself to smile. Someone in the universe was looking out for them.

His eyebrows dipped. Beth realized the room had gone silent.

Grady opened his mouth as large meaty fingers gripped her hair and yanked. She screamed, reaching for Grady as her body was airborne. Her scalp throbbed. Blaylock was gonna rip her hair out from the roots.

"Let me go, you bastard," Beth yelled, though her voice cracked from the thick build-up in her throat.

She kicked her legs, trying to land a hit on something. This only made Blaylock tighten his grip and made her eyes sting. She hoped the sensation of warm liquid running across her scalp was imaginary. Gripping his wrist with both hands eased his hold, but only a fraction. The man was made of tempered steel.

"Settle down, or I'll take my time, killing ya nice and slow." Nails on a chalkboard were preferable to the scratchy echoing hiss of Blaylock's voice. "I'll start with your eyelids. Slice 'em, then peel 'em off like flower petals, so you can watch the rest of the show without missing a blink."

The way he talked about her torture like they were catching up at the church potluck made her skin crawl. She peeked to make sure she wasn't covered in hundreds of wriggling maggots. She couldn't see any, but Blaylock's 'putrid foot boils and swamp-ass' cologne was a strong argument against her senses.

While the idea of having a bald spot on the top of her head wasn't great, Beth did as she was told. She didn't have anything to fuel her magic except her own lifeforce...and her track record for controlling how much she took from herself was zero to two.

It was best to bide her time. He'd have to release her for his next planned act of nefariousness, and she'd be able to get the drop on him.

The Sheriff continued through the door he'd destroyed and down the hall, opposite of the armory. His movements were almost robotic the way he stiff-legged stalked the hall. His straight-armed hold on her was very much a Frankenstein pose. It would take them forever to get wherever they were going, and her scalp had gotten the memo. Instead of an SOS, the ache had escalated to one long dash.

Beth couldn't stand it. She needed a distraction. To make her think of anything else other than the things lurking in the dark because the hallway narrowed ahead of her.

"Why are you doing this?"

Beth cringed at the stupidness of her question. He'd done it for a power he had no hope of comprehending, same as Curtis Putnam and Tom's and Grady's dads.

"In my dreams, I remember." Blaylock's broken-glass hiss made her shiver.

"Remember what?"

"Rust-colored skies above sands of anodized titanium and lakes of sulfuric acid," he wheezed as if a mummy speaking through layers of dust and sand. "My home."

Okay. Blaylock was out for lunch. He'd been reduced to a meat puppet, and the entity inhabiting his body pulled the strings.

There was no debating with something that wasn't human, but what could she use for a boost? Beth sent a trickle of her power outward like an insect's feeler, seeking some sort of life. There was nothing left except her friends.

Grady always said my stubbornness was a superpower.

"Fuck it," she whispered. "Are you wearing flame retardant clothing, by chance?"

Blaylock stopped in his tracks. Twisting her head to gauge his reaction was not an option, not with how tight his grip was. She did the only thing she could. She summoned the blue flame.

Shadows played on the wall, dancing happily as they devoured his shredded shirt sleeve. Beth closed her eyes as the sudden heat caused a rush of warm air. Even the acrid burnt hair smell she hated wasn't as bothersome, knowing the Sheriff would release his hold soon.

...any minute now.

The hallway was eerily quiet for housing a flaming zombie.

Instead, Blaylock resumed his stiff march. Beth growled in frustration. At least the flickering light from her fire kept the darkness at bay.

And the hallway was narrowing. Adjusting her hold on Blaylock's wrist, she treated his arm like a pull-up bar and swung her legs. Gritting her teeth helped to assuage the *idea* of pain, rather than the truth of it.

"What are you doing?" Blaylock's gruff voice almost broke her concentration.

"Swinging."

The entirety of her head was one big ball of agonizing ache. If this didn't work, Beth prayed she wouldn't die of an aneurism. When she was small, one of her aunts almost died from one. She'd said it was the worst pain she'd ever felt.

Well, Beth wasn't there yet, and there was more swinging to do.

Her toe grazed the wall, but Grady's voice coming from the other room had her heart doing jumping jacks.

Beth was on the back swing, bracing herself for the kick-off when her world was in rapid motion...in the wrong direction. The opposite wall collided with the left side of her head, filling her mouth with liquified pennies. She swallowed, adding a dash of spice to the rolling pitch in her stomach while her head felt like it had been cracked like a nut.

The only time she'd been punched in the face once was by Curtis Putnam, and it had hurt like a son of a bitch. This was much worse. Like someone had hammered an ice pick into the top of her head above her ear and the pointy end busted out the bottom through her jaw.

Beth's eyes were on auto-blink and the controls were set on 'random and rapid.' The echo of an ocean was stuck inside her ear with the salty seawater spilling out of her eardrums and down her neck.

Her stomach lurched. Blaylock's extraordinary hold hadn't let up, though the halls continued to flicker from her flames. Unable to keep it down, she emptied the contents of her stomach with some getting on her shirt.

Beth's other bodily fluids joined the party while the bass beat thrumming in her head dropped so hard stars swam in her vision. She was a thousand percent sure this was what dear aunty experienced.

Slowly, the stars gathered into groups and joined in a circle. Beth was in the middle of the pretty lights. They *called* to her. She started forward, and the closer she got, the further her pain receded like a bad dream.

When she reached out, a cluster floated onto her hand. It was warm and fluttered against her palm like the butterfly kisses her mother used to give her at bedtime.

"Eat me," the ball of happiness in her hand whispered with a childlike giggle.

Beth opened her mouth wide, popped it inside, and swallowed it whole. She crinkled her nose as a bitterness like rotten lemons coated her mouth.

Using her shirt to wipe the taste off didn't help. She no longer cared if the strange fireflies were pretty, she wanted to go back. Back to where Grady was.

Turning on her heel, Beth stomped in the direction she came, but nothing looked familiar. Spinning in a slow circle, a lump formed in her throat when she realized she had no idea where 'here' was or how to leave.

Even more disturbing were the stars. Not only had they corralled her into a tight ring, but they also went on for miles in every direction.

Pondering her predicament was like staring into the dark when—without warning—someone switched on neon flashing lights. The truth was spelled out, not in a matinee, but in clusters of magical knowledge that she'd put off for too long. The jerks had jumped the fence and were forcing her to finish the ritual. The timing couldn't have been worse, but Beth had dug the hole, now she had to lie in it.

"So, we're doing this *right now*, are we?"

Determination set her jaw and pressed her lips into a line. Beth slowly blinked, inhaling and exhaling deeply before plopping down where she stood. Holding out her hand, palm up, she leveled her gaze on the closest source.

"Fine. Let's get this over with."

Chapter 37

GRADY

Having Beth ripped from his grasp had jolted his body into action. Grady's movements were still sluggish, but she'd given him enough to function again. He'd have to sleep it off to heal properly, but first things first.

With each push and pull, his muscles tensed and flared with pain, but Grady finally managed to get to his feet. He was unsteady, having to hold onto the countertop until his legs stopped shaking.

While he waited, he looked around the room.

Rich sat propped against the wall. His eyes were wide as he jerked a pencil-sized piece of wood from his chest with a grunt. It clattered to the floor as Rich's gaze found him.

"Fennick is laying over there, but Blaylock took Beth," the former deputy relayed. Talking seemed to take a lot out of their friend.

"I've got her, Rich." Grady stretched his arms and legs, wincing as the taut muscles argued against usage too soon. "See to Fen."

Rich nodded, rolling to one knee and braced against the wall. Grady balled his free hand in a fist and demanded his body to work. When Eric Blaylock was dead, and Beth was safe, he promised to sleep for a whole day to make up for his stubbornness.

Victory was sweet when Grady took that first steady step and another. Beth's grunts of pain could be heard from the hallway. If her breathing didn't slow down, she would hyperventilate before he reached her.

When Grady got to the hallway, he did a double take. Blaylock was a walking torch, covered in Beth's blue flames. He did a full body shudder, covering his mouth to keep from regurgitating his dinner.

Grady swore off roasted pork for the foreseeable future.

Blaylock abruptly stopped his zombie walk to turn and face Grady. Blackened flesh clung to bone, dried and flaky. The rest either sloughed off his skeletal frame or hung by twisted strands of sinew.

As Grady studied the Sheriff, he realized the man's right arm was locked straight out. He had a fistful of Beth's hair while she dangled limply. Grady went temporarily blind as hellish fury demanded retribution.

Panther claws burst between his knuckles on both hands as Grady closed the distance. The first swipe separated Blaylock's hand from his arm. As soon as Beth was free, he dropped on his knees and slid his other arm around her waist. She flopped against his chest.

The bleeding gash against her face dialed his rage to incineration levels. He barely registered the blow to his back when he laid Beth on the floor.

Grady stood only to block Blaylock's punch with his face. He heard a crunch, and his nose felt odd, but Grady was here to pay the reaper. His upper cut to the solar plexus went through Blaylock's ribcage and got stuck between the bones when he tried to pull his fist out.

What was left of the Sheriff's lips curled in disdain and his blazing eyes flared. Grady twisted his hand back and forth, letting his large claws shred the innards.

The grin fell off the bastard's face real quick. Blaylock's skeletal free hand wrapped around Grady's wrist and pulled. Grady brought his other clawed fist in a downward motion aimed at the heart. Before Grady could enclose the shriveled heart in his fingers, Blaylock roared and brought his arms down against Grady's shoulders in a karate chop.

The force was enough to break the breastplate and free both hands, but it also brought him to his knees. As Grady considered his next move, he stared at the bloodied and scorched man. Blaylock was unrecognizable, save for the arrogant way he held himself. His calculating gaze narrowed on something behind him.

"Time to retire, you son of a bitch," Rich snarled. The sound of a shotgun cocking was Grady's only warning.

He dove, covered Beth's body with his own a second before the blast reverberated in the narrow space. Fiery bits of the Sheriff bounced off his back.

A timid tap on Grady's shoulder had him meeting Rich's concerned gaze. The man mouthed, "Dead."

"Thank you." Grady eased off Beth, his hand going straight for the pulse at her neck. He pursed his lips and nodded. "Good."

The adrenaline rush wore off while he huddled on the ground. Grady was going to need a crane lift if he was expected to walk any time soon, and they still had to raid the armory.

"Fuck."

"Exactly." Rich's muffled voice sounded as tired as he felt.

Grady worked to untangle Blaylock's fingers from Beth's locks, tossing the severed hand over his shoulder.

Blaylock had ripped out more than a few clumps of Beth's soft hair, which only sparked his anger all over again. Since he couldn't kill the bastard again, Grady redirected the energy to something he could, getting Beth home.

Grady rubbed his ears, trying to dispel the ringing to no avail. Giving up, he cocked his head toward the breakroom and asked, "Where's Fennick?"

Rich frowned, gripping the bridge of his nose before answering, "Gone."

The news made Grady's heart sink. He'd hoped Fennick would hang around a little longer, to guide and fight beside them. Their theory was incorrect, and Fennick lost his immortality anyway.

"Help, please."

Grady gestured Rich over. Together, they worked to carry Beth down the hallway to the armory. As they passed the breakroom, Grady's gaze wandered to where Rich last saw Fennick. A smeared bloody handprint was the only proof he'd been there at all.

"Can you hold her by yourself?" Rich asked, tipping his chin toward the reinforced outside door they came through to begin with. "That door is solid steel. I can lock it down, so no one besides us can come or go."

"Do it." Grady held Beth bridal style and squatted against the wall. His legs wobbled, but he managed to balance.

Rich slid the bolts in place and turned several locks until they clicked. "You sure you don't want to get her back to the Grove first?"

Grady gazed down at Beth, considering it. His chest buckled and tears pricked his eyes at the thought of leaving her there to wake alone. "No, way. I'm not leaving her side. We won't be long."

"You mean *I* won't be long." Rich corrected, tilting his chin down and raising his eyebrow. "Y'all are gonna wait right here while I load the goods."

The options weighed in his favor, but Grady felt shitty leaving Rich to do all the work. He could do both. "Just help me up, okay?"

When he was sure he could stand on his own, Rich stepped back. "Follow me."

Grady held Beth tight against his chest, stopping just inside the hallway when Rich gave him the universal sign for 'wait.' The former deputy went the opposite way to investigate.

The seconds ticked on, but Grady sensed no one else in the building. His arm muscles were aflame, and his legs cramped, both signs of overexertion. Grady was about to return to the mess hall when Rich popped back around the corner with an, "All clear."

Those two words set his jaw further at ease.

Grady continued his march behind the ex-deputy until they paused at an open gate. He peered around Rich, spotting a pair of boots.

They inched closer.

A body lay crumpled on the floor in a pool of blood. Four very distinct marks were cut into the fabric across their back, soaked in a deep red. The faint scent of sulfur clung to the air.

"Ungenth," Rich muttered as he squatted next to his fellow deputy. He closed their eyelids, picking the keys up from the ground. "I'll get what I can carry. You keep Beth comfortable."

"Can do." Grady nodded.

Rich helped him maneuver to the ground so the wall would support him. Beth was curled up in his lap. He swept the hair out of her face, clearing it away from the gash. If he got too comfortable, he'd pass out on the floor. The skin-to-skin contact seemed to ease some of his body aches. Afraid of getting too comfortable and passing out, he tucked his free hand around her waist and gripped his elbow.

Rich unlocked the lockers and grabbed two duffel bags from the shelf above them. The fabric rustled as he stuffed it with enough firearms to last them longer than a few days. Rich stepped further into the room, outside of Grady's sight and returned with a few KA-BAR knives and a handful of flares. He stuffed them into his pockets.

"Can you reach your stone to make a portal?"

"I think so." Grady wriggled his hand into his pocket, pulling the blood and sweat glued fibers apart until he found the stone. "Ready."

Rich sniffled and rapidly nodded, his eyes were wide like he was on the verge of shock. They couldn't afford to lose it, not with enemies on their doorstep and another ally short. The crushing weight of the world was strapped to Grady's back while the sun he orbited lay damaged in his arms. He felt like a kid still trying on his grandpa's clothes. They were in over their heads. Two kids from bumfuck nowhere who were new to adulting and were expected to save the world.

How did they get so lucky?

Grady sat on the ground with Beth across his lap. The bench of his makeshift outdoor shower was at his back. He hadn't expected the first time they bathed together to be fully dressed.

He lifted the water-soaked sponge and squeezed the excess, watching it return to the bowl. The liquid had turned a raspberry lemonade color, but her face and hands were clean. The thought of Beth being injured already twisted his gut into knots, but seeing her like this, the bloody gash above her temple and the giant red blotch taking up the left side of her face wrecked his soul.

The only saving grace was how soundly she slept. Beth wore a mask of peace despite her wounds.

Grady carried the sponge to the top of her head and squeezed gently. The steady stream of water washed away more blood, taking strands of her hair with it. He repeated the process until he was satisfied and emptied the bowl onto the ground.

"There. Mostly clean, love." Grady lifted her hand to his mouth and pressed a kiss to her knuckles. "When you wake up, I'll make sure you have all the warm water you want for a proper shower. I even have bottles of your favorite shampoo, conditioner, and body wash."

He wasn't sure why talking to Beth helped him cope, but it kept his mood from spiraling. Beth had done the same for Tom, giving him a sponge bath after he passed. This path skirted too close, blurred the lines. Grief paced on the other side, waiting to cross.

Instead, Grady ignored it and set onto his next task of getting Beth into clean clothes. He'd only undressed Beth a handful of times, but she'd always been awake to oblige. Given the circumstances, this time wasn't the least bit sexual. He was taking care of the love of his life where she wasn't able. It gave him a sense of purpose, fulfilling him in ways that learning magic or working to save humanity couldn't.

Grady slipped Beth's arms through the armholes of her cotton t-shirt. Next, he worked the hem up and off her head. Her skin was warm, arms pliant as he guided her arms into the sleeves of one of his button-up shirts. The reason for not using one of Beth's had everything to do with ease and nothing to do with how his chest filled with a swirling warmth having her wear his clothes. The same argument could be said of the smallest pair of sweatpants he owned that were cinched at her waist.

Lastly, he reached behind his head, feeling for the wide-toothed comb resting on the bench. His fingers closed over the cool plastic, but he hesitated when it came to the deed. Where did he start? Sure, she didn't seem to feel pain, but what about when she woke up in a day or two?

Gathering her hair near the middle, he started at the ends with short strokes and worked his way up. Whenever the comb snagged on a tangle, he'd loosen it with his fingers and resume.

When he finished combing Beth's hair, it was smooth and silky. However, his legs tingled with blood loss.

"Let's get you to bed." He muscled his way to one knee while propping Beth on the other and caught his breath. On a heavy exhale, his legs wobbled as he pushed off the ground to stand. "Don't worry, beautiful. I won't drop you."

With careful steps, he made his way to the cabin. The door was wide open, setting Rich's whistled song free. The man deposited his armful of blankets and pillows onto the dining table. Zeus lay asleep on a blanket by the crackling fireplace.

"Figured you'd wanna sleep next to Beth, so I brought these down."

"Thanks, man." Grady completed his quest by laying Beth in the center of the corner cot. When he straightened his back, it popped, relieving tension. "How are you holding up?"

"I'm alive," Rich chuckled, but his haunted eyes took the jest out of the sound. "Nothing a good meal and twelve hours of sleep won't fix. You?"

"About the same." Grady rubbed the back of his neck. "Look, I didn't get to earlier. Thank you. For not letting Blaylock kill us."

"He's had it coming for a long time." Rich put his hands on his hips and shook his head. "Y'all just gave me the strength needed to do what was right."

"Still, I appreciate what you did."

"Any time." Rich clicked his tongue and called for Zeus, "Come on, boy."

The bulldog opened one eye. Without moving a muscle, he assessed the lack of activity before settling back to his nap.

"I don't mind. He can stay if it's okay with you." Grady's jaw unhinged with a dizzying yawn. "Excuse me."

"It's fine. I'll be next door if you need me." Rich left the cabin, closing the door with a soft click.

Grady discarded his dirty clothes and grabbed the cloth on the sink. After a quick wipe-down, he slipped into a fitted t-shirt and boxer briefs. He gathered his makeshift bed and piled it on the floor next to Beth's cot. He wasn't leaving Beth's side. Not until she woke. Maybe not even then.

"Sleep well, beautiful," Grady whispered and kissed her cheek. "I love you."

HE WOKE WITH HIS back stiffer than a hickory plank, which was the hardiest wood. He should know, it was the only tree his maternal grandpa trusted when he built grandma's house from the ground up.

Grady sat up on a yawn and rolled his shoulders back to loosen the muscles. When he raised his arms and bowed his back, several cracks and a pop relieved the tension. The heaviness in Grady's head remained. All of Fennick's past had soaked into his memory banks like the ground after a good rain. The pain, betrayal, and—worst of all—the murder. Fennick had killed Barton Cooper for his power, leaving his son, Solomon, to mourn his father's death alone.

"Motherfucker," Grady whispered as he rubbed the sleep from his eyes.

The elder witch had been through so much in his six centuries, more than Grady could fathom. He'd also destroyed countless lives without batting an eyelash. It would take time to reconcile Fennick's sordid past with his most recent actions.

It would also make telling Beth he'd passed on to the Goddess trickier...*if* he had at all like Grady had initially thought. Things surrounding Fennick were muddied. Fennick's memories didn't include anything after the Ritual, but even though Fennick's guardian magic was broken, what remained bound them. He first learned of such a phenomenon after Myrtle's passing. The space carved for Myrtle's presence while she taught him magic had turned cold after the women performed the ritual of passing. Grady still noticed a faint presence whenever he concentrated on Fennick.

Getting to his feet, Grady moved Beth's arm, so he could sit on the edge of the cot. Much to his satisfaction, the bruises on Beth's face were gone. He covered her hand with his and pressed a kiss between her brows. Her warm skin with the hint of vanilla unwound the knots in his shoulders. He cupped her cheek with his free hand while resting his forehead on hers.

"Wake up, love."

Grady had no idea how long they were out. Physically, he felt capable of outrunning a speeding train or lifting a tank in each hand. The contrast between being beaten to shit, then waking fully healed was superhuman. He could get used to this.

After a long moment with no movement from Beth, he tried again, nuzzling cheeks with her. "Beth. Time to wake up, beautiful."

A thought chased away the frown forming on his face. This could be a sleeping princess situation, and he was the noble prince. He pressed a chaste kiss against her lips, letting it linger before pulling back to study her sleeping visage.

Beth's soft brown lashes brushed the tops of her cheeks. Her dusty rose lips curled upward at the edges as if locked in sweet dreams. The lock of pure white hair shimmered with the few streams of light peeking through the gap in the curtains. The rest of her honey-brown locks shined with golden and red highlights. She certainly *looked* the part of princess, except the part where she was supposed to wake from true love's kiss.

Grady frowned slightly and gently shook her by the shoulders. "Don't be a brat, sleepyhead."

His tone may have been playful but worry roused a swarm of angry bees in his gut. Beth had done the Ritual first. They'd had plenty of sleep, so why was he the first to wake?

The angry bees stopped buzzing and fell to the bottom like lead pellets as the missing clue fell into place.

Beth had altered her Ritual of Passing.

"Fuck."

Multiple times, Beth said she was tired and needed to sleep for a week. He'd dismissed her statements as jokes. Hell, she hadn't pushed any contrary feeling or thought through their connection, either.

Grady sprang to his feet and paced. Dizziness fogged his brain as he fought the obvious solution. Fennick had suspected something had gone wrong with Beth's ritual, but he hadn't come up with a solution, only a theory. Something to do with Heliotta's fractured state of mind and shit being a mess of incoherent information.

"Shit."

Fumbling with his jeans, Grady pulled his cell out and looked at the time. They'd been asleep for two hours, which was the equivalent to two days in the Grove.

His thumb hovered over Fennick's name. If he survived and ran, asking for his help wouldn't do any good.

He pulled up Rich's number instead and pressed send. After several rings, Grady hung up and winced. The man was probably asleep.

The thought was barely formed when Grady heard Rich's voice outside the cabin door.

"I'm safe, son, don't worry. When they get back, tell your momma and gramma I'll be in touch. Love you, too, Randy."

There was a soft knock. The doorknob turned, and Rich stood in the doorway, cell phone in hand. "Sorry about that. I hadn't talked to my son in a few days and he called, worried about the news—Wait, what's wrong?"

Grady eased the hand gripping the back of his curls loose with a shuddering breath, but it didn't loosen the tightness in his chest.

"Beth. She won't wake up and I feel weird about calling Fennick, though he's probably the only person who knows why she's still sleeping. For the first time since I don't know when, I'm not sure what to do."

The vomited words landed at Rich's feet with a splat. He tucked his mobile phone away in a back pocket.

"Two steps back. Beth sleeping is a good thing, right? It means she's healing." Rich gestured to her head, reminding Grady that her bruise should have been darkening to a purple by now.

"But, Fennick and I did the ritual after she did. Shouldn't she be awake before me?"

Rich frowned, his thinking hat smoked up a storm. "True, but she took on two people at once, *then* sat between you and Fennick. That kind of stuff takes a toll."

Grady was an idiot. Air rushed from his lungs, taking the strength from his neck with it. With his chin tucked against his chest, Grady faced the truth. Beth was simply sleeping things off.

"While you're digesting things, why don't you spill about Fennick? I thought you said he had 'gone on?'"

"I'm not so sure anymore. It's like—I can sense Beth through guardian magic. I can still sense Fennick, too."

"So, if you're sure he could help, what's stopping you from calling?"

Even though Grady knew the question was valid, he gritted his teeth. How much should he divulge about Fennick's past? Instead of answering the obvious question, Grady huffed and pulled up Fennick's number.

"All of this," Grady said, tapping the side of his head. "I'll manage, though. Calling now."

He pressed send before Rich could ask anything else. Grady averted his gaze, studying the newly stained wood floors while listening to the long rings. Eventually, they ended with the three beeps of death.

"He's not answering."

Panic rose in Grady's chest again, but this time it battered against his heart, taking his breaths in short, quick bursts. Rich put his hands on Grady's shoulders and squeezed.

"Son, you need calm down before you hyperventilate."

Rich was right. Beth needed the calm and calculating Grady, not whatever *this* was. Shame turned his cheeks red.

"You're right," he croaked, regulating his oxygen like a well-oiled bellows. Rich squeezed Grady's shoulder again and gave him space.

After a moment of quiet, Grady spoke, "I can't stand the not knowing, Rich. It's bad enough there's only two of us still standing, but I have no damn clue how to help Beth. By the way, how are *you* feeling?"

"Fairly well, considering I don't have super healing like you guys." Rich rocked his head from side to side. "As for the not knowing, I can sit with Beth while you see what you can find. Don't y'all have a whole cave of magical journals?"

Grady furrowed his brows as he studied Beth's sleeping form. He wouldn't be gone long, just a quick pop in and out. There were centuries of knowledge in the archives Fennick didn't have access to. The same knowledge was also locked inside Beth's head possibly doing harm.

All three cell phones screeched with an incoming national alert. Pins and needles flashed behind his eyes and cheeks, trying to push through his skin from the inside. The white rectangle on the screen was a stark canvas for the dreaded news printed in bold, black lettering spelling their doom.

"The Governor of Tennessee just issued an order to shelter in place." Rich frowned at his phone. The veins in his forehead popped out. "Why? Evacuating would save more lives."

"Son of a bitch," Grady cursed as he balled his fist and banged it against his thigh. "How long do we have before the shelter in place goes into effect?"

"Weather related lockdowns are as soon as possible. Biohazard or chemical spills are immediate." Rich studied Grady, his jaw slack and eyes wide with uncertainty.

Grady held Rich's gaze, watching worry seep into the cracks. There wasn't much he could do to help Beth without losing himself to the archives for days. Shit was hitting the fan now, and the goddess, Circe, had appointed him as a protector. It was time he stepped up to the task, not stick his nose in a book.

"Stay here with Beth. Call your family. If I can't keep things contained to Mayes Hill, they need to hide in the basement or a bunker until we can bring them through the portal." He turned on his heel to gather his shoes and a clean pair of socks. Adrenaline pumped through his body with the rhythm of war drums.

"Where will you go?" Rich asked, pulling a dining chair closer to Beth's cot.

"First I'm gonna get my truck, and then I'm gonna to check on Tom's family." Grady hadn't heard from Jack or Lillian since his check-in before incarceration. They'd sounded tired over the call, but that was to be expected after burying your only child.

"You sure that's a good idea?" Rich asked, clenching the back of the chair until it creaked. "Did you know Jack Newman was one of *them*? I read about him in your daddy's files."

"I do." Grady ground his teeth and took a deep breath. "If Beth can forgive him for trying to sacrifice her, I can, too. Besides, they're the only family I got."

"I hope you know what you're doing." Rich shook his head and dropped into the wicker chair, crossing his arms. "I've got things here handled."

Grady stood, stretched his neck, and popped his knuckles. He strode to Beth's side and dropped to one knee. Rapid eye movements behind her lids had his lungs expanding. It was a good sign, which helped him do the thing he promised not to do...

...leave her side.

"Once you have your truck and the Newmans, what next?" Rich's voice had lost its edge. He watched Beth with deep lines above his thick brows. "You know, you could stay here and let the officials take care of the problem."

Heat spread from his gut to the top of his head and out to his limbs. Staying would be the easy route, but he was tired of pissing around while the bad guys stayed ahead.

"No. They'll be able to slow the army down, sure, but it's my job to take them out."

Grady leaned over his lover and best friend, brushing his lips against her forehead. *"Come back to me soon, beautiful."*

"What if you go out there and Ja'azul's army is on our doorstep?" Rich pegged him with a hard stare.

Grady straightened, his upper lip curled on one side and his nostrils flared. If you'd asked him yesterday, he'd admit he was scared shitless to face this nightmare head on.

But he wasn't the naïve boy from Mayes Hill, Tennessee anymore. Grady was a lightbringer guardian, and he was ready to face his destiny.

"I'll be the welcoming party."

Epilogue

FENNICK

Fennick had run... Like the coward he was.

It was for their own good.

At least, that was his excuse.

As soon as Grady disappeared down the hall, Fennick had scurried away like a sewer rat during a flash flood. Beth's cries would forever be ingrained in his memory. He prayed she would forgive him one day, should they be reunited, but Blaylock's fist had been the catalyst. The impact to Fennick's temple jarred his mind, granting Ja'azul free reign. Cold fingers slipped along the edges of his skull, returning to their post.

Leaving had been in their best interest.

A quick burst of light behind his eyes had him stumbling against the brick wall outside. He saw an underground lake of fire... No, not *fire* but annihilation incarnate. Ungenth, Agnazar, and other hulking four-armed creatures he had not the displeasure of meeting crowded the space beyond sight. Four-legged dog-beasts from the bowels of Hell roamed among them, their wide mouths full of destruction as their predators eyes missed nothing.

As quickly as his vision left, it returned to normal. The insight left him panting, but his ringside ticket confirmed his and Grady's hypothesis: The door worked both ways.

Fennick's reasoned his time within the Grove's shield had strengthened his resistance. Once he was outside of the bubble, the scales tipped. They played a version of Tug-of-War where neither knew the rules. So far, Ja'azul was not cognizant of his intrusion, otherwise Fennick would have been, as the modern folk say, *toast*.

Unfortunately, Fennick feared his return to the Grove would stifle the two-way connection. He was in the unique position to learn if the enemy had a chink in its armor. He could form a strategy that would turn the tides.

Staying away also gave Grady and Beth time to process. They had the collective knowledge of all guardians. They did not need his assistance, even if it would be as a target for their aggression. His presence would only serve as a hindrance.

Still, knowing he could not train with Beth and Grady was like taking a lance to the heart. Logic was often in opposition of one's feelings.

They will be fine.

He pushed off the wall, groaning like an ox birthing young, and headed down the street toward the Lion and the Fox. There were aches in places Fennick had not known were possible, which was essentially *everywhere*. If memory served correctly, there was another healing tonic stashed in his office by the lab.

As night fell, the ominous fissure crossing the heavens more resembled an evil aurora borealis. The darkening sky made spotting foes falling from the crack difficult, however the slow-moving stream of northbound cars leaving Mayes Hill lit his way.

Fennick picked up his pace. Crippling guilt made every limping step he took more difficult than the next. His only path lie forward.

The irony of the situation left a sour taste on his tongue. The destruction of this planet was ultimately his doing. He had made a deal with the devil, harvesting souls around the world and throughout time. He could only hope to undo some of his transgressions through the form of fire and taking out as many of the enemy as possible.

Fennick continued his walk of shame when screeching tires and a gusty breeze sent his hair flying wildly around his face. Whirling around, he was met by the shining hood of a jacked-up forest green Chevrolet pickup truck. A 1972 classic, if he was correct. His gaze pierced the glass windshield to find a pair of smirking women.

The red head in the driver's seat hung her elbow out of the open window. She stuck her head out, revealing a lump inside her lower lip.

"Hey, handsome. Haven'ya heard there's an apocalypse. Ain't nobody hoofin' it with monsters runnin' 'round."

"I have heard; however, the lack of a vehicle is somewhat hindersome." In his haste, he had left his beautiful sports car behind.

"Hoo-wee! I like the way he talks." The strawberry blonde sitting in the passenger seat elbowed the driver in the ribs. "Let's take pretty boy with us, Greta!"

Greta swatted at her companion and shushed her with a look. She returned her attention to Fennick, sizing him up with a slightly narrowed gaze as she spat on the tarmac. Greta unceremoniously wiped the brown tobacco juice from her lip with the back of her hand. "Reckon we can handle this bit o' beanpole. What's yer name?"

"Fennick." He struggled with whether he should accept their offer or not. If they were endangered because of him, he would not be able to protect the women. On second thought, judging from the biceps on Greta's arms and the shotguns on the rack inside the cab, he figured they would be able to take care of themselves. "Are you certain I will not be a burden?"

"Not 'tall, long as ye know we ain't gonna put up with no ungentlemanly-like behavior." Greta punctuated her point by raising a single eyebrow. Something told

Fennick she was used to getting her way.

"I am not one to go against a lady's wishes."

"Unless you wont to with me, handsome." The passenger shot him a salacious smile and an exaggerated wink.

Fennick's cheeks heated.

Greta's upper lip twitched as amusement danced in her hazelnut eyes. She opened her mouth to reply, but her passenger jumped out of her seat with a bounce and gestured to her open door.

"Come on pretty boy, you can sit in the *middle*." The last word was pronounced as two words rather than one: 'mid' and 'dull.'

Fennick shoved his hands in his front pockets and hurried around the front of the truck. The strawberry blonde was petite but no stranger to hard labor either. Her cutoff jean shorts highlighted toned and tan legs.

"I'm Arlene." She held out her hand and Fennick took it, lifting her knuckles to his lips for a brief kiss. She fanned her face with her free hand. "Whooo, lawd! Ain't you just somethin! That, there, is Greta. We're the Pickman sisters."

"Nice to meet your acquaintances, ladies." He lowered his head in a curt bow. "I am Fennick. Fennick Rayon. But you may call me Fen."

"Boy! I wonder what else that fancy mouth can do!" Arlene guffawed. As Fennick climbed into the cab, she smacked his ass.

"Arlene. Have you no shame?" Greta grumbled, casting Fennick an apologetic frown when he settled onto the bench seat. Their thighs had less than a finger's width between them.

"Nope. Life's too short to be coy." Arlene climbed into the truck and shut the rusty door. She winked at Fennick. "And now we's got the end of the world to contend with. You gotta git while the gittin's good!"

Greta shook her head and floored the gas pedal. The tires squalled on the asphalt, causing the truck bed to fishtail. The driver efficiently handled the metal beast, correcting their course with ease. They sped past the grid-locked vehicles leaving town. He worried about someone jumping the line, but they had not yet.

"So, Fen. Where ya headed?" Greta asked, her hair flying around her face.

"Are you familiar with the Lion and Fox whiskey distillery?" To Fennick, the sisters were a breath of fresh air and seemed highly capable of self-defense. He supposed it would be beneficial to have them around.

"Sure thing, sugar. Daddy bought a case ever' year 'til the day he went to Heaven." Arlene did a poor job of crossing herself before kissing her thumb nail and raising it to the sky. "Whatcha need to go there for?"

Fennick chuckled at the gleam in Arlene's eyes. "I personally know the owner. We will be safe there."

"Hot damn, Greta! D'ya hear that? Fen knows the owner."

"Yeah," Greta replied, though she kept her eyes firmly on the road ahead. "Lady Luck must be feelin' sorry for us."

Arlene leaned out of the window, her ponytail whipping around, and whooped wildly into the wind.

Yeah, this is going to be interesting.

Fennick was lost on that thought when his cell phone rang. He flipped it over, wincing when Grady's name flashed across the screen. If he talked to Grady, the urge to return would shatter his resolutions. Hesitating, Fennick slid the phone back into his pocket without silencing the ringtone.

"Ain't ya gonna answer that?" His nosy companion asked. "Might be somethin' important."

"No. There is nothing I can do to help him except to stay away."

"Lover's quarrel?" Arlene pressed.

A laugh lodged in Fennick's throat. He coughed, "Not quite."

"Still, sounds like somethin' y'all need to work out before the shit hits the fan and ya ain't got another chance. Regrets ain't worth burning the energy to keep." Greta added her two cents, darkening the cloud hanging over his head.

"That, I know." Fennick crossed his arms and hunched in his seat. His flimsy shield was no match for such hard truths. "Trust me, they will be fine without me."

Maybe if I repeat the phrase enough, I will begin to believe it.

"Why's that? Did you do something so awful they's gonna—"

"Arlene May," Greta growled in warning, her fingers tightening on the steering wheel. "Mind yer manners, girl. Momma taught us better 'en that."

The eldest Pickman sister side-eyed Fennick. "'Sides, not everybody hurries to air out their secrets to strangers."

Fennick appreciated Greta's defense, though he saw it for what it was: a warning. Filing this tidbit away, he stared out the windshield, watching the taillights turn into one, long red line like the fireworms of old.

Cresting the next hill, Greta slowed to a stop. On the next hill over, a large armed vehicle barricaded the road. Several men in camouflage directed cars back toward town.

"What in the devil is going on?" Fennick demanded as heat welled from the depths of his stomach and flashed to his face. Without his lab, he was useless. He was already trying to recall the handful of backroads they could take to get to the distillery.

"'Bout damn time," Greta answered, a gleam in her eye. "That there's the National Guard."

"Looks like you'll be comin' to the farm with us after all." Arlene had her elbow on the headrest and faced Fennick with a playful smirk.

He opened his mouth in retort, but Arlene's grin dropped. She grabbed his shoulders with the strength of a Greccio-Roman wrestler rather than a slight woman and slammed his head onto her toned thighs. The position would have been pleasant, save for the fact they were strangers. In the past, advances from strangers were never an issue, but he was a changed man.

The shucking of a double-barrel shotgun was his only warning. His hands sheltered his tender ears in time. The blast gently rocked the truck. The cab had not yet settled and

Greta was already cocking and firing another.

"They're coming from everywhere. We need'ta move." Arlene shouted.

Her arms brushed against his back before he could sit up. By then, Greta had her elbow out the window and was reversing the truck at travelling speed.

"Hold on to yer butts," she said before slamming on the breaks and shifting into drive with one smooth motion.

Roadside gravel and dirt kicked up a storm as Greta followed her own road into the countryside. Arlene leaned out of the passenger window, picking off shadows moving faster than normal between bumps on the offroad. Fennick's head banged against the roof more than a few times.

After Arlene's third round, she cursed and fell back onto the bench seat. She pointed at the floorboard between his legs. "Grab the ammo."

Fennick must have hit his head rather hard, because it took him longer to realize the younger Pickman sister was speaking to him.

"Hurry up, hotness. These sons a'bitches keep comin'."

He thrust the hand not white-knuckling the dashboard underneath the seat. His fingers found a box, presumably holding said shells, and set it between them.

"Thanks, darlin'." Arlene winked as she made quick work of reloading.

As soon as the shotgun was full, she hung out the window again. Fennick tore his gaze away from the fiery minx to gauge her sister. Greta's jaw was set in concentration, but the twinkle in her eyes gave her away. The thrill of the moment, the exhilaration of forging her own path while her sister dealt with the threats as if they were keeping foxes from the hen house was electrifying.

Something deep in his chest stirred, causing something akin to heartburn. He pressed his fist to the center of his ribcage, hoping to alleviate the ache. Instead, it sparked and caught fire.

The Pickman sisters reminded Fennick of something he had forgotten centuries ago: the difference between feeling *alive* and simply existing.

He was a demi-god balanced on the crutches of humanity and whining about how unfair life had been. However, the Pickman sisters embraced the very thing he considered a weakness. Mortality was not a limit; it was an accelerant with which one could accomplish a great many things, given the drive.

These women had also given him the inspiration and bravery to embrace the unknown. It had been a long while since excitement vibrated Fennick's bones, and the aftermath would be glorious.

Afterword

Wow. To say Harbinger was a wild ride is a vast understatement. I liked the first edition, but—after listening to my readers and the editing team at BDA—the rewritten story is worlds better. While revisiting Harbinger has been fun, it's time to get down to the nitty-gritty. The third and final book, Zenith, will be where our heroes are tested beyond their limits. As the author, it is my solemn duty to document their journey and to pull them up when they get knocked down, because that is how we succeed...together. Love to you all!

Acknowledgements

As an author, I have come a long way since the first editions of both books in the Between the Birches Trilogy thus far. My writing style has gotten better, so has my storytelling. Most of the credit for this ability flex goes to my former awesome editing team (before BDA Publishing imploded). Katie Bell and Carter Elise Key, y'all saw past my bad writing habits to the decent writer underneath. You two helped me shed those layers and pushed me into hard mode, making sure Harbinger's rewrites kicked ass. Thanks for cheering me on and for making the comments section as fun as it was informative.

Azshure Raine...bet you didn't expect to be thanked in the second edition of Harbinger. Let it be forever put into print the 'I told you so' rights you earned when it came to the OG ending of Harbinger's first edition. You tried to tell me it was a bad idea. Guess we know where Beth gets her stubbornness.

Jana Rose, my magical email buddy! You were so appreciated and did a brilliant job of juggling all of us authors. Whatever you do, wherever you go, stay amazing!

A huge thank you goes to my awesome OG beta readers. Your attention to detail and grammar radars continue to astound me, and your diligence whips me into a better writer. Hugs to you all: Matthew Poslusny, Caroline Fleur, Alex Blacherne, & John Phillips.

Lastly, I cannot forget to thank my amazing ARC readers! Your support and reviews mean the world to me. Never stop being the awesome people you are: **Shar Rodriguez**, Bucky Wolfe, Jeanea Blair, Quinn Donahue, Kristi M. @flash_mama, Angie Dokos, Kimberly Morehouse, and Melissa Hawkins.

Lastly, to my wonderful readers. You stuck around while I fumbled for the light switch on this story, supporting me through the okay times until I found my stride. I hope you understand how appreciative I am for you all. Love and hugs!

Thank You

Thank You for Reading Harbinger, Book Two in the Between the Birches Trilogy!

If you have enjoyed the story so far, please consider leaving a rating or review on Amazon, Goodreads, or on social media. Your support helps to spread the word for indie published authors.

The trilogy ends with Zenith...
Coming 2027 from Lunar Ridge Publishing

OTHER TITLES AVAILABLE AT LUNAR RIDGE PUBLISHING:

Awakening, Book One, Between the Birches Trilogy
by K.P. Roberson (2025)
Harbinger, Book Two, Between the Birches Trilogy
by K.P. Roberson (2025)
The House on Lori Lane, A Young Adult Horror Short
by K.P. Roberson (2026)
https://www.lunarridgepublishing.com

About the Author

K.P. Roberson is a Georgia native living in the southern Appalachian Mountains with her very handsome and nerdy spouse, their two teenage spawn, and a very rotund cat who answers to 'Kitty.' She loves science fiction, fantasy, thriller, romance, and horror stories, especially if they are character driven. Her writings align with her tastes, but she also composed Stardew Valley fanfiction on Archive of Our Own (K8eCre8s). When not pounding away at her keyboard with a string of illicit words, she enjoys watching movies, listening to music, reading on her Kindle, gardening, hiking, and crocheting...which explains her love of weaving a good tale.

Where to find K.P. on Social Media:

Threads – @authorkproberson
Instagram – @authorkproberson
Facebook – @KPWritesFantasy
BlueSky – @kpwritesfantasy.bsky.social
Goodreads – K.P. Roberson
LinkTree – Author KP Roberson
www.AuthorKPRoberson.com